Praise for
When Sparrows Fall

"Rich, deep, and painfully honest. *When Sparrows Fall* is a lovely work of fiction that portrays a side to American freedoms that is too real to ignore."
—CINDY WOODSMALL, *New York Times* best-selling author of
When the Soul Mends

"Meg Moseley is the diamond in the haystack you've been looking for. She's a rising star who will have a permanent place on my keeper shelf. In her remarkable debut novel, *When Sparrows Fall,* Moseley spins a tale of depth, poignancy, and humor. I savored every page and after I turned the last, I simply sat for a while, basking in the aftermath of a story well told."
—DEANNE GIST, author of *Maid to Match* and *A Bride Most Begrudging*

"Meg Moseley has penned a fantastic debut with *When Sparrows Fall.* It's a story of darkness and light that she masterfully weaves so tightly, the reader can fully understand just how those seeking God can fall victims to the cult-like practices of false prophets. Still, in this thought-provoking, cautionary tale of extremism, Moseley drops in delightful moments of pure joy. Hers is a fresh new voice that readers—like me—should welcome with open arms."
—ALLISON PITTMAN, author of *Lilies in Moonlight*

"With her debut *When Sparrows Fall,* Meg Moseley writes with passion and daring about a young woman's fight for truth and spiritual freedom, providing a brave, new voice in Christian fiction."
—RIVER JORDAN, author of *The Miracle of Mercy Land* and *Saints in Limbo*

when
sparrows
fall

MEG MOSELEY

when sparrows fall

a Novel

MULTNOMAH
BOOKS

WHEN SPARROWS FALL
PUBLISHED BY MULTNOMAH BOOKS
12265 Oracle Boulevard, Suite 200
Colorado Springs, Colorado 80921

Scripture quotations are taken from the New American Standard Bible®. © Copyright The Lockman Foundation 1960, 1962, 1963, 1968, 1971, 1972, 1973, 1975, 1977, 1995. Used by permission. (www.Lockman.org); and from the New King James Version®. Copyright © 1982 by Thomas Nelson Inc. Used by permission. All rights reserved.

The characters and events in this book are fictional, and any resemblance to actual persons or events is coincidental.

ISBN 978-1-60142-355-9
ISBN 978-1-60142-356-6 (electronic)

Cover design by Kelly L. Howard.
Cover art by Michael Haegele/Corbis.

Published in the United States by WaterBrook Multnomah, an imprint of the Crown Publishing Group, a division of Random House Inc., New York.

MULTNOMAH and its mountain colophon are registered trademarks of Random House Inc.

Library of Congress Cataloging-in-Publication Data
Moseley, Meg.
   When sparrows fall / Meg Moseley. — 1st ed.
      p. cm.
      ISBN 978-1-60142-355-9 — ISBN 978-1-60142-356-6 (electronic)
   1. Widows—Fiction. I. Title.
   PS3613.O77876W47 2011
   813'.6—dc22
                                        2010051192

Printed in the United States of America
2011—First Edition

10 9 8 7 6 5 4 3 2 1

To my husband, whose love shelters my dreams.
In memory of my father and his mother,
who gave me the dream of writing.

one

If running late showed a streak of rebellion, Miranda Hanford was already in trouble. Pulling her van to the side of the narrow road, she tallied the other vehicles lined up on the shoulder. She wasn't the last to arrive at Mason's emergency meeting. She could steal a moment with Jezebel.

She picked up her camera and climbed out. Working quickly in the cold, she framed the last sliver of sun, as red as a forest fire above the pine-stubbled peaks. In the foreground, a maple sapling curled its bare limbs around the sunset, unwilling to let go—like sweet, stubborn Martha at bedtime, refusing to believe the day was over.

Miranda clicked the shutter. Before the sun abandoned the Blue Ridge to the night, she nailed five promising shots. She tucked the camera into its case and locked it in the van. An old lady who'd seen more of the world than her owner ever would, Jezebel deserved tender care.

Holding her cape closed, Miranda hurried up the long, steep driveway. Mason had called only the single women for this meeting. Six who hadn't married yet and two widows.

She hated that word. Widows were supposed to be meek, gray things with grandchildren and arthritis.

Around the last bend of the driveway, the lights of the house shone their welcome. Snow flurries swirled like silver glitter as she ran up the steps to the porch.

She knocked lightly and joined the women in the living room. They'd congregated in a semicircle of folding chairs near the feeble warmth of the fireplace, their hands clasped in their laps and their voices subdued. Like the others, Miranda left her cape on, but a draft crept under her skirt and up her legs like icy fingers. She sat beside Lenore Schwartz, the other widow.

"Where's Nicole?" someone asked.

No one knew. Abigail too was missing, her absence making the room colder still. If Mason's wife had been home, she would have been dispensing hugs and peppermint tea.

The ladies hushed when their pastor strode into the room. Mason crossed to the hearth and picked up the poker. He shoved the logs into compliance, making sparks fly.

Amid the smell of smoke and ashes, he hung up the poker. He cut a handsome figure, his temples barely touched with gray and his face remarkably unlined for his fifty-some years.

"Ladies, thank you for coming on such short notice. I want to share what I announced at the men's meeting last night." He paused, surveying the semicircle like a watchful shepherd inspecting his lambs.

One of the flawed lambs, Miranda shifted in her chair. It squeaked in the silence.

"I have a word from the Lord." Again, Mason took a moment to study the women. "I am to move from Slades Creek."

Mason leaving town? Miranda's heart made an unexpected leap, but Lenore bleated in distress and twisted her age-spotted hands together.

"We're moving to North Carolina," he said, "to a beautiful little town called McCabe. Where people take care of themselves and each other. Where the government stays out of people's business."

Miranda fidgeted again, and her chair betrayed her restlessness with another creak. If the government didn't stay out of people's business in Georgia, it wasn't likely to be much better in North Carolina.

"If it's the Lord's will, it's the Lord's will," Lenore said, "but I don't know how we'll get along without you and Abigail. We'll miss you terribly."

"No, you won't." Mason smiled. "You're coming with us. All of you. It's a new beginning for the whole church. There are jobs in McCabe. Inexpensive housing too, and clean air and water. It's practically paradise."

A wave of excited whispers rustled through the room, but defiance woke within Miranda and prowled like an angry cat. She couldn't leave Slades Creek. She wouldn't.

"I've already put our house on the market," Mason said, "and the other men will follow suit as soon as they can." He nodded at Lenore, then Miranda, the only single women in the church who owned homes. "I'll be glad to help you start the process."

Some of the men might have argued, but these women without men didn't. They embraced their marching orders with joy.

All but Miranda. She saw an escape route.

Yet, as Mason answered questions with a twinkle of amusement in his eyes, she felt a pang of loss. The church had become her family. She would miss the women, especially Abigail. Friends, secret-sharers, burden-bearers, these women were the sisters Miranda had never had. The mother she'd lost to an Ohio jail.

Once the discussion had played itself out, she spoke, veiling her agitation with a downcast gaze and a respectful tone. "I'll miss everyone—very much—but Carl wouldn't have wanted me to move."

The room hushed to a shocked stillness, punctuated by the snapping and hissing of the fire.

"I only want to honor his wishes," she added. "He always said we should hang on to the land, no matter what. For the children's sake. He said it's as good as money in the bank."

Mason's silver blue eyes flashed a warning. "We'll discuss it later, Miranda."

She studied the blunt toes of her sturdy brown shoes. Now she'd reinforced her status as a troublemaker.

But so what? Her pastor was leaving town. And soon.

She frowned. Why the rush? Well, Mason and Abigail could hurry. They had no family. No children to uproot from their home or leave behind.

Miranda looked up, startled, when a paper appeared before her, in Mason's hands. She took it, and he gave one to Lenore too.

"A checklist to help expedite the process," he said. "Weed out, fix up, sell. It's almost spring. The perfect time to attract buyers."

The photocopied list was written in Mason's neat, square printing. With bullet points. With tips for increasing the value of a home. With phone numbers of handymen, painters, and real estate companies. He'd even included the donation drop-off hours for the local thrift store.

He dismissed the meeting. Each woman folded her chair and leaned it against the wall beside the piano. Abigail's living room returned to normal except for her absence.

"Somebody needs to tell Nicole," Lenore said. "I wonder why she never showed up. And where's Abigail?"

Mason laughed and opened the front door, admitting a gust of cold. "Why should my wife attend a meeting of single ladies?"

Because she'd attended every other women's meeting, Miranda thought, wondering if Abigail's absence was related to Nicole's.

"Well, tell her we missed her." Lenore turned to Miranda. "You'll find another nice piece of property, honey. You'll find a new husband too. You're so young." Lenore seized her oversized handbag in one hand and her cane in the other and led the charge to the front door. "All you pretty young things, you'll find husbands there."

Miranda hung back as the chattering pack traipsed onto the porch, exchanging their good-nights. When Mason closed the door on the cold and faced her, she'd never felt so much like an ungrateful and obstinate child.

"Miranda, Miranda," he said with a heavy sigh. "I hope you aren't serious about staying behind."

"I am." She folded his checklist in half, then in half again. "I can't imagine uprooting the children. And the land has been in Carl's mother's family for generations. I can't sell."

"Land is only land. Your children are young enough to adjust to a move. So are you. You're young enough to start over."

The paper rustled in her fingers as she folded it twice more, making it a tiny rectangle. "I don't want to start over. I want to raise my family right here in Slades Creek."

"It'll be harder to raise your family if you don't have help from the church when you can't quite pay the bills."

"Yes, but—"

"And what if there's a good, godly man waiting for you in McCabe? What if God plans to play matchmaker? Don't take this lightly, Miranda. If you deny God the chance to act, you may be depriving yourself of a husband. Depriving your children of a father. You need to hear from God about this. It's a question that deserves fasting and prayer."

She would start fasting, all right. She'd fast down to skin and bones so no man in his right mind would want her.

"You'd better start packing," Mason said. "The move will take you beyond the chastisement of God to true repentance and blessings."

"Wouldn't the church be better off if a black sheep like me stayed behind? I know I've been a trial to you and Abigail."

"No, no. Black sheep or not, you're part of my flock. Of course you'll move. And you'll be careful not to sow seeds of rebellion in the others."

She hesitated, wary of his new sternness. "I need to do what's best for my children."

"Then you'll submit to the authority God has placed over you." Mason shook his head. "I've invested in your life for years, Miranda. I'm the one who made sure Carl had excellent life insurance, and I'm the one who writes the checks from the benevolence fund. You would have lost your property years ago if I hadn't looked after you, and now you won't listen to my guidance?"

He still spoke softly, but this wasn't the genial pastor who preached on Sundays and prayed for the sick and made a mean chili for potluck suppers. This was a different man. A hard, unreasonable man.

"What's right for the church as a whole isn't necessarily right for me," she said, quaking inside.

"Remember, Miranda, 'rebellion is as the sin of witchcraft.'"

The prowling cat inside her tested its claws. "I'm no witch, and it's not rebellion to make my own decisions."

"Before you make this particular decision, remember you're still paying for some of Carl's unwise choices."

Her knees went weak. "What does that have to do with it?"

"This is your opportunity to put some distance between yourself and the things you'd like to keep quiet. If the state ever gets wind of what happened, if DFCS steps in…"

She twisted her hands together behind her back. "I'll take my chances."

"Don't be foolish. As you said, you have to do what's best for the children. You want to protect them, don't you?"

Tears stung her eyes. "Of course. Always."

"Then you'll move to McCabe." Mason came closer, exhaling minty toothpaste. "I won't be held accountable for the consequences if you stay."

The veiled threat took her breath away.

She imagined a car in her driveway. A car that bore the state seal on its doors. At the wheel, a social worker who had the right to tear a woman's children from her arms and feed them to the foster-care system, backed up by the Bartram County Sheriff's Department. It happened, all too often. It happened even to parents who'd done nothing wrong.

"Agreed?" he asked. "You'll sell? You'll move with the rest of us?"

She shivered. She'd seen his anger before, she'd even been the target of it, but she'd never seen him as an enemy.

Now, though, he had threatened her children.

Slowly, she nodded. Fingers crossed behind her back. A liar.

Mason squinted, seeming to assess her sincerity. His somber expression warmed with that Hollywood smile. "Excellent. Now, don't make waves. Don't try to sway anyone into staying behind. Good night, Miranda." He dismissed her with a nod.

Speechless, she stepped outside, jamming the checklist into the pocket of her cape. Night had fallen, and the cold mountain air chilled her to the core. She stared numbly at a cardboard box in the corner of the porch, stuffed so full of clothing that its flaps refused to stay folded down.

Abigail must have started weeding out their closets for the move. Her Christmas pullover lay on top, the same red as the construction-paper hearts the girls had cut out for Valentine's Day. Abigail's sister had mailed it from Lincoln, but Mason said the color wasn't appropriate for a pastor's wife and the neckline was indecent.

Rubbish. It was perfectly modest.

Miranda tiptoed across the porch and snatched the sweater. She tucked it under her cape and ran down the steps. Now she was a thief too, but what was one more black mark against her?

She jogged down the steep driveway, slick with the barely-there snowfall. "I'm not moving. You can't make me." The jolting of her footsteps made her voice bounce as if she were jiggling a baby on her knee. That was what finally made her cry.

Her children. He had threatened to send the state after her children. They'd be like the family that had been in the news, their little ones scattered to different foster homes and the parents helpless against the authorities.

In the morning, she would ask her attorney about naming a new guardian. Someone outside the church. Someone with no ties to Mason. She had no family though, with Auntie Lou long gone. No brothers, no sisters, no cousins.

Jack? It might have to be him, but she couldn't call him yet. Couldn't risk giving him the idea of showing up on her doorstep again. Not until it was safe.

With unsteady fingers, she unlocked the van. She fumbled the key into the ignition and shone the headlights on the dark, twisting road before her. She hadn't felt so alone in years. Nine years.

It was even longer since she'd felt free.

Two weeks of fasting and early-morning prayer walks had left Miranda shaky but clearheaded. She eased the back door closed, allowing only a faint click that couldn't possibly wake the children, and hung her camera around her neck. Making no sound, she walked down the weathered steps. The wind snatched at her skirt and cape, flapping them around her like wings of blue and gray.

She hoped God knew she'd started her fast not because Mason had told her to, but because she wanted to hear God too. She wanted to hear Him tell her to stay in Slades Creek.

Fighting the dizziness that always accompanied a fast, she kept her eyes on her shoes as they nosed through long grass and the first violets. By the time the girls finished their morning studies and went outside to pick a teacup bouquet for the kitchen table, Mason might have called again. He didn't give up easily.

"I don't either," she said under her breath.

Her choices were limited, but she wasn't helpless. She could arrange for child care and hold down at least a part-time job. She could earn money with her photography, and she had the monthly income that she never would have seen if Mason hadn't talked some sense into Carl, years ago.

Yes, Mason was smart about money. He was smart about a lot of things.

He liked to document everything. He kept better records than God, she'd heard somebody say at one of the Sunday meetings. He'd probably hung on to his notes from that long-ago counseling session.

With the old fears nipping her heels, she slipped behind the barn and into the clearing. The camera rocked against her stomach and kept time with her footsteps and the swishing of her skirt. The faraway bleating of the goats faded as she ducked beneath the big dogwood and entered the dripping woods.

Thinking she heard footsteps, she looked behind her. No one was there, of course. It was only the wind making bare branches sway and creak.

She faced forward again. Her foot skidded across last year's dead leaves, slippery with moisture. She nearly fell but regained her balance and walked on. Rounding the last bend, she slowed to take in the view that never got old.

The mountain peaks still hid in the mist, but the sun was fighting its way through in a glorious dazzle of white light. She held her breath and savored the sensation of standing in a cloud that had descended to her little piece of the earth.

No matter what Mason held over her, she couldn't sell her family's land.

Venturing closer to the heart-stopping drop-off, she peered over the edge of the cliff to the rock-choked creek far below, crisscrossed with fallen trees. It had been years since she'd dared to stand so close to the edge.

The first time she and Carl had walked his late mother's property together, he'd reminded her that the cliffs were no place for children or even for sure-footed goats. When he was a boy, one of his grandfather's young goats had fallen the twenty feet to the bottom. She'd landed on a boulder, breaking her neck.

Miranda had swallowed, sickened by the imagined sound of slender bones snapping.

The far side of the ravine wasn't an abrupt fall like the near side, but it was treacherous too, especially when wildflowers came into bloom and disguised its dangers. Rock-cress, bloodroot, stonecrops, and bluebells would soon soften every cranny.

By the time the asters blossomed in the fall, Mason might have moved far away.

She reached into the pocket of her cape and pulled out his checklist, still folded in a neat, thick rectangle. She opened up the paper, just enough that she could crumple it, and pitched the lightweight ball into the air. The small white wad bounced off a mossy ledge and disappeared into a tangle of leafless brush.

"Lord, help," she said softly, as if anybody could hear her so far from the house. "Help me outsmart him."

There were no sounds but the soft splashing of water on rocks and a few birds singing. Far from the commotion of her household, she could almost believe that God would speak to her, but either He wasn't answering or He'd struck her heart deaf to punish her sins.

Mason heard God though, or claimed to. If he heard correctly, heaven had asked a hard thing of her. It wouldn't be the first time.

Miranda removed the lens cap from her camera. The fog was lifting. If she worked fast, she could capture the mountains veiled with fog but kissed by the sunrise.

There it was. The perfect moment. She tripped the shutter.

A new wave of dizziness blindsided her. She hung her head to send blood to it, the camera still held to her face, and smiled at the silliness of staying in picture-taking mode when she had only a clump of dry weeds in the viewfinder.

She fought to step away from the cliff's edge, but her feet melted beneath her. Someone dropped a curtain from the sky, shutting out the light.

two

Jack Hanford hated early-morning phone calls. They never brought good news.

Abandoning his briefcase and his half-eaten toast on the kitchen table, he went in reluctant search of his aging cell phone. Over the clatter of a trash truck in the alley and the distant roar of Monday morning traffic on the interstate, he tracked down the phone where it vibrated between piles of books and papers on the couch.

The screen showed an unknown number from outside the Chattanooga area. Not one of his colleagues, then. Not his ex, who wouldn't be calling anyway. Not her parents, who just might.

The phone buzzed again as he took it back to the kitchen and the mess in his briefcase. His students deserved a slightly higher level of organization on his part. February was nearly over before he'd adjusted to being out of January.

"Updated syllabus. Hold that thought. And stop talking to yourself."

The phone vibrated a third time. He lifted it to his ear. With his free hand, he resumed rifling through his papers.

"Hello." He checked the clock on the wall. If he wasn't in the parking lot in twenty minutes....

"Hello?" The caller sounded young. Nervous. He said nothing after the initial greeting.

"How may I help you?"

"I need to talk to Jack Hanford, please."

"Speaking."

"This is Timothy."

"Timothy?"

"Timothy Hanford."

Jack lost his place in the papers. The name took him back—how many years?—to two towheaded toddlers and a young mother with a sad smile and dazzling blue eyes. Wearing a gray cape and a circlet of blond braids, she'd reigned over a rickety porch in the mountains of north Georgia.

Miranda's son should have had no reason to call.

Dread slowed Jack's response. "Carl and Miranda's son?"

"Yes sir. Mother—" The boy's voice cracked but he continued in a terrible, stiff calm, as if he were reading from a script while somebody held a gun to his head. "Mother said if anything happened to her, I was supposed to read this letter."

"Why? What…what happened? Is she all right?"

"She fell off the cliffs behind the house. They're taking her to the…to the hospital." The kid sucked in a noisy breath and kept going. "Here's what the letter says. 'I pray you'll never need these instructions, but if anything should happen to me, call your father's half-brother, your uncle Jack Hanford. In my will, I have named him as the guardian of you precious children. I believe he is a good man who wants to do right.' That's all it says. Plus your phone number and stuff." Timothy exhaled, long and loud.

Guardian? *Guardian?*

Jack stared around the kitchen as if the sight of his bachelor digs could anchor him there, safe from startling developments and complicated relationships. A sniffle from his caller prodded him back to less selfish concerns.

"Is she going to be all right?"

"I don't know." Timothy sounded younger now. Frightened.

"Is anybody there with you?"

"A man from the sheriff's department."

"May I speak with him?"

"He's outside, talking on his radio."

"All right." Jack tried to harness his thoughts as they galloped away. "You're in good hands, for now. I'll be there as soon as I can, but it'll be, say, a two-hour drive. I'll have my phone, so call again if…if you hear anything."

"Okay." Timothy hung up without another word.

Jack snagged his raincoat off the back of a chair and ran out, hardly remembering to lock up. He remembered the way to Miranda's ramshackle log home though, up in the hills behind a tiny town with only two traffic lights. The route to Slades Creek was seared into his memory with painful clarity, along with the rest of his time there.

This was his chance to make amends for long-ago wrongs. A chance to restore what someone else had stolen.

He climbed into his car with a vague sense of conflicted triumph coloring his sense of impending doom. Carl had hated him. Now, without so much as a by-your-leave, Miranda had put him in charge of Carl's children.

"Lord, have mercy." Jack swung the car into the street, shifted into first, and punched the accelerator. "It can't get any weirder than this."

Unless she didn't make it, and then God help them all.

Having missed the morning traffic in Chattanooga, Jack made it to Slades Creek in ninety minutes. That still wasn't enough time to fully grasp the situation, but a patrol car at the end of Miranda's winding driveway was evidence that the call hadn't been a prank. To Protect and to Serve, read the motto on the car's door.

A large white van stood there too. Mud-spattered and disconsolate, it warned Jack of the burdens of parenthood. PTA meetings, soccer practice, piano lessons.

If Miranda had died while he was on the road, he had inherited those responsibilities. Those kids. A boy and a girl. To his shame, he couldn't remember the girl's name.

"God, I need some time here," he said under his breath.

His cowardly feet led him around the side of the house, where he spotted a path leading behind the barn. After a five-minute hike, he found cliffs dropping down to a shallow, rock-filled creek.

Two feet from the edge, his vivid imagination took him where he didn't want to go. She might as well have fallen from a two-story building. Hands in the pockets of his raincoat, he hunched his shoulders, not so much against the cold as against the dire possibilities.

Across the ravine, purple gray mountains faded into a smoky horizon streaked with remnants of morning fog. The vista must have been Miranda's last sight before she flew past rocks and brush and fallen trees on her way down.

An accident or a deliberate dive? He wasn't ready to face the answer.

A twig snapped. Jack turned.

A boy stood in the muddy path, his hands balled up in the pockets of a denim jacket. He was twelve or thirteen, his eyes a cold, clear blue. "Are you Jack?"

"I am. You must be Timothy."

"I heard your car. Why didn't you come to the house?" Timothy didn't sound young and scared anymore; the blunt question made him seem oddly adult.

"I needed a few minutes to think, that's all." Jack drew a slow breath of chilly air, delaying the news for one more moment. "Your mom...?"

"She was unconscious when they put her in the ambulance. That's all I know."

A pox on the small-town hospital that would keep the family so ill-informed. Maybe they didn't know who to call though. Especially if they had bad news.

"I'll keep praying for her," Jack said.

Timothy nodded, a quick jerk of his close-shorn head. Tears glazed his eyes.

Jack turned away, giving the kid his privacy, then shifted to watch from the corner of his eye. Teaching had given him a sensitivity to young people who were a tad off the track. This one bore watching.

"How do I know you're really who you say you are?" Timothy asked.

Jack swallowed a phrase that wasn't fit for young ears and dug in his pocket for one of his cards. Still not quite facing the boy, he held out the card. Timothy took it without comment.

"How's your sister doing?"

Timothy didn't look up. "Rebekah? She's all right. The younger ones don't really understand what's going on."

Younger ones…plural?

"I don't know, ah, how many of you there are…now."

The boy picked at one corner of the card with a fingernail and took his time answering. "Six."

Jack let out a low whistle. Miranda had better pull through.

"Why did Mother choose you to be our guardian?"

Still flummoxed by it, Jack rubbed his chin. "Well, now. I met her when you were two or three years old. I remember sitting on the porch, drinking lemonade. Passing the time of day."

"But if you're our uncle, where have you been all this time?"

"In Chattanooga, cramming the joys of literature into the hard heads of college students."

"That's not what I meant. You wrote all those letters, but you never came around."

"Your father strongly encouraged me to stay away, son."

"I'm not your son." Timothy took to the trail, his shoulders squared.

Squinting after him, Jack recognized the irascible tone and the inflexible body language. Timothy was only following Carl's example. Carl, who'd warned that the letters would go straight into the trash. Maybe they hadn't though, if Timothy knew about them.

Jack faced the ravine and the ever-changing Blue Ridge beyond. Glimmers of light on far-off glass and metal revealed the whereabouts of tiny towns tucked into the hills of Bartram County. Somewhere behind him lay the drowsy streets of Slades Creek. The place had grown to a six-stoplight town.

Somewhere behind him too lay Rabun County, his birthplace. The rainiest corner of Georgia, it snuggled up against the Carolinas and shared their beauty and their poverty.

Straight ahead, the mountains stretched away toward the comparatively flat sprawl of Atlanta, two hours south. The vista was beautiful—the light, the blues and greens, the shreds and patches of drifting fog—and everything held the wet, green scent of spring.

He inched closer to the edge and peered down at an outcropping of rock ledges. Slippery with moss and seeping water, they slanted this way and that, untrustworthy stairsteps that went only partway to the creek. Its banks and waters were muddied from the movements of many feet. The paramedics must have had a devil of a time transporting their patient.

Maybe she'd left the kids sleeping. A widow with six children wouldn't have much solitude, and sometimes solitude was a soul's lifeline. Other times, as Jack knew all too well, it was the lead weight that took a drowning soul to the bottom.

Dizzy, he backed up. After one last gander at the view, he returned to the wet, trampled path toward the house, pushing aside damp branches of dogwood and laurel.

A flash of bright white in the mud caught his attention. His card, crumpled.

Jack picked it up for proper disposal and walked on, entering the broad clearing where the wind bent tall grass to earth. On the other side of the clearing stood an ancient barn, a wooden shed of more recent vintage, and finally the boxy, story-and-a-half log home.

Wood smoke warmed the air as he made his way around to the front of the house. The two weathered rockers on the porch were exactly as he remembered them, but years had passed since he'd sat there with Miranda and her toddlers. Nine years.

In the drive, the sheriff's cruiser still blocked the van. The utilitarian vehicles dwarfed Jack's black rag top, a toy beside them.

He crossed the weedy lawn under the gnarled branches of a giant oak, then counted five wide steps to the porch where he'd first met Carl and his mean streak. Rooted in unfortunate family history, the animosity had been insurmountable. Miranda had made up for it though, in spades.

The rustic door held a wreath of dried flowers and golden wheat, something the earth-mother type might have handcrafted. Jack knocked, then waited, examining the wreath. Seven bunches of wheat, seven brown rosebuds—

The door creaked open. A large, graying man wearing a khaki uniform and a silver star filled the doorway and studied Jack with sad eyes. "Can I help you?"

"Yes sir, I hope so. I'm Jack Hanford. Carl Hanford's brother."

"Timothy told me you'd be here directly." The man's thick eyebrows drew together. "I never knew Carl had a brother."

"Most people don't know. I'm a half-brother, actually."

The officer ducked under the low door frame and stepped onto the porch, forcing Jack to retreat. "I'm Tom Dean. May I see your ID, sir?"

"Certainly." Jack pulled out his driver's license.

After examining the license, the man studied Jack's Audi. "Nice car. You aren't much like Carl, are you?"

"I don't know. I only spoke with him once."

"But Mrs. Hanford named you as the guardian?"

"According to Timothy, she did. I had no idea until a couple of hours ago when he called."

"Come out of the blue, did it?"

"Yes sir. I'm still trying to get a handle on it. I guess I'm the best she can do."

"Well, then." The deputy handed the license back. "Come on in."

Jack stepped inside. The house must have been a hundred years old. Inside, it was warm. Cozy. Directly in front of him, stairs rose to the second floor. To his left, a bright orange fire crackled behind the glass of a black wood burner. For a house full of kids, the place was blessedly quiet.

A long, dark trestle table stood on the far end of the room. He imagined it filled with children. There was an old-fashioned wooden highchair too.

"Any news on Miranda?" he asked.

"She was banged up pretty good. Unconscious. You could call the hospital and find out."

Jack nodded and continued his survey of the living room. Except for a few modern touches, it could have sprung from the pages of the Little House books he'd read to Ava's niece and nephews. Sturdy furniture, braided rugs, needlework. Wooden pegs studded the wall by the front door. They were draped with jackets and capes in a variety of sizes but a paucity of color. Shades of gray and blue, all of them.

An eight-by-ten photo of the kids hung above the pegs, and Jack counted six blond heads. He didn't know why he'd hoped for a lesser number; Timothy knew how many siblings he had. There were two girls, a little one and a big one, in matching dresses. Four boys in blue polo shirts. The smallest boy looked young enough to be in diapers.

A thud shook the wide-beamed ceiling. Feet thumped across a room upstairs, and young voices rose in a muffled argument. Someone else murmured something. The hubbub subsided and a faint tootling began. A recorder, perhaps.

Jack abandoned his study of the photo. "May I see the letter she left for Timothy?"

"Sure, but it looks legit. It's her penmanship. I found the same writing all through the kitchen, on recipe cards and lesson plans."

"Lesson plans?"

"For homeschool." The deputy led the way toward the table.

Jack followed, keeping his thoughts to himself. He gave grudging respect to parents who did the job right, for the right reasons, but he hadn't much patience with homeschoolers whose driving force was fear of the modern world. From the little he knew of Carl, it was easy to believe the man's family would have been on the radical fringe of the movement.

The table held a sheet of paper, a blue teacup filled with lavender violets, and a litter of construction-paper valentines in all sizes and all the wrong colors. The wrong colors, nearly the wrong month; it was disorienting, like seeing purple shamrocks at Halloween.

Jack picked up the letter. Written in the perfectly proportioned italics that he remembered from the two notes he'd received from Miranda, it read exactly as Timothy had given it over the phone, except it concluded with: *You have always been a good son. I'm counting on you, Timothy. All my love, Mother.* The boy hadn't read that part aloud.

She'd signed and dated the letter two weeks earlier. At the bottom of the sheet, she'd included Jack's full name, address, and cell phone number. All the information was current. He was somewhat suspicious of the timing but attributed his qualms to his overactive imagination.

"I wonder if this is official enough to put me in charge while she's out of commission," he said.

"It'll do for now, while you try to round up her lawyer. That'd be better than bringing in the DFCS folks. Department of Family and Children Services, that is. Once they jump in, it's hard to pull 'em off again."

"Do you happen to know the name of her attorney?"

"No, but if it's somebody in Slades Creek, it won't take long to track him down." The deputy hitched up his trousers. "You'll stay with the kids, then?"

"Of course, but for how long? I called in to work to explain that I have a family emergency, but I'll need to be more specific when I call back."

"Where do you work?"

"Chattanooga. It'd be a bit of a commute." Jack handed over his second card of the morning.

"My, my. A genuine PhD? We don't have many of those in these parts."

"We're pretty useless, most of us."

The deputy smiled. Then, sobering, he peered in all directions. "You could make yourself useful here," he said in a low voice. "Because I suspect Mrs. Hanford will need help for quite some time. It was a long, hard fall."

"Any idea how it happened? And who found her?"

"Timothy found her. We ran down there right after we got the call, and she had a big ol' camera hanging around her neck. Maybe she was setting up a shot and didn't realize she was so close to the edge. She—"

Shoes clattered down the stairs. A freckled scamp flew around the corner and came up short. Eight or nine years old, he had the air of having been interrupted in some kind of mischief.

"Hey, there," Jack said with a modicum of hope. Maybe they weren't all like Timothy.

"Hi." The boy jammed his hands into the pockets of his jeans and inspected Jack with frank but friendly curiosity.

Then came another kid. And another and another, until five fair-haired siblings had gathered at the foot of the stairs. Jack sought a resemblance to his late father, their grandpa, and found bright blue eyes and square chins. A surge of satisfaction hit, like the rush of fitting the last pieces into a jigsaw puzzle, but it lasted only until Timothy brought up the rear, unsmiling.

The deputy moved toward the door. "Anything you need from me?"

"Not right now. Not that I can think of, anyway."

"Good man. It'll all work out."

"Yeah."

The deputy gave the children a grave smile and a tip of his hat. As the door closed behind him, six pairs of eyes examined Jack.

"Guess I'd better introduce myself. I'm your Uncle Jack. Your dad's half brother. I don't know how much you know about the situation, but—" He stopped, loath to mention Miranda's will or anything else that smacked of death. "Your mom asked me to take care of y'all until she's better."

Nobody spoke, but somebody sniffled. He couldn't tell which one.

"Let's start with names and ages. Timothy, looks like you're the oldest. How old are you?"

"Twelve." He bit off the word as if he begrudged the bit of breath required to speak it.

"Who's next?" Jack asked.

"Me," said the older of the two girls. "I'm Rebekah." Her hands clamped down on the shoulders of the freckled scamp in a grip that he wouldn't easily escape. "I'm ten."

"You've grown a bit since last time I saw you, Rebekah." Jack moved his attention to her captive. "Next? Name, rank, and serial number, sir."

The boy smiled—the first one to smile. "I'm Michael. I'm eight. I ain't got no rank or serial number."

A smaller boy, not as freckled, gave Jack a gap-toothed grin. "I'm Gabriel. I'm six."

Two smiles and counting.

"And this is Martha." Rebekah released Michael and tugged a round-faced little girl into the limelight.

Martha was a small replica of her big sister. They both wore white T-shirts under long denim jumpers. Clunky shoes. Blond braids. The girls were miniature earth mothers.

"I'm four." Martha held up four chubby fingers. "And I'm learning my phonics." She spoke precisely, as if she delighted in pronouncing each syllable exactly right.

"Good girl. Phonics, that's the only way to go."

Her dimples blossomed. "Yes sir."

The youngest was a curly haired toddler. He studied Jack with calm disinterest, then dug in his pocket and pulled out a chunk of granite, glinting with mica. He displayed it on the flat of his hand for everyone to see but didn't say a word.

"That's Jonah," Rebekah said. "He's almost two."

Born shortly after his father's death, then. A come-after child.

The ages were easy to remember—two, four, six, eight, ten, twelve—but the names wouldn't be so easy. They were all Bible names. Somber saints and mischievous angels. It would take a while to remember which freckled archangel was Michael and which one was Gabriel.

"Is that last one potty-trained?" Jack asked. "Noah, is it?"

"Jonah," Rebekah corrected. "Yes sir, he's potty-trained. Mostly."

"Mostly." Jack jingled the coins in his pocket. "Okay, here's the deal. If y'all can show me how your mom runs the household, I'll help out the best I can. Sound good?"

No one answered out loud, but almost everyone nodded. Even the youngest, who was busy scratching his granite chunk with a grubby thumbnail. Timothy, however, stood motionless, his face a blank. Maybe he was reliving the moment he'd spotted his mom crumpled on the jagged rocks beside the shallow creek.

Years before, Jack had gone icefishing on a northern lake, impossibly clear and deep. Out on the glassy slab, nothing but a few inches of ice had separated him from drowning. Something about Timothy recalled that threat of a sudden fall into deadly waters.

Jack told himself to get a grip.

He crouched, lowering himself to Martha's level, the hem of his raincoat settling damply on the wide planks. "We'll make it through, Lord willin' and the creek don't rise."

Martha's eyes went round, looking oversized in her little face. "Which creek?"

He smiled. A literalist. "Any creek you want, sugar."

"The one my mama drowned in?"

"She didn't drown, sweetheart. She had a real hard fall, but the doctors will take good care of her. We'll keep praying that she'll be fine."

Martha leaned closer. "Maya isn't," she said in a confidential tone. "Maya fell. And died."

"Who's Maya?"

Her long-lashed, crystal blue eyes widened further. "I don't know. Timothy knows."

Jack sought Timothy in the crowd of kids. "Who's Maya?"

"I don't know anybody named Maya," he said.

Rebekah laughed softly. "A pretend friend."

Martha was the right age for it, but imaginary friends weren't supposed to die. They were supposed to be cast off like outgrown clothes.

Still crouched beside her, Jack looked up at the boys in the middle, trying to remember which archangel was which, then over at the littlest guy. Noah. No, it was Jonah. The big fish, not the big boat.

Timothy brushed past Jack and walked outside without another word.

three

Jack spent a solid hour on the front steps with his phone to his ear. Thank God, he could find a signal. He hadn't accomplished much though, besides irritating Farnsworth back in Chattanooga. She was skeptical of his story about being saddled with six kids.

He told her that if he barely had enough time to teach fiction, he certainly didn't have time to concoct it. She was not amused.

He closed his phone and wished Miranda's cupboards held coffee. He'd checked, and she was completely out.

Come to think of it, he hadn't seen a coffee maker.

Behind him, their voices muffled by the closed door, the kids bickered and laughed. Except for the slight undercurrent of worry, all was well. Timothy had come back from wherever he'd been, and under his and Rebekah's competent supervision, the younger ones had tackled their chores and a smattering of schoolwork.

At some point, Jack needed to run back to 'Nooga, grab a few of his

things, and check in at work, but he couldn't tell Farnsworth how long he'd
have to play baby-sitter. The hospital was being stingy with information about
Miranda. He might have to show up in person and prove he was kin before he
could pry a prognosis out of somebody.

Locating her attorney was his second priority. He had questions.

Across the driveway, the wind ruffled pale grass on the hillside. A small
patch of darker, taller grass lay on the slope like a bruise on a face, and a gray
sky brooded over it all, threatening rain. At nearly noon, it was still cold outside
but the chill wasn't a bad trade-off for a piece of solitude.

He jumped as the front door banged open and shut. Michael and Gabriel
raced outside so fast that they might as well have had wings.

"Boys," he hollered to their backs. "Don't go far. Stay away from the cliffs."

"Yes sir," the archangels answered as one. They vanished around the corner of the house without slowing.

Jack took a moment to sort them out. Michael was the older of the two.
Sturdy, freckled, and a bit resistant to schoolwork. Gabriel, six years old, had
fewer freckles. He was thin, restless, full of energy.

Martha trotted outside, wearing a hooded gray cape over her long denim
dress. Jack half expected to see elf slippers with curled-up toes, but she still
wore those clunky clodhoppers.

"What are you up to, Miss Martha?"

"Picking violets." She hopped down the steps, making a racket.

"Don't go far. Don't go anywhere near the cliffs."

"Yes sir." She ran in the direction the boys took, her elf cape billowing after
her.

Jack hoped the kids weren't as accident-prone as their parents, with a pre-
dilection for falling from high places. Their dad from the roof, and now their
mom from the cliffs.

He shook his head, and it gave him a throbbing reminder of his caffeine
deficiency. Miranda's kitchen didn't even stock real tea. He could hunt down

whatever passed for a Starbucks in Slades Creek, except he couldn't leave the children unsupervised—or could he? This business of playing guardian was outside his frame of reference.

He still didn't understand why she'd named him to the position. Carl hadn't wanted anything to do with him. Carl had even told him, through her politely worded note, to stop writing those letters, but Jack had never been good at following orders.

He went inside. Jonah squatted near the wood stove's warmth, singing nonsense to himself as he stacked brightly colored wooden blocks on the braided rug. Timothy and Rebekah were seated at the trestle table across the room. He kept his attention on his book, but she looked up, smiled, and laid down a quill pen. A genuine quill pen. She had a tiny glass inkwell and a blotter too. An assignment for her history studies, maybe, or the family lived in a time warp.

"Will the younger ones be okay out there?" Jack asked her. "I have a bad feeling about mixing small children and tall cliffs."

"They'll be fine. The rule is that nobody goes past the barn without an adult."

"And everybody obeys the rule?"

Rebekah nodded.

Jack eyed Timothy. The boy wouldn't look at him.

"Does your mom ever leave you two in charge?"

"Yes," Rebekah said. "Sometimes. For a couple of hours."

"If you don't mind, then, I'll run some errands once the boys and Martha come in. I didn't bring a change of clothes or a toothbrush, and I need to pick up coffee and such."

Timothy lifted his gaze, barely. "Mother doesn't allow caffeine in the house."

"Ah. But Uncle Jack requires it." With effort, Jack kept his voice mild.

"It's all right, Timothy," Rebekah said. "He doesn't have to live by our rules."

Her brother's lips moved with an unspoken comment:

Jack approached the massive shelves that filled the wall behind the table. They held homeschool books. Hundreds of them. Taking his time, he scanned their spines.

Judging by the titles, Miranda's version of school was heavy on math, grammar, history, and nature study but light on hard science and fiction. She owned dozens of biographies of godly souls, several well-worn Bibles, and a handful of Bible commentaries, but no novels unless he counted *The Pilgrim's Progress.*

"Does your mom keep fiction on different shelves somewhere?"

"No," Timothy said.

Jack took another look at the shelves. "Hold on, now. Y'all don't read fiction?"

"Fiction is unnecessary. Frivolous."

Boys that age didn't usually go around using words like that. He must have been quoting somebody. His mother?

Jack blew out a testy breath as rain started to patter against the windows. "The homeschoolers I've known would say good literature isn't even remotely frivolous. Have you ever read *To Kill a Mockingbird,* for instance?"

The kid kept his eyes on his textbook. "No."

"I'd be glad to bring you a copy."

"We don't read novels."

Of all the narrow-minded, ridiculous....

"Does your mom approve of, say...Dr. Seuss?"

"Who?" Rebekah asked.

Jack put his hands on his hips. "Please tell me you're joking."

Slowly, she shook her head. "What kind of doctor is he?"

He shook his head too. "I don't believe this."

The patter became a downpour, pelting the roof and windows. Michael and Gabriel raced inside, their hair darkened with rain. Martha followed, her chubby legs churning beneath her cape. She slammed the door and dumped a dripping handful of pale violets on the floor, then pulled down her hood and fiddled with the fastener at her throat.

"It's a big storm," she said with a grin. "I love big storms."

She spoke with exceptional clarity for her age. She was so bright, so interested in life—but she was deprived even of Seuss.

She was also having a terrible time unfastening her old-fashioned garment. Were ordinary jackets taboo as well?

Swallowing the caustic remarks stacking up on his tongue, Jack crouched before her. He conquered the loop-and-hook contraption that was bedeviling her, lifted the rain-speckled cape from her shoulders, and hung it up. He took his rumpled raincoat from a neighboring peg and shrugged his arms into the sleeves.

"Does anybody need anything from town?"

"Town?" Martha spoke the word with reverence, as if tiny Slades Creek were a magical destination. Then she squatted to gather her flowers. "No, thank you." With violets in both hands, she ran to Rebekah. "I want the tiny teacup today. The green one."

"Please?" her sister prompted.

"Please."

Neither Rebekah nor Timothy asked for anything from town either. She was already pulling a bright green teacup out of a cupboard; he was glaring at his book. Whatever it was, the book was certainly not frivolous.

About to spout off, Jack examined another family portrait on the wall. This one included the parents, when Martha was the baby of the family. Carl, a blond giant in suit and tie, looked like a paragon of respectability. That day on the porch, though, he'd been a boor.

Miranda had given the camera a shy and beguiling smile, her head down and eyes slanted upward in a pose reminiscent of early photos of Princess Diana. But Miranda's hair was atrocious, with long bangs forced into unlikely curls and a fat braid draped over her shoulder. No woman in her right mind would have volunteered for that hairstyle. Nor would a sane woman deprive her children of fiction and God only knew what else.

"Way to go, lady," he said under his breath. "Screw up your kids' lives, then donate 'em to me."

But what a gift. He wouldn't waste the opportunity.

He'd better find the hospital and learn her prognosis. Then he would look for basic necessities. Coffee, a coffee maker, a change of clothes, and toiletries. For the kids, he would try to find a decent bookstore somewhere in the godforsaken hollow called Slades Creek, and the books themselves could do the rest.

She floundered in a black sea of pain. Heavy fog weighed her down. Waves slapped her.

Don't make waves, somebody scolded.

She flew to the edge of the cliffs. The wind flapped her cape like a bird's wings. She was a starving bird, blown off course. Drifting between worlds, she floated past misty, spring green moss on rocks.

She opened her eyes to a smooth white wall. Spinning, spinning, spinning, it never went anywhere but never held still. Closing her eyes, she saw mossy rocks again and muddy tree branches flying past—and heard footsteps—

"Hey there, Miranda," a man said.

No, I'm Randi. Let me be Randi.

"Good Lord, girl, you took quite a tumble."

She forced her leaden eyelids open and saw him, from the shoulders down. In a wrinkled raincoat, the man weaved back and forth, moving but not moving.

Her eyes couldn't take it. She closed them. The inside of her eyelids rotated in a lopsided swirl.

He wasn't Carl. Carl never wore raincoats.

Carl was long gone. She remembered now. The chastisement of God. Her fault. So stubborn.

The letters. The sugar bowl. Jezebel.

She couldn't move. Her limbs were shackled. Her mind was heavy, clogged with pain.

"Miranda," the stranger said.

She dared another narrow peek at the spinning world. He still stood there, making that ceaseless, side-to-side motion.

"Are you awake?" He leaned closer. Dark eyes, curly hair. "I'm Jack. I don't know...but if you can..." His warm drawl drifted in and out, soothing her.

Jack. She knew that name. He was...who was he? She couldn't rouse her tongue to ask.

They'd given her...pain meds, they'd called it. So innocent. But Mason said drugs were witchcraft. They would lure her into giving her soul over. Out of her control. She'd go off the rails again and—

"Why did you name me as guardian?" the man asked. "You don't even know..."

Guardian. Jack. Of course.

She slipped into a dream, a memory, a long-ago day. Lemonade on the porch. They were talking, laughing. Sunshine in the storm.

He was kind. Sensible. He would keep the children safe.

"Miranda." His voice stroked her like a gentle hand on a cat in the sun, making her want to purr.

He had to stay. He was her lifeline.

"It's all right. I'll take care of the kids..."

But he would make waves. He would upset...somebody. She couldn't think who.

She wanted to run. She wanted out. She wanted the sunshine.

A white car pulled into her drive. The state seal....

Nausea rolled over her. She fought it. Consoling drowsiness curled in on her and pulled her into a soft pillow of black.

Too close to the wood stove for comfort, Jack propped himself against the smooth-planed planks of the wall and waited. He'd already given all the kids the simple and optimistic prognosis, but with the two little ones in bed, it was time to give the older four a more detailed report. He had no intentions of addressing the issue of their mother's psyche though.

Darkness seemed to run in the veins of the Hanford men and in the veins of the women they married. Even Ava, for all her upbeat energy, had sometimes shown a streak of melancholy that had scared him half to death.

Part of his mind occupied itself with counting the tight, spiraled rows of the braided rug. The other part stayed on Miranda's battered face and petite frame. And on the contents of the plastic tote he'd brought from the hospital. It held her ruined clothing and her trashed, mud-caked Nikon. The camera was a serious piece of equipment. Film, not digital, it had a vintage look. It must have cost a bundle when it was new, or even more as a collector's item.

Rebekah herded Gabriel and Michael down the stairs and toward the decrepit couch. The couch was a tweedy brown that wouldn't show dirt, which was fortunate, as the archangels had been in some kind of muddy trouble. They needed baths, pronto. All elbow jabs and jiggery pokery, they bounced their bottoms on the cushions. Their big sister, the peacemaker, squeezed between them.

Timothy came in from the kitchen but remained standing, his lean face expressionless. If he'd worn a horned helmet, he could have been a ferocious young Viking.

Knowing the smaller boys couldn't sit still for long, Jack started right in. He'd already decided not to mention the collapsed lung; it sounded too scary.

"Okay, here are the details. Your mom has a concussion, and she broke some ribs, messed up one shoulder, and tore up her right leg. She's lucky though. Instead of falling straight down, she must have slid from one ledge to another. She was groggy when I stopped by, but that won't last."

Gabriel's forehead puckered. "What's a concussion?"

"That's what they call it when you bang your head so hard that you black out. She'll have headaches and be tired and dizzy and sick to her stomach for a while, but her doctor says that's to be expected."

Timothy didn't move a muscle. The other kids sat on the couch like big-eyed owls on a branch, staring.

Jack was still trying to grasp the situation. "Who needs to know what happened? Family? Folks from church?"

Michael scowled at the floor. "People from church don't come around much."

Rebekah elbowed him. "There's our pastor. His name's Mason Chandler."

Jack wasn't eager for help from that quarter, but he tucked the name away in his memory. "What about relatives?"

Rebekah hesitated. "We don't have any."

Hard to believe. It might explain a few mysteries though.

"Isn't there anybody who needs to know your mom's in the hospital? Neighbors? Friends?"

The kids regarded him in mute puzzlement.

Jack asked more questions and learned that the children had never set foot in a school building or a McDonald's or a mall. A trip to the grocery store was an unusual event. Miranda did most of her shopping by mail order or from a food co-op that delivered to their door.

The kids had never touched a computer. They had never been to a movie or an amusement park. They had never been allowed to browse at the library—Miranda left them at home with Timothy in charge and selected their books herself—and that high-handed censorship was the clincher.

"All right." Jack resisted the urge to indulge in some salty language about his sister-in-law. "That's very…interesting. I'd like to know how—"

"Michael, Gabriel, you need a bath," Timothy said. "Go. Get the water started."

The archangels bolted. Timothy stalked after them, muttering that they needed supervision, although it wasn't likely. The only bathroom was downstairs, practically in the living room.

"The clean towels are in the laundry basket," Rebekah called.

She returned her attention to Jack. Her gaze was clear and direct, like he remembered her mother's. That was years ago, though, and he might have modified the memory to suit himself.

"Why did Mother pick you to be our guardian?" Rebekah asked.

That question, again. "Who did you expect her to choose?"

"I never thought about it." Rebekah frowned. "Do you even know her?"

Jack weighed how much to tell. Rebekah was an extraordinarily capable young lady for ten, but it wasn't likely that she knew much about real life.

"Okay, here's the story," he said. "Your grandpa's first wife was Celia, your dad's mom. When your dad was a little boy, your grandpa left them. He divorced Celia and married a woman named Eleanor. My mother." Jack took a breath and skipped his mother's fate. "My father died when I was in my twenties. After some years passed, I wanted more family than I had, so I stopped by to meet your dad."

"You'd never even met him?"

"Never, and I thought it was high time. He wasn't home, but I introduced myself to your mom. We sat on the porch and talked. Timothy was about three, and you were about a year old. You thought you were queen of the world because you'd learned to walk, but you wore yourself out and fell asleep in your mom's lap."

Rebekah smiled toward the window that overlooked the porch. "Then what happened?"

"We swapped phone numbers and planned to get together again. It was like finding a ready-made brother and sister-in-law for me, a brother-in-law for her. When your dad came home, though, he wasn't too pleased to meet me."

She met his eyes again. "How could you tell?"

"Well...he said I shouldn't come back. So that was the end of it." Except for the letters Jack had written, for years. Wasted effort, all of them.

"That still doesn't explain why she picked you."

"You're right. It doesn't."

"When she's feeling better, we can ask her."

"Yes, we can. Meanwhile, I located her attorney this afternoon, and he gave me the name of a reliable woman who can stay with y'all tomorrow while I run to Chattanooga. Mrs. Walker. Yvonne Walker. Do you know her?"

"No."

Of course not.

One of the boys shrieked angry words. Rebekah excused herself. Jack stayed put, having no desire to involve himself in the bath melee, but he heard everything.

"Get clean all over," Timothy ordered. "All over, Gabriel! Wash your ears."

Timothy was wound way too tight, but he'd had a terrible day. Apparently it had started with finding his mom at the bottom of the cliffs.

How had he known to search for her, though, so early in the morning? The unanswered questions kept piling up.

Rebekah's voice ran through her brothers' wrangling like a calm undercurrent in a tumultuous stream. After a few minutes, water gurgled down the drain. Timothy and Rebekah returned to the living room. Her dress was sprinkled with bath water, but he'd stayed dry.

The archangels followed, wearing damp skivvies and smelling like citrusy shampoo. They hadn't wasted much time in drying themselves, and their young limbs were shiny with water. Michael ran up the stairs while Gabriel darted to the front door and flung it open.

"I have to find my—" Cold air flooded in. Gabriel's feet thudded across the porch and down the steps in the dark. He reversed the process and hurtled inside clutching a slingshot. "Got it!" He slammed the door so hard that Jack cringed.

"Now your feet are filthy," Timothy said, pointing. "You need another bath."

"No." Rebekah slipped between them. She marched the half-naked boy into the kitchen and knelt to wipe his feet with a kitchen towel. "There. Clean all over. Off to bed, Gabriel, and say your prayers. Good night."

"G'night." Slingshot in hand, he stormed through the living room and up the stairs.

Rebekah stayed on her knees like a nun at her devotions, her habit made of denim. After a moment, she rose, slinging the dirtied dish towel over her shoulder, and walked toward the bathroom.

Jack guessed what she would do. Ten years old, she would play mom to her brothers. She would wipe the wet floor, tidy the towels, pick up the shed clothing.

Dazed, he thought of the pricey Glenlivet he'd bought the week before. If he'd had it with him, once the kids were out of his hair, he would have exercised his right to unwind somewhere in peace and quiet. Except, if Miranda didn't allow caffeine in her house, there was no hope whatsoever for a good Scotch whiskey. Demon alcohol.

He turned to Timothy. "Gabe's quite a handful."

"His name is Gabriel."

Nicknames were against their religion too? Jack kept his mouth shut, but he couldn't help thinking of the changes he would make if the kids were his. Lord willing, they never would be. But he was responsible for their welfare. He had to know where each one slept, at least. If the house ever caught fire....

He climbed the creaky, steep stairway. It was narrow, with a wobbly handrail. God only knew the condition of the electrical system and the furnace, if there was one, and he'd seen no sign of smoke alarms or carbon monoxide detectors.

He gained the second floor, half the size of the main floor and dimly lit by night lights. One of the bedrooms held two sets of bunk beds. In plaid pajamas, Michael and Gabriel huddled in the top bunks and argued softly with each other. Jonah was sound asleep in the bottom bunk on the left. Crowded close to the safety rail, he clutched a quilt to his chin. He was sucking his thumb, his mouth moving around it like fish lips.

"Good night, gentlemen," Jack said quietly.

"G'night," the archangels echoed in unison. They resumed their subdued argument without missing a beat.

The other bedroom held two twin-size four-posters, two dressers, and two school desks, all painted in pastel colors that glowed ghostly in the half light. Martha was sacked out, hugging the Seuss book he'd found in the grocery store down the street from Slades Creek's little hospital. It was the closest thing to a bookstore that he'd found.

She smiled in her sleep.

Jack grinned, rocking back and forth on his heels. Martha was already a book addict like her worldly uncle. A taste of *Green Eggs and Ham* would be good medicine for a literalist.

In his brief conversation with Miranda's attorney, Alexander Whitlow, Jack had learned that a guardian was required to abide by the parents' religious convictions for the children but had some freedom to make choices about their education. He hadn't asked Whitlow if a ban on Seuss would be called a religious conviction or an educational decision. It was a moot point anyway; Miranda's authority hadn't been transferred. Jack was simply Martha's uncle who happened to pick up a book to entertain her while her mom recovered.

Whitlow had not revealed why Miranda had changed her will, nor who the previous guardian or guardians had been, if any. He'd cited client confidentiality.

As Jack reached the bottom of the stairs, Rebekah emerged from the downstairs bedroom, carrying a wicker laundry basket heaped with bedding.

She smiled timidly. "I put fresh sheets on the bed for you." Her eyebrows wobbled up and down. "Uncle Jack," she finished, her cheeks turning pink.

Her bashful use of the honorific—new to her, but sadly nostalgic to him—moved him. He hadn't been an official uncle since his divorce cut him off, not only from Ava, but also from her sister's kids, and it still hurt.

"Thanks, Rebekah. I can sleep on the couch though. You didn't have to—"

"Oh, no. Take the bed," she said, sounding like a grown hostess. "That's what Mother would say." She hurried away, shifting the laundry basket to her skinny hip.

No doubt Miranda wouldn't want him anywhere near her bed, but he checked out the room. The high four-poster was spread with an intricately pieced quilt in shades of blue and green. A stiff, symmetrical swag of dried flowers hung on the wall, flanked by three little needlepoint pictures on each side. The frames were lined up with an inch separating each one from its neighbor. Miranda seemed fond of regularity and order, or maybe that was Carl's influence.

Everywhere were family photos, some posed and some candid. Many of them were artsy black-and-whites with a photo-journalistic flair out of sync with the stiffness he saw elsewhere.

Rebekah may have been right about having no relatives, because Jack saw no photos of anyone but Carl, Miranda, and the children, and there weren't many of Miranda. She must have been the official family photographer, behind the camera more often than in front of it.

Now her vintage Nikon was trash.

Now a man she didn't know had taken charge of her children.

That explained the panic he'd seen in her eyes when she fought through the pain medication and connected with reality. Maybe she'd begun to question her crazy decision.

She might question it even more once she woke in her right mind, or in whatever passed for a right mind in her strange world. A world where children didn't use computers or read fiction. Where they didn't even know Dr. Seuss.

Tomorrow, Jack would enroll six young students in Normal American Life 101. He couldn't stay long, but while he did, at least he could say he was homeschooling them.

four

Miranda struggled out of a groggy sleep and recalled a man standing beside her bed. "It's all right," the stranger had said. "I'll take care of the kids."

No, not quite a stranger. Jack. Unless she'd dreamed him.

What was he doing in her bedroom?

She fingered the bedding. It was wrong. A fuzzy blanket instead of her soft quilt and smooth sheets. And her hand hurt.

Everything hurt.

She fought to open her eyes. Her head drummed with a dull ache that was pierced by daggers when she made the slightest movement. She turned anyway and saw closed blinds on an unfamiliar wall. Everything kept spinning and thumping.

She closed her eyes. The throbbing continued. Desperate to know where she was, she turned slowly in the other direction before she opened her eyes again.

A pale blue curtain hung from the ceiling. A room divider.

A hospital room. That antiseptic smell. That quiet bustling.

Past hours came back in bits and pieces. Intense pain encasing her chest, her shoulder. Ice packs, bandages, IV lines.

A move from one room to another. A nurse who hummed and a room-mate who snored.

A doctor who pried her eyelids open and mumbled at her.

Something rustled. The room divider swayed. A thin woman in a green shirt loomed over the bed, out of focus, and fiddled with the IV bag.

"You awake, hon?"

"I…I think so."

The nurse smiled. "Maybe not, then. Do you remember what happened?"

Miranda lay still, trying to sort memory from nightmare, and nightmare from dream. "I fell?"

"You sure did. You've had a concussion, not to mention a collapsed lung and some broken ribs and a separated shoulder. Pretty impressive road rash too. Did you know that?"

"Not…exactly. Did I have a visitor?"

"I don't know, hon. I'm working nights."

"Yeah, you had a visitor." A woman spoke from the other side of the divider. "A man. Dark hair. Good-lookin'."

Jack? She hadn't dreamed him. He had the children, then?

He would think she deserved to lose them. A good mother wouldn't have left her children alone in the house. Not even for a prayer walk. But what had she been praying about?

She moved her head too quickly and cried out. The room spiraled, pressing in on her.

The nurse hovered near. "You have a button to push for your meds, whenever you need more." Warm fingers took Miranda's hand and guided it toward the side of the bed, then curled it around something cold and hard. "Like this, see? There, now. You'll feel better soon." The nurse lowered Miranda's hand to the bed.

Lying motionless, she tried to think. Everything was fuzzy. And growing fuzzier. Now her bed was a boat, tilting and circling in a giant whirlpool. Nearly going under.

She was thankful for the numbness creeping up on her. But she mustn't rely on *pharmakeia*. It was a false peace. It wasn't peace at all.

Too late. The whirlpool spun faster, sucked her in, and spat her up in Abigail's living room. Nicole was there, her dark eyes shining. She held a folded red sweater to her chest.

That's Abigail's sweater! Miranda snatched it and ran.

You Jezebel, Carl scolded. *Now you're a thief too.*

You're dead, she told him. *Be quiet. I don't have to obey you anymore.*

He faded away. She was drowning in the black hole again, trying to catch her babies in the cuddle-quilt as they fell from the sky. One…two…three….

They fell from heaven, dodged earth, and raced through a lower sky toward hell. Something choked her scream into a weak bleat that traveled no further than her prayers.

Jack stumbled into the kitchen, rubbing his face awake. "O, I have passed a miserable night, so full of fearful dreams, of ugly sights, that, as I am a Christian faithful man…"

It was annoying, sometimes, the way his mind spouted Shakespeare at random moments.

Something about sliding between Miranda's flowery sheets hadn't set right with him, and he'd hardly slept. He'd kept imagining how his life might have changed if her fall had killed her.

One thing was certain. If anything ever happened to her now, he couldn't put the children in foster care. Martha? Jonah? Unthinkable.

He couldn't raise six orphans either.

Jack looked out the window at a dormant vegetable garden and an arbor hung with brown, bare grapevines. Farther away, fog softened the outline of a wooden swing hanging from an oak that still bore last year's caramel brown leaves. Three smaller oaks stood deeper in the fog. One broken limb hung straight down like a body at the end of a rope.

It was only Tuesday. Too early in the week for morbid thoughts. He turned away from the window.

Thankful that the local Kroger stocked everything necessary for the perfect cup of coffee, Jack poured beans just past the four-cup line in his brand-new grinder and hit the switch. An explosive racket shattered the quiet. Quickly, he lifted his finger from the switch.

No sounds of life came from upstairs. Thank God. He didn't need half a dozen rug rats underfoot when he was hardly awake. But he couldn't wake up without coffee.

He toyed with the desperate idea of pulverizing the beans with the marble mortar and pestle on the windowsill, then recognized the insanity of that notion. Grimacing at the noise, he hit the switch again. Nobody stirred, but he'd better start grinding the beans the night before.

While the coffee brewed in his new, no-frills coffee maker, he took a closer look at Miranda's domain. The kitchen held a king-size fridge and a modern electric range. Sunshine, filtered through fog, sneaked into the room over plain white curtains that covered only the bottom half of the window.

The walls were warm, knot-holed planks, and her decorating taste ran toward cheerful yellows and greens. The door of the fridge held twelve pieces of artwork and penmanship practice, lined up in two neat columns that nearly reached the floor. Everything looked clean, orderly, and reasonably prosperous, but something was missing. He couldn't put his finger on it.

Maybe it was the very orderliness of the room that bothered him. He preferred the irregular, off kilter, haphazard stuff of life. He liked, as Hopkins put it, all things counter, original, spare, strange.

Jack examined an ugly pink and purple ceramic plaque that hung above the stove. Clumsily painted pansies nearly eclipsed the florid lettering:

A wife who's always neat and sweet
Makes her husband's life a treat.

Jack rolled his eyes and turned his back on the monstrosity.

Soon he was at the table, drinking black coffee from a brown mug. With his eyes closed, he could almost fool himself into believing he was in his own kitchen—

"What's a half person?"

Startled, he looked down at a sleepy face framed by messy pigtails. Martha wore a flannel nightgown, and she'd draped a small quilt around her shoulders like a faded red and blue shawl.

"Mornin', Miss Martha."

"Good morning," she said in her precise way. She placed her elbows on the table and propped her chin in her hands. "How can there be a half person?"

He smiled at the glimpse into a four-year-old mind. "Like a half-brother?"

She nodded.

"I'm a whole person, but I'm only a half brother to your dad because we had the same father but not the same mother. Do you understand that?"

She scrutinized him as she mulled the concept. "No."

"Don't worry about it. I'm ten times older than you are, and there are a lot of things I still don't understand."

She pointed to the cereal he'd unloaded on the counter the day before. "What's in that blue box?"

"Frosted Flakes. Do you like Frosted Flakes?"

"What's that?"

He nearly choked on his coffee. "It's a kind of cereal. What do you usually have for breakfast?"

"Toast or hot oatmeal. Or hot buckwheat when Mama's fasting because she doesn't like it so then she isn't tempted."

"Fasting? Why does she fast?"

"Because she wants to hear God." Martha's tone implied that he was a big dummy for needing to ask. "That kind there, is it any good?"

"What a pessimist. Of course it's good." He searched for a bowl, finding the right cupboard on his third try, and fixed her a serving of Frosted Flakes.

She dropped her quilt to the floor. "We can't get sticky fingers on the cuddle-quilt," she explained. Then she sat across from him and devoured the cereal, milk dribbling down her chin. Finished, she let out a sigh of bliss. "That was yummy."

"Told you so."

"It tastes like sugar." She grinned. "I like you, Uncle Jack."

"I like you too."

"Pastor Mason says sugar is bad, but he doesn't come around much." She scraped one last spoonful of milk from the bottom of the bowl. "I don't think he likes us."

Before Jack could process that, Rebekah came downstairs and greeted him shyly. The archangels arrived in the midst of a good-natured squabble, followed by Jonah in red pajamas, bumping his way down the stairs on his rump. Timothy came last, avoiding Jack's eyes.

Michael inhaled noisily. "What's that smell?"

"That isn't a smell, son. It's an aroma. The aroma of freshly ground Arabica coffee beans from tropical mountain slopes. At this hour, it's my reason for living."

Michael put his nose nearly in Jack's coffee and inhaled again. "Can I try some?"

"Once your mother's home, you can ask her if it's all right."

But Jack decided to have no scruples about sharing his sugar-coated cereal. Although Timothy only took a banana from the counter and left the room, the other kids enjoyed the unexpected treat. Martha had seconds. What would have been a week's supply for Jack was gone, just like that, and he'd never had a bite.

He was an adult though. He had wheels. He could escape, any time he wanted, into a world that held Frosted Flakes and anything else his heart desired.

"Listen up," he said when the children were about to scatter. "I need to run to Chattanooga, but I don't want y'all to be home alone that long, so I've found a woman to stay for the day. Her name is Mrs. Walker, and I hear she's a nice lady but she runs a tight ship. That means no misbehavin', understand?"

Nobody argued. Rebekah wiped Jonah's sticky face and hands and liberated him from the highchair. Without prompting, the other kids rinsed their bowls and started their chores.

Timothy fetched logs from the stash on the porch, stoked the wood stove, and tidied the hearth. The archangels swept and vacuumed. Rebekah washed dishes—there was no automatic dishwasher—and planned supper. Jack had never known a ten-year-old whose day started with planning a meal for a family.

At nine, a white car bucked around the last curve of the bumpy driveway. Jack stepped outside, pointing, to direct the driver to park behind the van and leave the Audi unblocked. She complied and climbed out. Silver-haired Yvonne Walker was seventy if she was a day, but she wore jeans and a bright red top. Her lipstick was as vivid as her shirt.

"Hey, there. Are you Jack? I'm Yvonne. Land sakes, but that's a long driveway. I never even knew there was a house hid away back here." Hauling an immense canvas tote bag, she sashayed toward him, chewing gum at a rapid rate.

He ushered her inside and introduced her to the kids. She had their rapt attention as she gathered them around the table and started to unpack her tote. First out was a romance novel with a garish cover.

"That's for me. So's this." She pulled out a six-pack of Diet Coke.

Then, winning Jack's heart forever, she produced what she called "entertainments." Jigsaw puzzles, a Rubik's Cube, Play-Doh…and books. Board books. Classic picture books. Seuss. Even a few easy chapter books. Jack could have kissed her wrinkled cheek.

With Yvonne firmly in charge, he could leave with a clear conscience. He settled behind the wheel of his car, an eBay bargain with low mileage and a defunct stereo. Within ten minutes, he'd blown through downtown Slades Creek, such as it was, and was headed northwest.

The mountains of Bartram County were very much like the ones he'd known as a boy in the next county. Each switchback curve held an interesting ravine or a waterfall or a glimpse of distant cliffs. The views were spectacular, but the pockets of poverty were heartbreaking.

The run-down houses and trailers of the mountains hadn't seemed trashy when he was a child. Children were that way, though, oblivious to the concerns of the adult world. So the adults had to do the worrying for them.

His new worries accompanied him all the way to Chattanooga.

It was nearly eleven when Jack unlocked the back door of his cluttered bungalow. As always when he'd been away for a while, he half expected Ava to greet him with a kiss. Or with another round of tears and recriminations.

His briefcase still lay on the table, exactly as he'd left it. Already, it seemed as if his work belonged to some different world.

He hurried down the hall, past the room they'd envisioned as a nursery. Since Ava had left, it had become a catchall, a repository for junk and old dreams of a baby or two.

Weaving back and forth between office and bedroom, he grabbed clothes, toiletries, and the books and papers necessary to keep up on his committee work and his writing. He made several trips to the car, finishing with a battered paperback copy of *To Kill a Mockingbird* and the cigar box from his desk.

Inside again, he fired up his laptop to check e-mail and the news. Doing the bare minimum, he finished quickly, then typed a few words into a search engine. Within minutes, he'd printed nearly forty pages of information about certain circles of not-quite-mainstream Christians. Even at first glance, parts of it were highly disturbing.

About to drive away, the laptop and printouts stashed in the trunk, he remembered the Glenlivet and ran back for it. It should have gone in the trunk, but he tucked it carefully under the passenger seat instead.

It was a ten-minute drive to the tree-filled campus that was a second home to him. He nipped into the dragon's lair, but Farnsworth wasn't in her office. Grateful for small blessings, Jack loitered in the hallway and pondered his immediate future.

If he took a leave of absence, he'd be out for the rest of the semester. His colleagues would be great about covering for him, but he hated to impose on them. Who could cover for Miranda though? Timothy and Rebekah? Even if their mom came home in a day or two, they'd be shouldering burdens far beyond their years for weeks.

That settled it. He solicited the leave-of-absence paperwork from Farnsworth's admin and nailed down some temporary workload arrangements, subject to change. With that process underway, he picked up a slew of work from his own office and ran for his car.

As he drove across the campus, a dark mood descended on him. He faced a long haul through the mountains, his destination a run-down log home on a lonely hillside. He'd be stuck there for days, maybe for weeks. He had no friends in Slades Creek. No adult company. Nobody but six sheltered kids. And, soon, their mother, who fasted so she could "hear God." Jack couldn't imagine hearing a personal message from God. It didn't fit into his theological framework.

He tried to picture this Mason Chandler whose teachings Miranda followed. A stern, bearded figure like an Old Testament patriarch, perhaps, and equally devoted to rules. Not that rules were intrinsically bad.

Jack's thoughts meandered with the winding roads. He recalled his search for coffee in Miranda's cupboards. Instead of coffee, he'd found a container of St. John's wort capsules. They might come in handy.

An hour and a half later, he reached Slades Creek, zipped through town without hitting any red lights, and continued south. The sun was sinking to-ward the horizon as he turned onto Larkin Road, not quite a quarter mile from Miranda's place, and passed a small herd of goats that must have belonged to her neighbors. White scraps of movement in the twilight, they looked more like ghosts than farm animals.

Yvonne met him at the door with her tote bag slung over her shoulder. "Those children aren't being raised right." She glared at him as if he were to blame. "They're sweet, every last one, but they're almost *too* good. My word, they've never seen a movie. Not even a kids' movie. They don't know any songs but Scripture songs. The girls don't own jeans. They don't even—"

"Shh." He sent her a warning look over the box of papers in his arms. "I know, I know."

She came onto the porch and planted her bejeweled hands on her hips. "Well, what do you plan to do about it?"

"I don't know, but I'm working on it."

"Work a little faster, hon."

"I have to proceed carefully. We're dealing with sincere religious convictions."

"Being sincere doesn't make 'em right. You know their mom's in that strange church, don't you?"

"Do you know Miranda?"

"No, but I've figured out which church she's in. When my daddy was in his right mind, he never went around bad-mouthing other preachers, but he always said Mason Chandler had some strange ideas."

"Such as?"

"Chandler is the Lone Ranger type. He doesn't take orders from anybody, but he orders the men around, and the men order their wives around. Those poor women don't have a thought of their own." Yvonne leaned closer. "They're not even allowed to *vote.*"

"Excuse me?" Jack set the box on the porch and straightened. "This is the United States of America. It's a free country."

"Not in some households. Look into it, Jack."

"I will." He pulled out his wallet and extracted a generous payment meant to keep her on his side.

Yvonne pocketed the money, thanked him, and hauled her tote to her car, where she faced him. "The kids never go anywhere, never do anything. Can you imagine *their* children?"

Hermits or rebels. Or worse.

"Say, did their mom happen to call?" he asked.

"No, nobody called. The phone didn't ring. Not even once."

The phone never rang, friends never stopped by, and Miranda would consider it a sin to escape into a soap opera or a romance novel. No wonder she popped St. John's wort capsules, the earth-mother version of Prozac.

"Have you ever heard of homeschoolers who ban fiction?" he asked.

"No!" One hand on her car door, Yvonne stared at him. "One of my girls homeschooled her kids, and sometimes I thought she spent half her grocery money on paperback novels." She nodded toward the house. "These aren't your normal homeschoolers, hon."

five

A dream of tumbling down a mountainside woke her and slid away. Still half-asleep, Miranda sought something solid. Something that wouldn't fall out from under her. Time slipped and slued, fishtailing like a car on ice, spinning her through the recent past in no particular order.

A roommate, snoring. A nurse, checking vital signs. Opening and closing the divider.

The rattles and clinks of food trays. Food smells. Doctors, asking too many questions.

She took a deep breath and gasped at the agony that knifed her chest.

"Hurts to breathe, doesn't it?" A gray-haired nurse popped into view. "Broken ribs are the devil himself. Remember, now, don't be afraid to mash the button for more meds. It's controlled so you can't overdose."

"I'm...fine."

She couldn't remember what had happened. Yesterday? Or the day before?

A fragrance of flowers came from the other side of the divider. Sweet and light, like the girls' violets—

The children! She had to call home. That's what she had to do. Dial 532… no, 352. No, it was…. The digits jumbled themselves in her head until she wanted to scream.

"Excuse me, nurse?" Her voice was rusty, her throat dry. "I can't remember my own phone number. Could you find it for me, please?"

"That's a concussion for you. Sure, I'll track it down. Give me a few minutes." The nurse left the room.

Miranda lay still. Tears seeped onto her cheeks. She couldn't use her right hand to dry the tears because her shoulder hurt so badly that she couldn't lift her arm. Slowly, she raised her left arm. It trailed an IV line. An ID bracelet rasped against her wrist.

A sob caught her in the ribs like a giant's fist. She felt as if she'd been in a fight, pounded by some merciless bully. But what had happened?

Think.

That was it. She'd been trying to think. Day after day, she'd gone to the cliffs, alone. Praying. Planning. The days blurred, and she couldn't remember much about her last walk. Just that the sun had burned through the fog as she'd stood by the cliffs. Maybe, dazzled by the cloudy white sunshine and lightheaded from fasting, she'd fainted.

Who had the children? Nothing else mattered.

Jack had them. Because she'd written that letter and she'd changed her will. Because Mason planned to move the entire church to North Carolina. That was almost as crazy as some of Carl's ideas, but Mason had warned her not to stir up trouble. So she'd dragged Jack into it. By now, he must have decided *she* was the crazy one.

She opened her eyes to convince herself that she was awake and in her right mind.

She hadn't dreamed it. Mason had threatened her.

"Your visitor was a good-looking guy," her roommate volunteered from the other side of the curtain. "Your husband?"

"No. My husband passed away a couple of years ago. That was his brother."

"Oh, I'm sorry about your husband." The woman paused. "His brother is cute."

The nurse breezed back into the room. "Here's the number. It's an ungodly hour though. You'd better wait." She left a slip of paper on the bedside tray and hurried out.

"But I have to check on my children!" A sob racked Miranda's throat and shook her ribs into pain so intense that a wave of black rolled across her vision. She fought it off.

"The nurse ain't God," her roommate said. "You can call right now, if you want to."

Miranda tried to shift her position and yelped. "I can't reach the phone."

"I'll get it for you." A middle-aged woman swam into view. Wearing a blue and white hospital gown, she padded to the bedside. "Hi, I'm Sue."

"I'm Miranda."

She heard a rustle as the woman picked up the paper, and then the *tap-tap-tap* of fingers on buttons. The phone nestled in Miranda's hand and was guided to her ear.

She waited, anticipating Timothy's voice. It was his job to pick up the phone when she wasn't home.

On the second ring, a man answered with a low, grumpy "Hello."

"Who is—oh." Her scrambled brain had already forgotten Jack would be there. "Is this Jack?"

"It is. Who's calling?"

"This is Miranda."

"Miranda. Is everything all right? Do you need me to run up to the hospital?"

"No. The children. How are the children?"

"They're fine. Alive and kicking."

"Are they up yet?"

"At five in the morning?" A short laugh. "No. I wasn't either. I'm glad you called though. I have questions."

"It's too early for that," she said quickly. "I'll call back later so I can talk to the children. About eight?"

"Sure. Let me give you my cell number so you can reach me anytime."

"Wait. Sue? Can you write down a number for me?"

Miranda repeated the numbers after Jack. On the other side of the curtain, Sue parroted them once more as she wrote them down.

"I've got it." Miranda's nose itched as tears dried on it. "Has anyone else called? Or come by?"

"No. Not a soul."

"This may sound strange, but I'd like to ask you not to rock the boat while I'm gone. Don't, um, make waves."

He laughed. "You're asking the impossible, darlin'. They call me Jack 'Tsunami' Hanford."

"They do?"

He laughed again, making her feel like a fool. "No, I just made it up. I like the sound of it though."

She had to play along. "Yes, it has a ring to it. Well, I'll...I'll let you go."

"All right. And Miranda—you're welcome."

"Oh! Thank you, Jack. Thank you so much. You'll never know how much I appreciate—"

Too late. She was speaking to a dead phone. She deserved his shortness with her, but it still stung.

He'd better not be short with the children, or he'd hear about it.

As she lowered the phone to the bed, a man walking down the hallway chuckled and said "Bottom of the ninth." A woman laughed and made a soft reply.

She sounded happy. Normal. She wasn't worried about tangling with a pastor who wanted to drag his entire church out of state. She didn't have to rely on a smart-mouthed professor who had no idea what kind of trouble he might cause.

Miranda needed him though. The children needed him. Jack was the wall between them and Mason's threat.

Unwilling to disturb her roommate again, Miranda wept quietly, the agony escalating with every stifled sob. She ached to be with her children. This hospital stay was like an evil foretaste of a worse separation.

At five minutes to eight, Jack rounded up the kids and told them their mom would be calling. "And everybody will have a chance to talk, all right? You can pass the phone around."

They gathered at the kitchen table and waited. Sometimes they were a tad too compliant, as if their behavior had been shaped by a rod on their backsides, though Jack had no problem with that. He had been raised that way, with moderate success.

At two minutes past, the phone rang. He grabbed it. "Jack's Diner. The best breakfast in town."

Gabriel busted loose with a belly laugh. Within seconds, everybody started laughing. Everybody but Timothy, who stared off into space, and Miranda.

"I want to talk to my children," she said after a frosty silence.

"Certainly, madam. Here, start with Martha. She's about to blow a gasket."

Martha nearly dropped the phone in her excitement. "Mama! Guess what? Uncle Jack gave me a book! And Frosted Flakes!"

He slunk away, smiling. In Martha's sheltered existence, maybe he *was* nearly a tsunami.

"Hey, look." Gabriel pointed toward the window. "Pastor Mason's here."

It was mighty early for a pastoral visit. He must have heard about Miranda's accident.

Jack watched from a window as an old burgundy Buick rolled to a stop behind the van. A tall, solidly built man climbed out and frowned at the Audi. Probably pushing fifty, the visitor wore a dark suit and a white shirt but no tie. Lacking the full beard that Jack had imagined for him, Mason Chandler bore no visible resemblance to an Old Testament prophet. A televangelist, maybe, or a game show host.

Jack pondered some of his experiences with ultraconservative churches. He'd found two schools of thought regarding facial hair for men. According to one view, it was sinful to shave. According to the other view, it was sinful not to. Chandler's mug was as hairless as a baby's bottom, and so was Carl's in every photo.

Jack ran a hand over his jaw and considered losing his razor for a while.

The man moved his attention from the car to the house, studying it with narrowed eyes, and started walking.

Jack stepped onto the porch. "Good morning."

The man broke stride but recovered quickly and jogged up the steps. "Good morning. And who are you?"

"Jack Hanford." He offered his hand. "Carl's brother."

Chandler shook hands but scrutinized Jack as if he might have been guilty of an overnight tryst with Miranda. "Mason Chandler. Miranda's pastor. Is she home?"

"She's in the hospital. She fell from the cliffs."

Mason's eyebrows rose. "How did she manage that?"

That was entirely the wrong question. Jack's needle drifted toward the orange zone.

"She was taking pictures, apparently."

Mason shook his head. "Miranda and that camera."

"In case you're interested, she's going to be all right."

"Thank God. I'll be praying for her. How did you get involved, Jack?"

"On Miranda's orders, Timothy asked me to help out."

"Why you, Jack?"

Like a used car salesman, Mason used first names at every opportunity. The habit grated on Jack's nerves.

"I'm the children's guardian," he said.

Mason's face hardened. "When did that happen?"

"Recently."

"How long do you plan to stay?"

"For the duration."

"That's not necessary. The church can take over."

Jack's needle jumped to the red zone but he hung on to civility. "No, thank you. We're doing fine."

"You must have more important things to do with your time, Jack."

"Not at all. I'm glad to help. Apparently I'm the only family she has."

"The church is her family now."

Then it was a dysfunctional family. The clues were adding up.

The door creaked. Jack looked over his shoulder.

Gabriel peered through a three-inch gap but didn't speak. Even when Mason gave him a warm "Good morning," Gabriel only nodded, closing the door with an unwelcoming click. The kid had good taste, if not good manners.

Mason began his retreat. "Nice meeting you, Jack. I'll stay in touch."

"You do that. I'll be here."

After the Buick rolled away, Jack paced the porch until he'd put a lid on his temper. When he went inside, the kids were off the phone, and they'd scattered. All except Martha.

Cute as a bug, she was curled up on the couch, her hair still in those messy braids. She'd pulled her long nightgown all the way over her feet, and she'd draped what she called the cuddle-quilt around her shoulders. Her lips moved as she sounded her way through the Seuss book. Sometimes, she spoke a word out loud, savoring her mastery of the symbols that stood for sounds that made words that built worlds. She owned those worlds, but her mother kept her locked up, safe from the big, scary, real world where bad things happened.

Bad things could happen in a run-down log home on an isolated back road too. Like a very bad thing once happened in a small brick house in an ordinary town where a boy looked into his mother's eyes and saw unthinkable darkness but did nothing.

"Not this time," Jack said quietly. "I'll make a fool of myself first."

Martha looked up with a smile so happy that it broke his heart.

six

It was still dark out, and oddly quiet compared to the thrum of Chattanooga. Waiting for the coffee to brew, Jack drifted through the previous day.

The family could have survived without him. Timothy acted as the man of the house, keeping the wood stove fueled and lecturing Jonah about staying away from its hot surfaces. Rebekah did a fine job of washing clothes and putting meals on the table, but her gratitude for Jack's help made him realize what a load she was carrying.

Ten. She was *ten*.

The younger ones carried on as best they could, doing their junior-size chores, but they were getting a little ragged around the edges. They missed their mom.

And Miranda? She'd called several times, perfectly lucid. Uptight, but lucid. No one else had called. Just that early-morning visit from her pastor. The memory was almost enough to put Jack in a foul mood.

Sitting at the kitchen table, he eased into his day with a paper from a student who always took a highly original view and set out to prove her point with style if not with impeccable logic. T. S. Eliot himself might have enjoyed her thoughts about the psyche of J. Alfred Prufrock.

Jack leaned over the paper, red pen poised. He would make her think harder and dig deeper. When parents entrusted their young people's minds to R. Jackson Hanford, PhD, they got their money's worth.

His troubles retreated to a dull rumble in the back of his mind while he played with words, ideas, arguments. He loved teaching. Loved his students. Most of them, anyway. Most of the time.

Halfway through the paper, he tripped on Eliot's line about Prufrock's thinning hair. It conjured up memories of a dad with a receding hairline and an existential crisis of his own.

Jack ran a hand through his hair. It was still thick, a legacy from his mother's genes. His temples were going gray, though, and he was barely past his fortieth birthday. At forty, his father already had two failed marriages behind him. Jack had one, and that was one too many.

Struggling to focus on his student's paper, he saw instead his father's odd, blank expression. It had cropped up with increasing frequency after his not-quite-ex-wife's memorial service. Roger Hanford had blamed himself, for good reason, but he wasn't the only one at fault.

Outside, the wind lifted its head. Rain began to fall, light but steady. Jack poured more coffee and dug into his work. When he heard feet on the stairs, he was startled to see daylight at the window above the half curtains.

Rebekah was shepherding Jonah down the stairs. "Hurry up. If you don't make it in time…"

"No." Jonah's sleepy fretting was like a fiddle played out of tune. "Don't hafta."

"Yes, you do."

They reached the bottom of the stairs. Rebekah wore a long, floral-print dress, while Jonah shuffled along in his red footed pajamas, clutching a blue jay's feather.

Rebekah smiled. "Good morning, Uncle Jack."

"Good morning. Hey, Jonah."

Jonah only pouted as they proceeded to the bathroom. Not a morning person, obviously.

The rain poured harder, a depressing flood of gray. The archangels woke, evidenced by bumps, thumps, and all manner of shrillness upstairs. Timothy's voice joined theirs, in a lower register. Every time the boys' footsteps thudded on the ceiling, the noise jarred Jack.

Rebekah and Jonah emerged from the bathroom. She installed him in the highchair, conned him out of the feather, and gave him a banana. With Jonah settled, she started heating a pot of water on the electric stove.

The kids would need room to eat breakfast. Jack gathered his papers into a neat pile. He could always think better when he had room to spread out his work, as if that made room for bigger thoughts. That was another habit he needed to lay down for a while.

The other children showed up as Rebekah was doling out oatmeal. She offered it to Jack too, but he would have preferred to eat mud.

"Thanks, but I'm not ready to eat yet," he said to soften his refusal. "Maybe I'll fix something later in the..." He saw a toaster, a food processor, a huge slow cooker, and his coffee paraphernalia but no microwave. "Y'all don't have a microwave?"

"No," Rebekah said. "Mother won't have one in the house."

"Why is that?"

"Father said...it's something about the way the microwaves heat the food. They make the molecules vibrate, and it might be harmful."

Jack swallowed a comment about Carl's grasp of basic science. "When you heat food in a pot on the stove, the molecules vibrate too."

Rebekah studied him with light, luminous eyes. "Oh! I guess they do."

He reminded himself that she was only ten.

And that her mother might forbid her to go to college.

By nine o'clock, the kids had finished chores and hauled out their school-books. Jack soon concluded that their education was adequate in most ways, stellar in others, and sorely lacking in some respects. When Rebekah ran across a reference to Ebenezer Scrooge in an essay, she couldn't grasp the gist of the paragraph because she'd never been exposed to Dickens.

At least Miranda didn't require the busywork that public schools used as a means of crowd control. One point for her, but quiet, all-absorbing busywork would have come in handy. He couldn't send the kids out to play in a rainstorm.

By ten, they had cabin fever. The rain came down without stopping, and so did Jonah's tears. Sitting amid his blocks, he screamed in useless rage. Rebekah, usually so good at soothing toddler angst, teetered on the verge of a meltdown herself. The archangels bickered. Even Martha, the sunny one, found reasons to whine.

Only Timothy kept his mouth shut. Hunched over a grammar lesson, he clicked his pen, over and over. *Click. Click. Click.*

"Hush up, y'all," Jack said quietly. Nobody paid him any mind.

Click. Click. Click.

Martha abandoned her phonics workbook and opened the fridge. "Some-body drank all the orange juice," she wailed. "I didn't get any. Not *any*." She segued into broken-hearted weeping that sent Jack into auditory overload.

Click. Click. Click-click-click-click-click.

Jack slapped his own pen down on the table. "That settles it. Ladies and gentlemen, I'm taking y'all to Walmart."

Martha silenced herself, midsob. Jonah stopped shrieking and wiped his wet cheeks with gooey fingers. All the kids gawked at Jack as if he'd announced a trip to France. And a guillotine.

"It's Thursday," Timothy said. *Click.* "A school day." *Click.*

"Indeed, every day's a school day. The world is our classroom. We'll take a field trip."

"There's no Walmart in Slades Creek," Rebekah pointed out, sensible as always.

Jack smiled at his astonished charges. "There's one in Clayton." And it carried clothing. Normal clothing. There was a thought.

Martha closed the fridge and sniffled. "Uncle Jack? Can we buy Frosted Flakes? Please?"

"Yes. And orange juice." He turned to Rebekah. "And something easy for supper, because you do too much cooking for a girl your age."

Click. Timothy slapped his book shut. "Mother buys organic. She doesn't want us eating junk, *Jack.*"

"He's *Uncle* Jack." Martha stuck out her tongue at her brother. "And he's nice. You're not."

"Now, now. Don't be ugly." Jack handed her a tissue, then tossed the box to Rebekah so she could deal with Jonah's snotty countenance. "Blow your noses, you little ruffians, and let's get this show on the road."

Nobody argued. Not even Timothy. The children were so compliant and well organized that Jack was leading them to the van in only five minutes. Like the Pied Piper.

That story didn't end well for the parents.

Walmart might as well have been Tiffany's; the children, refugees from a third-world country. Dazzled, they stared at everything—and everyone—and their fellow shoppers stared back.

Jack shouldn't have cared. He didn't know anybody in their neck of the woods, so he shouldn't have minded being seen in the company of two girls in elf capes and four polo-shirted boys who might have escaped from 1960.

There was a bit of gender discrimination afoot. The boys, in their store-bought jackets and jeans, blended in more easily than the girls did in their home-sewn dresses and voluminous capes. It hardly seemed fair.

Jonah sat in the seat of the cart while Michael and Gabriel pushed it, shoulder to shoulder. Martha clung to Jack's hand, her cape sweeping the leg of his jeans with every step. Rebekah and Timothy followed a few paces behind. Jack sensed that they'd taken up the rear so they could keep him under surveillance.

So far, the cart held orange juice, three boxes of Frosted Flakes, bagged salad, and applesauce in individual plastic tubs. All Martha's requests. Nobody else had asked for anything.

Questionable items lurked throughout the store. To Miranda, nearly every-thing might have been questionable. Jack wouldn't have been surprised to learn that she objected to frozen dinners on general principles. He herded his flock toward the freezer section, anyway, and contemplated smuggling a portable microwave into the house at some point.

But why should he have to smuggle it in? He'd be bold. He'd call it a sci-ence lesson.

"What do y'all like best?" he asked. "Lasagna? Pizza? Burritos?"

The resulting argument did his heart good. The kids had definite opinions.

After stocking up on freezer meals, then two gallons of milk for the Frosted Flakes, he tried to direct the children toward the checkout. Martha spotted the meager book department first. She drew in an awestruck breath and yanked his hand.

Jack let her tug him along. Her siblings followed and filled the aisle.

Martha spied the early readers. She dropped his hand and sat on the floor as if she were in a public library and about to commence reading for free, for as long as she pleased. She started with *The Cat in the Hat*, a classic beloved by generations of kids for its anti-adult propaganda.

On the other hand, Ava had said it taught her kindergarten classes that it was okay to let a stranger into the house as long as they cleaned up the evidence before Mom came home. What Mom didn't know couldn't hurt her.

What Miranda didn't know…. When she came home, though, she would know.

Jack tugged the book out of Martha's surprisingly strong fingers and replaced it with *One Fish, Two Fish, Red Fish, Blue Fish.* "This one's better," he said, hating himself for being a censor like Miranda.

Martha started to argue, but the colorful fish snagged her attention. He replaced the first Seuss book on the shelf, above her eye level lest she be tempted again.

Rebekah had picked up a historical romance. The cover art depicted a buxom, satin-clad lass who appeared to be fainting in the arms of a lusty highlander.

Jack swiped the romance and replaced it on the rack, upside down and backward. "Why don't you try…" The cookbooks saved him. "This!" He planted a Mexican cookbook in Rebekah's hands.

He checked on the boys. Thank God, they'd gravitated toward the outdoor magazines that featured hunting, fishing, and other wholesome, manly activities.

"Look, Uncle Jack." Martha jumped up, holding the Disney version of Cinderella. "What's this one about? I want it. Please?"

"Sweetie, I can't buy you every book you haven't read. You need to have your own library card and pick your own books. A library card, that's the best little piece of plastic you'll ever own."

With a sigh, she settled on the floor again, her cape pooling around her, and leafed through the book. Fiction, not to mention magic. Miranda wouldn't have approved.

A teenage girl entered the aisle and gave Jack a bold once-over. Her hair was an unnatural black, and the same morbid color clothed her from head to shiny boots. As well endowed as the lass on the paperback, she bore a rose tattoo above her left breast, a ring in her lower lip and a spiked dog collar around her throat. Jack was accustomed to seeing such styles, but he could only imagine how Miranda would react if her kids gave her a report.

The teenager stepped around Martha, then stared at Rebekah. And back to Martha, with a sneer.

Jack tried to see his nieces as a stranger would: braids, matching jumpers, and old-fashioned capes. All three young ladies attracted attention, but in the Goth girl's case, it was by her own choice. Not by her mother's.

Rebekah straightened her shoulders and met the teenager's sable-rimmed eyes. Martha also examined her. And wrinkled up her nose. The little Pharisee.

Smelling of cigarettes, the girl in black brushed against Jack's shoulder as she walked past. "Some people don't know what century they're livin' in," she said under her breath but no doubt intending to be heard.

"Forsooth, fair damsel, good manners yet remain in style," he said, earning a snort from the girl as she turned the corner.

"She was staring at us," Martha said, loud and clear. "I hate it when people stare at us."

He seized his chance. "Martha, Rebekah, you want to pick out some jeans? People wouldn't stare if you wore—"

"No, thank you," Rebekah said. "Mother wouldn't like it." She returned the cookbook to the shelf and took charge of the shopping cart with Jonah still fidgeting in it. "We're leaving. Martha, put the book back. Timothy, round up the boys. Let's go."

Now Rebekah was the Pied Piper. Martha held on to the side of the cart and trotted to keep up with her sister's longer stride. Timothy and the archangels followed them to the nearest checkout. Jack trailed behind, put in his place by a ten-year-old who might as well have been leading all of them back to prison.

"Anybody hungry?" he asked. "There's a McDonald's, right here in the store. Let's hit it."

Rebekah paused in the unloading of the orange juice to look him right in the eye. "No, thank you. Mother wouldn't like it."

"No, she wouldn't." Jack descended into gloom, though he didn't even like McDonald's.

Freedom. That was what he liked. What he wanted for the kids.

Martha craned her neck for one last glimpse of the bookshelves, like Eve longing for her lost garden. Jonah, seated in the cart, tried to reach the gum and candy rack, while Michael and Gabriel foiled his efforts.

Timothy stood apart, his hands in his pockets, and scowled at the groceries as they traveled the short conveyer. He wanted to protect his family, yet he hungered for a wider world at the same time. All of them did, or they wouldn't have latched on to those books and magazines.

Mother wouldn't like it.

Jack was starting to see what he was up against. Miranda had every right to raise her children as she saw fit. They were hers. He was only the uncle with no rights in the matter.

But rights or no rights, he had to do something.

His phone vibrated. He answered, making no effort to disguise his testy mood.

"Jack? Where are you? Why aren't you answering the phone?"

"I just did, Miranda."

His phone beeped a warning. It was on its last breath of battery power.

"I meant the house phone," she said.

"I am not at the house."

"Where are you? I've been trying—reach you." The dying phone cut in and out. "The doctors—tests look good—discharging me today."

"Glad to hear it. I'll run the kids home, and then I'll pick you up."

The phone made its last-chance beep.

"I...wh...but...er...*are* you?"

"Walmart. Those all-American purveyors of dangerous books and frozen pizzas."

No reaction from Miranda.

He checked the screen. Dark. Dead.

Pretending the phone hadn't expired, he returned it to his ear. "I'm bustin' some kids out of prison," he said into the useless instrument. "And hang on to your hat, Mrs. H., because you're next."

An aide had put Miranda's hair in a French braid so loosely that it was already a mess. At least she had clean clothes to wear and her spare cape. Jack must have brought them on an earlier visit, when she was sleeping.

She'd called the house again, and Timothy assured her they'd come home safely. Jack was on his way. Too edgy to sit still, she hauled herself out of the bedside chair and hobbled to the window. Her head throbbed and her vision swirled. She ached all over, and her ribs stabbed her with every breath, but she was done with narcotics. She needed to be alert. In control.

Still resenting the sling that supported her right arm, she braced herself against the windowsill with her good hand and looked out on the rainy day. She was on the second floor with a view of a narrow, brown lawn, the visitors' parking lot, and a short stretch of Lee Street. A truck rumbled past, sending sheets of rainwater splashing over the curb, but the hospital's thick walls muffled the sounds of the outside world.

A young woman, drenched with rain, jaywalked between a pickup and a car. In a brown parka and worn jeans, with a phone to her ear, she dodged puddles in a gamey, cheerful way that made Miranda smile.

Her wish list kept growing. A cell phone. Jeans. And instead of a cape, a parka. A red one. Once Mason had moved away, she would go on a shopping spree for herself and for the children.

She never had extra money, though, and she'd have even less when the checks from the church stopped coming. She didn't even want to think about her medical bills.

Miranda squinted at the local paper her roommate had left folded up on the corner of the bed. It was no use trying to check the want ads for work until her vision cleared. She'd never dreamed that a concussion could cause so much trouble.

Footsteps approached her room. There was a light knock, and a dark-haired, dark-eyed man entered, wearing a rumpled raincoat. She knew him immediately—yet she didn't know him. Although he bore some resemblance to the idealistic young man who'd come in search of family, years ago, this Jack carried himself with an intimidating air of confidence.

Speaking with him on the phone had been awkward, but this was worse. She couldn't think of a blessed thing to say. Couldn't think of a blessed thing to *think,* except: This was Jack "Tsunami" Hanford, and she was in trouble.

Laugh lines crinkled around his eyes. "Hey, Miranda. Remember me?"

"Hello, Jack." The room resumed its merry-go-round routine. "Thank you for everything. Thank you so much."

"Glad to help. How are you feeling?"

"Like I've been run over by a freight train."

"The kids can't wait to have you back. They'll want to pamper you half to death."

"That sounds good. I've missed them."

"I can imagine. They're great kids. Very well-behaved. Never having been the sole custodian of a passel of young 'uns, I'm grateful for that."

Despite his education, he still sounded like a country boy. In fact, he sounded very much like Carl, whose southern accent had once charmed a lonely Ohio girl.

Still at a loss for words, she bit her lip. She hadn't imagined facing Jack in person.

"You weren't supposed to show up unless I died," she blurted. "Not that dying would have been a better outcome—" Seeing his frown, she stopped. "You don't think I *meant* to fall, do you?"

"The thought occurred to me. Did you?"

"Of course not. I must have fainted."

"Miranda, if you're depressed, it isn't anything to be ashamed of. It's—"

"I know what it is. But I'm not depressed. Not now."

"I want to believe you."

"Please do. I want to stop talking and hurry home to my babies." She waited, holding her breath. If he believed she was suicidal, and if that rumor somehow reached DFCS….

He slid his hand inside his raincoat. From a shirt pocket, he extracted a slender black pen and a paper. "First, we have business to tend to."

She exhaled. "What kind of business?"

"You need to sign this." He unfolded the paper and held it in front of her.

To her unfocused vision, it was only a block of his cramped and nearly indecipherable writing followed by a list of some sort in Rebekah's neat penmanship. The lines wobbled and blurred. "What is it?"

"This authorizes me to obtain emergency medical attention for the kids if the need should arise. Rebekah listed names and dates of birth, and I understand they're a healthy crew with no allergies or medical conditions. Is that correct?"

"Yes, but why would you need this? You won't be staying more than a day or two."

"I'm not quite so optimistic. You can't even drive yourself to the store. Or to your checkups with various and sundry physicians."

"I'm still not sure it's a good idea."

"I would only use it in an emergency. For instance, if Rebekah whacks off a finger with one of those butcher knives she's always slinging around."

"But—"

"Or if Jonah does a face-plant into the wood stove."

"Yes, I suppose—"

"Sign, please." He placed the paper on the tray table beside the bed and offered the pen.

She wiggled the battered, swollen fingers that extended from the sling. "I can't grip a pen."

"Yes, you can."

With a pleasant smile, he placed the pen in her left hand. She considered tucking the pen right back in his shirt pocket, but that would have required reaching inside his raincoat.

"Come, now," he said. "Don't argue about signing a simple form that deals with the short-term when you've already named me as the children's guardian."

"But that won't go into effect unless I die."

"And you'll live for another seven decades or so, I hope." He gave her a boyish grin and tapped the pen with one finger. "Please cooperate with me." His grin faded. "God forbid that I should ever need this paper, but you're living proof that accidents happen."

She lowered herself into the chair. "You're right. I should be thanking you instead of arguing." Despite the way the room rotated around her, she made the pen connect with the paper and produced an ugly, crooked scrawl.

Jack reclaimed the pen and paper. "I'll run down to the pharmacy and pick up your 'scripts."

"My what?"

"Prescriptions. Might be a while."

"I don't need the prescriptions."

"Wrong." And he was out the door.

seven

Jack's sleek black convertible was lithe and sure on the curves, but Miranda wished he would slow down. He navigated the slick roads in the pouring rain as if he'd driven them all his life.

Of course he did. He was mountain-bred like Carl.

The fall must have jostled some memories out of hiding. She kept remembering the first time she saw Carl's blond head bent over his books between classes. The oldest student on campus, he'd towered over the boys her age, not just in stature but in maturity. When the news came, he'd helped her buy a plane ticket. He spoke with her professors, drove her to the airport, and picked her up when she came back from Auntie Lou's funeral. He'd been a fortress.

Miranda hadn't known, then, that a fortress could be a prison.

Rain on the windshield made blurry stars of oncoming headlights, but then the wipers cleared the glass and the lights became sharp white knives slicing into her. Blurry stars, then brutal knives, they alternated every two seconds, but she had to keep her eyes open.

Jack hadn't spoken since they'd turned onto the county road. She gave him a cautious look and knew he was unaware of her discomfort. He tapped a rhythm on the steering wheel in time to some private song, his mouth graced with a faint smile.

Her muscles clenched with panic. She would never be able to explain him to Mason—or vice versa—and Mason would show up soon. Even before her accident, he'd rebuked her for procrastinating. She hadn't listed her house or called a handyman. Her excuses had worn thin.

The car swooped through another pass, making her feel as if she were in a blender. She clung to the black leather seat with her left hand and turned slowly toward the rain streaming down her window. With the slightest movement, pain hammered her.

"Could we clear up a few questions?" Jack asked.

"We could try."

"Why did you name me as guardian?"

"It doesn't matter now. I didn't die." Too late, she realized her answer was both flippant and illogical.

"Yes, we've already established that you didn't die—thank God—but why me, a divorced curmudgeon with no experience in raising children? And you don't know me. We've had only one conversation, nine years ago. A conversation that ended with Carl ordering me off the property."

"I've always been sorry about that. We were going through a rough time, and…he wasn't quite himself."

"I'm happy to know that wasn't the real Carl, but back to my question. Why me? Why not your own relatives?"

She pictured her mother's pleasant, uncomplicated face. Her honey brown hair in a classic, simple style. Her closet, jam-packed with expensive clothing and shoes.

"I don't have any relatives who are fit to take care of the children," Miranda said.

Jack murmured something, but she didn't catch it.

Wooded slopes, silvered by the rain, whipped past. Woozy, Miranda faced forward again, into the violent brightness of the oncoming lights. She leaned back against the head rest but couldn't decide if it was better to brace against it or try to relax her muscles.

"Why didn't you discuss it with me first?" he asked.

"I thought I would call as soon as…as soon as things…well, soon. But then I fell."

"You changed your will only a couple of weeks ago. Were you expecting a calamity like your fall?"

"No, but I might have brought it upon myself. I'd been taking a lot of walks to the cliffs."

"What inspired you to change your will though?"

"The previous guardians are moving out of state."

"And you decided the children would be better off with me? A stranger to them and nearly a stranger to you?"

"After Carl asked you to leave, when you started writing to him…your letters made me feel that I knew you, at least a little."

From the corner of her eye, she caught the swift movement as Jack turned toward her. "You read my letters?"

In rebellion. In secret. If Carl had known, he never would have believed that she thought of Jack only as a brother. A brother who made her smile.

She nodded, and a jolt of pain hit her skull. "I read them."

"Did Carl?"

"Only the first one. I wish he would have given you a chance."

"After he told me to stop writing, did my persistence cause any trouble?"

She hesitated. After that first letter, Carl had told her to write back and tell Jack not to bother. She'd obeyed, written the note, but Jack's letters hadn't stopped coming until she'd told him Carl was gone. Maybe they'd saved her sanity.

"No," she said. "There was never any trouble."

Now, though, trouble sat in the driver's seat. And he was staying under her roof.

Approaching a passing lane, Jack swung the car to the left. He overtook a slow-moving UPS truck, a brown blur in the rain-speckled glass. The car swept back to the right lane, far too close to the deep ravines. If he lost control of the car…if she never made it home….

What if they *both* died, mother and guardian? DFCS would take the children. Like they'd taken the Padilla children in Rabun County. In that case, though, the parents were alive and fighting to reunite the family.

"Slow down!" She clutched the seat with her left hand.

"Sorry. I've got a lead foot sometimes." He reduced the car's speed.

She still clung to the seat.

Jack turned right at the blinking yellow light that signaled Larkin Road. For a little while, there was no sound but the hiss of tires on wet pavement, backed by the rhythm of the wipers and the drumming of the rain. In the strained silence, she wondered if half her nausea was caused by nerves.

"You never called me when Carl died," Jack said. "You only wrote a note, weeks after the funeral."

"I'm sorry. I should have let you know, right away, but I must have been in shock. Then Jonah was born, six weeks later. I still remember the flowers you sent, though, and your note was so kind. You said you wanted to help."

"And I could have helped, if you'd returned my call."

"You called me?"

"I left a message. You never responded."

"But there was never—oh! You must have called just before Gabriel destroyed the answering machine. You know how four-year-olds are. He kept taking things apart. Toys and clocks and gadgets—and the answering machine."

Jack laughed. "That doesn't surprise me. The little devil. I wonder how many messages you lost."

Not many. The phone seldom rang, then or now. But life might have been very different if she'd known Jack's offer of help had been more than polite words to accompany the flowers.

They reached the last bend of Larkin and, she hoped, the end of the interrogation. There was her mailbox. Her driveway. She braced herself against the bumps and jolts of the rutted gravel, but tensing up only made it worse. Finally, the car rounded the last curve, and the lights of the house blazed like gold in the gray of the storm.

Jack braked to a gentle stop and killed the engine. Rain made a steady patter on the roof of the car. "I should have brought an umbrella."

"I don't care if I get wet."

"Good, because you will."

He climbed out. The slamming of the door was like a slap to her aching head. She fumbled for the latch. Before she could locate it, Jack was there, opening the door. She gulped fresh, rainy air and prayed her stomach would settle.

"Well." He rubbed his jaw. "This might prove to be difficult."

It would. The steps to the porch might as well have been Mount Everest. Leaving the hospital, they'd had a wheelchair, the help of an orderly, and no steps to deal with.

She flexed her right ankle, and pain shot down to her toes and up her calf to her knee. She clamped her lips closed.

Bending over, Jack slid a hand under her knee and nudged her bad leg so it faced the opened door. The forced intimacy was awkward, but she moved her good leg into the rain, her foot onto the muddy ground.

"Let's get your feet planted," he said. "There. Now, raise your arms a bit. Can you, with the sling?"

"Yes, but what—" She yelped as he pulled her to her feet.

"Sorry."

She fought to keep from blacking out. She wanted to focus on the house— her goal, her refuge, her whole world—but Jack was inches away, blocking her view. His lips were moving, saying something, and they'd doubled themselves. Two mouths, two noses, four eyes. Her eyes crossed as she tried to bring the two Jacks into one.

"Good thing you're about as big as a peanut," he said. "And good thing I picked up your prescriptions."

A fat raindrop hit her cheek. "I don't need prescriptions," she said between clenched teeth.

"I beg to differ." He scooped her up, one arm under her knees, one around her torso.

She stifled another cry, her head bumping his damp shoulder. Someone swung the front door open. Jack carried her up the steps and over the threshold with her skirt and cape flapping. Through the veil of her hair, she caught a glimpse of Timothy's worried expression.

"Make way," Jack said. "Somebody go pull down the covers."

Michael ran ahead. Gabriel was underfoot, his thin face alight as Jack swung Miranda in a half turn that made everything spin.

"Rebekah," he said. "Help me out, please. Undo your mother's cape."

"Thank you, sweetheart," Miranda whispered as Rebekah hurried to obey.

"Welcome home." Rebekah tugged at the cape, trying to pull it away, but it was pinned against Jack's chest. As Miranda was. Her ribs snagged on a spike of pain with every breath.

"Never mind. She can lie on it, for now." Jack eased her through the narrow doorway of her room, then lowered her onto the bed. "Doin' all right?"

On the verge of screaming, she fought her way back to control. "I'm fine."

"You're not an especially good liar, Mrs. H." He straightened. "I'm sorry, but if I hadn't hauled you inside, you'd still be out there."

"I know."

His rain-sprinkled face was etched with concern. "Every movement hurts, doesn't it?"

The unexpected sympathy threatened to undo her. She nodded.

"Then may I recommend one little pain pill?"

Before she could argue, the rest of the children surged into the room. Jack raised one hand, stopping them in their tracks.

"Quiet! One at a time. Gently. No hugs. Not even half hugs."

They came forward, one at a time, and patted her hand or kissed her cheek. When she thanked Timothy for rescuing her, he shrugged.

"I only dialed 911," he said. "That's all."

Then he must have left her at the bottom of the cliffs. He'd had no choice but to run back to the house, hating himself for abandoning her.

Fresh tears blurred her sight. "You did exactly the right thing, Timothy."

He lost his smile and slipped out of the room before she could ask how he'd known he needed to look for her.

Martha brought the cuddle-quilt and tucked it tenderly if inefficiently over Miranda's legs. Finally Jonah came, the one she most wanted to pull close, but he didn't touch her. He laid his head on the bed. From that sideways perspective, he frowned at her.

"Don't worry, Jonah. Mama will look better soon. How are you, my big boy?"

He didn't answer. She could only blow him a kiss. Without smiling, he straightened and ran out.

"Scat, everybody." Jack made shooing motions toward Michael and Gabriel. "Later, y'all can plague your mama. For now, she needs rest."

"I do not. I need my children."

"They'll keep. Rebekah, hand me those pillows before you go." He propped Miranda's right foot on two pillows, straightened the quilt, and gave her toes a squeeze through the soft fabric. "Now I'll bring you a pill."

She hesitated, craving the relief. It wouldn't be wise though. If Mason stopped by, she'd need a clear head. "No, thank you."

"Medicines, used as prescribed, are a good thing. Your body will mend faster if it doesn't have to deal with pain too."

"No."

Jack threw up his hands and walked out.

"Bekah," Jonah called from the living room. "C'mere, Bekah."

With an apologetic glance behind her, Rebekah followed Jack.

He was a bull in a—no, he was a steamroller in a china shop. Miranda's breaths came short and fast as she tried to master the sobs that racked her chest. Bit by bit, she regained control.

Lifting her head, she squinted at a dark, blurry object on her bureau. A black shaving kit came into focus. A plaid shirt hung on the arm of her chair.

An unfamiliar scent clung to her pillow. A subtle, spicy aftershave. It smelled good. Too good.

The evidence that Jack had been sleeping in her room was disorienting, as if some alien force had invaded her territory. Except, of course, she'd invited him. She'd practically forced him to come.

Mason hadn't come though. He might have decided she'd earned another shunning. Or maybe Timothy hadn't spread the word about her fall or about Jack. It would be better that way.

She trained her attention on the sounds that drifted in from the living room. *"My, my, my baby,"* Martha crooned in a singsong, muffled by distance, while Rebekah chattered about something. The girls' voices faded into the background as Gabriel and Michael started one of their endless arguments.

The commotion rose, it fell, it rose again. Thanks to Jack, the children were still together, in their own home. For how long though? Because Mason would keep pressuring her to move.

Why did he want to drag a black sheep along? It made no sense.

Her eyelids began to yield to exhaustion. She jerked them open. Hoping for even a glimpse of her children as they went about their business, Miranda fought to stay awake.

With Miranda dozing and the kids busy with play or chores, Jack installed himself in one of the rockers on the porch, where the phone signal was decent.

He returned a few calls and learned that his colleagues were doing an admirable job of sharing his workload during his absence; nonetheless, Farnsworth was royally irritated. No surprises there.

Miranda's timing was off. She should have picked the week of spring break to take her dive.

Jack breathed in, savoring the aroma that somehow escaped from the kitchen to the porch. Tonight, Rebekah was having her first experience with frozen lasagna, ready-made garlic bread, and bagged salad. If he could persuade Miranda to eat, she might agree to a pain pill too.

"Fat chance," he said, then read a text message from one of his grad students. She was having trouble with a paper and wanted to meet for coffee. Jack sent his answer, suggesting a consultation over the phone.

The last of the rain fell in sporadic drips from eaves and trees. In the distance, a goat bleated. A squirrel chattered in the big oak, and a young rabbit ventured onto the wet grass, its long ears twitching.

That was what the house lacked: animals. A log home in the mountains, complete with a ramshackle barn, should have had a pet or two. The family didn't even own a goldfish. But if Miranda didn't want pets, that was her decision.

She would be up to making her own decisions again soon. Once she'd recovered, she would send him on his way, and everything would be back to normal.

Except everything had changed. He was blood kin, not to Miranda, but to the children, and he would never forget them. He would want to come back and make sure they were all right. He would want to introduce Martha to a few hundred good books, teach Rebekah how microwaves worked, teach Timothy…how to smile?

Then there was Miranda. An oddball homeschooler. A beautiful, bruised enigma.

Jack read another text message, replied, and listened to the squirrel.

A sheriff's cruiser nosed around the curve and bumped up the muddy driveway. As Jack got to his feet, the deputy parked and climbed out. It was the same man as before, large and sad eyed. Jack had forgotten his name.

"Good evening," the deputy said.

"Hey, there. Come on up and grab a chair. They're dry."

"Thanks, but I can't stay long." The deputy came up the steps but remained standing in the cautious, battle-ready posture of soldiers and lawmen. "How's Mrs. Hanford?"

Jack gave the man's name tag a surreptitious look. "Nice of you to check up on her, Officer Dean. I just brought her home. She's pretty beat-up, but there shouldn't be any lasting damage."

"That's good news. The family's doing all right?"

"Doing fine. They're great kids."

"I remember that. I was on duty the day Carl died." Dean rubbed one finger against his temple. "Late last night, it dawned on me. That was almost exactly two years ago."

The unspoken question hung there, breathed into the stillness from their matching thoughts. Jack wouldn't be the one to ask it out loud.

Dean cleared his throat. "Have you seen anything that would shed some light on Mrs. Hanford's frame of mind in the days leading up to her, ah, accident?" He said the last word lightly but precisely, giving the effect of putting imaginary quotation marks around it.

"I wasn't around, remember? Have you asked Timothy?"

"Yes, and I would like to believe his version of events."

"And that is…?"

"He told me she has a history of fasting, getting dizzy, and falling. So he was worried about her that morning, knowing she was fasting, knowing she liked to walk to the cliffs before the little ones woke up. He followed her. At a distance, he said, because if she'd spotted him, she would've told him to mind his own business."

"I've been wondering how he happened to find her at the bottom of the cliffs, but he never wants to talk."

"Typical of that age, I guess. Well, they're a fine family."

"Yes, although I have a few disagreements with the worldview that Carl imposed upon them."

Dean studied him for a moment. "You really didn't know Carl?"

"No sir. There were some hard feelings between my dad's first and second wives, so he thought it prudent to raise me in the next county. Different schools and all. How well did you know Carl?"

"I didn't, really, but I saw the two of them around town, sometimes. He'd be walkin' all over her, and she'd be takin' it." Dean's face hardened. "The one thing Mrs. Hanford doesn't need is another man ordering her around."

"I agree."

A long silence followed, making Jack newly aware of the property's seclusion. No traffic sounds. No barking dogs. Nothing but bird songs and wind in the trees. It had to be a lonely place for a widow and six kids.

"Do you know much about Miranda's church?" Jack asked. "The head honcho is named Mason Chandler."

"I know who he is, but I haven't had any dealings with him." Dean squinted against the sun. "It's not illegal to be different."

"You'd agree that his church isn't exactly mainstream?"

"That's a good way to put it."

"But the man isn't criminally inclined?"

"Not that I know of, but let me put it this way." Dean shifted his weight from one foot to the other. "I'd rather pet a copperhead than buddy up to Chandler." The radio clipped to Dean's uniform squawked, and a dispatcher rattled off a series of garbled words and numbers. He drawled a response and nodded at Jack. "I'll have to answer this call."

"Thanks for stopping by."

Dean pulled a card from his pocket, scribbled something on it, and offered it to Jack. "That's my personal number. Call any time, or stop by the station. We're in the city hall building. The coffee's always on, and the checkerboard comes out when things get slow."

"One of the advantages of living in a small town."

"You bet. We like to keep things simple." Dean strolled to his car. "Keep a close eye on those kids," he said over his shoulder. "Keep countin' noses."

"Yes sir, I will."

As Dean's car pulled out of sight, Jack made his way across the wet grass to the dead branch that hung from the young oak. Now, with no fog to veil reality, there was nothing sinister about it. It was only a broken limb, dark with decay and slick with rain. He twisted at it until it broke, the pith of it still green, then dropped it on the weedy grass in front of his shoes. His feet were soaked right through the leather, chilling him.

Walking back to the house, he pictured a blond giant of a man on the roof, hammering shingles. Carl's foot had slipped. His hands clawed and clutched but found nothing to hang on to. His wife and children heard the sounds of disaster and ran outside, but it was too late.

Unlike the rest of the house, the roof was in good repair. Somebody had finished the job. The job that finished Carl.

Jack sat in the rocker again and tried to shed the gory pictures his imagination had produced. Even a jerk like Carl shouldn't have died that way.

But if he'd been such a jerk, why had Miranda married him? Only a year out of high school, maybe she hadn't known much about men or—

Glass shattered, the sound launching Jack out of the chair. He was inside in two strides and running toward her room.

eight

Jack skidded into the room, his wet shoes sliding on the planks.

Miranda lifted her head from the pillow, her eyes big and scared. "What was that?"

"I don't know." If his heart had been a jackhammer, it would have slammed through the floorboards already.

Shouts of alarm came from upstairs, and he ran. Timothy crowded past him and bounded up the stairs, followed by Rebekah with her long dress rustling like a prairie schoolmarm's.

Jack caught up with them in the doorway of the boys' room. Michael and Gabriel stood side by side, their backs to the door. A softball lay on the braided rug in the center of the room. On the bare floorboards by the wall, a picture frame lay face down, surrounded by shards of broken glass.

No blood. No catastrophe. Not this time.

"Y'all were playing catch?" Jack asked. "Inside?"

The archangels turned around, hanging their heads. "Yes sir," they squeaked in unison.

"No more of that. Clean it up, gentlemen—carefully."

They ran, arguing about who would hold the dustpan. Timothy followed them out, but Rebekah moved toward the broken glass.

"Hold on, now," Jack said. "They made the mess, so they'll clean it up."

She nodded but bent over and leaned the picture against the wall, loose glass tinkling. The frame held a black and white photo of a lily. It was a good, interesting composition but all wrong for a boys' room.

After Rebekah left, Jack lingered. He'd never seen the room in daylight. No self-respecting boy would have chosen to hang his baby quilt on the wall, but three of them hung there, with a name embroidered in the lower right corner of each one. Timothy. Michael. Gabriel. These quilts were a smaller version of the cuddle-quilt the kids were always dragging around with them.

At least they were done in masculine color schemes. Browns, dark blues, rich greens. Jonah's, in shades of gray and blue, lay on one of the lower bunks, still in use. Red and blue plaid comforters, all alike, covered the beds.

"What happened?" Miranda called with panic in her voice.

Nobody answered. Not even Rebekah or Timothy. Jack smiled at their loyalty. They didn't want to rat on their brothers, so they'd left it up to him.

He descended the stairs, asking himself what he would have done if the sound of breaking glass had signaled a true emergency. He wasn't up on first aid.

The archangels charged up the stairs with broom and dustpan. Jack pressed against the wall to let them pass, then proceeded to Miranda's room.

"What happened?" she asked again. Her skin was pale beneath the bruises and scrapes.

Of course. The sudden crash had sent her and the older kids into a harrowing flashback to the sounds of disaster. Maybe she relived Carl's accident with every loud noise. Maybe she saw him every five minutes in Timothy's eyes or in Michael's smile. Only two years past Carl's death, the memories would still be powerful whether they were good or bad.

"Everything's all right," Jack said. "The archangels were playing catch—"

"*Who?*"

"Michael and Gabriel. They knocked a picture off the wall, and the glass broke."

"Nobody's hurt?"

"Everybody's fine. They're sweeping up."

"You left children to clean up broken glass by themselves?"

"Would you feel better about it if I supervised?"

She nodded, screwing up her face in pain from that tiny movement. "Yes, please."

At least she'd said "please."

Jack grabbed a trash bag from the kitchen and climbed the stairs again. The boys were doing a fine job, but he stayed, holding the bag open and pointing out a few pieces of glass they had missed.

"No more playing catch in the house," he reminded them. "Now you need to vac—"

Before the word was out of Jack's mouth, Michael barreled past to fetch the vacuum.

Downstairs again, Jack deposited the bag of broken glass in the kitchen trash and decided to administer a pain pill to Miranda. Like it or not, she needed one.

The homey aroma of baking lasagna surrounded Jack as he made a quick tour of the room to gather necessities. The bag from the hospital pharmacy. A spoon. An individual plastic tub of applesauce from Walmart. The mortar and pestle from the windowsill.

While the vacuum growled upstairs, he sneaked onto the porch and pulled the heavy-duty pain prescription from the bag. He ground a pill with the mortar and pestle, then tapped the powder into the applesauce and stirred. Flecks of white dotted the fruit, but he wouldn't allow Miranda a close look. He could do nothing about the taste.

He made a clandestine return to the kitchen. The girls were there, Rebekah instructing Martha in the best way to tie a bow, but they ignored him as he replaced the mortar and pestle on the windowsill and the pharmacy bag on top of the fridge.

Applesauce and spoon in hand, he went to Miranda's room, stopping in the doorway. This was private territory. The room she'd shared with her husband. The bed they'd shared. It still held two pillows, as Jack's bed still did.

A bureau of dark wood held a photo of a youthful Miranda holding an infant in miniature overalls and a blue shirt. That was Timothy, no doubt, because by the time Michael came along, Miranda wouldn't have looked quite so young.

The older Miranda lay motionless and tiny in the big bed. Thank God, she'd grown out those ridiculous bangs. Her braid had come undone. Wisps of flaxen hair framed her cheeks and trailed onto her slender shoulders. Jack's fingers itched to finish the job of setting her hair free. To touch it—

He gave himself a mental slap. She was his sister-in-law. Mother of six. Weird homeschooler whose religion forbade nicknames, fiction, and attractive clothing. She was a mess.

Not that he could point fingers at anybody. Guilt ridden, hypersensitive to noise, compelled to count things and talk to himself, he had issues too.

"All God's children got issues," he said quietly.

Her eyelids fluttered open. "What?"

"Sorry. Talking to myself." He hesitated, battling his conscience, but the pill ploy was for her own good. He pulled the frilly upholstered chair from the corner to the bedside and sat. "I brought you something to eat."

"No, thank you."

"Just a few bites of applesauce." Overcoming another twinge of guilt, he dipped the spoon into the fruit. "Open wide."

"No."

"Yes." He teased her lips with the spoon.

She pulled back. "I'm not hungry."

"If you don't eat, you can't build up your strength and boot me out."

The light of battle gleamed in her eyes. She went for the spoon.

He pulled it out of her reach. "No, let me feed you. You're right-handed?"

She nodded her head slightly on the pillow and winced.

"Thought so. If you're a righty trying to be a lefty, you'll make a terrible mess."

When she opened her mouth to argue, he slipped the spoon between her lips. Now she was mad. With some luck, she'd be too angry to taste what she was eating.

"Bite number two," he crooned and attacked again. And again and again. She glared but didn't argue. Hungrier than she wanted to admit?

It was a tad too personal, this spoon-feeding. He could have enjoyed it, though, if it were something more exotic than applesauce. An Italian ice, for instance. Or, instead of spoon-feeding, he could imagine grapes, from his fingers to her soft lips—

"Whoa, Hanford."

"Hmm?"

"I—nothing." He focused on the remaining applesauce.

She wrinkled her nose. "No more. It tastes funny."

"Store-bought never tastes as good as homemade. I noticed some fruit trees out front. Are any of them apple trees? You ever make your own applesauce?"

"Yes."

He didn't know or care which question she'd answered. He only wanted to take her mind off the taste.

"I've never had my own fruit trees," he said. "My mom grew strawberries though. She made freezer jam with 'em." He kept rambling until he scraped up the last of the applesauce and prevailed upon Miranda to open her mouth one more time.

She swallowed and shuddered. "Ugh."

With his mission accomplished, he couldn't resist teasing. "Now that you have something in your stomach, you can take a pain pill."

"No, thank you."

"All right. If you're sure. I'll check on you in a few minutes."

She gave him an almost imperceptible nod. Even that small movement made her cringe, justifying his decision to slip her the painkiller.

He returned to the kitchen. The girls had left, but Timothy was there, digging into a plastic bag on the counter. He pulled out a piece of homemade bread, then seemed to forget that he held it as his attention drifted to something outside the window.

"Maya," he said softly.

The name Martha had mentioned. Timothy had said he didn't know anybody named Maya—but now he did? Maybe he was so lonesome that he'd adopted his little sister's imaginary friend. That was too weird. Too lonely.

Timothy sighed and bit into the bread.

Jack took four large, silent steps backward, into the living room, then cleared his throat and breezed into the kitchen as if he'd just arrived. "Ah, the appetite of a growing boy."

Timothy turned around, his expression stony. "Why do you keep trying to change the way my mother wants to live?"

"Excuse me?"

"You tried to make her take pain pills."

Jack managed not to look at her mortar and pestle. "Where did you get that idea?"

"I heard you. When you brought her home."

Whew. "Sometimes, pharmaceuticals are necessary."

"Pastor Mason says *pharmakeia* has the same root as the word that means sorcery. It's in Deuteronomy."

"Don't believe everything you hear."

"I don't. Especially if it comes from you."

Jack set the spoon in the sink and dropped the empty applesauce tub in the trash. "Have you ever thought about trying to get along with me, son?"

Timothy took another bite of bread and spoke around it. "I'm not your son, *Jack*."

"Why do I keep forgetting that?"

Shaking his head at the animosity that kept building between them, Jack pulled some work out of his briefcase and escaped to the porch, his only available refuge. Inside the house, he was an intruder with no space of his own.

After reading the first paragraph of an article three times without retaining it, he set it aside. Across the drive, a young tree was covered with black leaves—but then the tree exploded in a flurry of wings and chatter. The leaves were starlings. They wheeled en masse against the sky, then flew back to their perches, and the tree appeared to bear leaves again.

He stared past the bird-filled tree at the hillside and the mountains beyond it. When he'd counted the purple green peaks three times, getting a different number each time, he went inside. There were no kids in sight, but he listened for sounds of life upstairs. The two little ones were prattling together while the archangels wrangled about something. He wasn't sure of the whereabouts of the two oldest.

Jack returned to the bedroom. Miranda seemed to be sleeping, and that was exactly what she needed. Her left hand lay on her midriff. A simple gold wedding band caught the light.

She opened her bright blue eyes, set above high cheekbones like a model's. Even with the bruises and scratches, and despite dressing like a farm woman from a past century, she was—

A mess. And he was supposed to be taking care of her, not ogling her.

He placed his hand on hers. "How are you feeling?"

Her lips moved tentatively, then released a single word. "Tired."

"Want me to snip off your hospital bracelet?"

"Please."

On her bureau, he found small scissors beside a pile of embroidery thread in neat packets. He slid one of the blades between her bruised skin and the plastic, made the snip, and removed the bracelet. *HANFORD, MIRANDA E.,* it read, then gave her date of birth.

She was coming up on her thirty-fourth birthday. So young to be the mother of six and raising them alone.

Her dreamy smile demonstrated the softening effect of the narcotic. "Where'd you meet Ava?"

A startling question. Jack settled into the bedside chair, taking his time. "A soup kitchen. I mean—not *in* it, but because of it."

Miranda frowned. "Was she poor?"

"No, not at all. I volunteered at a soup kitchen one Christmas. And Ava's mom was working there. She dragged me home to her own Christmas dinner and introduced me to Ava."

"She was pretty."

"I sent pictures, didn't I? Yes, she was pretty."

He waited for the next question, but it never came. Well, good. The reasons for the split were no fun to talk about.

"Should we ask Rebekah to sleep in here tonight, in case you need anything?" he asked.

A moment passed. "'Kay, but she already...does too much."

"She's a good kid. She loves you. They all do."

Her eyes watered, but she didn't answer.

She made him think of a paper lantern, burning brightly but easily ripped to shreds or turned to ashes. She was all wrong for a bullheaded bruiser like Carl.

"Tell me how you met Carl," Jack said.

Again, that slight delay in answering. "Bible college. Eas'burn."

"I've heard of Eastburn. Did you graduate?"

"Got my degree...in one year."

He frowned, unaccustomed to such prodigies. "Really."

"Got my MRS." She flashed deep dimples.

Jack laughed. "By George, the woman has a sense of humor."

Her smile slipped away, but her silence was amiable enough.

"How old were you when you married him?"

The medicine had definitely kicked in; she'd developed more lag time between question and answer. Or she was ignoring him.

"Mmm…nineteen," she said at last.

"And Carl was…?"

She took two slow breaths before answering. "Twenny…nine."

"A little old to be in Bible college, wasn't he?"

"Went back t' finish up. Few more credits."

Jack nodded, recalling his own pursuit of credits and degrees. "Remember the day I came by, hoping to meet him?"

Her eyelids drooped. "He was rude…t' you."

"True. He didn't want anything to do with me. That leaves me wondering why you named me as the kids' guardian." He waited, hoping for a candid answer this time.

"I already tol' you. I didn' have anybody else." Her mouth curved into a barely-there smile. "An' you were kind…an' you tol' me you love truth. All truth."

"Did I?" Not far past his thirtieth year, he'd probably said it with the flair and egoism of youth. "I do love truth, still."

Her smile twisted to the left and vanished. She ran her hand over her face. "I feel funny."

Jack's conscience assailed him. The medicine was for her own good though. She needed the respite from pain.

He stroked her left hand, careful to avoid a red scratch that ran from the first knuckle of her pinkie to the delicate bone of her wrist. There probably wasn't a square inch of skin that didn't hurt. When she'd slammed from one ledge to another, she could have broken both arms and her legs. And, if she had, would her pastor know or care?

"Miranda?"

Her glassy gaze found him. "Mmm?"

"You like being in Mason's church?"

Her lips parted and trembled. "Not…'zackly."

"And why is that?"

"A col' war."

A cold war meant threats, bluffs, fears on both sides. But surely Mason wasn't afraid of this tiny, bruised woman, so beat-up that it hurt her to frown. It hurt just to look at her. Maybe, with her pristine system under the influence of strong medicine, she was hallucinating her cold war.

"Stay awake another minute, now," Jack said.

"'Kay." Her eyes weren't quite focused. She was still with him, but she was fuzzy.

It was the perfect opportunity to ask one more question. The big one.

"It's beautiful out there by the cliffs," he said. "Beautiful but dangerous. Sometimes I wonder if a person, a lonely person, might be drawn there for the wrong reasons."

She stared past him, saying nothing. The silence stretched on and on, and eventually she closed her eyes.

"Miranda?" He touched her hand again. "The fall. Was it an accident? Really?"

"Yes," she breathed. "Didn't mean to. Just loved…the cliffs." A frown knotted her forehead.

"Miranda, honey? Still with me?"

An even longer silence. Then her eyelids fluttered open. She focused on him, blinked, and came close to smiling.

"Steamroller," she said. She faded out with one more word, so soft that he couldn't catch it.

He ran his finger over her hand, but she made no response. Her forehead was smooth again except for the marks left by the sticks and stones that had caught her on the way down.

Elbows on his knees, chin in his hands, Jack studied her. He had more questions than ever, but she'd convinced him that she wasn't suicidal.

nine

No trace of light competed with the blackness behind Miranda's closed eyelids, but she was afraid to open her eyes. Even the dark would spin.

She touched the bedclothes to anchor herself. Thank God, she was home. She had proof: The worn quilt beneath her fingers. The comforting smell of wood smoke.

The headache that woke her thudded in time with her pulse. She wasn't as groggy as she'd been in the hospital, but she felt dull, like a knife that had lost its edge.

Inches away, a soft sound startled her. She held her breath until she recognized Rebekah's sigh, heavy with sleep. Of course. Jack had said he would ask her to stay—

Jack! Miranda's eyes flew open on pitch-black that whirled around her.

He was in the house. Sleeping on the couch?

She conjured up his expression as he'd sat beside her bed. Kind but stubborn.

Stubborn about what? He'd said something about strawberries. Apple trees.

Applesauce. Jack had insisted she eat it.

There was always a man telling her what to do. Carl, Mason, and now Jack, just when she had the scent of freedom in her nostrils.

She crinkled her nose, remembering. The applesauce had tasted wrong, somehow. Another aftereffect of the concussion. Her taste buds had gone awry, along with her vision and her sense of balance.

At least her ears still worked right. She lay motionless, testing that assumption.

Familiar night noises reassured her. The wind in the trees, the occasional creak of the old house.

And footsteps. Someone was pacing in the living room. Back and forth, back and forth. It wasn't Timothy's nearly noiseless tread. It was Jack, then.

She raised herself on her left elbow, inch by excruciating inch. The headache hammered her skull. Across the dark room, the blurred amber digits of the alarm clock wavered. She couldn't read the numerals.

The footsteps came closer, slow and steady like Carl's pacing on the long, haunted nights when he couldn't sleep. Except Jack was lighter on his feet.

"Jack? Is that you?"

The hall light blazed. Rebekah moaned and flung an arm over her face but didn't wake.

"Miranda," Jack said quietly. "Are you all right?"

Shielding her eyes with her hand, she could make him out. Half in the light, half in the shadow. Her vision played tricks on her. Jack seemed to advance and retreat, edge closer and retreat again, all the while standing motionless in the doorway.

She squinted to conquer the sickening sensation of movement. "What time is it?"

"About three."

"Why are you up? What are you doing?"

"Waiting on you, madam."

"You're up in the middle of the night?"

"I'm working. Doing some research. Sometimes I walk around. It helps me think."

"At three in the morning."

"Yes." The half of his mouth that was visible eased into a tolerant smile. "In a house full of kids, the daylight hours don't provide a lot of peace and quiet."

Of course. He'd changed his routine, disrupted his work, to accommodate her.

She lowered her hand, her eyes adjusting to the brightness. She needed to thank him, but she would only break down and make a fool of herself.

In the silence, Rebekah sighed again in her sleep.

"I'm sorry," Miranda whispered.

"Don't be. It's normal for kids to be noisy." Jack leaned against the door jamb, bringing his whole face into the light. "Do you miss him?"

"Who?"

Jack raised his eyebrows. He nodded toward the wall where the family photos hung. "Your late husband."

Heat flooded her cheeks. "Oh. I—yes, of course."

"I'm sure. Can I bring you anything?"

"No, thank you. I'm fine."

"I'll talk to you in the morning, then. Holler if you need anything."

The light went off. He retreated down the hallway, his footfalls softening when they reached the rug in the living room.

The house was so quiet that she could hear the ticking of the mantel clock as it crept toward morning. A day closer to seeing the church move out of town—but why the entire church?

Miranda eased herself down again and hugged the cuddle-quilt. Jack had removed his belongings from the room, but the scent of his aftershave still lingered on her pillow, teasing her. As if she could think about a man that way now, with the future tangled up with the past and her family in the middle of the snarl.

So far, Mason held all the advantages, including the fact that she couldn't make sense of his game. If he wanted to move away, that was fine, but she didn't understand why he insisted on taking the whole church. Even a family that didn't want to go.

No one in the church would side with her against the move. Of all the women, Abigail had the most gumption, but she was married to the man.

Not Wendy or the other elders' wives. They would be loyal to their husbands, who were loyal to Mason.

Lenore? She didn't have a lick of sense.

There was Nicole. Being single, she didn't have to worry about a husband's loyalties, but she'd always put Mason on a pedestal. Sometimes she acted like an infatuated teenager, although she was in her thirties. No, Nicole wouldn't fight the move. She'd probably volunteer to help Mason and Abigail pack.

Leaning her cheek into her pillow, Miranda inhaled that teasing scent again. Jack couldn't help. He wasn't part of the church, and he wasn't even a friend. He'd come only because she'd drafted him. She could no more confide in him than she'd go to the police. If he heard the worst of it, he would probably be a good citizen and save her the trouble.

She inhaled, racking her ribs with agony. She exhaled, and the wind picked up as if her exhalation had breathed life into it.

There would be more rain before morning. Falling through leaves and branches. Running down tree trunks. Soaking into the rocky ground.

Carl had said the memories would fade. As if what they'd endured together could drain away like rainwater and be forgotten.

But she would never forget that day, and neither would God. Even if He condemned their decision, surely He remembered why they'd made it. It was a strange consolation.

That puzzled "Who?" was pretty good evidence Miranda didn't miss her late husband, no matter how hard she'd tried to back-pedal. For some twisted reason, that cheered Jack immensely. He caught himself whistling as he moseyed back to the kitchen.

At the table, he tried to remember details of the two notes she'd mailed him, penned in those elegant italics. The first one had said Carl wanted him to stop sending letters and cards; all future correspondence would go straight into the trash.

After Jack had continued the letters and cards for another seven years, Miranda's second note had explained Carl's accident. Her message had been short and devoid of emotion, and Jack had assumed she was frozen with grief. It might have been apathy instead.

Judging by Carl's reading materials, he'd held some odd beliefs. Those beliefs were echoed in some of the articles Jack had found on the Internet.

On Miranda's shelves, he'd also found her college yearbook. He opened it and browsed, paying extra attention to the photos of Carl and Miranda. Carl looked like a solemn and well-scrubbed missionary, the type that rang doorbells on Saturday mornings, while Miranda had the fresh-faced look of a young college girl, her hair long but unbraided. She might have worn long skirts even then, but the photo showed her only from the shoulders up.

By the time he neared the end, he'd concluded that the typical Eastburn student might not drink, dance, or smoke, but probably wouldn't be afraid of fiction or pharmaceuticals either. The school didn't appear to be a magnet for crazies.

Someone was breathing over Jack's shoulder. He nearly slapped the yearbook closed, then decided not to. He wasn't doing anything wrong.

He turned and met Timothy's chilly stare. Dark circles hinted at ongoing insomnia for him. A Hanford trait, perhaps.

Jack released his breath. "Doesn't anybody in this household have normal sleep patterns?"

"Eastburn is the college my parents went to."

"Correct. Why are you up at this hour?"

"I heard somebody talking. Is Mother all right?"

"She hurts all over but won't admit it."

"She's not a whiner," Timothy said with a note of pride in his voice. He pulled out a chair and sat on the edge of the seat. "Why are you looking at her yearbook?"

"Call it research."

"About what?"

"I'm looking for anything that might help me understand what your folks were like in their younger days. Which groups and clubs your mom belonged to, for instance."

Timothy's gaze iced over. "Why are you obsessed with her?"

"I'm not obsessed."

"I don't believe you." Timothy scraped his chair back, a raw, grating noise. "I knew I couldn't trust you. I knew it."

"I'm sorry you feel that way, son."

Fists clenched, Timothy rose. "I'm not your son. Stop trying to be my father."

"I'm not. I'm still adjusting to the idea of being your uncle."

Timothy padded away on bare feet, making no noise until the stairs creaked beneath his weight.

Obviously, he respected his mom. Like a well-trained guard dog, he commanded respect himself. And, being the alpha male of the pack, he resented the newcomer.

Jack rubbed the tense muscles of his neck. "Don't blame me, buddy," he said. "I didn't volunteer for this gig."

He continued reading the papers he'd printed at his house. If he were a normal homeschooler, he'd be furious with the few who gave the whole movement a bad name. Not all homeschoolers were nut bags, but many of the nut bags in a certain off brand of Christianity were homeschoolers.

The fringe elements weren't unified. Some groups were more extreme than others. Many of them were nearly mainstream except for eschewing much of modern technology and requiring beards. Or forbidding them. Others maintained Web sites and discussion boards that gave a clear picture of their teachings, and some of those teachings turned Jack's stomach.

Some deprived women of higher education and the right to vote. Some favored white supremacy, couched in patriotic terms. The common denominator was a focus on the home. Homeschool, home church, home birth—with the father as the absolute ruler of the household. He was the patriarch, and woe to the wife or child who defied him.

Miranda, a bride at nineteen, would have been no match for a despot ten years her senior.

Too tired to think, Jack put away the books and papers and shut off the light. He lay on the couch and wrapped himself in an old quilt Rebekah had rounded up for him.

No sound came from Miranda's room. She must have gone back to sleep, or she would have been calling his name, wanting to know why she'd heard voices in the kitchen.

Come to think of it, he and Miranda had spoken quietly so they wouldn't wake Rebekah. If Timothy heard them from upstairs, he must have been awake already.

Jack could sympathize with anybody who couldn't sleep. He'd endured many a night of wrestling with his regrets. He'd spent months, years, blaming himself, his father, God, and Eleanor Hanford. But none of it would bring her back from the dead.

Sometimes, he thought he'd made peace with the facts, yet something still wasn't settled inside him or he wouldn't so often have asked God to embrace a woman who might have stepped outside His mercy.

It couldn't hurt to ask God to take pity on a troubled soul. Like Luther, Jack regarded it as no sin to pray for the dead. Luther, though, had believed that a time or two would suffice.

Dear God, if this soul is in a condition accessible to mercy, be Thou gracious....

Deciding, once again, that the Almighty was outside of time and could sort out the prayers of mankind and answer from eternity as He saw fit, Jack turned toward the window and its patch of black sky. He prayed for his mother first, then for his father, gone for years now.

Jack prayed for the living too, including Ava. And he prayed for Timothy and Miranda. Especially for Miranda.

Birds woke in a blue gray dawn before Jack ran out of prayers.

ten

Miranda stretched out a trembling hand to brace herself against the kitchen counter. The wooziness was not going away as quickly as she'd led Jack to believe.

Thursday had flown by in a whirl that left her shaky on the inside. Unsettled, disoriented. Like a stranger in her own home, she'd watched Jack supervise the children's work, settle their quarrels, and answer their questions.

Today, she saw even more of his influence. Here in the kitchen, it was Frosted Flakes and frozen pizzas. In the living room, it was his books and papers. And the Dr. Seuss book he'd given to Martha.

Miranda hadn't seen a Seuss book in years, but now, every time she glanced at the silly illustration on the cover, the jaunty rhymes popped into her head. Not that there was anything wrong with Seuss. Or with Shakespeare, Jack's other favorite.

He was full of contradictions. His southern accent and folksy sayings betrayed his mountain roots, but then he would quote a line from *Hamlet* or throw a ridiculously long word into a simple conversation. Even if she hadn't had a concussion, he would have made her dizzy.

For now, all the commotion was in the backyard, where Jack was teaching the children a variety of raucous outdoor games. Carl wouldn't have allowed them to play before they'd even started their schoolwork, but she saw no harm in it. They sounded happy.

The glass carafe of Jack's coffee maker still held a few inches of cold coffee. Its very blackness was enticing.

She couldn't use her right arm, still in the sling. With her left hand, she lifted the carafe to her nose and inhaled. She hadn't tasted coffee since she was nearly nineteen. She'd owned a bright blue mug, personalized with white letters.

Nobody was watching her for once. Nobody would know. Nobody but God, and somehow she doubted He would care.

She could have reheated the coffee easily enough if Carl hadn't forbidden microwaves. As it was, though, she'd have to pull out a pot and heat it on the stove. She was too wobbly to accomplish even that simple task. It was too much.

The carafe suddenly seemed to weigh ten pounds. Afraid she would drop it, she clattered it back down and gripped the edge of the countertop so she wouldn't fall.

She couldn't stand up to a fruit fly. She would never be able to stand against Mason. It would be far easier to give up. To move to McCabe.

God might have arranged her fall to humble her and show her He was on Mason's side. The Bible said God sided with widows and orphans, but maybe she wasn't godly enough.

"Please, God," she said softly. "Tell me what to do. Speak to me. Speak."

It sounded like a command given to a dog. She made a silent apology to the Lord, then strained to hear His inaudible reply.

Nothing.

Her prayers never went anywhere. They were locked inside her skull, never escaping to fresh air, much less going all the way to heaven.

Still gripping the countertop, Miranda looked up at the homemade wedding gift she'd grown to hate.

A wife who's always neat and sweet....

Being "sweet" had been her undoing. If she'd stood up to her husband, she wouldn't have found herself under Mason's thumb.

Moving slowly, she reached for the plaque and curled her fingers around the edge of it. With one upward yank, she pulled it from the nail. She dropped the plaque into the trash. It landed, hard, on an empty juice bottle, but neither of them cracked.

She wouldn't crack either. She couldn't afford to.

Outside, Martha shrieked. "Ollie-ollie over, I'm home free!" she screamed.

Miranda's breath caught in her throat. *Home. Free.*

To be both home and free—that would be heaven. That was what she wanted for her children. No matter what Mason threatened, she couldn't uproot them from her land.

Jack walked into the kitchen, breathing hard from running races with the archangels, and started a fresh pot of coffee. The last one in, he wasn't in the mood to "do school," as the kids called it, but he didn't buy Miranda's claim that she was up to handling it. She only wanted to take charge again because she didn't trust him with her children's education. And no wonder.

Her tidy domain showed the gulf between their lives. The children's penmanship-practice scriptures decorated the fridge; earlier, he'd proofread an article for publication that would have curled Miranda's hair right out of its braid. Chaucer wasn't for prudes.

She limped into the room with Martha tagging along, gave Jack a wan smile, and settled into her chair. "Time for school."

"Are you sure you don't want to wait until Monday?" he asked. "What's one more day?"

"It's one more day toward meeting the state's requirements for the year. Martha, love, would you like to ring the bell?"

"Yessss!" Martha fetched a fist-size brass bell from one of the lower book-shelves. Holding its clapper still with one hand, she tiptoed to the bottom of the stairs, then shook the bell into a clangor that sent Jack's blood pressure skyrocketing.

"School!" she screeched. "Time for school!"

"Holy smokin' Moses," Jack said, his ears still ringing after the bell had quieted. "Miranda, please tell me y'all don't start every day with that racket."

"Only when everybody scatters right after breakfast. I'm sorry. Our house must be much noisier than yours."

Her anxious expression prodded him into a little white lie. "I don't mind."

The other children popped out of nowhere to assemble around the table. Jack huddled over his coffee while Miranda drafted Timothy to open his Bible and read aloud from Paul's letter to the Ephesians.

With only half his mind on the familiar verses, Jack pulled Miranda's dog-eared Bible from the center of the table. He'd flipped through it once before and perused the neat notes in the margins. None of them appeared to be the ravings of a religious fanatic.

On the flyleaf, she'd written *Randi Ellison* in a schoolgirl version of her beautiful penmanship. She'd run out of room, crowding the name into the margin. The lack of planning revealed an endearing youthfulness, as did the tiny hearts that dotted the *i*'s.

The Presented By line said *To Randi from Auntie Lou* in different writing.

Timothy stopped reading, midsentence, and glared at Jack. Jack closed the Bible and returned it to the center of the table, and Timothy resumed reading.

Jack turned his attention to the red, spiral-bound notebook that held at-tendance records, but he didn't open it. No need to; he'd already examined it at his leisure.

Someone—Miranda?—had drawn on the cover. Quite artistically too. Flowers. Trees. Stairsteps and zigzags and overlapping circles or squares. Most of the doodles were in sets of seven. The number of completion. The mark of a perfectionist.

Timothy droned through the verse about wifely submission. Jack wanted to argue that it didn't say a woman had to give up her right to vote—or drive—or work—but he kept quiet.

Finished with the chapter, Timothy closed his Bible. Miranda said a brief prayer and told the kids to get busy. And they did. Timothy took himself off to the couch with a pile of books. In the kitchen, Gabriel searched a dictionary while Michael grumbled over a math problem. Martha colored in a phonics workbook and sang the alphabet song with the volume and enthusiasm of a professional cheerleader. Jonah hummed as he smacked a fist into red Play-Doh on the highchair tray, and Rebekah stood at the sink, filling her inkwell from a larger container of ink.

Jack couldn't imagine teaching multiple grades simultaneously. Six basic subjects multiplied by five grades, plus one busy toddler, equaled countless headaches. He assumed that the archangels and Martha required the most help, but Timothy and Rebekah hadn't outgrown needing their mother's guidance either.

Miranda owned an impressive array of supplies. Worksheets, penmanship guides, maps, flashcards, posters, pens, pencils, paper. Games, puzzles, history time lines. The materials had overtaken a large freestanding storage unit. That didn't count the shelves crammed with books—none of them fiction, of course.

"…E-F-G," Martha sang at the top of her lungs, waving a fat blue crayon in the air.

"I can't think," Timothy said from his outpost on the couch. "Stop it, Martha."

"Amen," Jack said. "Pipe down, Miss Martha. Please."

She lowered her volume, barely. "H-I-J-K…"

"There it is." Gabriel underlined a word with his forefinger.

"L-M-N-O-P!"

Needles of pain pinched Jack's temples. A noise-induced headache was coming on fast.

Miranda, though, seemed oblivious to the uproar as she faced Michael across the table. With her left hand, she rubbed the nape of her neck where delicate wisps of hair escaped her braid. "I can't remember where we left off. What are you working on?"

"This." Michael pointed to his math text as if she could read upside down.

"Refresh my memory," she said.

Jack's phone buzzed. Farnsworth. He retreated to the porch and dealt with her demands as swiftly as possible, but it was a good five minutes before he could return to the kitchen.

The archangels engaged in a spirited arm-wrestling match while Miranda sat with her eyes closed and listened to Rebekah's quiet recitation of the Gettysburg Address. A challenging assignment for a ten-year-old, but she nailed it. Word perfect.

Unaware of her silent audience, Miranda smiled. "Very good, Rebekah."

Martha resumed belting out the alphabet song, with Jonah joining her in a fair imitation. Michael whomped Gabriel's skinny arm onto the table and crowed in victory.

"Hush up, y'all," Jack hollered. The bedlam subsided. "Miranda, you're trying to do too much, too soon. How about if I borrow a couple of your noisiest young 'uns to run errands this afternoon so you'll have some peace?"

She opened her eyes but seemed very far away. "That sounds wonderful."

Her wistful tone wrenched his heart.

Bless her, Lord, he prayed. *Bless her, bless her, bless her.*

Slowly, it was dawning on him that he shared that job with the Almighty.

Opening his car door, Jack glanced back at the house and saw Martha scowling down from an upstairs window, her lips moving. No doubt she was repeating the same complaint she'd voiced when he chose the archangels for the trip to town.

It wasn't fair, she'd said. *She* wanted a ride in his pretty car.

He waved. She pouted, then waved back and disappeared from view.

With some luck, Miranda would take advantage of the archangels' absence and catch a nap. The two older kids were perfectly capable of watching over the two youngest.

Jack hoped he could handle Michael and Gabriel. They were in high spirits, as if they were headed for a circus instead of a boring round of errands.

"Don't expect anything exciting," Jack said. "We'll just drop off your mom's film and pick up a few groceries."

The boys' enthusiasm didn't diminish as they climbed into the Audi. Gabriel sat in back, the sun making a halo of his buzzed blond hair as he pressed his nose to the window. Michael sat up front and played with the knobs of the stereo.

"Why doesn't the stereo work?" he asked.

"It came that way. I bought it as-is through eBay."

"What's eBay?"

"You've never heard of eBay? It's—" Jack stopped. Michael might not know the definitions of *online* or *emporium* either. "It's a market for buying everything from books to cars."

"Why don't you fix the stereo?"

"Because stereos jangle my nerves. So do noisy fans, TVs, and inquisitive children."

"Oh. Okay." Michael opened the glove compartment and slammed it shut, then thudded his heel against something and bent over to investigate. He came up with the forgotten Glenlivet.

"Put it back, please."

"What is it?" the boy asked.

"That's, ah, an adult beverage."

"Why do you keep it in your car?"

"I forgot it was there."

"Why did you put it there?"

"I was bringing it from home."

"But what *is* it?"

Jack was beginning to remember how to explain things to kids. The shorter, the better. "It's Scotch. Put it back, please."

Michael complied. Jack waited for yet another question—*What's Scotch?*—but either Michael already knew, or he'd hit his quota of inquisitiveness.

First stop was the photo counter at the pharmacy in downtown Slades Creek. While Jack scribbled his name and number on the film envelope, the boys hung close, bursting with bewildering remarks about somebody named Jezebel. She must have gone missing, whoever she was. A dog? A cat?

"Whoa, y'all. Who's Jezebel?"

"Mother's camera," Michael said. "Where is it?"

"Back at the house, smashed to smithereens. Why do you call it Jezebel? Does your mom make a habit of naming inanimate objects?"

"Huh? No, just her camera."

"There must be a story behind that."

"She bought it from some old lady, a couple of years ago," Michael said. "And Pastor Mason didn't like it. That's all I know."

Jack tucked the film receipt into his wallet, dropped the envelope in the slot in the counter, and started herding the boys toward the door. "It was quite the camera in its day."

Gabriel grinned. "Sometimes, Mother burns supper or forgets to start school 'cause she's taking pictures. It's her favorite thing to do."

"Soccer used to be her favorite thing," Michael said. "She told me she was good at it. In high school."

"I wish I could have seen that." Jack pictured Miranda as a petite teenager in a soccer uniform, her long hair swinging in a ponytail. Wholesome, athletic, and normal.

"We ain't got no soccer ball," Michael added.

"Your mom never says 'ain't.' Where did you pick that up?"

"My friend Daniel talks that way, just to be funny, but I can't see him anymore. His family left the church."

"And that means you can't stay in touch?"

"Uh-huh."

"Is that church policy or just your mom's choice for this particular family?"

"I don't know."

"What's Daniel's last name?"

"Gilbert. They live right down the road. Daniel's big brother is Timothy's best friend."

Timothy had a friend? Jack filed the information away for future reference as they walked toward the car. They piled in, with Gabriel claiming the front seat. Jack pulled into traffic and did a double take. He hadn't expected to find a genuine car wash in Slades Creek. His car was filthy from its trips up and down Miranda's unpaved driveway.

He turned in, checking the setup. Modern. Touchless. Nothing that could scratch his baby, so he lowered his window at the pay station and fed money into the slot.

Gabriel leaned closer to gawk at the process. "What are you doing?"

"Washing my car."

"I've never been in a car wash."

"Me either," Michael said.

"Never?"

"No!" Gabriel bounced up and down. "What's it like?"

"You're about to find out."

As excited as if they were on a roller coaster, Gabriel unbuckled his seat belt and scrambled into the backseat. The boys clung to each other, all jitters and grins.

Jack looked at them in the rearview mirror. "Pretend you're Jonah in the belly of the whale."

"*Our* Jonah would be scared." Gabriel craned his neck to take in the washing apparatus that loomed ahead. "I'm not scared."

"Fish," Michael said. "It was a big fish, not a whale."

"Oh," Jack said. "Right you are."

As he put the car in neutral and it locked into the track, he remembered the car washes of his boyhood: a driveway, a soapy sponge in a bucket, and a garden hose. His dad had loved to turn the occasion into a water fight.

The car wash swallowed the car and created a twinge of claustrophobia. The boys chattered and laughed as a cloud of fresh-smelling soap surrounded them with a gentle hiss. A flood of water thundered all around. A great wind buffeted the windshield and blew the last of winter's brown leaves out from under the wipers and into the cold spring air.

The wind returned, making droplets bead on the glass. Wind and water, water and wind.

Jack closed his eyes, listening to the subdued roar of the artificial storm, and tried to remember his dad's laughter as he'd manned the hose in the driveway, twin strips of cement with grass in the middle. Old Mr. Olson next door was eternally watering his grass but never washed his car, while Roger Hanford was eternally washing his car but seldom watered his lawn. The men had joked that they averaged out about right.

Back then, Jack had idolized his dad. He was a family man, a churchgoer, an all-around nice guy who often burst into song or told funny stories. Yet he'd abandoned his first wife and their young son to start a new family. Then he abandoned his second wife for yet another woman, and darkness descended on the little brick house.

Jack opened his eyes. The boys were still reveling in the novelty of the car wash. One last sweep of the blower tugged two more leaves free. They floated away.

"'As dry leaves that before the wild hurricane fly,'" Jack said.

Michael snickered. "Why are you talking about a hurricane? There's never hurricanes in the mountains."

Jack viewed the boy in the mirror. "You've never heard that poem?"

"What poem?"

"''Twas the night before Christmas…'" Jack waited for some sign of recognition.

Michael gave him a blank look.

"You've heard of Santa, haven't you?"

"Yeah, but he's made-up."

"Correct, although he's based on a real person. Ever heard of Rudolph?"

"Rudolph who?"

Jack groaned.

He tossed them a dozen questions in various realms. They'd never heard of Pippi Longstocking, Christopher Robin, Hillary Clinton, or Michael Jordan. Worse, they had no clue who was fictional and who wasn't.

Yet they knew Sacajawea, Paul Revere, and even Alan Shepard. Jack had encountered college students who knew less US history than these two wiggle worms, but the gaps in their education worried him. If Miranda neglected some subjects or skipped state-mandated testing, she was breaking the law. Some states required supervision from certified teachers, especially for parents who hadn't graduated from college, but he didn't know Georgia's rules.

The car edged forward, into the cold sunshine, and Jack put it into gear.

"Let's do it again!" Michael said.

"Sorry, buddy. Once is enough."

"It'll get dirty again when we go on the driveway," Gabriel mourned.

"We can pull it onto the grass and hose it off," Jack said. "Sort of like Rebekah wiping your feet after your bath, remember? Clean all over."

The archangels settled back in their seats, content with their sheltered world where a car wash was an exciting destination.

eleven

Sunlight striped a wall that wouldn't quite come into focus. The slant of the bronzed light told Miranda that her nap had stretched through the afternoon until nearly sunset.

Through the closed door, rustles and thuds and giggles came from the living room. She heard Rebekah. Martha. Jonah. And…a woman. Abigail?

After months of being on probation, of sorts, Miranda hadn't expected anyone from church to stop by. Now Jack had littered the house with his duffel bags, briefcase, books, laptop, papers. His shoes. His shaving kit. Not even Abigail would believe it was an innocent situation.

"Rebekah? Rebekah! Come here, please."

No answer. Only a new flurry of muted laughter.

Miranda climbed off the bed. She moved slowly down the hall, then stopped.

A skinny, gray-haired woman in jeans and sweatshirt stood in the living room with Jonah and the girls. The room looked as if a Goodwill truck had dumped a load in the middle of the floor. Jeans, shirts, dresses, shoes. Four black trash bags lay empty, and two more waited to be emptied.

Martha was inspecting a pale blue bra. She lost interest and slung it onto the coffee table, where its lacy straps snaked across Timothy's math book and sent one of her paper hearts sailing to the floor.

The woman handed a black T-shirt to Rebekah. She held it up to gauge its size while Jonah pawed through a bag and dragged out a raspberry red garment. He dropped it and resumed digging, like a shopper raiding the clearance tables at a department store.

Miranda took a halting step into the room. "What's all this?"

Rebekah looked up. "You finally woke up! See, Uncle Jack was right. You do need naps."

"I suppose I do." Miranda turned to the stranger. "Hello, I'm Miranda."

"Hey, there. I'm Yvonne Walker. Jack asked me to stay with the kids a few days ago while you were in the hospital. How are you feelin', hon?"

"Better, thanks."

"Sorry about the mess. This stuff is from my grandkids and great-grandkids. I have more than I can sell in our yard sale, so you can take all you want."

"Thanks, that's very kind, but we have plenty of clothes."

"Sure, but don't you love hand-me-downs? At least let the girls take what they want for dress-up." Yvonne drew a breath and rattled on. "It's so nice that Jack's staying with y'all. He's a cutie, isn't he? I hope the neighbors won't talk."

Miranda's face burned. "There's nothing to talk about."

"Of course not." Yvonne picked up a bright blue sweater. "This would fit you, you lucky duck. Must be heredity. Babies ruin some women's bosoms, but not yours. You sure do try to hide your assets though." She folded the sweater and placed it on the arm of the couch. "Oh, I brought magazines too. They're in that Walmart bag. I don't need 'em back."

"Look what else she brought us, Mama." Martha pointed toward the kitchen table.

The table held a canning jar filled with a bright mix of mums and alstro that Yvonne must have picked up at the grocery store.

"Thank you," Miranda said. "What a neighborly thing to do. Nobody's given me flowers since—"

Since Jack. He'd sent flowers weeks after Carl's funeral.

Yvonne smiled. "Flowers are always good medicine. Well, I'd better run. Nice meeting you." She found a path between heaps of clothing and stopped with her hand on the doorknob. "Say, could you use a kitten? Let me know. Bye."

"Bye, Miss Yvonne," Martha yelled. "Thank you for the pretty clothes!"

"You're welcome, baby. I'll be back." The door closed. Yvonne's feet drummed across the porch. An engine started, and tires scuffed the gravel.

"I like her," Martha said. "She's fun." Her eyes went round. "Mama! Did she say *kitten*?"

"I—yes—but—no, I can't deal with that right now. Rebekah, where are Jack and Michael and Gabriel?"

"Still running errands, I guess, and Timothy's upstairs working on his math." Rebekah dumped out the contents of another bag and picked up a shirt. "I can't believe how long you slept, but Uncle Jack says that's normal for a brain injury and..."

Miranda tuned it out. Uncle Jack says this, Uncle Jack says that. He was a know-it-all who placed far too much credence in doctors and their propaganda.

Aching all over, she lowered herself into Carl's chair and surveyed the mess. If Mason stopped by, sniffing around for rebellion, he would find it in abundance.

All the bags were open now. It was like the old days when she and the other young mothers had passed around hand-me-downs and swapped maternity clothes. But these garments were stylish. Some were bright with sequins. Some were cheerful prints; a few were black, severe, and sexy. Others were classics, like the clothes her mother had favored.

Miranda shook her head. "What's keeping Jack and the boys? Why aren't they home?"

"Let's call, so you'll stop worrying." Rebekah fetched the phone from the kitchen, dialed a number and handed over the phone with such briskness and authority that Miranda felt like the child instead of the parent.

Jack answered with the boys laughing in the background. "We're on our way, posthaste, and rest assured I'm not corrupting the boys any more than is absolutely necessary."

"You'd better not—"

"Miranda, Miranda. Relax, darlin'. See you in a minute; we're nearly home." He hung up.

"I forgot to tell you," Rebekah said, taking the phone. "Pastor Mason called. He said he'll call back later or just stop by."

Miranda's pulse accelerated. "Did he say when?"

"No."

"Did you tell him about my fall? Or about Uncle Jack?"

"No. Was I supposed to?"

"No! No, that's fine, Rebekah."

Martha held up jeans with yellow daisies embroidered on the hip pockets. "Look, Mama."

"Put them back, please." Miranda stood up too quickly, and her vision swam.

Martha obeyed, then pulled a lacy pink dress from the bag. "A party dress! I love it."

It was nearly the same shade as a prom dress Miranda had once longed for. "You don't need a party dress, Martha."

"But it's the most beautiful dress in the world. I want it, Mama." Martha held the dress up to her chin. "I want it so bad."

"Covetousness is wicked, sweetheart. It can lead to—to—just put it back, please."

"I hear a car," Rebekah said.

Miranda froze. She held her breath until she recognized the distinctive sound of the Audi. But Mason could be driving down Larkin Road, right behind Jack.

"Uncle Jack's home!" Martha dropped the dress and ran to the door.

Jonah trotted after her, wearing a squashed cowboy hat. Far too big for him, it fell over his face. He tripped on a pile of clothing and lay there, laughing.

"Rebekah, help." Miranda's voice cracked. "Help me maintain order here, please. Let's put everything back in the bags."

On her knees in the clothing, Rebekah wasn't listening.

Michael and Gabriel rushed in, spouting a tangled story about a car wash and a dog in the park and chocolate milkshakes. Jack followed, his hair windblown, his shirt wrinkled, and his eyes twinkling.

"Mercy me," he said. "Where'd all this loot come from?"

"From Miss Yvonne," Martha crowed. "I *love* Miss Yvonne!"

Jonah clambered to his feet and planted the cowboy hat higher on his forehead. Jack snatched the hat, clapped it on his own head, and scooped up Jonah.

"Nice hat," Jack said.

Jonah giggled, retrieved the hat, and slithered to the floor.

"I love these shoes." Rebekah wobbled across the clothing-strewn room, wearing high heels. Already tall for her age, she looked years older than ten.

"Looks like Miss Yvonne wants to speed up the process of bringing y'all into the current century," Jack said, smiling.

Fine, but not until Mason had moved away.

Rebekah picked up a faded red T-shirt with shaggy-headed singers portrayed in black above the band's name. "The Beatles? Who are they?"

"I've heard of 'em," Gabriel said, peering into one of the bags. "They're a kind of car."

"A kind of car." Jack's smile vanished. "Miranda, you might as well be raising your family in a cave."

She swayed, and the room distanced itself from her. She groped for the back of Carl's chair, found it, and hung on tight until the room returned to normal.

Normal? This? No, it was crazy. It was too much. The hand-me-downs. Jack's influence. The move. Mason's threat—and her plan to lay low until he'd moved away? Jack would ruin her strategy without even trying, unless she made him her ally.

Michael and Gabriel were playing keep away, tossing a tiny silver evening bag back and forth over Martha as she shrieked for it. Timothy came downstairs and roared at the younger boys to stop. Jonah giggled, strutting around the room in a lavender T-shirt decorated with *LOVE* in hot pink sequins. It hung past his knees, like a dress. Rebekah ignored the hubbub and burrowed to the bottom of a black trash bag like a puppy digging a hole under a fence.

If Mason were to walk in....

"Look at 'em," Jack said over the uproar. "The little sinners." He glanced at Miranda. "That's not an insult, you know. Sinners are all God has to work with."

She couldn't bear the noise and the movement and the never-ending headache. "Settle down. Stop it!" Her words were lost in the din.

"Pipe down, y'all," Jack thundered.

Silence reigned. Gabriel relinquished the evening bag to Martha without grumbling. All of them, even Timothy, gave Jack their complete attention.

"Carry on, young 'uns," he said, "but show some restraint, please."

Miranda crooked her finger. "We need to talk, Jack."

"We certainly do." He threaded through mountains of garments and offered his arm. "Little pitchers have big ears. Let's try the porch."

He escorted her outside, into cooler air. He closed the door, shutting out the children's noise. She took the nearest rocker and considered how much to tell him.

Not much. If she told him anything at all, he would demand details.

"I'm very grateful for the help you've given us, Jack. You've been very kind."

"I sense a *but* coming."

"No, I really do appreciate the way you've disrupted your life for our sakes, but you've disrupted our lives too, and I need to explain—"

"Your lives could use a little disrupting." He took the other chair and started rocking. "I'm taking a leave of absence. I'll have to be on campus now and then for committee work and so forth, but for the most part, I'll be at your service. Chauffeur, baby-sitter, teacher."

"Thank you, but that's not necessary."

"Not to worry. The policy is laid out in the faculty handbook, and it's generous. A family emergency is a legitimate reason to take a leave of absence."

"This is not an emergency. We'll get along fine without you."

"Starting when? Who'll take you to your medical checkups? Who'll drive to the store when you run out of milk? By the way, why don't your friends stop by? Or don't you have any? The children don't seem to have friends either. You could at least let them play with the Gilbert kids. Why punish the children because the parents left your church?"

How did he know about the Gilberts? "You don't see the big picture."

"Oh, I'm afraid I do. Anyway, my leave of absence is a done deal. I submitted the paperwork already."

"Without asking me first?"

"Yes, like you named me as the guardian of six children without asking me first."

Oh, he was quick. She had to stay on her toes.

"Fine, but if you're going to stay longer, you'll have to abide by my house rules, and the first rule is that you remember it's my house."

"I can't argue with that one."

"And I'm in charge. You aren't." She took a quick breath, afraid he'd interrupt. "I want the children to put the hand-me-downs back in the bags."

Abruptly, he stopped rocking his chair. "Why? What's wrong with those clothes?"

"Nothing, but please don't argue with my decision."

"But why—"

"Don't argue. It's my house. My family. My rules."

He started the chair creaking again, back and forth in a slow, steady rhythm. "The children are family to me, and I worry about their isolation and the gaps I see in their education. The lack of fiction and extracurricular activities, to name a couple of examples. Most homeschoolers haunt the library and participate in everything from debate team to chess club and ballet, but your kids? The archangels had never been through a car wash until today."

She shot a glance at his sporty little car, gleaming in the last rays of the sun. A reminder of his carefree existence. "Thank you for your concern, but you don't own my children."

"Neither do you, darlin', and I'm afraid you need some help with their education."

"Am I not living up to your high standards? I'm recovering from a concussion, Jack! You still haven't seen our typical school day. Even if you had, you have no right to interfere."

"I only want to make sure that my nieces and nephews are receiving a well-rounded education."

"They *are.*"

"Yet Rebekah has never heard of the Beatles. If that's not cultural illiteracy, I don't know what is. If you want me to be the guardian, I'll start tomorrow. I'll take the whole kit and caboodle to 'Nooga and introduce them to the real world."

"You're not taking my children anywhere."

"Not yet." He stood up. "Sounds like a bar-room brawl in there. Let's go break it up."

He offered his arm to help her up. She didn't want his help, but she needed it. Like she needed it a hundred times a day. Once she was on her feet though, she removed her hand from his arm. He grasped her elbow. She shook him off.

As she limped into the warmth of the house, she tried to see her household through his eyes. The mess. The commotion. The relaxed homeschooling that must have looked like educational neglect to a professor.

Jack had never seen what DFCS could do to a family. He wouldn't understand why she'd rather tangle with a grizzly than with a hostile social worker. If she didn't meet Jack's impossibly high standards, he might report her.

twelve

Moving slowly in the dark and blessed silence, Jack placed the bottle and the glass on the table between the twin rockers. Weary to his bones, he filled his lungs with cold air, exhaled, inhaled again, and lowered himself into the chair.

When six riled-up kids didn't want to go to bed, they kept popping up, like they belonged in the Whac-A-Mole game at a carnival. But they'd been quiet for half an hour now, and Miranda was in her room, either asleep or plotting his demise.

She had a right to be angry. He shouldn't have mouthed off.

His eyes adjusted to the moonlight. Except for crickets and spring peepers, he was alone with his Glenlivet. He couldn't keep an open bottle in the car unless he stashed it in the trunk, but that would make him feel like a lush.

One of his duffel bags? No. He'd already caught Jonah snooping in their side pockets.

If one of Miranda's house rules was a ban on alcohol, she hadn't mentioned it. He could plead ignorance. One of her cupboards, then. A high, out-of-the-way cupboard. If by some chance she stumbled across his booze and decided to be offended, that was her problem.

At peace with his decision, Jack poured a finger of Scotch. He was glad it was too dark to see much. It was a sin to pour the good stuff into a scratched and clouded tumbler.

He took a sip of the smoky, peaty potion. "Relax, Hanford."

Impossible. Nerve-racking images warred with each other in his mind.

That helter-skelter version of school. Boys who'd never seen a car wash. The hand-me-downs. The brouhaha about his leave of absence and the kids' education, and finally the stuffing of those forbidden fashions back into the black trash bags, much to Martha's distress.

How could a few bags of clothes set a woman off like that? Cheeks flushed and eyes blazing, Miranda was beautiful and incensed and not quite rational. A concussion was a brain injury though. Mood swings could be part of the package. Or she was born a shrew, and he was playing Petruccio to her Kate. Except matrimony wasn't his objective.

He closed his eyes and enjoyed the solace of his second sip. The wind in the trees began to wash the noise from his brain.

By the time he'd mused his way through his allotted portion, fatigue had joined forces with the alcohol. He would sleep like the dead, even on that dastardly excuse for a couch. Even on a Friday night, when his demons sprouted fangs and claws.

They still lived in the back of his mind, dark cousins of the fears that had plagued him when he was Martha's age. He'd believed there were ghosts in his toy box. A bogeyman in his closet. A slimy, silver gray water monster in every storm drain. An embryonic Grendel had lived in Jack's childhood nightmares long before he'd read *Beowulf* and recognized an old enemy. *Gastbona*, soul slayer.

They'd surfaced again, every one of them, on a Friday when he was thirteen. They'd never quite left him.

Suddenly hungry for warmth and lights, he went inside and opened the cupboard above the stove. Reaching in to put the Scotch away, he bumped something, knocking it over. His hand closed around a smooth object with sharp points here and there. He pulled it into the light.

It was a creamy white porcelain angel, six inches tall. Traditional and elegant. Nothing about it said "earth mother." Nothing about the angel matched the style of that cheesy plaque either.

Jack raised his eyebrows. The pansy plaque was missing. It might have been broken, knocked off the wall by a rambunctious boy, or Miranda might have trashed it simply because it begged to be trashed. Maybe her tastes were changing.

He still wanted to know who she'd been before she met Carl. Where she'd come from. Where she was going.

Jack placed the winged figurine on the table, then fetched a sheaf of papers from one of his duffel bags and a handful of Carl's books and booklets from the shelves.

Miranda's worries wouldn't leave her alone. Sometimes social workers took children from good homes based on nothing but anonymous accusations. If a man bristling with educational credentials reported a homeschool mother for problems he'd seen with his own eyes, she didn't stand a chance.

She flung back the covers in the dark. She had to think about something else or she'd go insane.

She switched on her lamp and pulled one of the magazines out of the Walmart bag. What a hypocrite, sneaking a magazine in the middle of the night when she'd made the girls give up the hand-me-downs.

As soon as she opened the magazine, she knew its pages hid a perfume sample. Unable to resist the scent, she hunted it down. It was a new brand. Not one of the classics that she might have remembered. The ad included a blurry closeup of a man and a woman, their shoulders bare, their lips barely touching. The blur was a deliberate attempt to produce atmosphere and mood, but it didn't enhance the image.

No one had opened the fragrance strip yet. She slid her finger under it and tugged it open. Its fresh, floral scent teased her nostrils and took her back to high school, back to those few short years after she'd met Jesus but before she'd met Carl, when life had been ripe with dreams.

Just before their three-day honeymoon, she'd bought a tiny bottle of White Shoulders with the last of her own money. But Carl had said perfume was as seductive as immodest dress and might lure a man to sensual thoughts. He'd poured her gardenia-scented treasure into the sink of the hotel bathroom. Having just promised to honor and obey, she hadn't argued.

She should have though. It might have set a healthy precedent.

She flipped through the magazine, unable to focus her attention on recipes or weight-loss tips or the latest fashions. Nothing gripped her interest.

Turning another page, she found an article that was considerably more intriguing than nine new ways to cook with yogurt: the phenomenon of May-December romances. Older men, younger women. Having married an older man, she was curious.

According to the article, some young women wanted a father figure. An older man could provide both romance and security, and if he was also an authority figure, he could be especially appealing to a woman who didn't have a good relationship with her father.

That made sense, maybe. Miranda had never known her father. Maybe she'd been primed to fall for Carl. Ten years older and wiser, he'd had a commanding way about him.

She kept reading. A young woman's need for a lover and a father figure, combined with a middle-aged man's need to relive his youth, could lead from innocent flirtations to reckless behavior.

That was a far cry from her own experience. Carl's behavior was anything but reckless, and he was only twenty-nine. From her teenage perspective though, he was a much older man. He'd made her feel grown-up. Important. Honored to be the object of his affection.

She turned the page and frowned as she read on. If the relationship was forbidden, involving marital infidelity or an age gap that was too large to be socially acceptable, the thrill was greater still. When a young woman fell for a much older man, she was likely to fall hard. He, flattered by her interest, would encourage it. With both parties adding fuel to the fire, the romance could heat up in a hurry.

I'm not afraid of a little heat, Nicole had said, linking her arm through Mason's. *I want to know your mystery ingredients.* He'd smiled and said he wanted her secret spices too.

Miranda's heart thumped at the memory and the inappropriate suspicion that followed. But that was ridiculous. They'd only been talking about chili.

Closing the magazine, she placed the recollection in context. Abigail's kitchen after the chili cookoff in the fall. Abigail was still outside clearing the picnic tables when Miranda stopped in the doorway, searching the counter for a bare spot where she could set a basket of leftover cornbread.

If Mason and Nicole were only discussing food, they shouldn't have dived for opposite ends of the kitchen when they realized they weren't alone anymore. He went to the sink and washed his hands. She opened the fridge, her dark hair tumbling onto pink cheeks.

Miranda's heart beat faster as she recalled other snatches of overheard conversations. Furtive smiles. Body language that whispered secrets beyond recipes.

Mason—and sweet, naive Nicole? Nicole, who blushed and simpered when he gave her a fatherly wink. Or maybe those winks weren't fatherly.

Nicole lived alone with a cat while she waited—and waited—and waited—for God to send her a husband. And there was Mason, a handsome, smooth-talking man in a position of authority. A man who was, on occasion, a little too charming in the presence of the single women, especially when his wife wasn't in the room.

"No," Miranda said out loud. Surely these fears about Mason were only some kind of concussion-related paranoia. Refusing to dwell on evil imaginations, she opened the magazine to an article about inexpensive family vacations. But she couldn't concentrate.

Rustlings came from the kitchen. Jack, probably. Making himself entirely too much at home. Browsing through her school records, maybe, looking for something to show DFCS.

Her fears came roaring back. Ignoring her smashed ribs, she eased her legs over the edge of the bed and put her weight on them. Still working her robe over her shoulders, she moved down the hall.

Light spilled into the living room from the kitchen. The couch was empty.

Jack sat at the table with his back toward her, flipping through a thin pile of papers. One of her Christmas angels stood beside his elbow, and he'd taken some books from her shelves.

Of all the nerve.

She crept close enough to squint over his shoulder at the paper in his hand. A heading, in bold print, read *Scriptural basis for submission.*

At least he wasn't snooping in her school records.

"From smoke into the smother," he said softly. "From tyrant duke unto a tyrant brother."

A board creaked beneath her feet, betraying her.

He jumped. "Miranda. Are you all right?"

She fumbled to hold her robe closed over the sturdy flannel of her nightgown. "Do you rummage everywhere? What are you doing with that angel?"

"I was stashing my Glenlivet in the cupboard. Found the angel and took a closer look."

"Your Glen—what?"

His smile managed to be both innocent and challenging. "My booze. Don't worry, I never abuse the privilege. But shouldn't you be in bed?"

"I can't sleep. Don't tell me to rest. And don't tell me to take a pill."

His smile faded away. "I worry about you."

"Please don't."

"Very well, then. Since you're up…" He pulled out a chair for her, but she ignored it. "I would like to know what you believe. And why."

"Believe about what?"

"Various teachings. Some of them I found online and printed at my house." He indicated a sheaf of papers on the table. "The author of this particular batch is the same man who wrote some of your books."

"Why are you snooping through my bookshelves?"

"I didn't snoop. They were in plain view. Please, can we talk about these things?"

It would be better than lying awake, imagining horrible things about her pastor. Miranda sighed and settled into the chair beside Jack's, careful to hold her robe closed. Her ribs complained with every movement.

"All right," she said. "Go ahead."

Jack ran a finger down the page. "Let's start with this statement. 'Obedience to God-given authority is the linchpin of society. Children are to submit to their parents; wives, to their husbands; believers, to the spiritual authority over them.' Agree or disagree?"

She agreed with the general principle, so she nodded.

"All right; next one. 'Marriage vows are to be honored at all times, and God's blessing of conception must never be avoided or refused.' Agree or disagree?"

"I agree about the wedding vows, of course, and I believe every child should be welcomed as a blessing from God."

"Do you believe every married couple must have as many children as possible?"

She repressed a shudder at the memory of childbirth and the dark days afterward. "No."

Jack nodded. "Okay, how about this one? 'A married woman's calling is to serve her husband and children at home, while a single woman should remain in her parents' home and serve them until she is married. She should not pursue higher education because her calling is higher still as she is her husband's God-given helpmate.'" He raised his eyebrows and waited.

Her eyes watered. Poor Nicole. Even if she was guilty of nothing more than infatuation, she might have been better off if she'd gone away to college. "That's a mixed bag. It all depends on the situation."

"Okay," Jack said. "Now, here's an interesting belief. 'A woman should not vote, as her opinion is represented by her husband if she is married or by her father if she is single.'" He waited, tapping one finger against the table.

"Carl let me vote."

"No, the Constitution lets you vote. It shouldn't have been Carl's decision. If I'd told Ava she couldn't vote or had to agree with my vote, she would have kicked me to the curb."

Miranda shrugged, trying to imagine any woman kicking Jack anywhere. "Go on."

"All right. Some fathers believe a teenage girl shouldn't get her driver's license because her future husband, when he comes a-courtin', might prefer that she doesn't drive. Are you familiar with that belief?"

"It's a new teaching that's making the rounds lately. I think it's extreme."

"That's one way to describe it." Jack shuffled through his papers. "The folks who abide by the extreme rules…do they think their obedience will make them a little more saved?"

"I don't know, but obedience honors God."

"Are they obeying God though? Or are they obeying men who claim to speak for God? Men who might be wrong?"

She kept quiet, remembering Mason's pronouncement about the move. *I have a word from the Lord.* Carl had used the same phrase to justify the worst decision of his life.

Jack gestured toward the books and booklets scattered across the table. "Where did these come from? From Mason?"

She felt like a suspect being grilled by a shrewd and unsympathetic lawyer. "No. Carl had most of them before we were married. I'm not sure where he got them."

"Would Mason agree with them, in essence?"

"Yes."

"Then he's no better than a common thief."

That was one of the phrases they'd thrown around, she and her mom, in that horrible argument about the prom dress. An unexpected flood of shame heated Miranda's cheeks.

"What do you know about common thieves, Jack?"

"Enough to know Mason's worse. He hasn't stolen your possessions. He's stolen your freedom. Your ability to think for yourself. And all in the name of God."

Maybe he'd done worse too. Miranda felt like a child standing on the beach with the sand being swept out from under her feet.

Jack picked up the angel, turned it over, and inspected the oval label on the bottom. "One of the books teaches that failure to conceive is God's punishment for sin, and that neglecting to tithe opens the door to infertility and miscarriage. Do you agree?"

Those views didn't make sense when she held them up to the light of real life. Mason always put ten percent of his salary right back into the church's coffers, yet he and Abigail had never been blessed with children.

Of course, if he was an adulterer… But then, if his philandering was a recent development, there was no cause-and-effect. Miranda hoped she was wrong about him, anyway. It was only a crazy hunch with no facts behind it.

She started to shake her head in sheer weariness but stopped. Jack would take it to mean "No" to his question, and she simply didn't know what to believe anymore.

"Miranda, do you agree or disagree?"

She couldn't recall the original question. "I…I don't know."

He blew out a short breath. "You don't know."

He righted the angel and clenched it, squeezing the life out of it. She wanted to tell him to be gentle. To honor what it represented.

"You don't know," he repeated. "You think there may be some truth to those teachings?"

Desperate to end the conversation, she nodded.

Jack spoke a sharp word under his breath, and the angel's wing snapped in his hand.

thirteen

A brown dragonfly zigzagged in front of the dirty windshield as Jack drove across a narrow bridge. The shallow creek was the same one that flowed at the bottom of Miranda's cliffs, a couple of miles away.

Mason Chandler's number wasn't in the phone book, but Miranda's address book had yielded the necessary information. Jack had also noticed a listing for "Gilbert," crossed out with a single line of bright red ink. He'd entered the Gilberts' number into his phone and the Chandlers' address into his memory.

He found Hollister Road tucked into a steep valley between rocky hillsides. Taking a right, he drove slowly, reading numbers on mailboxes until he found the one he wanted. A realty company's sign stood beside the Chandlers' mailbox.

He parked on the shoulder and took a flier from a holder below the sign. The price seemed low for the area's property values. Considering what that might mean, Jack folded the flier and tucked it in his pocket. He hiked up a steep, winding driveway thickly bordered with evergreens. Like Miranda's place, it was almost too secluded.

Around a curve, a small brick house came into view. An aluminum flag-pole stood in the middle of the yard, the American flag rippling in the breeze. Smoke drifted from the chimney, but no lights were on, even in the fading light of late afternoon.

The burgundy Buick stood beside a blue pickup truck, its paint flaking and faded. The truck's door sported the words *Chandler Electrical Contractors* and a phone number. There was nothing wrong with a man of the cloth run-ning a business on the side, but judging by the condition of the truck, the electrical business didn't contribute much income.

The house and yard were well-kept, if devoid of charm. Through a gap in the trees, Jack saw a plot of cultivated ground. A garden, waiting for spring. Even in summer, it must have been starved for sunlight.

At the door, he tried the bell. Nothing happened. The electrician's door-bell was broken.

Jack knocked. Waiting, he counted tiny pine cones in a dried-flower wreath that resembled the one on Miranda's door. Mrs. Chandler must have also been into earth-mother crafts. Being married to Mason though, she wasn't likely to make Jack's list of favorite people.

Fourteen pine cones. He was tempted to pull one off, merely to make it an odd number, but he refrained. He'd done enough breaking of delicate items lately. Every time he remembered the hurt on Miranda's face when the angel's wing snapped, he wanted to kick himself.

Footsteps approached. A dead bolt slid back. The door swung open to re-veal a short, plump woman of sixty or so in a dark, conservative dress. Silver braids topped her head like a crown. Jack thought immediately of Queen Vic-toria in mourning.

"Mrs. Chandler?" he asked, suddenly unsure.

"Yes?"

"I'm Jack Hanford. Miranda's brother-in-law."

She frowned. "Why are you here? Is everything all right?"

"Yes, she's improving every day."

Mrs. Chandler drew a sharp breath. "Improving? What's wrong?"

"You never heard about her accident?"

"No." She took a quick look over her shoulder and lowered her voice. "What happened?"

"She fell from the cliffs and wound up in the hospital."

"The cliffs? Oh, poor Miranda. Is she still in the hospital?"

"No, she's home, and there's not much wrong with her that a little time won't fix. I've been helping out."

Another furtive peek behind her. "Are you sure she's going to be all right?"

"Absolutely. She's doing well except she won't take her pain pills."

Mrs. Chandler clasped her hands and worked them against each other. "I'm so sorry I haven't been there. How are the children?"

"They're as lively as ever. When I left, they were finishing their Saturday chores."

"I have a big pot of soup if you need anything for tonight."

"Thanks, that's very kind, but what I'd like most is to speak with your husband."

Her eyes, flickering toward the blue pickup, might have shown the sheen of tears. "He's...not available."

Jack hesitated, reluctant to press her for a more direct answer. "I can try again sometime."

She was in a hurry to close the door. "Tell Miranda I'll be praying for her," she said so softly that she might have thought someone was listening.

This time, he was sure of it. Those were tears. The queen was in mourning.

"I'll tell her," he said. "Please, before I go, may I ask—"

"Thanks for stopping." She shut the door.

After regarding the closed door for a moment, he started down the walk.

Before he came to the curve in the driveway, he looked behind him. The lace on the left side of the door flickered. Almost simultaneously, the lace on the right moved.

Two people were spying on his departure. Mason, who'd neglected to tell his wife that one of their flock had fallen off a cliff, and the wife, who'd tried in vain to keep him from hearing a hushed conversation about that fall.

Jack flipped his phone open. The Gilberts might provide a few more pieces of the puzzle.

Miranda wanted nothing more than to lean back in the rocker and let the spring peepers sing her into numbness. The frogs' shrill voices were almost soothing after the rowdiness inside. The children were finally in bed though, and if they knew what was good for them, they would stay out of her hair. So would Jack.

Last night and again today, he had apologized profusely—for meddling, for criticizing, for breaking the angel's wing—but once she'd convinced him that she'd accepted his apologies, he'd climbed right back on his high horse.

The door opened. Martha popped her head out. "Mama?"

"What now? This makes three times you've gotten out of bed."

"Yes ma'am, but I fell out of bed and scraped my knee."

Jack loomed behind her, silhouetted against the light. "Come on, Martha. I'll take a look."

"It's all her imagination, Jack."

A dry chuckle. "Vivid imaginations must run in the family."

"Honestly, she doesn't need a thing."

"How do you know, madam?" The door closed sharply behind him and Martha.

That child could talk him into anything: another bedtime hug, another glass of water, first aid for a made-up injury.

Five or ten minutes passed before Jack came out again. From the dim light coming through the living room windows, Miranda could tell he was carrying two small bowls. Keeping the bowl, he placed the other one on the table near her good arm. They held portions of the rice pudding Rebekah had made for dessert.

"Peace offering." Jack settled into his chair. "Courtesy of Rebekah."

"You don't need to bring me a peace offering. I've accepted your apologies. All forty-three of them."

"I thought it was forty-four, but who's counting?" He took a bite and waved his emptied spoon in the air. "Rebekah's an amazing cook."

Leaving her bowl on the table, Miranda maneuvered her first bite to her mouth. "She is."

The pudding recipe wasn't a keeper though. The off flavor made her think of almond extract that had turned rancid, if that were possible. Maybe the milk had gone bad. Or her taste buds still weren't back to normal.

She glanced at Jack. He was frowning into the distance.

"It tastes funny, doesn't it?" she asked.

"Tastes fine to me." He resumed eating.

Bite by dutiful bite, she ate hers too. He leaned toward her occasionally as if he wanted to be sure she was eating her dessert like a good girl. She imagined flicking the last spoonful at his nose. His reward for sticking it in her business.

"Guess I'll have to run to the store tomorrow," Jack said. "Rebekah used the last of the milk for the pudding. How do you manage to feed so many mouths, anyway?"

"I do a lot of canning and freezing from my garden in the summer, and I buy in bulk."

"But how can you afford to live here at all?" He let out a grim laugh. "There I go again, butting into your business. I'm s—"

"Don't apologize, please. There's no mortgage, and Carl had excellent life insurance that gives me some monthly income. The property taxes are low too, because of the goats."

Jack stopped with the spoon halfway to his mouth. "Goats?"

"It's zoned agricultural because I own goats. You might have seen them, down the road. They're on my land, but my neighbor does the work and has the milking rights. I don't like goats' milk anyway."

"I had no idea your property went so far."

"I'm land rich but cash poor."

"With the price of milk these days, I think I'd learn to like goats' milk. Especially with six mouths to—"

Martha put her head out again. "Hi."

Miranda clattered her spoon into the empty bowl. "Martha Elizabeth Hanford, this makes *four* times. Didn't I tell you I'm done talking to you? Go to bed!"

"I don't need to talk to you, Mama," she said with offended dignity. "I need to talk to Uncle Jack."

His grin was a triumphant flash of white teeth in the darkness. "Yes, Miss Martha?"

She scampered to him in her long nightgown and stood with her hands clasped behind her. "What did you sneak into Mama's bowl?"

"What?" Miranda straightened. Pain scorched her rib cage.

Jack didn't look at her. "Obey your mother, young lady. Head straight back to bed."

"But I saw you stirring something into Mama's bowl. What was it?"

Miranda slapped the arm of her chair, making him jump, making her hand hurt beyond belief. "Answer the question, Jack."

He wouldn't look at her. "Martha, you're messin' with my heretofore impeccable reputation."

"Jack Hanford, my daughter asked you a question. Answer it."

"You won't let a man get away with anything, will you? It was only a pain pill, ground up."

"Martha, go to bed and stay there." She turned on him with a horrible new suspicion. "How many times have you drugged me?"

Finally, he met her eyes. "It wasn't drugging in the criminal sense. Your doctor prescribed a medication for you. You needed it. I simply neglected to mention that I was administering it."

"How many times?"

"Three times. Applesauce, yogurt, pudding. It's a problem, this belief that medicines are somehow—"

"No, the problem is that you sneaked drugs into my food!"

"When you hurt all over, you're hard to live with. Oh, pardon me, I didn't mean to say anything so scandalous. I wouldn't want Martha to think we're living together."

"Mama, what's he talking about?"

"Nothing."

Martha scooted closer to him. "Uncle Jack, why's Mama always mad at you?"

"Because I'm always doing something stupid. Don't worry, sweetie, it'll all blow over."

"Don't be so sure about that," Miranda said. "Martha, go to bed. Now. And if you come downstairs again, I'll…I'll take away your scissors and paper for two days."

Martha's face fell. She slipped inside, closing the door with a thump.

Jack drummed his fingers on the arm of his rocker. "I'm sorry. It's just that I hate to see you in such misery. And so exhausted. That was my fault, keeping you up half the night with my questions."

"Don't pretend to be compassionate. It's about control. It's about tricking me into doing things your way. This cancels out all those apologies."

He let out a sharp sigh and rose. "I'd better vamoose. Can I bring you anything first? A cup of the hot hay water you call tea?"

"Do you really think I trust you to bring me anything to eat or drink?"

"I guess not. Good night, then, Randi."

"You—what—where did you come up with that?"

"It's written on the flyleaf of your Bible."

"You stay out of my Bible!"

"Yes. Certainly."

He lifted his fingers to his brow in a crisp salute, then ran down the steps and into the darkness. The Audi's engine growled and the driveway came alive with lights. The car backed up, swung around in a tight turn, and sped away.

"Don't hurry back," Miranda said.

She'd have to get rid of the prescriptions. The older children might know where he'd put them.

Fighting the dizziness that never quite disappeared, Miranda went inside, leaving the bowls and spoons. Jack had brought them onto the porch; he could take them in again, with his two good hands.

Unless she locked him out.

It was past midnight. A faraway owl hooted as Jack climbed out of the car. The house was dark. Nobody had left the porch light on for him.

He retrieved half a dozen bags from the trunk and climbed up the five broad steps. He set two gallons of milk on the porch and tried the door.

Locked. And Miranda had never given him a key. Now she never would.

She wouldn't hear a knock. Thanks to the narcotic in the pudding, she would be dead to the world for a few more hours, but one of the kids might hear his knock and take pity on him.

He knocked, lightly at first and then harder when no one came. He began contemplating his limited breaking-in skills.

Once more, he made a sharp *rat-a-tat-tat,* the bags growing heavy in his hands.

The stairway light came on. Moments later, footsteps approached.

"Who is it?" It was Rebekah, sounding scared.

"Your long-lost uncle."

She opened the door. Wrapped in a bulky blue bathrobe, she rubbed her eyes. "Where were you?"

"The Walmart in Clayton. Sorry to wake you. I don't have a key."

"It's okay." She yawned. "I wanted to talk to you anyway."

"Yeah? Shoot."

She followed him into the kitchen and helped put groceries away. "When I came down for a drink of water, Mother asked me to take the pills from the hospital and flush them down the toilet, but is that all right?"

"Of course. That's her decision. She's your mother, and you should obey her."

"But is it all right with you?"

"That shouldn't matter. Unless she asks you to do something that's illegal or immoral or dangerous, you should do as she asks."

"Okay, but I can't find the pills."

He opened the cupboard over the stove, careful of the pathetic, one-winged angel that stood guard over his Scotch and the pills. Miranda had ordered him to put the figurine away without mending it.

He reached behind the bottle for the prescriptions, one heavy-duty narcotic and its weaker cousin. Miranda hadn't taken a single pill of her own volition. He removed the lids, wondering if this ten-year-old raised on home remedies had ever dealt with childproof caps, and placed the containers in Rebekah's hands.

"Go ahead," he said. "Flush 'em."

He watched from the hallway while Rebekah made the pills disappear. Just as they swirled away in the water, he wished he'd grabbed one of the strong ones for himself, so he could sleep straight through the rest of the night. It was best to get rid of them though. Pills could be as dangerous as a loaded gun on a nightstand.

Rebekah dropped the empty containers into the bathroom wastebasket and shut off the light. "There. That will make her happy." She started toward the stairs.

"Wait, Rebekah. May I ask you a couple of questions?"

She studied him with that direct and trusting expression. "Yes."

He fingered the plastic lids like worry beads. "Can you tell me about your family's history with the church? How long you've been in it, for instance."

"As long as I can remember."

"And has your mom been one of the pillars of the church? Or more of an outsider?"

"I think she's a pariah. Is that the right word?"

"If you mean an outcast, it's the right word. And I must say you have an excellent vocabulary."

"Outcasts, yes. That's what it feels like. Everybody's nice to us at church, but nobody ever calls or comes over."

"Because of something your mom did? Or your dad?"

"I don't know."

"When did it start happening?"

"I don't know. A couple of years ago?"

Two years ago, Rebekah was only eight.

Two years ago, Carl died. Six weeks later, Jonah was born. If there was a clue in the timing, Jack couldn't see it. Except….

"That must have been a rough time for your mom. Losing her husband, then having a baby."

"Yes sir. It was hard." The poignant understatement made Rebekah seem older than ten.

He played with the lids, matching up their ridged edges perfectly. If only it were that easy to match answers to the random questions that bounced around in his head.

"Do you know anything about your mom's camera?" he asked.

"Sort of. She already had a camera that wasn't so fancy, but then she bought Jezebel. The lady she bought her from taught her how to use her."

Jack blinked at the profusion of feminine pronouns. Two women and one camera, all in the same sentence. "And how did it—she—Jezebel—get her name?"

"I don't know. I just know Mother loves her."

"Speaking of names, what about the rule against nicknames? Where did that come from?"

Rebekah yawned again. "Pastor Mason says they're disrespectful."

"All right. I have a million questions, but they'll keep. You'd better get to bed."

"Good night." She started up the stairs, as graceful as a princess.

Jack wanted some liquid consolation to keep him company while he disobeyed Miranda's orders. He poured a finger of Scotch and drew the angel and its wing out of the cupboard. He settled at the kitchen table with glue from the school cupboard. His fingers big and clumsy on the delicate porcelain, he applied a thin thread of glue and matched the broken edges. Like sliding pieces into a jigsaw puzzle.

Holding the edges together with one hand, he lifted the clouded tumbler in the other and nursed the Glenlivet, listening to the ticks and creaks of the old house as it rocked in the wind's arms.

After a few minutes, he tested the wing. Nearly solid. The repair would make a weak wing though. The angel needed to be in a safe place. Locked away in the darkness.

Continuing to hold the wing together, he looked across the room at a photo of the kids. Not long ago, they'd been strangers. Now they were like family. They *were* family. Blood kin, forever. Four boys, two girls.

He was counting again. Constantly, in the back of his mind, he counted faces, shirts, buttons, anything at all. He took after his grandma, who'd admitted to the compulsive counting of tomato plants, tomatoes, and canning jars.

Sometimes he tried to calculate how much mental energy he expended on his endless mind games, but those very calculations became another counting ritual.

Once he was sure the mend would hold, he replaced the angel and the Scotch in the cupboard. Then he stood in front of the fire, warming his hands and weighing his options for busting Miranda out of a church that made her a pariah yet kept her loyalty. It made no sense.

If he could prod her into arguing, their arguments would raise questions. If she would dig deeply enough, she would find the answers. She would own them.

Except, given her slightly twisted perspective, she could easily come up with the wrong answers.

Coyotes yipped, surprisingly close to the house. Just over the nearest ridge, maybe. They were thieving, murderous animals that ate small pets, but he loved the way they howled their attitude to the night. He just hoped they wouldn't go after Miranda's goats.

Smiling at the idea of goats as a kind of tax shelter, he headed for the couch but stopped at the sound of feet on the stairs. Didn't any of the Hanford offspring sleep through the night?

He'd already learned to distinguish different footsteps. These were Martha's. She moved quickly, lightly. A girl on a mission. A trip to the bathroom, probably, but she would take full advantage of finding him awake and beg for a drink of water or a fresh bandage.

He waited. Sure enough, Martha appeared at the bottom of the stairs. She wrapped her arms around the bulky newel post like a shipwreck victim clinging to a mast. "Uncle Jack? Hear the wolves?"

"They're coyotes, sweetie."

"They're wolves. Michael says so."

"They're only coyotes. Don't worry. They can't come inside."

"I'm still scared."

"But you're safe, even if you're scared."

"But I'm *still* scared." The drama princess darted a glance at the front door as if the coyotes might be slavering on the other side of it, then made a mad run for him.

He scooped her up. Her warm head sagged against his shoulder, evoking sharp memories of another little girl who used to call him "Uncle."

Martha took a deep, shuddering breath. "Aren't you scared?"

"Of coyotes? No."

She was silent for a moment, listening. "What *are* you scared of?"

"Lots of things. I can't abide dark, enclosed spaces, for instance. Or flying in small planes. Or spiders."

"Me too. I hate spiders." She reared up her head, big blue eyes crossing as she matched the tip of her pinkie to the tip of her opposite thumb. "The eency-weency spider," she quavered, making the age-old movements. "Spiders make my tummy all squidgy. I hate it when they come weencing out of dark corners."

"So do I."

"There are spiders in Mama's Christmas cupboard, sometimes. Is it almost Christmas?"

"No, not for a long time. Easter's coming though," he added quickly when he saw her disappointment. "Maybe you can stop cutting out hearts and start doing Easter eggs."

She ignored the suggestion. "Mama has pretty things in the Christmas cupboard, but I can't play with them. I may look, but I may not touch."

Jack smiled at her perfect parroting of Miranda's warning. "I'm sure you don't dare."

Already, the coyotes' chorus was fading into the distance. Somewhere nearby, their eerie cries might be waking another child. Possibly Michael's friend. Michael had said the family lived right down the road.

"Do you remember the Gilbert family, sweetie?"

Martha frowned. "No sir."

"They must have been before your time. Okay, sugar, it's time for you to go back to bed."

"But the coyotes—"

"They're gone. Listen."

She stilled. Straining his ears, he heard nothing but a soft wind in the pines.

"Those useless critters went back where they came from," he said. "Now you need to go back where *you* came from. Bed."

She sniffed and made a face. "Your breath smells funny. Didn't you brush your teeth after supper?"

Shocked at the slur on his personal hygiene, he drew back and stared at her. "Yes, I did. Even used mouthwash."

Then it hit him. She smelled the Glenlivet.

He fought a smile. "Guess I'd better brush 'em again."

"You better."

"Now, get to bed and stay there." He deposited her on the floor.

"Yes sir." Slow as Moses, she plodded toward the stairs, then stopped beside the black bags filled with hand-me-downs. "I still want that pink party dress." Her chin quivered. "I want it so bad, but Mama says it's wicked."

A pink Cinderella dress? Wicked?

Jack managed to speak gently. "She does, does she?"

Martha nodded sadly and proceeded up the stairs as one last, silvery howl hung in the night.

fourteen

Feigning sleep could be an interesting way to begin the day. While the family tiptoed around the couch, Jack kept his eyes closed and his ears open.

The girls' voices came from the direction of the big brown chair, where Rebekah was combing snarls out of Martha's hair. Martha was as cross as a frog in a sock.

"Ouch, Rebekah! Don't yank."

"Sorry. One braid or two?"

"Two." A pause. "Please," Martha added more sweetly. "I hope we're going to church. I want to wear that pink dress."

If Jack had any clout, she would wear it. Soon. But not to Mason's church.

"Mother isn't up to going," Rebekah said. "We haven't gone in forever. I miss Rachel."

Jack's nose itched from a faint, flowery scent that clung to the cuddle-quilt. Someone had left it on the couch, and he'd appropriated it to supplement the other quilt. Barely bigger than a crib quilt, it didn't do much good.

The cuddle-quilt seemed to be the family's common property. Somebody was always dragging it around, like Linus with his security blanket. Jack had even seen Timothy wrap it around his bare feet when he lay on the couch reading.

The hinges of Miranda's door squeaked. It was like hearing someone breathe in, and not breathe out.

Then it came, the answering squeak as she closed the door. She rarely left it open unless she was in the room. As if she kept something worth guarding in there. It made Jack want to explore. But he wouldn't. Even the nights she'd been in the hospital, he hadn't so much as opened her closet door.

She greeted the girls softly. They answered her and went back to their conversation.

"I'll cut out lots of yellow hearts today," Martha announced. "Lots and lots."

"Don't," Rebekah said. "You've already made way too many, and they're supposed to be red or pink anyway. Not yellow."

"The red and pink paper's all gone."

"Valentine's Day was last month. Isn't it time to stop?"

"No."

Martha's obsession with construction-paper hearts was driving Jack nuts. She taped them to the fridge, the mantel, the stairway railing. He couldn't keep himself from counting them in batches. She must have had several hundred already.

As Miranda's uneven footsteps approached the couch, he concentrated on keeping still. No twitching of his eyelids, no movement of his mouth. His right ankle itched. He ignored it.

He half expected her to order him out of the house with more furious words about the meds in the pudding. That had been a very bad idea.

She passed him without slowing and headed for the kitchen.

He cracked one eyelid. Her back was toward him, her braid messy from a night's sleep. Presumably, Rebekah would fix it for her. Miranda, with her injured arm still restricted in a sling, couldn't braid her own hair.

Martha, in profile, sat on the arm of the chair and scowled at something while Rebekah knelt on the seat and plaited a braid. The other half of Martha's hair hung nearly to her waist.

He lifted his head to see the object of her displeasure.

The bags that held those wicked hand-me-downs. They still stood in a squat lineup, waiting for somebody to dispose of them. He wouldn't do it. Not unless Miranda gave him a direct order. Even then, he would argue.

He returned to playing possum. The itching on his ankle intensified. As a distraction, he focused on the ever-present scent of smoke and ashes from the wood stove.

Upstairs, something thumped on the floor. The boys were stirring, but he could stretch out his phony sleep for a few more minutes. A man who could fake exhaustion long enough might overhear an incriminating statement or two, or perhaps a clue about how long he could expect to stay in Miranda's doghouse.

Miranda didn't know who had let Jack in, or at what hour, but if she'd had anything to say about it, he would have slept in his car.

When she returned to the living room, he was still sprawled on the couch with the quilts pulled up to his chin. His right hand was tucked behind his head, and his left hand drooped toward the floor. How could he sleep through the girls' chatter?

She moved closer. His hair was tousled and messy. Dark lashes lay peacefully against bronzed skin. If she hadn't been so disgusted with him, she would have enjoyed her chance to examine him up close.

His coloring must have come from his mother, because she knew from an old photo that Roger Hanford had been fair-skinned and blue-eyed, like Carl. Jack had those dark, dark eyes, hard as bullets when he was angry but sweet as chocolate when he laughed with the children.

His mouth made a firm line softened by the barest hint of a smile. She leaned toward him in search of the family resemblance. The square jaw was a bit like Carl, and the easy curve of the lips was familiar.

She hadn't kissed a man in two years. Hadn't even looked, really—

She jumped, startled by a small hand on her hip.

Martha stuck out her lower lip. "Can I wake up Uncle Jack? Then he can talk to you about my pink dress." She looked over her shoulder at the black trash bags.

"Shh. I've already made my decision," Miranda whispered.

"But it's so pretty."

She'd be beautiful in that lacy confection, a delicate pink like the inside of a seashell. She'd be just as sweet in those tiny jeans with the embroidered pockets—but Mason might stop by.

"I'm sorry," Miranda said. "The subject is closed."

Tears pooled in Martha's eyes. "But I want—"

"Shh! Don't argue. You need to obey me cheerfully, immediately, and without questioning."

"Why?" Martha wailed.

"Because God put me in authority over—"

The quilts erupted in a flailing of limbs. Miranda jumped back in tandem with Martha as Jack sat up, obviously wide awake, wearing nothing but chest hair and plaid pajama pants.

"Bull. Lady, you're full of it."

Fighting discomfort and dizziness from her sudden move, she forced a smile. "Good morning to you too."

"Good morning." His dour expression vanished as he grinned at Martha. "Good morning, sunshine."

"Uncle Jack, you scared us!" Smiling through her tears, she waved at him as if they were separated by a broad expanse.

He waved back with equal enthusiasm. "Miss Martha, you give a man hope for the next generation." Then he glared at Miranda. "Unquestioning obedience is dangerous. What if you've taught your children to be so compliant that they've lost their God-given defenses against evil?"

Her retort was lost in the tumult as Gabriel and Michael ran into the room with Jonah on their heels. Rebekah followed. They surrounded Jack in an uproar of greetings and demands.

He retaliated with his own. "Back off, troops. Somebody turn on the coffee, please. Somebody else, hand me my duffel bag. What's the weather today?"

"Cold an' clear." Michael raced for the coffee maker. "Can I try some coffee?"

"If your mother says you can," Jack said with a tight smile. "She is, after all, your authority figure."

Gabriel scrambled behind the couch. "Which bag?"

"Blue one."

Gabriel retrieved it and shoved it at Jack. "Get dressed."

"Aye, aye, sir." Jack sauntered toward the bathroom with the duffel bag, the flannel pants hanging crookedly from his hips.

The bare back of a fit man was one of the world's most gorgeous sights, right up there with the long legs of a thoroughbred or the curve of a gull's wings. He was beautiful.

No. She couldn't entertain admiring thoughts about a man who drugged a woman's food and criticized the way she raised her children.

"We're not done talking, Jack," she called after him.

"Not even close, m'lady." The bathroom door closed with a firm click like a reprimand.

Michael stood before her, pressing his hands together in supplication. "Mother? Can I try some coffee?"

"May I," she corrected automatically. "And say 'please.'"

"Please, may I have some coffee?"

"No, Michael. I'm sorry. Caffeine isn't good for growing children."

Martha tugged Miranda's skirt. "Will Uncle Jack go to church with us?"

"We're not going." Even if Miranda had wanted to go, she couldn't risk

Jack and Mason tangling with each other. But her absence—again—might trigger a visit from Mason.

"Are we going to have the Lord's Supper at home?"

"I don't know, Martha."

Gabriel giggled. "It's morning, so it's the Lord's breakfast."

"Hush. Don't be irreverent."

This was Jack's doing. The irreverence, the mockery.

And the laughter. Sunshine in the storm. Miranda's heart ached sometimes, craving more.

Behind the bathroom door, the water came on. Jack burst into song, muffled somewhat by walls and water, with a customized version of "Oh! Susanna."

"Oh! Miranda, don't you cry for me," he bellowed. *"For I've come from Chattanooga with my laptop on my knee…."*

The children laughed but Miranda couldn't.

The lyrics and melody stuck with her as she headed for the kitchen. She knew all the words—the correct words—because she'd learned them as a child in school, but her children only knew Scripture songs. Carl had said those silly folk songs were pure foolishness, and he didn't intend to raise his children to be fools.

I had a dream the other night, when everything was still.
I thought I saw Susanna a-comin' 'cross the hill.
A buckwheat cake was in her mouth, a tear was in her eye.
Says I, "I'm comin' from the South. Susanna, don't you cry."

Except for Martha's little tunes and Jonah's humming, Miranda couldn't remember the last time anyone in the family had broken into spontaneous song. Not a single time.

So what? So Jack liked to sing. His influence wasn't all bad, but it wasn't all good either.

After a few minutes, he came out of the bathroom, wearing jeans and a flannel shirt worn unbuttoned over a white T-shirt. He carried his blue bag to the couch, moving out of Miranda's line of vision. Then, trailed by five children, he came into the kitchen.

His hair was curlier when it was wet. He hadn't shaved, and he resembled a scruffy student more than a fortyish professor.

With the children crowding him, he took a mug from the cupboard and poured coffee. "Young 'uns, your mother and I need to chat in private. Vacate the kitchen, please. Scram."

They obeyed. Cheerfully, immediately, and without questioning him.

He lifted the mug to his lips and let out a sigh that might have been in enjoyment of his coffee or might have been exasperation. "So, if Martha wears that pretty pink dress, it's just the beginning of our troubles. The girls slide down that slippery slope. Wearing mascara. Shooting up heroin. There's a link somewhere. I'm sure of it."

Words exploded in Miranda's mind like corn in a popper, but they refused to line up in the right order. "You—you—I never said—don't you put words in my mouth, Jack Hanford, because I do have a temper."

"So do I. Why did you tell Martha the pink Cinderella dress is wicked?"

"I never said the dress is wicked. I said covetousness is wicked."

Jack blinked. "Oh. Oops. I must have lost something in the translation."

"You certainly did."

"I'm sorry." He took a sip of his coffee and studied her. "You're right to be wary of covetousness, but would you agree that there's nothing inherently wrong with a lacy pink dress?"

"Of course."

"Good. In my opinion, Martha's mama would be quite lovely in pink lace." He winked.

Miranda felt herself blushing, and it only made her angrier. "You can keep your opinions to yourself."

"What's going on here, Mrs. H.? In theory, you see nothing wrong with wearing a beautiful dress, but in practice, you wear rather…utilitarian cloth-ing. Because of Mason's rules?"

"Is it any of your business?"

"No, but I've noticed that you don't seem very fond of the man, so why do you kowtow to his teachings?"

If she let Jack open that can of slimy worms, he'd ask more and more ques-tions. Dangerous questions. Desperate to change the subject, she shot up a prayer for help.

The solution presented itself immediately. And every word would be true.

She straightened her shoulders. "I do have some issues about stylish clothes. I associate them with stealing. Years ago, my…I had a…a very close association with someone who had a habit of shoplifting."

"Ah. A friend of yours was a thief?"

"Well…yes. You could call her a friend."

His expression softened. "And has this…friend…ever been caught?" he asked gently.

It took her a moment to comprehend his mistake. "Yes," she said, keeping a straight face. "She was caught a number of times."

"I'm very sorry to hear that."

"So was she."

"Well, I would never hold these youthful indiscretions against your friend."

She tried to look properly grateful and repentant. "That's very gracious of you."

The children flooded back into the room—everyone but Timothy—all talking at once. Jack smiled at the children eddying around him as if he were thankful for the interruption.

"I'd like to tackle the yard work," he said. "Could somebody tell me where I'll find gardening implements and such?" He glanced at Miranda. "Unless house rules say that nobody works on Sunday."

"Do as you please."

"The rakes and stuff are in the shed," Michael said. "The key's in the brown crock on the mantel."

"Thanks, Mike." Jack topped off his coffee mug and raised it high. "Cheers, y'all."

He was out of the kitchen in a flash, whistling, with the children trailing him. The key clinked as he tipped it out of the crock. The front door closed behind him, and the children let out a collective sigh of disappointment.

"Jeremiah and the valley of slaughter," Timothy called from the living room.

Miranda's arms prickled with goose bumps. "Excuse me?"

He came into the kitchen, holding his father's Bible. "A reading for home church. I did the ol' stab-a-page routine and landed in Jeremiah, the sixth chapter." He smiled crookedly.

At least he had a sensible explanation for what he'd said. "The Bible isn't something we play like a game of chance, Timothy. It's to be treated with reverence."

"Jack's irreverent, and he gets away with it." Timothy turned and walked away, as jaunty as Jack.

Weary of arguments, Miranda sank into a chair and fingered the drab fabric of her dress. *Utilitarian,* Jack had called it. He'd meant *ugly.* And now he thought she was a thief.

By sunset, Jack's back ached. A day of manual labor had punished his muscles harder than a gym workout ever could. The rewards were significant though.

On a patch of bare ground behind the house, he'd gathered some of the yard debris in a pile of manageable size for burning. He pulled matches from his pocket, kicked the dry brush into a more compact shape, and lit it in several places. Within minutes, the fire was crackling and blazing as orange as the sunset.

He sat on one of the logs he'd dragged over to serve as seating and pulled off the bulky suede gloves that he'd found in Carl's shed. Stained and worn, they must have held traces of his DNA. The half brothers shared Roger Hanford's genes but had little else in common.

Carl must have been a stickler for organization. He'd kept a scrupulously neat collection of tools, hardware, gadgets, and ropes in his shed. One wall held plastic bins for nails and hardware, neatly labeled. Tools hung from a pegboard on another wall. Two years past his death, everything remained tidy.

Jack rotated his aching shoulders. It had been a long day.

Although Miranda had told him to do as he pleased, apparently it was her habit to confine the family to the house on Sundays. Several times, he'd stolen inside to grab a drink of water or a bite to eat or just to see if she needed anything. Each time, the kids paused in their quiet pursuits—board games and the like—and watched with long faces as he walked out again.

The last time he'd ventured inside, the boys were nowhere to be found but Rebekah was quilting like a little granny and Martha was pouring imaginary tea for imaginary friends. Miranda looked up from her Bible but didn't speak until he did. He suspected she was simultaneously appreciating him as slave labor and condemning him as a Sabbath breaker.

But quilting was work. If he'd broken Miranda's Sabbath rules, so had Rebekah. Not that Sunday was the biblical Sabbath anyway, but most legalists didn't bother to get their facts straight.

As the sun winked out of sight behind the mountains, Gabriel raced around the corner of the house, beating a line directly for the fire. Michael charged after him. The girls followed at a more sedate pace. They stopped a few feet from the fire and stared into the flames while the boys found sticks to poke with.

There was a reason people told tales around campfires. The flames hypnotized. Knocked down barriers. Loosened tongues. Far from Miranda's hearing, even Timothy might have revealed a chink in his armor. Except he hadn't shown up.

"Is your mom strict about not playing or working on Sundays?" Jack asked.

"No," Michael said. "It's just that there's six of us and only one of her, and sometimes she wants a break from worrying about where everybody's run off to. So she makes us stay inside on Sundays, but then we have to do quiet stuff all day so we won't drive her crazy."

Only one adult to supervise six children amid the multiple hazards of a place in the country. That was indeed a problem, but Miranda's solution made Jack smile. It was so...Miranda.

"Smart woman." He stretched his legs toward the heat. "Maybe she can join us next time, if she's up to it. And we'll roast marshmallows."

Martha wrinkled up her nose. "What's that? It sounds bad."

"You've never heard of marshmallows? Roasted marshmallows are the food of the gods, sweetie. They're as good as Frosted Flakes."

"Nothing's as good as Frosted Flakes." She smiled at the fire and began to hum softly.

"Timothy's not joining us?"

Michael snorted. "No, and I'm glad. He's grouchy and bossy and weird."

Jack waited, hoping somebody would stick up for Timothy. Nobody did, and if he was already a tad off the track, becoming an outcast in his own family wouldn't help.

"Y'all need to cut him some slack." Jack wondered how plainly he could say it without implying that Timothy was an oddball. "Sometimes, maybe he feels as if he doesn't quite fit in, even with his own siblings."

"What's that?" Martha asked. "Siblins."

"Siblings? That means brothers and sisters. Anyway, everybody needs to be a little more understanding, all right? Be kind."

Martha massaged her lower lip with her teeth. "Even when he's not nice?"

"Especially when he's not nice, because that means he's having a hard time."

Nobody else commented.

Jack poked the fire with a stick, making sparks fly. "Have y'all ever gone camping?"

All four kids shook their heads.

"Ever slept in a tent?"

Four blond heads shook again.

"Ever gone fishing?"

"Father took me once," Michael said, "but I don't exactly remember it."

"I like to fish," Jack said. "Y'all want to go with me sometime?"

Gabriel and Michael erupted in eager agreement. They wanted to do it all. Camping, fishing, sleeping in tents.

"Bear hunting?" Jack asked, and the boys whooped until he confessed he was teasing. "We'll try to do the rest though," he said, ashamed of himself for raising false hopes about bears. "Sometime soon."

Rebekah rose. "I'd better put Jonah to bed. Mother still shouldn't do the stairs."

"You barely got here," Jack said. "Once Jonah's down, come on back. The fire won't go out for a long time."

Flame shadows flickered across her pensive face. "If Mother doesn't need me for a while."

She walked into the dark void between the fire and the lights of the house. Jack knew she wouldn't come back.

He could build another fire, another night. He could borrow a tent and camping gear too. They could have a real campfire with roasted hot dogs and marshmallows. They could sit up late and tell ghost stories—except he'd forgotten Miranda.

If she was like the other earth-mother types he knew, she would put her foot down about the marshmallows, saying they were pure sugar. She would say hot dogs had nitrates. And, if she thought *pharmakeia* was sorcery, she would say ghost stories were of the devil. But a mother could do worse than to deny a child a hot dog and a ghost story.

It was interesting that such a strait-laced individual had a history of thievery. Not that she'd admitted to it exactly, but the way she'd stumbled over the word *friend* was a dead giveaway.

Martha made a cradle of her arms and started singing. *"Rockabye, rockabye, rockabye my baby. Rockabye, rockabye, sweet—Maya baby."*

Funny, how she threw in a tiny hiccup of a pause to make the rhythm come out right to her ear. Interesting too that the pretend friend had died and come back to life as a baby.

He'd never seen her cradling a real doll. Baby dolls, like fiction, might have been forbidden. A teaching of the church? Or Carl's lingering influence?

"Do y'all remember your dad at all?" Jack asked.

"He was tall," Gabriel said.

Martha stopped singing. "We have pictures. Have you seen them?"

"Yes, I have. You were too young to know him, weren't you?"

She nodded.

Gabriel fidgeted on his log. "He read his Bible a lot, and he ate a lot. That's about all I remember, but I was just a little kid then."

"A little *child*," Martha said primly. "Remember what Pastor Mason says. Kids are goats. We're children, not goats."

Michael jabbed a long stick into the fire. Sparks blossomed like miniature fireworks. "Sometimes, Father got mad. Really mad. And he spanked us hard. But Mother almost never spanks, and when she does, it hardly hurts."

"Because she's quiet and gentle," Martha said. "Like ladies are supposed to be."

Jack smiled. Quiet and gentle, maybe, but sometimes, Miranda was a mama bear who would savage anybody stupid enough to mess with her kids. He liked that. He liked it a lot.

"So, how does she keep y'all in line?" he asked.

Michael shrugged. "Mostly, she takes away privileges or makes us do extra chores."

"Seems to be working," Jack said. "I've never seen such a bunch of good eggs."

Martha let out a shout of laughter. "We're not eggs!"

"No, but you are definitely a literalist."

"What's that?"

"Ah...somebody who adheres to the explicit substance of an expression."

"Huh?"

"Never mind, sweetie, but rest assured that you're a very good one."

Content with that, she resumed singing the lullaby to her phantom baby, then switched to a Scripture song. *"Rejoice in the Lord, O ye righteous,"* she piped, off-key.

She was perfectly normal. Too young to have been warped. Timothy, the oldest, showed the most signs of having been affected by the legalism and the isolation. Jack had a feeling, though, that Timothy was a good, solid boy who happened to be going through a rough time.

Jack prodded the fire with his stick. Bright orange motes flew skyward and faded into ashes that continued rising. Gray snowflakes, they defied gravity.

Ashes to ashes, dust to dust. He remembered his mother's cremation, hastily arranged by the husband who'd just dumped her. Roger Hanford's first ex-wife had turned religious. His second turned to pills.

Jack remembered his dad as a good-time Charlie. When in doubt, sing, he'd always said. He'd often grabbed his wife for an impromptu dance around the living room, and Jack had laughed with them, thinking he had the best dad in the world. Roger Hanford was a great guy except for his unfortunate habit of chasing anything in skirts.

There were no perfect fathers. No perfect sons.

Pulling in a breath of smoky air, Jack counted the years since he'd lost his mother. And he'd lost her, all right. Like losing a library book. He'd been irresponsible. Careless. So busy with his all-important eighth-grade pursuits that he hadn't bothered to make a phone call.

The dancing flames cast a spell of silence over Martha and the archangels. They didn't volunteer any more information, and Jack didn't ask any more questions. He had plenty to think about.

fifteen

Jack downed the last of his morning coffee, set the mug in the sink, and turned to find Martha scooting into the kitchen on her rump, backward, for no discernible reason.

"Uncle Jack, is Mama still mad at you?"

"No, I think we've cleared the air."

Abandoning her unladylike locomotion, Martha sniffed. "What was wrong with the air?"

"That's a figure of speech. It means talking things over. Or clearing things up."

"Oh." Martha stood and reached into a big, square pocket on the front of her denim skirt. She pulled out a delicate glass snowflake that shot rainbows of color as the sun hit it.

"Is that a Christmas ornament, young lady?"

"Yes sir, but I'm not playing with it. I'm just looking at it."

"And touching it and hauling it around with you. Breaking your mom's rule. Hand it over."

"But it's so beautiful."

"It is. Show me where you found it, please."

Martha stuck out her lower lip but relinquished her treasure. She led him into the living room, opened a tall pinewood cabinet that stood near the wood stove, and pointed to a shoe box on one of the middle shelves. She must have dragged a chair over to reach so high.

Jack deposited the snowflake amid ten or twelve similar ones, each one in its own nest of white tissue paper. Every shelf in the cabinet was loaded with decorations. Coils of lights and old-fashioned bead garlands. Candles. A red and green plaid tablecloth. A glittery silver star for the top of the tree. It did his heart good to see that Mason hadn't banned Christmas celebrations.

"Looks like your mom goes all-out when Christmas rolls around."

"Mama loves Christmas. She bought these angels last year." Martha pointed to a row of porcelain angels like the one he'd found in the kitchen. "Aren't they pretty?"

"Very," he said, annoyed with himself for automatically counting the angels on the shelf. Six, all alike. "But stay out of the Christmas cupboard or you'll be in deep trouble."

"Yes sir."

The impeccable politeness of the well-brought-up southern child. *Yes sir. No sir. Please, thank you, you're welcome.* Such beautiful manners, mixed with sly disobedience. He understood completely; he had been a well-brought-up southern child as well.

"Find something else to do for a few minutes," he said. "We'll start school soon."

"Yes sir." She ran off, apparently holding no grudges against him.

Miranda entered the room a few minutes later, and Jack helped her round up her students. They sailed through their daily preliminaries and got on with the lessons.

Martha and the archangels engaged in a three-way squabble about something as they opened their books. Jonah meticulously stuck tiny balls of

Play-Doh on his shirt. Rebekah was distraught because she'd made an ink smudge on a fresh page of her journal. And Miranda struggled to open a gigantic paperback textbook one-handed.

Jack stopped beside the highchair to have a quiet word with Jonah about the proper uses of Play-Doh, then reached around Miranda to open the textbook. It was a reprint of an exhaustive nature guide from 1905. Jack swallowed a remark about the veracity of scientific findings in 1905.

"Which page do you need?"

"Chapter 11." She sounded weary already.

He found the right page. The entire chapter was devoted to earthworms. He scanned the first paragraph and shook his head. "When there are so many simple ways to construct a sentence, why did these old geezers love their pedantic, convoluted sentences and polysyllabic words?"

"Like the words that just came out of your mouth, professor?"

He smiled down at the neat part in her hair. "Touché."

She slid the book across the table to Gabriel, who bent over the dictionary and scratched his pencil across a sheet of paper. "When you're done with your vocabulary words, please read chapter 11 and answer the study questions."

Gabriel nodded and continued writing.

Jack bent over to put his lips close to her ear. "A six-year-old can't read that."

She pulled away from him. "Gabriel can. And he does."

Jack straightened and took a respectful step backward. "I'm impressed."

"It's about time."

"It's a shame that such a good reader is limited to nonfiction."

She snapped her pencil's lead against the table and the tip flew across the room. "Children, take a break."

Michael grinned. "Already? Wahoo!"

Pencils rolled across the table, chairs scraped back, and feet hit the floor. The boys grabbed jackets and the girls donned their capes. Except for Jonah, still in the highchair, the kids abandoned the kitchen in record time and fled to the great outdoors.

Jack strolled around the table to view Miranda from a safe distance. "I'm sorry, but I can't reconcile myself to the idea that you've outlawed fiction."

"I haven't."

"Is that so? Yet you don't provide it, and your children can't provide it for themselves unless they make up their own like Martha does."

"She does not."

"She pretends to have tea parties. She sings lullabies to an imaginary baby. If we wrote down those scenarios for her, they would be a form of fiction, would they not?"

"So to speak."

"And you don't mind that, yet you're opposed to letting the children read fiction?"

"That was Carl's rule, not mine."

"Why do you stick with his rule? Do you think fiction is sinful? Dangerous? It's more dangerous to try to raise your children in a sinless bubble. Why won't you let them live in the real world?"

Her cheeks were pink, the tips of her ears were red, and she'd pressed her lips tightly together as if to keep them from spewing naughty words. "Stop lecturing me."

"I'm trying to be helpful."

She whispered two syllables that sounded remarkably like an unladylike word that cast aspersions on his ancestry. "Helpful? *Helpful?* You think it's helpful to keep pointing out that I don't meet your standards for homeschooling? You think it's helpful to threaten to take my children? Next thing I know, you'll be reporting me to DFCS!"

She hurled her pencil. It caught his left shoulder with surprising force and bounced to the floor.

Jack blinked at the mama grizzly. "I never said...I said...I don't recall exactly what I said, Miranda."

"I do, and it gives me nightmares."

He racked his memory but drew a blank. "Whatever I said, I'm sorry. I want the best for you and the children. That includes covering all necessary subjects and arranging for standardized tests and so forth. In short, I need your schooling to comply with the law."

"The law, yes, that's fine, but DFCS is above the law. Have you ever seen them go after a family? They snatch the children first and ask questions later. They take the word of an anonymous caller as the gospel truth, and the parents are presumed guilty."

"Sometimes, parents *are* guilty, and children's lives depend on intervention from social workers."

"Social workers don't always rescue children from abusive homes. Sometimes, they steal children from good homes and put them in abusive homes."

"That must happen only in a minute percentage of cases. Nonetheless, please believe me, Miranda. You're doing a wonderful job, in general, and I would never report you."

"A week from now, you'll say it again."

"Say what again?"

She arched her eyebrows. "Ah don't recall exactly what Ah said, M'randa."

Jack winced. The spot-on mimicry made him painfully aware of his country-boy twang.

He took a piece of notebook paper, leaned over the table, and scrawled: *I, R. Jackson Hanford, will not take Miranda Hanford's children from her, nor will I report her to DFCS or to any other governmental agency.* After a moment's thought, he made the period a comma and added: *for anything, so help me God.*

He signed it, dated it, and slid it across the table. "There you are, and I'll trust you to be a law-abiding homeschooler so you won't ask me to violate my conscience."

"Two more copies, please."

He complied, wondering what she intended to do with them. Once all three copies were in her custody, her shoulders sagged as if she'd dropped a heavy burden to the floor.

She handed one copy back to him. "Keep it. To remind you to keep your promise."

"I don't forget my promises. But I do apologize for worrying you." He shook his head. "I'm always apologizing for something."

"Hmm. I wonder why."

He chose to ignore that. "About Carl's rule. Do you think he was right to ban all fiction?"

"I believe I should be careful about what my children read." She stopped, biting her lip and staring into the distance. "But honestly, I don't know how to choose good books. I…I don't have any experience. My mom wasn't much of a reader, and I only had one year of college."

He felt as if she'd opened a massive door, just a crack, and might open it further if he didn't growl like a pit bull and scare her into slamming it shut again.

"Would you like some help with that?" he asked cautiously.

After a moment, she nodded.

"I'd be happy to run them to the library and supervise their choices. It would give you a break. And I'll be careful about what I expose them to."

She started rounding up crayons, awkwardly, with her left hand. "If they come home with godless trash in their hands—"

"They won't."

"If they do, I'll never trust you again."

"You can trust me," he said. "Like you trusted me when you named me as the guardian."

She stuffed crayons into the box, every which way. A red one snapped in half. She crammed the broken pieces in and mashed the lid down. She looked up but didn't speak.

"On my honor," he said, "I will keep godless trash out of their hands. Would you like that in writing? in triplicate?"

"No. Go ahead. Take them to the library and use your best judgment."

"All right, then." In a hurry to escape with the kids before she changed her mind, Jack took his copy of his pledge into the living room. The girls and the archangels were nowhere in sight, but Timothy was prone on the couch. Book in hand, but not reading it.

Jack cleared his throat. "You overheard that bit of unpleasantness, didn't you?"

"Yes." Timothy rolled over and met Jack's eyes. "When are you leaving?" he asked quietly.

"For Chattanooga?"

"No." Timothy darted a glance at Miranda. "For the library."

"This afternoon, unless your mother kills me first. And that's a distinct possibility."

Jack tucked the paper into his briefcase. When he looked up, Timothy was smiling. Whether it was a sign of camaraderie or that the kid liked the idea of losing his uncle to murder, it was a nice change.

Miranda lowered herself gently onto the couch and savored the quiet. It had been years since she'd been completely alone on her property. Even now, she wasn't truly alone; Jonah was napping in her bed. But, until he woke or Jack brought the others home, she would enjoy her solitude and relish her victory.

No doubt Jack thought he'd won because she'd let him take the children to the library, but she was the victor. He'd promised, in writing, that he would never report her.

He lived in a different world though, with different standards. There was no telling what kind of garbage he would allow the children to bring home.

"God, please protect them from evil," she said. "Give Jack some common sense. Remind him to respect my wishes. And help me recover quickly, so everything can go back to normal." Her voice cracked. "And please, please, make Mason leave me alone."

There. She had prayed; God either heard her or didn't. Would answer or wouldn't. These days, that was about as far as her faith could stretch.

She leaned toward the coffee table. Some of Jack's papers lay under a scattering of Martha's hearts. Miranda brushed a few of the hearts away. Her vision still swam sometimes, and Jack's ragged penmanship didn't help, but she could read his notes on the top paper. Some hapless student was coming under fire.

Why? Back up opinion w/ facts.

That sounded exactly like Jack. His own opinions, of course, he regarded as absolute truth. She tried to decipher another scrawled line but could make out only two words, *Not true.*

The handwriting in his letters had always been messy and cramped, as if he'd been in a hurry to jot down a thought and fly to the next one. *Dear Carl and Miranda,* he'd always written, his salutation wisely including both of them even in birthday cards for one or the other. Jack must have sensed that Carl's jealous streak hadn't left room even for brotherly friendship.

Exploring further in the paper, she found more of Jack's pithy comments and questions, demanding facts, logic, references. *Dig deeper,* he exhorted in bright red ink. *Define terms!*

Straightening the papers into a neat pile, she glanced at the author's name. It was *Jack's* paper? He'd directed his critique, not toward a student, but toward himself.

Smiling at her new perspective on him, she retrieved one of the women's magazines she'd hidden under the couch. This time, she'd avoid any articles that might threaten her peace of mind.

Again, she found a perfume sample. She ran one finger over the white matte surface of the fragrance strip, then rubbed it over her left wrist. The scent was light and sweet, like violets. Like springtime without sorrow. It made her feel starved for sunshine.

She wrapped herself in her cape and took the magazine outside. With the bedroom window cracked open, she would hear Jonah when he woke.

Jack's shiny black car stood uselessly in the drive. He had taken the van. She didn't have keys to his car, nor did she have two good hands at the moment, nor did she know how to drive a stick shift. Carl had believed that was an unwomanly skill. Even if she didn't have a child sleeping in the house, she couldn't have escaped.

Tired of the porch, she proceeded to one of the two white Adirondack chairs that sat on the grass, their paint peeling. Above her, a hawk cried. Dark against the sky, the bird dipped and wavered, and the sun shone through its tail feathers, making them brick red. The hawk looped and circled over the woods and finally soared out of sight. Free to choose its own course. Free to make choices, bad or good.

Sometimes she wasn't even sure she wanted freedom. Freedom wasn't safe.

She opened the magazine—to a two-page ad for lingerie. It reminded her of Jack's comment about pink lace. He hadn't said anything racy, yet his wink and the twinkle in his eye had made her blush.

At least she hadn't rebuked him. If she had, and he hadn't meant a thing by it, then they both would have known that she, not Jack, was entertaining impure thoughts about lacy lingerie.

She closed the magazine. She should have brought her Bible outside instead, to cleanse her mind.

Jack probably had a girlfriend back in Chattanooga, anyway. A polished, professional woman. The kind who paid for real manicures and real haircuts in real salons. She would shop at department stores with her own money. She would make her own decisions about jeans and red sweaters and big, shiny earrings. She wouldn't be a frumpy housewife who wore home-sewn clothes and hand-me-downs.

The purring of an engine caught Miranda's ear. Abigail's car pulled around the curve in the driveway. Miranda's heart leaped—but Mason was at the wheel. He was alone.

She hid the magazine under her cape. Feeling like a turtle, she pulled her hands and arms in too so he wouldn't smell the fragrance on them. Then she went cold all over. She couldn't hide Jack's car.

Mason climbed out of the Buick, the wind whipping against his trousers. Paying no attention to the Audi, he gave Miranda a warm smile. "Hello, Miranda."

"Hello." A heavy strand of hair fell into her face. She felt like a messy child who'd been playing with Mommy's perfumes. And Mason—why was he pretending he didn't see the unfamiliar car sitting there? Didn't he see her scrapes and bruises?

"Are you feeling better?" he asked.

"Yes…you've heard about my fall?"

"I stopped by when you were in the hospital. Jack filled me in."

Mason knew about Jack? Jack hadn't said a word about it.

Her pulse speeding, she gave Mason a casual nod. "I see."

Mason took the other chair, crossing his legs at his ankles. "Where is everybody? The van's missing."

"Jack took the children to town."

Mason ruminated on that for a moment. "As you can imagine, I was surprised to find him staying here. I was even more surprised when he told me you'd named him as the guardian of the children."

"He's a Hanford. He's family."

"True, but I'm concerned about his influence. You haven't been in church for weeks."

"That isn't his fault. First, we had that bout of chickenpox. I had one contagious child after another for weeks. Then I fell. Then Jack came." She took a quick breath. "How's Abigail?"

"She's packing. She's looking forward to the move. That's what we need to discuss, Miranda." He ran his forefinger over the weathered arm of her chair as if to point out that it needed a fresh coat of paint. "You'll get a much better price if the place is in good shape. Have you taken even the first steps on the checklist?"

Until that moment, she hadn't recalled wadding up his list and tossing it over the cliffs. "No, I haven't. It's still hard to get through the day without dealing with anything extra."

"If you'd started the process before your fall, the place could have been on the market for weeks already." He pulled two business cards from a pocket and handed them to her. "These folks will put you on the fast track."

She squinted at the cards. One of them read *Palisades Properties.* The other one advertised a handyman's services. Their numbers had been on the checklist.

"Miranda, I still sense a certain resistance," he said. "You don't want to be the last one to sell and move, do you?"

"No." She didn't want to sell and move, period.

"Then you'd better get busy."

Why was he so determined to make her move? Some reckless impulse dropped the question onto her tongue. "Is Nicole moving?"

"You let me worry about Nicole. You need to worry about Miranda."

No sign of nerves or guilt. He was so smooth—or he was innocent.

He stared off into the distance for a long time, then spoke softly. "I'm sure you don't want to face the elders again."

She shook her head. Robert Perini was the only tender-hearted man among them. She'd squirmed on a hard metal chair while Mason scolded her and the other men sat still and silent as a jury. Tiny, colicky Jonah had cried until Abigail took him to the back room, but he'd still refused to be comforted. Miranda's aching breasts had leaked milk as she'd endured what she remembered now as the Inquisition.

All because she'd refused to give up her camera.

Mason stood, towering over her, the late sun catching a faint sheen of perspiration above his upper lip. "Ever since you lost your husband, you've leaned on the church for a great deal of support. Financial support, moral support. If you stay behind, you'll be on your own." His silvery eyes bored into her.

"That will be difficult if DFCS starts poking around. I hope it won't go that far, but it could."

Stunned, she stared up at him. "Are you threatening me?"

"Not at all, but I'll always do whatever my conscience requires, even if it means exposing someone's wrongdoing."

She hesitated, her pulse racing. "What if my conscience requires that I expose yours?"

"Who has the most to lose?" he shot back.

Then he was guilty—of something. An innocent man wouldn't have responded that way, wouldn't have to calculate who had the most to lose.

Miranda couldn't speak. She could hardly breathe.

His nostrils flared. Then his face softened with a sympathetic smile. "It's happening again, isn't it, Miranda? The mixed-up thoughts. The topsy-turvy emotions. If you're not careful, you'll find yourself in trouble again."

About to argue, she stopped herself. If he thought he could manipulate her into confusion and compliance, he might leave her alone a little longer. She could buy time by playing along.

She hung her head so he couldn't read the contempt in her eyes. "I need to examine my heart."

"You do indeed. I'll be praying for you, Miranda."

"Thank you."

She watched his shiny black shoes until they turned in the long grass and moved toward Abigail's car.

Long after he'd driven away, Miranda sat there, weighing her risks and responsibilities. They were many. If she was meant to stay in Slades Creek, she would pay a high price.

She tore both business cards in half, then in quarters, a task that became painful when one of the nearly healed cuts on her right hand broke open again. Some of the pieces were smudged with blood when she tossed them into the wind.

Facing a cold breeze, Jack led Miranda's brood out of the library and tucked her library card into his wallet. He'd picked up applications for the kids in the hope that she would sign them. If he'd thought ahead and brought proof of Miranda's residence, he could have taken advantage of having the same surname and signed the forms himself.

Everybody climbed into the van. While the engine was getting its wits together, he turned on the heat, buckled his seat belt, and checked in the mirror. "Ready to roll, troops? Everybody strapped in?"

"Yes sir," five young voices chorused, drowning out the irritating roar of the heater's fan.

Jubilant with the success of his mission, he pulled the van out of the tiny parking lot. The vehicle was stuffed with kids and books. Lord willing, none of the books were godless trash, but it was hard enough to keep track of five kids without inspecting each selection.

He glanced at Timothy, riding shotgun. At the last minute he'd nearly stayed home, but he'd been unable to resist the lure of free reading materials.

"What did you find?" Jack asked.

"Science. History. Mostly history."

"You want to be more specific?"

"World War II. Stuff like that." Timothy conveniently neglected to mention the psychology and anatomy books between his feet.

Ah, the joys of adolescent curiosity. Jack could guess which chapters Timothy would read first, far from his mother's supervision.

"I noticed you weren't in the children's section," Jack said.

"The good history books are in the adult area. You have a problem with that?"

"Absolutely not. I don't believe in the strict policing of reading choices, nor do I approve of censorship, for the most part. I believe in digging for the truth. If you earn it, you own it."

Timothy nodded.

Encouraged, Jack went on. "My dad was a history buff, and I have dozens of history books that belonged to him. I'd be happy to share them, if you're interested."

Timothy shrugged.

"Uncle Jack," Martha called. "I love going to the library, but it would've been more fun if we were in your pretty car."

Jack looked in the rearview mirror. Hugging a brightly colored book, she sat in the middle seat with the archangels and smiled out the window at the passing sights.

"Y'all wouldn't fit in my car, sweetie. It only holds four people, and the ones in the backseat had better not be very big."

"Oh. But sometime I want a ride in your—" She shrieked. "Look! A palm reader's sign. I *hate* palm readers."

Jack laughed as he cruised through the intersection on the yellow light. She'd seen the red Don't Walk hand.

"That's not a palm reader's sign, Martha. It's connected to the traffic light, and it warns people on the sidewalk when the light's about to turn red."

"Oh. Good, 'cause palm reading is bad. That's divination, and it's wicked."

How could a four-year-old know a word like "divination" but remain ignorant of basic sidewalk safety?

Down the street, she cried out again. "A blimp! I love blimps."

A gray, blimp-shaped balloon flew high above a car dealership. Behind the tether, a jet carved out a white trail against the sky. The tether and the jet trail appeared to be on the same trajectory, but the jet kept going, soaring free. The balloon's line jerked and arched and pulled back, attached to the earth. A fake, it was going nowhere.

On the outskirts of town, Jack looked in the mirror. Michael and Gabriel had already dug into *Kidnapped* and *The Borrowers,* respectively. Martha had opened one of the Berenstain Bears stories and was tracing the words with her forefinger.

The kids were reading, unfettered by ridiculous rules. That was the first step toward cutting the tether and setting the family free.

"Gabe, how's your book so far?"

Gabriel nodded furiously without looking up and turned a page.

"I loved the Borrowers series," Jack said. "I remember reading in the closet with a flashlight and wondering if there were borrowers in the walls."

Martha looked up. "What are borrowers?"

"Smart little people, a few inches tall. They hide in old houses and borrow things from big folks like us."

She gasped. "In *our* house? Where?"

"I'm afraid it's only a story," Jack said. "Make-believe."

"Oh." The disappointment in her voice was pitiful.

"But we can pretend…"

"Yes! I love to pretend."

"I'll read it to you when Gabriel's finished with it," he offered.

"Okay! Uncle Jack, I'm so happy because you came to stay with us."

"And I'm happy to be staying with you," he said over a ridiculous lump in his throat.

Martha clutched her book to her heart and let out a sigh of bliss. Behind her, with the backseat all to herself, Rebekah swayed with the motion of the van, engrossed in a paperback copy of *Jane Eyre*. Jack hoped Miranda wouldn't fuss over the fact that Mr. Rochester had fully intended to enter into a bigamous marriage. It would be difficult reading for a ten-year-old, but if Gabriel could comprehend that horrible chapter about earthworms, surely Rebekah could enjoy Charlotte Brontë.

Jack hadn't forgotten the youngest child either. Among other titles, Jack had grabbed *The Book of Jonah* by Peter Spier, partly for the shared name and partly for the cover art, a fantastically scary fish sure to thrill Jonah when he woke from his nap.

If Miranda wanted to throw a fit, she could throw a fit. She could even confiscate their finds, but the kids had spent the afternoon glorying in the treasures of a public library without their mama looking over their shoulders, and they wouldn't forget it.

"Almost home," Jack said. "And we'll watch it hit the fan."

"Watch what?" Timothy asked. "Oh. That." His mouth curled into a mischievous grin, and for one little moment, they were allies.

sixteen

Jack ran up Miranda's steps with the pharmacy bag in his hand and stopped on the threshold to savor the change wrought by yesterday's trip to the library. Overnight, the noisy household had become a place of quiet, book-induced rapture.

Finished with the day's schoolwork, the kids had returned to their pleasure reading. Timothy had taken his haul upstairs the night before, but the rest were headquartered in the living room.

Jonah lay on his back with his feet propped up on the coffee table, humming like a contented little bumblebee with the Spier book a few inches from his face. The archangels were sprawled on the rag rug. Rebekah and Martha, absorbed in Brontë and Seuss respectively, snuggled together on one end of the couch, while their mother took the other end.

Only Miranda wasn't reading. She stared into space, oblivious to Jack's return. For the last twenty-four hours or so, she'd been gloomy, her eyes haunted with something he couldn't name.

What had happened in the last twenty-four hours? Not much. He'd pledged, in writing, that he wouldn't report her to anybody, and he'd led the library excursion. As far as he knew, that was it.

"I'm back," he said.

She jumped, touching her fingertips to the hollow of her throat. "Oh! I didn't hear you come in."

Closing the door behind him, he lifted the plastic bag higher. "I have something for you."

"If it's another pain prescription, I don't need it."

"It's not." He squeezed in between her and Martha, who ignored him in favor of Seuss, and pulled the photo envelope from the bag. "Your camera was beyond help, but we saved the film."

"Oh, Jack, thank you!"

Warmed by her enthusiasm, he hurried to extract the pictures from the envelope. "Tell me if I'm going too fast."

The first few photographs were outdoor group shots of the kids, so well posed that they appeared to be candid. In the best of them, Jonah lounged in one of the Adirondack chairs with his siblings gathered around him, all of them glancing toward the camera as if it had just happened to catch their attention.

"A great shot of a great family," Jack said.

"They're pretty wonderful, aren't they?" Miranda said wistfully. "Such beautiful girls, such handsome boys."

"Stop talking, Mama," Martha said, turning a page. "You make it so I can't think."

"Yeah, don't talk about us," Michael said. "It's embarrassing."

Jack wadded up the photo receipt and bounced it off of Michael's head. "Listen up, young 'uns. Your mother and I plan to go on talking. And embarrassing you. If you don't like it, you'd better leave, because it'll only get worse."

The archangels exchanged irritated glances and got to their feet. Martha huffed and slid off the couch. Rebekah followed, still reading. The two boys and two girls took to the stairs with their books. Only Jonah stayed, still humming.

"Worked like a charm," Jack said.

Liking the cozy setup, he didn't scoot over to the space the girls had vacated. Miranda didn't move either. Their knees knocked against each other, their shoulders touched. She sighed, and her shoulder moved up and down against his.

"Okay, 'fess up. Ever since I took the kids to the library, you've been wallowing in gloom. Are you afraid I didn't vet their choices adequately?"

"No. If you think they're good books, I'll trust your judgment."

"You trust me?"

She didn't answer right away. "Yes," she said, finally. "I do."

"Good. Then you can tell me why you're moping."

"I'm not moping."

"Let's call it worrying, then. Are you paranoid about trouble with the authorities?"

She was watching Jonah with a faint frown. "Because we homeschool? It's not paranoia. Even when we're completely legal, they keep a close eye on us just because we buck the system."

"And this has troubled you for quite some time?"

"Yes."

"Ah. Then you still haven't explained the recent increase in moping. What's that about?"

"Oh, it's nothing," she said, a little too briskly.

Jack bit back another question. He'd segue into flattery instead.

He moved on to the next photo. "Your kids all have the same chin. Even in the girls, it's sort of pugnacious. It shows up in pictures more than it does in real life."

"The Hanford chin."

He ignored that. "They have your eyes. Very pretty eyes."

She ignored that.

"You seem to know your way around a camera," he said. "I like the way you used tree branches like a window frame in this one."

"I'm always looking for frames." Her voice came alive, and this time her animation was genuine. "I like any kind of window. An actual window or something in nature. I love to watch the vignettes in the frame change as I move."

"You must like off-center shots too or you wouldn't take so many of them."

"I do. They wake up the eye in ways a centered, symmetrical shot can't." She looked up.

Squashed close together as they were, he had to twist his head down at an odd angle to see her. But it was worth it. She gave him a shy smile that very nearly demanded a kiss.

Trying to talk himself out of that idea, suddenly he couldn't remember exactly what he'd been trying to worm out of her. "I don't like too much symmetry either," he said, afraid he'd be babbling like an idiot in no time. "I like random, irregular things. Appaloosas. Crooked tree limbs. Stories that don't have neat endings, that leave doors open, that make me think about possibilities."

"You're funny. Next picture, please."

He complied, feeling like a fool but glad that he'd made her smile. "This is a good shot of Timothy."

"Yes, it is."

Timothy hadn't smiled, but he'd met the eye of the camera squarely, as he looked at people when he spoke to them. Jack was still working on that. He was in his thirties before he'd learned he made a habit of looking *at* eyes instead of looking into them. A subtle distinction, but it made a difference.

He continued flipping photos. A pine with a twisted trunk. A hawk in the sky. A shaft of sun turning a cobweb to a string-art creation of light. Then, five shots of a vivid mountain sunset, the sun lower in the sky with each click of the shutter.

The outdoor photos captured the mountains in the grip of winter. No green but the pines. Some were taken on sunny days, others on overcast days. Most of them had a morning look, somehow.

"You're a very good photographer, Miranda."

"Thank you."

The next-to-last photo was a vista of the Blue Ridge, shrouded in fog. It might have been taken from the cliffs. The final shot was a blurry image of straw-colored weeds.

He held those two side by side. The faraway mountains in one; the weeds in the other. "Do you remember taking that last shot of the mountains?"

"Yes, I do, and I remember getting dizzy."

"Then you fell."

"And that was the end of poor Jezebel."

"You're the funny one, Miranda. You're more interested in the camera's fate than in your own. That fall could have killed you, you know."

"But it didn't. So that's that."

"Thank God. But why were you out walking so early in the morning?"

She kept her head down, hiding her expression, but he could tell from her voice that she'd stopped smiling. "I was praying."

"And you were praying about—?"

"You are incredibly nosy." She squeezed his hand so swiftly that he might have imagined it. "But you have a good heart."

"Sometimes."

With her battered fingers, she picked up the last picture and studied it in silence. Not that there was much to see, as far as Jack could tell. Weeds, out of focus and blurred with movement.

"Jack?"

"Yes ma'am?"

She'd tilted her head again to look up at him. The connection was down-right scary.

"Why didn't you tell me Mason came by while I was in the hospital?" she asked.

Jack looked away. He shrugged, the movement making his shoulder bump hers. "I saw no need to tell you. Is that what's been bothering you? Something about Mason?"

She dropped the photo on the top of the stack in his hand and edged away from him, making him feel that she'd built an invisible box around herself, shutting him out.

"I see no need to tell you," she said, and that told him more than she'd probably intended.

⌒

Armed with Yvonne Walker's address, Jack drove down Piedmont Road on Friday afternoon. He'd spent most of Wednesday in Chattanooga, catching up on committee work, and he'd spent half of Thursday driving Miranda to checkups in Clayton while Yvonne stayed with the kids. Today's errand, though, was both pleasant and local.

Yvonne had a kitten.

Most of the houses on Piedmont were small and well-kept, though some of the yards bloomed with junk instead of daffodils. He swung around a curve and spotted balloons and a yard sale sign at the mailbox of a trim white house. A smaller sign read *FREE KITTENS* with the *S* crossed out.

Only one left. "A brat cat," Yvonne had said. "You'll love her."

He parked on the shoulder and climbed out. A faded red canopy, obviously reincarnated from a prior life as the property of a funeral home, sheltered a hodgepodge of household goods on a pair of rickety tables. Yvonne was nowhere in sight.

He picked his way between a galvanized bucket and a dented birdcage. He'd hated birdcages since he was thirteen, would rather make the world his aviary than trap a living creature that way, but he refrained from kicking it.

Boxes of books sat on the ground toward the rear of the canopy. He crouched on the thin grass to investigate. Most of them were cookbooks, romances, and musty textbooks, including a science text that was permanently opened to the periodic table of the elements. Nothing was worth even a quarter, but Jack stayed in his crouch and took in the view.

The lower hills, just starting to green up, stretched toward blue green mountains and a cerulean sky. In the middle distance, a valley cradled a creek that zigzagged toward lower ground.

Something about the way the water curved out of sight behind the trees reminded him of a narrow lake where he'd hidden in a clump of willows and spied on a baptism, long ago. The white-robed figures and the voices singing without instruments had made him feel shut out, like a time traveler whose modern mind was too sterile, too barren, to grasp an ancient mystery. The lake could have been the Jordan River, and the preacher could have been John the Baptist.

But this was only a yard sale in Georgia. Jack straightened, his head brushing against the overhang of the funeral-home canopy. A faded canvas tabernacle in the wilderness.

A skinny old man in overalls came around the corner of the house, barefoot. The top of his head sprouted a crest of gray hair, like a tufted titmouse. His gap-toothed grin resembled Gabriel's. The man was freckled too but with age spots.

"Glory be to God," Jack said quietly, in Hopkins heaven. *Whatever is fickle, freckled....*

Yvonne followed the man at a fast trot. "Hey there, Jack! Now, Daddy, don't go inside with muddy feet."

The old man stopped short and stared at his feet as if he'd never seen them before. "I wouldn't, I wouldn't."

"Sure, you would."

"Nope, nope," he said. "We'll have us an old-fashioned foot-washin' first."

Yvonne's daddy was remarkably spry for a man who must have been closing in on centenarian status. He hurried onto the lawn and sat in a decrepit easy chair with a price tag on its arm.

"He's got all the sense of a turnip," Yvonne said under her breath. She squinted at Jack as if he were some rare zoological specimen. "Now, is it true, what Rebekah told me the other day? You're a college professor? a PhD?"

The idea still startled him sometimes, as if he'd woken in the middle of a luckier man's life. "Yes, but I'm still clawing my way up the ladder to tenure. Serving on committees. Writing my brains out. Bowing and scraping to my superiors and so on."

"I thought you were just a plain ol' schoolteacher. You don't act like a PhD. You act like a regular guy."

"That might be because I'm a regular guy."

"Okay, I just wanted to make sure Rebekah wasn't pulling my leg."

"She wasn't. Now, where's that kitten?"

"Miranda wants her?"

He cleared his throat. "I…ah…I haven't actually asked. I want to surprise her."

"Men!" Yvonne planted her hands on her hips. "What if somebody has allergies? Or maybe Miranda hates cats. Some people do."

"True."

"You're not taking her until you've talked it over with Miranda."

Chastened, Jack hung his head. "I guess you're right."

"Oh, for heaven's sake, don't look so heartbroken. The kitten's in the dining room, snoozing on the windowsill." Yvonne pointed toward the house. "See?"

He nodded. From a distance, the kitten was only a small, vague mishmash of colors stretched out on the other side of the glass.

"She's not the prettiest thing," Yvonne added, "or the sweetest, but she's more fun than a barrel of drunk monkeys, especially when she's riled up. I've been calling her Hellion."

"That'll go over big. I could call her 'Hell' for short and see if Miranda throws anything."

"Be nice, Jack."

"Yes ma'am. Sorry."

"It's hard enough being a homeschool mom, but being a single mom with six kids? I'd be on my way to the loony bin. Or a long vacation in Tahiti, if I could afford it."

Jack's imagination swerved toward Miranda in a bikini on a tropical beach. For being the mother of six, she was remarkably trim and fit—or at least he guessed she was. Her sacklike wardrobe didn't reveal much.

"How's she doing today?" Yvonne asked.

He shrugged. Ever since he'd asked Miranda what was bothering her, she'd been hiding behind those invisible walls. Living in an invisible box that kept him at a distance.

"Physically, she's better every day," he said. "Her docs are happy with her progress."

"Help me fold shirts," Yvonne ordered, pressing a purple sweatshirt into his chest. "Is she antsy to go back to Chandler's church?"

"Not right now. Thank God." Jack tucked the shirt under his chin and began folding it. "If she asks me to chauffeur the family to his Sunday services, I'll respectfully decline." Having wrestled the shirt into some semblance of neatness, he placed it on the table behind him.

"I wish she'd try my church. We're, you know, normal." Yvonne laughed. "I guess everybody thinks they're normal though. Even the weird ones."

"True."

"Long time ago, before my husband passed away, we knew a gal who got mixed up with a strange church. We were afraid she'd wind up in a place like Waco or Jonestown." Yvonne snapped the wrinkles out of a T-shirt. "Then she went and died of cancer instead."

"Everybody has to die somehow."

"Yea, verily," her father rasped from his ratty throne. He pointed a long, bony finger at Jack. "Yea, verily, hear the word of the Lord."

"Oh, Daddy," Yvonne said. "We'd better cut back on your TV time. You're watching too many preachers." She lowered her voice. "Once a preacher, always a preacher," she told Jack. "He's been retired for twenty years, but he thinks he's still at it."

"I'm sure he's as well qualified as some."

"He used to be. Used to know the Bible backward and forward, but something can go wrong in the mind like something can go wrong in the liver."

Her phone rang in her pocket. She answered it and wandered into the garage, abandoning Jack with her father.

There was nothing wrong with the elderly gentleman's ambulatory powers; he sprang from the chair and hustled across the lawn, stopping a foot from Jack. Never comfortable with any invasion of his personal space, Jack backed up. He bumped into the table, shaking it.

Yvonne's dad came closer. Smelling of peppermint, he placed a dry, warm hand on Jack's forehead and examined him with wide blue eyes.

Jack lifted a hand then lowered it again, unwilling to deliver even the gentlest of shoves. "Back off, sport."

"Hear the word of the Lord for you," the preacher croaked.

Jack's nerves made his laugh sound froglike. "Sorry, sir, but I'm not in the camp that believes God channels personal messages through humans."

"That don't matter to Him, son."

"I'm not your son," he blurted.

"No. No, you're not. You're His. A good son. Now, hear the word of the Lord."

Goose bumps dotted Jack's arms. He wanted to scream that he'd come for a kitten, not for some prophecy birthed in senility.

The man's eyes were like crystalline windows that reflected their light into the dark corners of Jack's soul, where the Friday-night demons lived. It was impossible to run. Impossible to hide.

"Silence is brother to lies," the old man said. "The truth is sister to mercy." He lifted his other hand, cradling Jack's head between dry palms. "This time, say the words you've been given to say. Do the deeds you've been given to do. This time, hear Me and obey. Thus saith the Lord." The preacher ruffled Jack's hair and trotted back to the decrepit easy chair.

Finished with her call and having witnessed the tail end of the home-grown prophecy, Yvonne hurried out of the garage. "Sorry about that," she said. "Ignore him, hon."

Jack forced a laugh. "Don't worry about it."

Snatches of her father's message buzzed in Jack's mind like static as he headed for his car.

seventeen

From her rocker on the porch, Miranda had tracked the bedtime routine by the sounds: water running in the tub, an occasional quarrel, and Jack's voice rising over it all. Calm had descended, and she assumed the children were in bed.

Another quiet Sunday had come and gone. She'd half expected Mason to show up after church and scold her for playing hooky for so long, but she couldn't bear the thought of sitting under his teachings. Ever again.

Joining a different congregation would feel like a betrayal though. Like abandoning family for strangers.

Through the wall, she heard the rush of water in the pipes again—and Jack, singing. It was too muffled to make out the words, and she didn't know the tune.

After a while, the water and the singing stopped. He would come outside soon.

All day, he'd been sweet to her. He'd softened, somehow, or maybe she was learning to enjoy his teasing even when it leaned toward sarcasm.

Except for a chorus of frogs, the chilly night was quiet. Too quiet. She set the rocker going, and it filled the air with the familiar rhythm of wood rolling against wood. She'd always loved snuggling here with her babies after supper, with the wind cooling her face and the sunset bathing her in peace.

But it was long past sunset now. A half moon rose above the trees.

She pulled the cuddle-quilt up to her chin. In the thin strip of pewter gray sky between the bottom timber of the porch roof and the top of the trees, the stars were coming out. When she tried to focus on one, it faded. If she looked to the side of it, she saw it in her peripheral vision.

The door creaked. Jack came out, wearing a bulky jacket and carrying something in each hand. Light from the window glimmered on shiny surfaces in the half dark. He set everything down with a faint clinking. A glass, a bottle, and a saucer. It was too dark to see details.

"What's that?"

"Glenlivet. The good stuff. Would you like to try it?"

"No, thank you."

"Are you sure?" He poured a small amount, sat back, and sampled it. "I think you'd do well to avail yourself of its sedative properties."

"I don't need sedation."

"But I do." He laughed. "Come on. Try to regain your usual sunny disposition."

"Now you're being sarcastic."

"I wish I wasn't, darlin', but we all have our vices. Speaking of which, I would like to indulge in a cigar. Or would that unleash your inner harpie?"

She smiled at the banter that would have offended her not long ago. "Cigars cause cancer, you know."

"As rarely as I smoke one, I'm more at risk of being run over by a bus. Please, may I?"

"Oh, go ahead. Smoke, I mean. Don't get run over by a bus."

"Thank you." He set the glass down, dug in his pocket, and pulled out a small cigar, a box of matches, and a tool that resembled miniature garden clippers. With the air of engaging in a mystical ritual, he snipped off the end of the cigar, then pulled out a wooden match and struck it against the side of the box. He bent over the flame, cigar in his mouth, and slowly rotated it, puffing. After a few seconds, the rim of the cigar glowed bright orange in the semi-darkness and the smell of tobacco filled the air.

He dropped the match on the saucer. "Perfect. There's nothing like the simultaneous enjoyment of a fine cigar and a fine Scotch."

The air already reeked. She waved her hand in front of her nose and coughed.

"Stop faking the cough, Mrs. H. You're upwind."

"It's so strong that I don't have to be downwind. I didn't expect it to be so smelly."

"Smelly? You insult my excellent taste in cigars. Would you like to try one?"

She burst out laughing. "No! Just hurry up and finish that thing."

He chuckled and continued to smoke in placid silence, using the saucer as an ashtray and occasionally lifting his glass to his lips. His puffs were few and far between, and she sensed again that it was a ritual. The measured sips, the measured puffs; he was drawing out the process as long as he could.

He set his glass on the table. "I noticed some St. John's wort in the cupboard," he said. "Are you the one who takes it?"

"Is that any of your business?"

"No." He paused. "St. John's wort, the earth mother's Prozac. Herbs are the health-food version of the pharmaceuticals you refuse to take."

"It's not the same thing."

"No? You have your St. John's wort to lift your spirits and your chamomile tea to help you sleep. I have my coffee to wake me up and my occasional nip of Scotch to soothe my nerves. They're all mood-altering substances. Sometimes our moods need to be altered."

"You're very good at altering my moods, Jack. You make them worse."

He laughed out loud. "You think I'm a Philistine, don't you?"

"Not exactly."

"Not 'zackly?"

She couldn't see much of him in the half dark. Either he was trying to be funny, or she'd underestimated the effect of a small amount of alcohol.

"You'd probably label me as an antinomian," he added, taking up his drink again, "but I'm not."

"Oh, you and your big words. What's an antinomian?"

"You didn't learn that in Bible school?"

"If I did, I've forgotten."

"Look it up. As I tell my students, if you want to own your answers, you have to earn them."

She smiled, remembering the stern notes he'd written to himself. *Dig deeper. Define terms.* "I suppose you always verify your facts before you draw conclusions?"

"I try to anyway."

"What conclusions have you drawn about me?"

He was silent for a moment, then spoke slowly. "You're stubborn. Smart. Kind. A loving mother. A sincere Christian. A person of integrity."

"Except for that little matter about my friend, the shoplifter."

He cleared his throat. "Yes, well, perhaps you skirted around the facts. Just a bit."

"Or maybe you didn't verify the facts."

"How could I, when you didn't give them to me?"

"Okay, you're right. I skirted around the fact that my 'friend' was my mother."

The liquid in his glass made a sloshing sound. *"Mother?"*

"I've never stolen anything except once when she told me to wear a pair of jeans out of the dressing room under baggy pants. I did it, but under protest. And when she stole a prom dress—"

"Prom dress?"

"Would you please stop repeating everything I say? Yes, when I was in eleventh grade, my mom stole a prom dress for me. Exactly the one I wanted. I couldn't enjoy it though. I was afraid I'd wind up in jail."

"And did you?"

"No, but Mom did. Not that time, but several other times. That's why I went to live with my great-aunt for my senior year. She sent me to Bible college, where I met Carl, with all his rules about modest dress and godly music. After my mom's problems, his rules looked like righteousness."

"This explains a lot." Jack's voice held a note of relief.

"Are you glad to know I'm not a thief?"

"I wouldn't have held it against you, but I'm glad you trust me enough to tell me the whole story." He emptied his glass, set it down, and took her hand.

Startled, she looked down at their clasped hands; barely visible in the darkness, their shared warmth served as a physical token of friendship.

A familiar rumbling shattered the quiet night.

Headlights flashed between the trunks of the pines and snaked through the curves of the drive. Mason's truck pulled into view, its pale blue paint luminous in the light of the moon.

"That's Mason." She pulled her hand free and hid it under the quilt as if her skin now bore Jack's fingerprints.

"He needs some muffler work. That truck's loud enough to wake the dead. Does he often drop by at this hour?"

"Not at my house," she said, wondering about Nicole's cozy apartment. No chaperone there but a cat.

"I hope everything's all right."

"Everything's wrong, Jack. You're staying under my roof. You're smoking. You're drinking. I don't see how it could look much worse."

He patted his thigh. "Come sit on my lap, sweetheart. That should do it."

She startled herself with an unladylike snort of laughter. "You're terrible."

"Yes ma'am, but why are you so worried about what Mason thinks?"

Anger raced through her in a white-hot flood. She shouldn't care anymore what Mason thought. "I'm not worried," she snapped.

"Liar," Jack said cheerfully.

The truck's engine coughed and quit. The headlights died, returning the yard to darkness. Jack stood up, cracked the front door open, and switched on the porch light and the security light that illuminated the stretch of grass between the front steps and the driveway.

"Turn off the lights," she said, eyeing his empty glass and cigar.

"Why?"

"Just turn them off."

"I thought you weren't worried about what Mason thinks." Leaving the lights on, Jack shut the door. "By the way, several days after I told him about your fall, I met his wife, but she still hadn't heard. Strange, isn't it, that he hadn't told her? And she looked as if she'd been crying."

"Abigail—when did you—never mind." Miranda inhaled, trying to suck courage from the night air, and winced as her ribs rebelled.

"She said she'd be praying for you," Jack added.

Miranda had no time to answer before Mason emerged from the truck and started toward the porch.

"Good evening," he said. "Are you feeling better, Miranda?"

"Yes, thanks," she said, her voice tight.

"Thank God." Mason climbed the steps. "Hello again, Jack."

The men shook hands, and Mason turned to Miranda again. "Are you in much pain?"

"Not too much."

"Have a seat, sir." Jack propped himself up against one of the porch's columns. "Join the conversation. It's always fascinating." He was smiling. As relaxed as could be.

"Thank you, Jack." Mason sat, planting his feet firmly. Not allowing the chair to rock. "And thank you for being here to take care of one of my flock."

"It's a pleasure."

"It's a concern as well, of course."

"And why is that, padre?" Jack sounded too friendly, like a cat that purred as it stalked its prey.

"You know how people talk," Mason said, staring up at the starry sky. "I'm not accusing anybody of anything, but we're commanded to avoid even the appearance of evil. It doesn't look good, Miranda, to have a man staying under your roof."

She rose so quickly that her chair rocked like mad. So did her head. "I may have a number of things on my conscience, but certainly not *that*. Of course Jack can stay under my roof. He's family." Woozy, she limped toward the door.

Jack held it open. "I'll vouch for Miranda's character, Reverend," he said, smiling at her. "She's a good example for her daughters. And a good example for her sons of the kind of wife they'll want to find someday."

"Of course," Mason said. "But wouldn't it be better, Miranda, if one of our own women stayed with you instead?"

"No, thank you," she said, then addressed Jack but raised her voice so Mason would also hear. "You've been a godsend, Jack. I don't know what I would have done without you."

Jack's smile broadened to a wicked grin. "I don't, either. Good night, Randi."

The forbidden nickname must have singed Mason's ears, but Miranda didn't care anymore. She escaped inside. Jack shut the door after her, and she turned to face it.

"And what do you have on *your* conscience, Reverend Chandler?"

Outside, Jack laughed about something. He had no idea what was at stake, and she didn't dare tell him.

Jack studied Mason for a moment—the perfectly combed hair, the neat suit, the black dress shoes—and sniffed. The man smelled like toothpaste and a powerful deodorant soap. If he'd reeked of aftershave too, he would have strongly resembled a teenage boy out to impress a girl.

Deciding on barbed civility as his best approach, Jack made himself comfy in Miranda's chair. "May I offer you a Scotch? Or, if that's not to your liking, I'd be glad to fix you something else. Coffee? Hot cocoa?"

"No, thanks," Mason said. "Now, tell me the truth, Jack. What's going on here?"

"Child care, housework, and good conversation. We haven't engaged in any hanky-panky—yet."

"That answer reveals your heart."

"Can't you take a joke? Like she said, I'm family." *And you're not. Swine.*

"Miranda's church is her family. We're the ones who should be here, caring for her and the children."

"Mmm," Jack said. "And that's why you're here so late? After the kids' bedtime?"

"I happened to be passing by." Mason splayed his hands flat against the rocker's arms, as if bracing himself to rise.

"Why didn't you come around weeks ago? If I'd been in an accident like Miranda's, my pastor would have been at my bedside in an hour. Where were you?"

"It isn't my fault she didn't call me."

"You might want to ask yourself why she didn't. You never called her, once you knew, and you never sent your wife over. You never even told your wife."

Mason shook his head. "That's not true. I told her."

"When? After she'd finally heard it from me?"

Mason let out a slow breath. "Jack, I'm sorry we seem to be getting off on the wrong foot. I hope we'll get along better in the future."

"I suppose that's possible." *On some other planet.*

Mason got to his feet and pulled keys from his pocket. "I'd better be going. Good night, Jack."

"Good night." Jack rose too. His glass was empty but he lifted it anyway. "Cheers!"

Mason didn't reply. He walked down the steps with great dignity but wasted no time climbing into his truck and igniting the noisy engine. As the taillights wended their way between the pines, Jack sat down and picked up his cigar. It had gone out. He lit it again, then closed his eyes and tried to absorb everything.

Mason was slick. A tad too courteous and smooth…until somebody crossed him. And there was no missing the tension between him and Miranda. Her narcotics-induced "cold war" comment might have been accurate.

Jack caught himself puffing his expensive cigar as if it were a cigarette. Burning it hot, ruining the flavor. He put it down, poured a second finger of Scotch—a rarity for him—and took a deep breath of the mountain air.

He couldn't enjoy any of it. Not until he'd had a chat with Miranda.

Grinding out the cigar, he tossed back the rest of his drink, then gathered bottle and tumbler. Inside, he left the booze on the coffee table and caught Miranda as she was about to enter her bedroom.

"Why doesn't Mason treat you with some respect?" he asked. "He was way out of line to imply that we had something to be ashamed of."

She retreated a few feet into the room and turned around, breathing hard. "Yes, he was out of line, but I hope you weren't rude."

"No ruder than he deserved. But explain the cold war, darlin'."

Her eyes widened, then narrowed. "Men always complicate my life. They tell me what to think. what to do. One of them even slipped drugs into my food."

Jack fiddled with the box of matches in his pocket and assessed her again. Pale skin—except for the flush of anger in her cheeks. Dark circles under her eyes. A tendency to sway like a reed in the wind. If he still had the drugs, he'd be tempted to slip her another dose.

"You know that was for your own good," he said. "If you pass out in the middle of a phonics lesson tomorrow, I'll call your doctor and tattle on you for entertaining visitors until all hours."

She straightened her spine and lifted her chin as if a puppet master had jerked her into perfect posture. "I didn't invite either of those visitors to my porch."

"No? I seem to remember an early morning phone call that invited me to join your household. Actually, 'commanded' would be more accurate."

"Whatever you want to call it, I'm very grateful. Good night." She closed the door.

"Come back here," he said to the smoothly planed planks. "I still want to hear about your cold war. If you won't explain, maybe Mason will."

The door opened a crack, and he found himself regarding one crystal blue eye.

"Remember when I asked you not to make waves?" she asked.

He leaned forward, bringing his face a few inches from the crack. "Yes. Is Mason the boat you don't care to rock?"

The door opened an inch wider, revealing a narrow strip of her face. "He's the boat I don't *dare* rock."

"Too late. Between the two of us, we nearly capsized him."

Her lips parted with a sharp intake of breath, but she said nothing.

Jack bent nearer. If he could talk her into opening the door a few more inches—

She shut the door, nearly catching his nose.

He stepped back, abandoning the imagined kiss. "Miranda? Why did Morgan put you in such a foul mood?"

There was no answer except her footsteps limping across the floor in an uneven rhythm. As their pattern faded into silence, an old song popped into his head.

Waltzing Matilda, waltzing Matilda, you'll come a-waltzing, Matilda, with me…. The lyrics had always struck him as a passive-aggressive assumption that this Matilda, whoever she was, would let somebody drag her into a waltz. It should have been posed as a question instead.

He walked slowly toward the living room. "Waltzing Miranda, waltzing Miranda," he sang under his breath.

Mason was waltzing Miranda along, against her wishes, but she still didn't trust Jack enough to tell him what was going on.

eighteen

Jack had bought a tiny jar of bubble solution for each of the children. Martha, Gabriel, and Michael laughed and screamed, chasing bubbles across the grass. Rebekah stood still, her cape flapping in the wind that carried hers away.

Jonah, with a minimum of instruction from Jack—don't drink it, don't get it in your eyes, and don't dump it—had taken to it right away. Still, Timothy hovered near, supervising and trying to act as if he were too old to join in the fun.

"Bubble juice is to kids as catnip is to kittens," Jack said, stretching out his legs.

Miranda wished he hadn't chosen to sit in the Adirondack chairs. After nine or ten days, it wasn't likely he would find a bloodied scrap of a business card in the grass, but if he did, she'd be hard pressed to explain.

"Thank you," she said. "You're always picking up something for us. Books, bubbles, my photos…"

"Speaking of photos, may I ask why you named the camera Jezebel?"

She shook her head, remembering Robert Perini's quiet suggestion. If she was forbidden to use the Jezebel camera to earn money, it was only fair to make it up to her by helping out with the church's benevolence fund. As much as she'd appreciated the gesture at the time, the small checks had only made her feel more indebted to Mason.

"I bought the camera from a retired photojournalist," she said. "A woman who traveled all over the world. Even when I was only taking pictures in my own back yard, I tried to imagine all the sights the camera had seen. It helped me see everything with new eyes."

"But you haven't explained where the name came from."

"It was my little joke about working women." She waited, expecting another question.

"Oh, no," Martha wailed. "I spilled half of it."

"You still have half," Jack called. "Enjoy it."

She whirled around, flouncing her skirt and cape, and went back to blowing bubbles.

"I knew that would happen," Miranda said.

"So did I. I bought a couple of jumbo refills, but I haven't let the kids see them."

"For not having children, you seem to understand them pretty well."

"I spent five years as an uncle. Ava has a niece and two—"

Martha screamed. "Oh, no! I spilled the rest! It's all gone, every *drop*!" She clapped her hands over her mouth, muffling heartbroken sobs.

"I predict a theatrical career for that one," Jack said. "But look. Her devoted servant is coming to her rescue."

Timothy was already by Martha's side, offering his jar and wand. She grinned through her tears. He gave her braid a gentle tug, then went back to supervising Jonah.

"He does love his siblings," Jack said. "He watches after them like they're the lambs and he's the sheepdog."

"Yes, he does. You and Timothy have a lot in common."

"No, he's a lot more responsible than I was at that age." Jack shook his head. "He's a good kid. Mad at the world though. Do you know why?"

"No."

"Carl died only two years ago, and God only knows how that still affects Timothy. You might need to get him into counseling."

Anything but counseling. She shivered.

"My dad put me in counseling when my mom died," Jack added. "It helped."

She didn't answer. She tugged her cape more securely over her legs.

"Cold? Would you like a quilt? A cup of hay water?"

"No, thank you. I'm fine."

"Except something's bothering you."

"Just a few things. A miserable headache, dizziness, ribs that hurt every time I move—every time I *breathe*—not to mention bruises and scrapes and scratches. And I am so tired of wearing this sling."

Jack smiled. "Sorry I asked."

The children had scattered all over the yard. Martha quickly blew and dribbled and spilled her way to the bottom of Timothy's jar of bubbles. She dropped it on the grass and wiped her soapy hands on her skirt.

"Push me in the swing, Timothy? Please?"

"Sure." He followed her to the old wooden swing that hung from the tallest oak. Once she was situated, he gave her a solid, steady push. Her cape billowed behind her as he pushed her into a higher and higher arc.

It was like going back to childhood, or to a dream of childhood as it should have been. The wind sang in the trees, joined by the friendly creaking of the swing's ropes. If Miranda focused only on the moment, it was a happy moment.

But Mason kept encroaching on her thoughts. The way he'd threatened another session with the elders. The way he'd asked who had the most to lose. Something plagued his conscience. If she could find proof of it, whatever it was, she'd have ammunition to use against him. Even if it wasn't equal firepower.

That was mutual blackmail though, ugly and ungodly. On the other hand, it wasn't right to let a church blindly follow a man who wasn't trustworthy.

Jack was saying something about child-rearing practices, but she hadn't been listening.

"Excuse me?" she said.

"I was just saying they're kind to each other, usually, and they have good manners. They're excited about bubbles and bikes and baking a perfect loaf of bread. They aren't numbing their brains on video games or ruining their spelling by texting their friends. I can honestly say I'm proud to be their uncle."

"Thank you, Jack. And I'm very thankful that they have you."

Across the lawn, Michael and Gabriel argued cheerfully about something. Rebekah walked backward across the grass, watching her bubbles float away. Jonah still sat in the chair, blowing a steady stream. Her last-born child, he looked very much like her firstborn.

As Timothy pushed Martha, she started singing, her voice jerking loud and soft with the swing's movement. It was too far away to make out the words.

Timothy gave her a savage push that shoved the swing sideways. "It's not funny."

"Is too!" Martha went on singing while the swing rocked out of its usual orbit.

"So much for kindness and good manners," Jack said.

Timothy yanked one of the ropes, then let go. Thrown off kilter, the swing twisted in a crazy spiral. Martha screamed as if she were in mortal danger although she was perfectly all right.

Her brother backed away from her flailing shoes. "Shut up, Martha!"

"Stop being mean to your sister," Miranda said, but the wind swallowed her voice.

"Be a gentleman." Jack's voice carried clearly over the wind. "Gentlemen don't treat ladies that way, and they don't say 'Shut up.'"

Timothy glared at him. "You're always telling us to hush up. What's the difference?"

Jack shrugged. "Good point."

Miranda made a megaphone of her hands. "No more roughhousing, Timothy, and no more smart remarks. Do you hear me?"

He nodded. Folding his arms across his chest, he watched Martha's back while the swing straightened its course.

When the swing had slowed, she bailed out, her cape ballooning behind her and her dress flapping. She landed with a thud, windmilled her arms to catch her balance, then faced Timothy and planted her hands on her hips. "I'm nice to you even when you're ugly," she screamed. "Uncle Jack says we have to be nice to you, 'cause you're different."

Timothy shot a furious look at Jack. "Yeah, I'm different. Glad you noticed, *Jack*." He stalked inside the house, the door slamming behind him.

Miranda turned on Jack. "What were you thinking? That was a terrible thing to tell his sister!"

"Hold on, now. One night, around the fire, the other kids started calling him a grouch. It bothered me, so I asked them to be kind. Now Martha has given a slightly inaccurate quotation, taken a wee bit out of context, and we've got the wheels comin' off this chariot."

"We certainly do, thanks to you."

Jack spread his hands wide. "Timothy has been hostile toward me since I showed up. Why would I deliberately say anything to make it worse?"

Miranda hesitated, weighing the likelihood that he'd been misquoted. "You wouldn't, but for a man who earns his living with words, shouldn't you choose your words more carefully so you can't be misquoted?"

He opened his mouth then shut it again. Eyes on the ground, he nodded. "You're right. I'm sorry."

"I'm sorry too." Miranda watched Martha chase Gabriel's bubbles, her spat with Timothy already forgotten. "I'm sorry Timothy and Martha ruined a nice afternoon by scrapping with each other. That wasn't your fault."

"I guess it's natural for siblings to clash." Jack let out a short laugh. "The one time I spoke with Carl, he picked a fight with me."

"I wish he hadn't."

"Well, it's too late for me to get along with Carl, but I'd like to get along with Timothy, at least."

The sadness in Jack's voice made the decision for her.

The younger children were upstairs, asleep or reading. Jack, grumbling about some kind of deadline, sat in the living room, his fingers flying over his laptop's keyboard. And Timothy stood in the doorway of Miranda's room, his hands curled into fists and his chin tilted with the belligerence she knew so well. No doubt he expected a rebuke and a loss of privileges, at the very least.

He was nearly a teenager. Any day now, he'd want to start shaving.

Seated in the bedside chair, Miranda attempted a smile. Timothy didn't return it.

"Come in and close the door, please."

He obeyed and resumed his stubborn stance. So much like his father, but without Carl's unreasonable harshness.

She recalled Carl's heavy hand on her back, shoving her into Mason's office while the little ones clung to her legs and cried. If only she'd disobeyed.

If only, if only.

"You're the oldest," she said. "I need to start treating you differently."

His face tightened but he didn't reply.

"Starting tonight, you may stay up until ten."

His eyes narrowed as if he expected a trap. "But what's my punishment?"

"None, this time. You bear more responsibilities than the younger children, and you're old enough to enjoy more privileges too."

Timothy scuffed a toe across the rag rug. "I thought you were going to punish me."

"I should. You were mean to your little sister. You were rude to your uncle and to me."

He hung his head. "Martha drives me crazy. She's always bugging me. Always saying these weird things…"

"She's four. Show her some grace. I know you love her, so start acting like you do."

"Yes ma'am. I'm sorry."

"Now, about your attitude toward your uncle."

"I know, I know." Timothy's voice cracked. "He's Father's brother."

"Half brother. I'm going to explain the situation. It's not something to share with your brothers and sisters though. Do you understand?"

Timothy raised his head. "Yes ma'am."

She moved to the bed and patted the quilt, signaling him to sit beside her, but he ignored the cue. "All right. Your grandfather left his first wife, your father's mother, for another woman. Jack's mother. Your grandmother spent the rest of her life feeding her hurt and hatred to your father, and I believe you picked it up from him. But is that fair? Is Jack responsible for his parents' wrongdoing?"

"No ma'am."

"When you were three, he stopped by to meet your father. They'd never met, which was ridiculous because they lived in neighboring counties. But your father wouldn't speak with him."

Timothy's forehead wrinkled. "Not at all?"

"Just long enough to ask him to leave. Jack didn't give up though. He wrote letters. Your father read the first one and told me to write back, to say that if any more came, he would throw them in the trash. I gave that message to Jack in a note, but I tried to be polite about it. His letters kept coming. When each one came, I read it and hid it, in case your father changed his mind some-day. Jack wrote for years, and your father never knew."

Timothy's expression turned smug. "I knew though. Remember when I said I was old enough to walk down to the road and get the mail? And you said I wasn't?"

She nodded, remembering a small, quiet boy who never asked for much but didn't give up once he'd set his heart on something. "You were eight."

"You finally gave in, but you told me not to stand there and look through it. Just to grab it and take it to you. But I always looked, and I noticed you acted funny whenever there was a letter from this guy named Jack. Like you were hiding a big secret."

"It was an innocent secret. I saw Jack as a brother. I hoped your father would relent and want to know him after all. But even after I stopped hoping for that, I kept reading the letters. They brightened my life. Can you under-stand that?"

After a long, doubtful pause, Timothy nodded. "I guess."

"He wrote for seven years, until I let him know your father had died. Then there was one more note. A sympathy card. Jack offered to help, but I never took him up on that offer—until the poor man suddenly found himself in charge of six children. He dropped everything to come when you called. Don't throw his kindness back in his face."

"Why didn't you pick somebody from church?"

She ran a finger across a seam of the quilt. "We might not always be part of this church, but Jack will always be part of the family. He's your father's brother. How would you like it if somebody treated Michael the way you've been treating Jack?"

Timothy looked toward the most recent family portrait, the one that had captured Michael's irrepressible grin. "I wouldn't like it."

"All right, then. Please work on your attitude."

He met her eyes. "I'll try."

"Thank you. I trust you to make an honest effort. I think you and Jack have a lot in common, actually, and that may be why you clash."

Timothy indulged in the hint of an eye roll but didn't argue.

She pointed toward her closet. "In the back, on the highest shelf, you'll find a box that's labeled 'sewing scraps.' If you'll get it down, you can look through Jack's letters with me."

Timothy found the box and brought it to the bed. She pushed the fabrics aside—scraps from a dozen different projects—and revealed neat rows of envelopes, carefully slit at the top.

"I kept them in chronological order, in case your father ever wanted to start at the beginning and read them all."

"I think he would have been mad that you opened his mail."

"Maybe, but it was my mail too." She chose an envelope at random. "See? They were all addressed to Mr. and Mrs. Carl Hanford."

She checked the postmark. It was dated three days before Carl's last Christmas, when he'd finally loosened up enough to allow wrapping paper that depicted Santa Claus. Poor Carl. Maybe he'd had the scent of freedom in his nostrils, but he'd died before he could pursue it.

Timothy started with the first letter.

Jack might not have approved. He might have wondered what had become of the letters, might have assumed or even hoped they'd gone straight to the landfill, as Carl had threatened.

She glanced at the closed door and pictured Jack sitting in the living room, writing on his laptop. Unaware that someone still cared about the words he'd penned years before.

Each letter had been a shaft of sunlight shining through a crack in the walls Carl had built around his family. Carl had never relented, but Jack had kept hammering away at those walls.

Timothy's new bedtime came and went as he and Miranda browsed through the letters. Jack must have decided to pretend that Carl's hostility had never existed, because most of the messages were upbeat and friendly. Occasionally, though, there were a few lines that hinted of loss and sadness.

Finally, Timothy read the last one, the sympathy card, and looked up. "This one's sort of sad," he said slowly, as if he were weighing every word. "It says, 'I wish I'd had a chance to know my big brother.'"

Miranda nodded, unable to speak.

After a long silence, Timothy stuffed the card back into its envelope and dropped it on the bed. "Jack's still a bossy bully." He left the room before she could reply.

She ran her fingertips across Jack's return address and then across Carl's name, scrawled in that messy penmanship. "I wish you'd known your brother, Jack," she whispered. "You might have changed him."

If Jack had come in time, he might have changed everything.

nineteen

Miranda sat on her bed, leaning against the wall with a pillow behind her back and a sick lump of dread in her stomach. Her unexpected visitor might bring up a variety of unpleasant topics. The move. Those suspicions about Mason. Miranda's own secrets—except Abigail didn't know those, did she?

Abigail's footsteps signaled her return from the kitchen with the tea tray. She set it carefully in the place she'd cleared on the bureau.

Hardly aware she was doing it, Miranda framed a mental shot of Abigail, her face in three-quarters profile and her hands moving busily over the tea things. A portrait of a woman who'd spent her life serving others. Even her austere dress and old-fashioned crown of braids spoke of practicality.

"I don't remember," Abigail said. "Do you take anything in your tea?"

"No, thank you."

Abigail poured Miranda's tea into one of the bone china cups from Auntie Lou. "There you are."

"Thank you." Grateful to be free of the sling, finally, Miranda took the cup and saucer in both hands and studied Abigail. It was a rare woman who looked anything but drab when she went gray. Mason was several years younger than his wife, and the age difference had become more apparent recently.

After pouring her own tea, Abigail closed the bedroom door and sat in the chair beside the bed. "I'm sorry I didn't give you any warning."

"Don't be sorry. It's good timing."

Jack had left for Chattanooga with Michael and Gabriel. Jonah was napping, Timothy and Martha were reading in the living room, and Rebekah was upstairs, practicing on her recorder. No one was within earshot. Still, Miranda was glad Abigail had shut the door.

"I wish I'd known about your fall sooner," Abigail said. "I thought you stayed away from church so long because the children were sick. I should have checked on you."

"How did you find out?"

"About your fall? Your brother-in-law stopped by a few weeks ago and told me—and then Mason told me. He hasn't mentioned it to anyone else, as far as I know." Abigail looked over the rim of her teacup. "He's afraid the ladies will bring meals, and you'll infect them with your opinions. I put a bug in Wendy Perini's ear though. Don't be surprised if she shows up."

"Please, Abigail, don't do anything that will get anyone in trouble. Has Mason decided I've gone off the rails again?"

"Not exactly. He's just afraid you'll speak up against the move, and he'll have a mutiny on his hands. You don't intend to move, do you?"

"No."

"I can always rely on you to be honest. That's why I've come to you, our black sheep." Abigail started to lift her cup to her lips, then lowered it to the saucer instead and stared out the window.

Trying to grasp Abigail's ominous words, Miranda fidgeted against the headboard and nearly spilled her tea.

A blue jay flew past the window, squalling, and the noise jolted Abigail out of her reverie. "I'm afraid I have some bad news about my marriage."

It was true, then. Wanting to cry, Miranda ducked her head in an awkward nod. "I'm very sorry."

Abigail gave her a puzzled look. "You act as if it isn't a surprise."

"I've seen a few clues."

"Do you know who the other woman is?" Abigail's voice was flat and lifeless.

"I have a hunch."

"Nicole?"

Miranda nodded again, her throat sore from holding back the crying jag that ached to be released. She imagined Nicole in the apartment she shared with a fluffy black cat. The red geraniums in the window box. The bright white Priscilla curtains. Nicole at the window, her dark eyes searching the sidewalk as she waited, not for the husband she'd thought God would send her someday, but for an older man. Another woman's husband.

"Does Mason know…that you know?"

"Yes," Abigail said. "He claims it was Nicole's fault. She looked for ways to be alone with him, to entice him. I don't believe it for a minute. This isn't the first time he's stumbled. In Nebraska, years ago, there was a similar situation. The elders there confronted him, but he would rather change towns than change his heart. And he expected me to forgive him and tag along."

"I'm so sorry. I don't know what to say."

"Neither do I," Abigail said with a cracked little laugh.

She rose and returned to the tea tray, where she stirred a spoonful of sugar into her tea, the spoon clinking against the china. She took a second spoonful of sugar, and that was as startling as her new frankness. Abigail's kitchen hadn't held sugar in years, unless she, like Miranda, had a secret stash of it.

"Does anyone else know?" Miranda asked. "The elders?"

"I certainly haven't told them. And it's over now. Nicole has left the church.

She's going to her parents' church again, and her father told Mason to leave town if he wants to keep it quiet."

Miranda clattered her cup down on the saucer. "What? That's why he's uprooting the whole church? And the church will go on thinking he heard from God, when he only heard from Nicole's daddy?"

"That's an interesting way to put it."

"Well, is it true? Is he moving so he can hide his sin?"

"That's part of it." Finished stirring her tea, Abigail sat down again. "It would be awkward to run into Nicole, of course, but I think she'll keep quiet for the sake of her own reputation. And I'm not going to talk about it. But the affair isn't the only reason for the move."

"What's the rest of it, then?"

"He's tired of the home-church setup." Abigail balanced her teacup on her knee. "He wants the legitimacy of having our own building. A larger, more conventional church. People ignore a church that has only a few cars in the parking lot, but crowds collect crowds. If he can move the whole flock, he'll be well on his way."

"So he's moving the whole church? Even me, when he knows I don't want to go? That's the part I don't understand."

"He's made a commitment to buy a building there. You own a big piece of prime acreage, free and clear. If you pay a tithe on the sale price of your property, there's his down payment."

"I don't believe it." Miranda rubbed her face with her hands, as if that could erase the conversation from her ears.

"Thirty years ago, I never would have believed any of it." A sad smile played on Abigail's thin lips. "When we were first married, Mason was a gem. Some men are, you know. But I wasn't able to give him children. He was sure it wasn't his fault. He was righteous. He prayed, he studied the Word, he tithed, he did everything right. Therefore my barrenness must have been my fault."

"You don't believe that, do you?"

"No, but he does. Or he used to. I'm not sure what he believes now, because he can't claim to be the blameless one anymore. Now, of course, I'm long past the childbearing years." Abigail lifted her hand to pat her gray braids. "I'm old enough to be a grandma. Oh, what does it matter? I've forgiven him—and I have to forgive him again every time I think about it—but I have scriptural grounds for divorce."

"You're leaving him?"

"I've started packing, right under his nose. He thinks I'm preparing for the move." Abigail's mouth tightened. "In all the years of our marriage, he has hit me twice. I don't intend to provoke him into a third time. One of these days, I'll load my boxes into my car and drive. By the time the church starts asking questions, I'll be gone."

"Will he still move to McCabe without you? Will the church follow him?"

"Probably not, once they know their pastor preys on innocent young ladies." Abigail shifted the cup and saucer to her other knee, sloshing tea on her skirt. She didn't seem to notice.

"But they might not find out in time. They're putting their homes on the market. They'll find buyers. They'll quit their jobs. That's not fair to them."

"I'm sorry, but I only want to get out of town before he knows what I'm doing." Abigail's voice shook. "Don't tell anyone."

"If you don't want me to talk about it, why did you tell me?"

"To encourage you to put your foot down. You belong here, Miranda. This is your home." Abigail wiped tears from her eyes. "But Nebraska is mine. Once I've left town, you can tell the church what I've told you."

"But if I tell—" Miranda stopped short.

Once the church knew the truth, she would have nothing to use against Mason. Worse, with his marriage and his ministry falling apart, he would have nothing left to lose. He would be dangerous.

Not for the first time, she wondered what had become of the notes he'd taken during that miserable counseling session nine years before.

The afternoon trip to 'Nooga with the archangels wasn't strictly necessary except to escape the incessant piping of Rebekah's recorder, but that was reason enough for Jack.

The boys kept busy on the drive by counting the mile markers and pointing out the sights, including a billboard for the aquarium. The realization that they were counting things made Jack chuckle; the compulsion may have been hereditary. But the fact that they'd never been to an aquarium troubled him. Too expensive for Miranda? Or too far removed from her family's cloistered world?

The boys hollered when they spotted the state line. The closer they came to Chattanooga proper, the more awestruck they became. They'd never seen so much traffic. They were impressed by the bridge over the Tennessee River too. In a few minutes they were on Jack's street. From three houses away, he saw Ava's paperwhites and yellow daffodils spilling down the bank.

Deprived of babies, Ava had plunged into landscaping sprees and decorating projects. She'd decorated the soul out of the place, doing her level best to turn a man's simple house into a woman's fussy showplace. Bit by bit, he was stripping it of its froufrou elements and returning it to its former simplicity. Ava's boot prints on his heart weren't so easily erased.

He ushered the boys inside, then took in the view from the living room to the kitchen. Evidence of his book addiction lay everywhere, but the boys were more likely to notice a few other items. The latest *National Geographic* on the end table, for instance. He couldn't remember whether or not it included photos of scantily clad natives.

Two empty Guinness bottles stood on the kitchen counter, and a nude hung on the wall in the hallway. One of the few things that hadn't been sold when his mom died, the print was tasteful enough, but there was no telling how the boys might describe it to Miranda. She was probably in the same camp as the parents of one of his students, who'd censored her textbooks by placing black tape over certain photos—like Michelangelo's *David*.

Jack breezed past the boys and opened the door to the backyard. "Y'all go outside, all right? See if you can find the varmints digging up my lawn. Moles, probably."

They raced outside, nearly bowling over the wrought-iron chairs on the patio.

On the kitchen table, Jack found the dry crust of a sandwich he'd abandoned on one of his earlier trips. He tossed the crust onto the patio for the birds and dropped the Guinness bottles in the recycling bin. After he'd rounded up some of his belongings and loaded them into the car, he returned to the kitchen and looked out the window to check on the boys.

A brisk breeze blew a scrap of paper across the bricks of the patio. Half a dozen birds flew in, so lightweight that they could have been paper scraps too, and started fighting over the bread.

Jack's phone rang. The Gilberts' number. Jack had forgotten he'd left a message.

"Hello, this is Jack Hanford."

"Terry Gilbert, returning your call. I understand you're Miranda's brother-in-law?" The man didn't sound especially friendly.

Jack plunged into an explanation of who he was and why he'd made Miranda his business. "Michael tells me your family left Mason Chandler's church," he added. "Could you give me your honest opinion of it?"

Gilbert's dry laugh spoke volumes. "Do you have a few hours?"

"I have as much time as you want to give me."

"I can give you the short version."

"Please, go ahead." Jack sat at the table. Waiting for his caller to speak, he ran his thumb along a crack in the table's surface. It held multicolored glitter and a faint trace of orange Play-Doh, remnants of the days when his other niece and nephews had come to visit him and Ava.

"Mason's a control freak," Gilbert said. "When my wife and I disagreed with him about a few things, he said we had bitter, rebellious spirits. We were harboring secret sin. I think our worst sin was that we'd checked our minds at the door when we joined the church."

"You'd say it's a church, then. Not a cult."

"That's a hard call. You're treated like a child, so you act like one. You can't speak up. You're not worthy to think your own thoughts. You just shuffle along with the herd because if you don't, you might get booted out. Or shunned."

"I think that's what happened to Miranda, a couple of years ago. Rebekah said she was made a pariah."

"I don't know about that. It must have happened after we left. Once you're out, you don't get any news."

"What made you leave? What was the last straw?"

Gilbert didn't hesitate. "Terrible child-training advice from a man who's never had children. He thinks parenting is all about control. My wife and I are still homeschooling, but we've gone back to what it's supposed to be about. Individuality. Independence. Learning."

"Excellent. Miranda needs friends like you. And her kids miss your kids. If I can talk her into calling, would your wife be willing to chat?"

"I'm afraid Miranda will try to drag us back into the church."

"She wouldn't."

"Don't be so sure about that. Mason has a way of getting his claws into people."

"Have you found another church?"

"No way. Not even interested. I can't sit there and listen to somebody telling me what to believe. They're all wolves in sheep's clothing."

"Come, now. Most members of the clergy are trustworthy."

"Believe that if you want, but I'm done. Good luck."

Before Jack could respond, the connection went dead.

Pocketing his phone, he blew out a sharp breath. All those questions he'd asked Miranda weeks ago might have stirred up her doubts, leaving her vulnerable to the cynicism that had infected Terry Gilbert's wounds.

Sick at heart, Jack rose and went to the window. On the patio, the birds scrapped over the bread crust. It was almost as big as they were. One bully kept dragging it away, hogging it.

Dappled things. Finches' wings. Fragments of the Hopkins poem beat in Jack's head. The birds were sparrows, though, not finches.

Four sparrows out in the open. Two under a table. One on the back of a chair. One sparrow flew away. Two new ones soared in. No, three. He couldn't keep up. God could count grains of sand and stars in the sky, every leaf on every tree that had ever grown on every continent, but Jack couldn't keep track of a handful of sparrows.

In his imagination, he heard Thomas Dean. *Keep countin' noses,* the deputy had drawled.

Jack counted two squirrels. One crow.

The boys—where were they?

He hit the back door at a run, scattering sparrows to the sky. No sign of the archangels. No voices. Just the brown, dead lawn.

He tore around the side of the house, shouting the boys' names. How would he explain to Miranda that he'd lost two of her children?

"Uncle Jack, Uncle Jack! We found a snake hole!"

Michael's voice. The boys raced around the corner and across the grass, their faces flushed.

Jack sagged against the nearest tree trunk and offered a heartfelt prayer of thanks. "Great. Always happy to hear about snake holes."

The archangels' polo shirts had come untucked. Dirt disguised their freckles. Their jeans bore grass stains and mud. Gabriel's shoes dragged untied laces. Both boys looked entirely disreputable, like small, blond Huckleberry Finns in search of trouble. Jack had never been quite so fond of them.

"Let's go to your school now," Gabriel said. "I wanna see it."

"Sure," Jack said. But he wouldn't let them out of his sight.

He was beginning to understand why a parent might want to control a child. When you kept a child under your thumb, you weren't as likely to lose him. It probably worked for adults too.

twenty

Miranda checked the clock on the living room wall. She might have a few hours before Jack and the archangels returned from Chattanooga.

Archangels? She'd picked up Jack's nickname for the boys.

In the backyard, Rebekah pinned the freshly laundered cuddle-quilt to the clothesline, where it would sweeten in the sunshine. Another load tumbled in the dryer. Other chores had gone by the wayside, but at least Rebekah had started the laundry.

Had *started* it. Wouldn't necessarily finish it, judging by the way she kept losing herself in her latest library book.

As Miranda walked into the kitchen, Rebekah raced inside, picked up her paperback from the coffee table, and plopped down on the couch. She'd plowed through *Jane Eyre,* then *Rebecca of Sunnybrook Farm.* Now she'd started *A Little Princess: The Story of Sara Crewe.* Funny how she'd started with the hardest and had worked her way down to a slender, easier-reading book.

"Mama," Martha called down the stairs. "Can I play bride?"

That would be a big, messy production, but Miranda was inclined to be indulgent. Martha had been terribly disappointed when Jack denied her plea to join him for the long ride in his pretty car. And it would keep her busy, giving her mother more time to work her scheme.

"Yes, you may play bride," Miranda said.

"Where's my veil?"

"Rebekah, would you mind getting it down for her? I'm afraid to try it. The ribs…the shoulder…"

Rebekah furrowed her brow and turned a page. "If she's a pretend bride, why can't she have a pretend veil?"

"When you were four, you wanted real lace too. It's in my closet, on the top shelf by the door. Thank you, sweetheart."

Rebekah tucked the book under her arm and went off to find the dingy curtain panel that she had once used for dress up. She emerged from the bedroom with the lace draped over her arm and took both it and the book upstairs.

After five minutes, she still hadn't come back. No doubt she wanted to disappear for a while so her mother couldn't make any more demands on her.

Timothy was already upstairs; Jonah was the only one within earshot. Still, Miranda savored the freedom of using her "new" cordless phone, a replacement for the plug-in phone Gabriel destroyed when he was four. Carl had never seen the need to slip away from the family for a private phone call, but he'd never planned to blow up his pastor's life either.

While Martha's unique version of the wedding march floated down the stairs, Miranda took a few minutes to collect her thoughts. She'd been fasting and praying, but now it was time to act.

She sat at the table with the phone and the church contact list. She intended to reach every woman on the list. Except Abigail and the elders' wives. They were too risky.

The married women might or might not convey their doubts to their husbands; that was out of Miranda's hands. And she could do nothing about the single men because she couldn't think of a good excuse for calling them. She had the perfect pretext for chatting with the women though.

Miranda decided to start with one of the chattiest, friendliest people. Lenore Schwartz.

Lenore answered on the first ring. "Where have you been, girl? It's been weeks since you've been in church. I don't care how many children you have, the chickenpox can't last *that* long."

"About the time the last one was past being contagious, I took a tumble and—and got a little banged up."

"Oh, honey! Are you all right?"

"I'm doing fine, thanks. Say, do you ever share your recipe for three-bean soup? Mine never comes out like yours does."

"Oh, sure. I know it by heart. It was Ronnie's favorite, God rest his soul. You have a pen and paper handy?"

"Yes," Miranda said, though she planned to use the pen only to check off names.

"You take three-quarters of a cup of dry pinto beans…"

"Three-quarters pinto," Miranda echoed as if she were writing it down.

"Three-quarters of a cup of garbanzos. Oh, but you might need to triple it for your family."

"Right. Will do."

It was a terrible time to talk about food, while her stomach begged her to end the fast, but it had to be done. Miranda pretended her way through the entire recipe, thanked Lenore, and arrived at the true purpose of the conversation.

"Have you put your house on the market yet?"

"Not quite," Lenore said. "I had the repairs done, and I had an agent walk through and set a price, but the listing papers are still sitting here on my desk. I just can't make myself sign."

"Why not?" Miranda's heart beat faster.

"I don't know if Mason's word from the Lord is for all of us. You know? It doesn't seem right, somehow, a word that covers everybody. Why, look at the LeBlancs. If the Lord led them to buy their house just six months ago, did He change His mind already?"

"Good question."

"Now, don't you go telling anybody I'm having doubts, Miranda. I'm just prayin' it through."

"Me too. I know McCabe is supposed to be a beautiful little town, but how can it be very different from Slades Creek?"

"Amen," Lenore said. "Mason keeps saying it's like heaven there, but honey, there's no corner of God's green earth that's safe from sin."

And Miranda had thought the woman didn't have a lick of sense.

Upstairs, a scream rent the air. "I am *not*!"

"I need to go, Lenore. The girls are fighting."

"That's what girls do." Lenore sighed. "Oh, I'll miss my girls and my grandkids if I move."

If. The tiny word encouraged Miranda. Lenore remained undecided.

Before they'd finished their good-byes, Martha stomped down the stairs, spitting mad. She yanked the lace off her head, making her hair stand up with static electricity.

"Rebekah's mean. She says I'm making too much noise."

"Maybe you are."

"I'm not! I'm just singing."

"Stay down here, then, because I love to hear you sing. Let me fix your veil."

Martha submitted to the rearranging of the lace. Miranda stepped back to admire the effect.

"There. You're a beautiful bride."

"Thank you," Martha said, her woes forgotten. "I need a bouquet."

"Here." Miranda pulled the dismal remnants of Yvonne's flowers out of the vase on the counter. The alstros had gone in the trash long ago, but the mums were hanging on. Miranda shook the water from the stems and placed the wilted blooms in the bride's hands.

"Ooh, pretty. And I need some other stuff."

"Okay, sweetheart. Have fun."

As Martha rummaged in a cupboard, Miranda checked the first name off her list. Lenore had provided the perfect question for the next call: Had God changed His mind about the beautiful house He'd led the LeBlancs to buy only six months ago?

Miranda tried to remember what Lisa LeBlanc brought to potlucks. Baked spaghetti, usually. Miranda's children hated it, but that wouldn't keep her from asking for the recipe.

Vaguely aware that Martha was creating more havoc than necessary, Miranda dialed Lisa's number. If Martha wanted to destroy the house, fine. A tidy house wasn't important in the grand scheme of things.

"Lisa? Hi, it's Miranda. Do you have time to give me your recipe for baked spaghetti?"

"Sure, but…oh, Miranda! I've missed you. And you're the only one I can talk to."

Miranda's heart sank. More infidelity? Another broken marriage?

"What do you need to talk about?" she asked gently, prepared to scrap her plan, at least in Lisa's case.

"I can't move. I just can't." Lisa started to cry.

Miranda had never been so happy to find a friend in such misery.

With their attitudes much the worse for wear, Michael and Gabriel raced upstairs before Jack could close the front door behind him. For all his panic when he thought he'd lost them, he was glad to see the last of them for a while. The ride home, nearly two hours long, had transformed them.

"Monsters," Jack said, scowling up the stairs after them. "Devils."

Two steps into the living room, he noticed a sprinkling of small, white grains of…rice?

Rice. Everywhere. Spilled across the couch cushions. Sprinkled on the coffee table. Lying in drifts on the floor. It was a wonder the boys hadn't slipped on it when they ran in.

Bits of some bright material mixed with the rice. He leaned over to examine them.

Wilted flower petals, pink and yellow. Jack looked up. The bouquet from Yvonne was gone.

Martha sat peacefully at the table, cutting her endless hearts. A piece of white, lacy fabric was draped over her head. She was so sweet, in her quirky way. After the hours he'd spent in the company of the archdevils, she was the picture of innocence.

"Hey, Miss Martha."

She smiled at him, her eyes dreamy, but didn't speak.

"Rebekah," he called. "Where are you? Where's your mother?"

"She's in her room." Rebekah's glum reply came from the kitchen.

He walked toward her. She stood at the sink. With a wickedly long knife, she sliced one of a large quantity of yellow squash. Jonah sat in a corner, playing with blocks amid a smattering of rice.

Jack scratched his head. "Who dumped rice everywhere?"

"Martha," Rebekah said. "She was playing bride. Throwing her own rice. And then she played flower girl and threw petals."

"Well, now. That's what I call an original sin."

"Every time I ask her to clean it up, she wanders off somewhere."

"I do not," Martha said indignantly. "I'm just busy."

"You certainly are," Jack said.

Construction-paper hearts were strewn everywhere. On the table, on the floor. Taped to cupboards, held to appliances with magnets. All the colors of the rainbow, plus black, brown, and white. A skinny orange heart escaped its moorings on the fridge and floated to the floor.

Jack walked back to the bride with rice crunching under his feet. "Miss Martha, life isn't all skittles and beer. I'm glad you've had fun today, but it's time to clean up."

"I made one for you." She handed him a lopsided blue heart.

I love my Unkul Jack, she'd printed laboriously on it in red marker, running the second *k* right off the edge. On the table lay a green heart with *I love Mama* in bigger letters.

He tucked the blue heart into his shirt pocket. "Thank you, but if you love your mama, you'd better tidy up your messes. Start with this one, and then I'll help you take care of the rice."

"Later."

His ears must have gone bad. "Excuse me?"

"Later. 'Scuse *me*." Martha climbed off her chair. As she squeezed past him, she burst into song. *"Rejoice in the Lord, O ye righteous,"* she sang, one hand clamped to her head to keep her veil in place.

"Righteous, nothin'. Get back here, you little sinner."

"For praise is comely for the upright...." Her happy voice trailed behind her as she sashayed through the living room, the veil swaying.

"Martha!" he roared, to no avail. She was gone, tromping up the stairs. Still singing.

He took a long, slow breath and let it out. In theory, he believed in a child's right to test her limits, to explore independence to the very borders of rebellion. In practice, though, he leaned toward paddling the brat. Except she wasn't his.

"She's horrible," Rebekah said, still slicing squash with no great regard for the safe handling of knives.

"She's four. Careful, there. I'd rather not make a trip to the emergency room."

The blade kept flashing. "I haven't cut off any fingers. See?" She laid down the knife and held up her hands.

He counted automatically. Four fingers and a thumb on each hand. "Not yet."

She picked up the knife and started in again, with even greater vigor.

"Watch it, Rebekah. You'll slice your finger off."

The knife clattered into the sink. "You're worse than Miss Minchin!" She stormed past him in a swirl of denim skirts and ran for the stairs.

"Miss...who?"

No answer.

"Oh," Jack said, with a vague memory of Ava's young niece breathlessly reciting the plot of one of her favorite stories. Something about a noble orphan and a tyrannical headmistress or some such thing.

He walked over to the coffee table to review Rebekah's choices from the library. Sure enough, she'd read three books in a row that featured brave young ladies who endured cruel mistreatment at the hands of hardhearted adults.

And he'd thought Martha was the drama princess.

Upstairs, Gabriel screamed, and Michael responded in kind. A thump followed; a head against a wall, perhaps. Jack decided not to interfere. Both archangels deserved a good thumping. Better in their room than in his car.

He swept the kitchen and dumped a mixture of paper scraps, paper hearts, rice, and flower petals into the trash. Furtively, he trashed the vegetables with the rest. He couldn't abide yellow squash.

Pancakes. A foolproof recipe he knew by heart. With some luck, he'd find that Miranda allowed pancake syrup. If not, he'd settle for her strawberry jam, nuked into syrup—except there was still no microwave to nuke it.

He washed his hands, but orange mud streaked the kitchen towel that hung from the oven door. He opened the drawer for a clean one. The drawer was empty. Rebekah must have forsaken her duties as laundry maid.

He wiped his hands on his jeans. Ransacking the cupboards, he found bowls, a cast-iron griddle, measuring cups, ingredients. Within a few minutes, the batter was ready but he'd forgotten to heat the griddle.

Then Miranda was at his elbow, smiling as she peered into the bowl. "Pancakes?"

"Pancakes." He scrutinized her, trying to understand how she could smile when her children were clearly going berserk.

"Did you have a good trip?" she asked.

"In most respects, yes. And what did you do all day?"

"I spent hours on the phone, getting recipes from some of my friends from church. Then I fell asleep, I guess. Where's Rebekah? I thought she'd planned soup for supper."

"She's upstairs. I believe she's on strike."

"Where's Martha?"

"Also upstairs. As of a few minutes ago, she was alive and well but in great need of a paddling."

"Where's Timothy?"

"Don't know."

"The archangels?"

"The devils? Upstairs, thumping each other."

No negative reaction to that either. Her smile just wouldn't quit.

Jack cocked his head to the side, trying to reconcile this vibrant, cheerful woman with his dire imaginings of soul-deep wounds and shipwrecked faith.

"Did you notice the rice?" he asked, jutting his thumb toward the living room.

She looked around blankly. "Rice?"

"The white stuff underfoot. According to Rebekah, we have a young bride in our midst."

"Oh. That would be Martha."

"You think?"

"I think," Miranda said with a mischievous smile. "I certainly do."

Even if he couldn't explain her mood, he could take advantage of it. "Is anybody in your family allergic to cats?"

"No, but why do you ask?"

"Yvonne's giving away a calico kitten. About eight weeks old. Is there any chance you would like to adopt her?"

Miranda's smile fled. "I don't know. A pet is a big commitment."

"I can run to town and pick up all the trappings. Food and litter and such. And I can give the kids a ferocious lecture about taking care of her themselves."

"That would last about a week. I just don't know. Besides that, she'd have to be spayed. And she'd need her shots."

Jack sighed. "All right, all right. I'll pay for the spaying and the shots. The first shots, anyway. I'm not subsidizing this cat's existence for life."

"Why do you want me to take her, then?"

"Kids need pets."

"Kids *want* pets."

He reached for his phone. "Forget it. I'll tell Yvonne to give the kitten to somebody who'll appreciate it."

Miranda gripped his forearm with surprising strength. "No. That kitten's all mine."

"What the—"

"I only gave you a hard time because you expected me to be a kill-joy."

"Because you have been one."

"Oh, all right, maybe I have, but I'm loosening up a little."

"Excellent. I'll call Yvonne so she'll save the little beast for us—for you."

Quick footfalls on the stairs heralded the approach of one of the children. Miranda sent him a warning look; he tried to ask the question with his eyes: *the cat should be a surprise?*

She nodded, giving him a fleeting smile—shy, winsome, flirtatious—and removed her hand from his arm.

Martha trotted into the kitchen. She'd shed her veil and was dragging the cuddle-quilt instead. "I'm bored."

"Let's play a new game," Miranda said. "We'll pretend we're starving prisoners searching for rice and hiding it in a bowl. Every precious grain of it."

Jack handed her an empty bowl. "I don't think anybody got the mail today. Before I start the pancakes, I'll go see." He waggled his phone at her.

"Good idea. Thank you." She gave him a conspiratorial wink.

She'd winked? At a man? At *him*?

He winked back. Her cheeks reddened with gratifying speed. Her smile lingered.

Jack smiled back, picturing her with the bruises and scratches gone, hands on her hips as she argued with him. His imagination produced jeans and a T-shirt. A decent haircut. Makeup. If she would get out of prairie-princess mode, she'd be a knockout.

She turned her back on him and took Martha's hand. "The other prisoners are starving too," Miranda said. "Let's hurry."

Rice crunched under Jack's feet as he passed mother and daughter on his way to the front door. Halfway across the porch, he remembered Yvonne's father who believed he spoke for God. The old guy probably believed he could handle poisonous snakes without coming to harm or raise the dead if the snake theory didn't work out. He wasn't a real prophet. Not that such a thing existed anyway.

Still, when Jack reached the bottom of the steps, he took a slow, calming breath before he called Yvonne's number.

A cracked and ancient voice wavered, "Hello?"

Jack wanted to hang up, but the kids needed that kitten.

"Hello," he said. "May I speak to Yvonne, please?" He braced himself for another pronouncement from on high while mocking himself for expecting it. The preacher wouldn't know who was calling.

"Silence is brother to lies," the old man said. "The truth is sister to mercy. This time, say the words you've been given to say. Do the deeds you've been given to do. This time, hear Me and obey. Thus saith the Lord."

Shaken, Jack closed his phone. He'd try again later.

twenty-one

Waiting for Yvonne to call back and set a time for picking up the kitten—preferably when her crazy daddy wouldn't be around—Jack had grown desperate to beat the paralyzing boredom of Miranda's quiet-Sunday rules. He'd resorted to snooping through Saturday's mail where it lay untouched on the kitchen counter.

Right on top was an envelope with the church's name and a PO box for the return address, and then the electric bill, addressed to Carl as if he were still alive. Only twenty-four electric bills ago, Carl had still lived under this roof. Miranda wasn't far removed from his daily influence. And what an influence it had been.

He must have had some good qualities though or she wouldn't have married him. Ava, lost to divorce instead of death, had some fine qualities and sometimes Jack remembered her with a pang of bittersweet regret that was close kin to the taste of new love.

Standing at the kitchen counter with the envelopes in his hand, he tried to remember Miranda as she'd looked on the day Carl came home from work and found her chatting with a visitor. Carl had waded into an innocent conversation with the verbal equivalent of a swift uppercut to the jaw, but he'd aimed his first swing at Miranda, not at Jack. She'd obeyed Carl immediately, taking the two toddlers inside while he strong-armed Jack off the porch for no good reason.

Except there must have been a reason. Whatever it was, it hadn't kept her from naming Jack as the kids' guardian.

Maybe the guardianship had something to do with getting even with Carl.

Jack resumed looking through the mail. Most of it was junk or catalogs hawking seeds, homeschool books, nutritional supplements, modest clothing—

Modest clothing? That earned a double take. The angelic, teenage cover model wore a bulky, bloomer-style swimsuit that could have been recycled from Edwardian days.

Fascinated, Jack propped himself up against the counter and started browsing. In disbelief, he flipped through page after page of little-girl style dresses with ruffles and lace and wide collars, modeled by little girls *and* by women. Then there were those ridiculous swimsuits. Aprons. Head coverings. Modest sleepwear for men and women—

"Why?" he asked.

And modesty vests.

"Modesty vests?" He skimmed the paragraph describing the garment, then read it a second time and doubled over with laughter.

Behind him, the floor creaked. "What's so funny?"

He marshaled a solemn expression and turned around. Miranda stood beside the table, possessing a trim but womanly figure he couldn't help but notice, no matter what she wore. The brief explanation of the necessity for a modesty vest had only ignited his imagination. He blushed like a virgin in a bawdyhouse.

One more burst of laughter escaped him.

She frowned. "What's so funny?" she asked again.

"Ah…it's…" He cleared his throat. "Okay, you asked for it." He held up the catalog for her to see. "These people sell modesty vests." He managed not to snicker, but it was a near thing.

Her face colored. "They haven't managed to sell one to me."

"Glad to hear it." Jack tilted his head and imagined her in jeans and a T-shirt. Again. It was becoming a habit, and he knew why. By controlling her choice of clothing, Mason controlled her freedom to choose, period. But it wouldn't be prudent to say so.

She nodded toward the mail. "Were there any medical bills? Or a check?"

"Just the electric bill. And something from your church." He handed her both envelopes just as Martha trotted into the room.

Miranda made a face. "I was hoping I'd get the bigger check today, the one from Carl's annuity. This one's so small it's ridiculous. The church gives me a little check, and I give a teensy tithe right back."

Martha tugged at her mom's skirt. "What's a tithe?"

"It's a certain percentage, a certain part of your money that you give back to God."

"Uncle Jack, do you do that?"

The issue was a shibboleth in some circles, but he wouldn't lie. "No, Miss Martha, I don't tithe, but I give. How much I give is between me and God, but I don't believe He would smite my flocks or curse my crops based on how much I do or don't give."

Her forehead furrowed. "Are you a farmer?"

"No, sweetie. Flocks and crops…that's a figure of speech. But if I did have flocks and crops, and if they failed, I wouldn't blame it on my decision not to tithe."

"Your uncle is generous," Miranda said. "He doesn't cheat God or anyone else." She walked out of the room, hardly limping anymore.

While he was still enjoying the novel sensation of being on Miranda's good side, Martha sidled closer. "Mama's still fasting," she confided. "But she's trying not to be grumpy."

"Yeah, I noticed." It worried him. Since the night he'd made pancakes, four or five days ago, she hadn't eaten. "She's still trying to hear God talk, eh?"

"Yes sir."

He scooped Martha up and plunked her down on the counter so she was nearly at his eye level. "I wish we could hear that conversation. Do you think she and God ever talk about you?"

Martha grinned. "Maybe."

"I'll bet they say nice things about you."

"And you." She poked his chest with one finger.

"Maybe."

But he didn't tithe. He drank a little and smoked an occasional cigar. He mocked modest clothing. He snooped through Miranda's mail, drugged her food, and teased her without mercy. And those were his minor flaws. It would be a cold day in hell before the Almighty said anything nice about him.

Martha frowned at him. "Uncle Jack, why are you sad?"

"I'm not sad."

"Yes, you are. In your eyeballs." She pointed at his left eye, making him flinch. "Right there."

"No, Miss Martha, you're imagining things."

"No. I see it." She squinted at him, shifting her attention from his left eye to his right and back again. "Did you do something bad?"

"That's a strange question. Why do you ask?"

"I get sad when I've been bad. You know?"

Disarmed by her sweet honesty, he sighed. "Yes, I know."

"Like when I dropped Mama's new teapot. That was pretty bad." She drummed her heels against the cabinet door. "Did you do something really, really bad?"

"Well, when I was little, I threw a rock through the neighbor's window just to see if it would break."

Martha's eyes widened. "Did you get a spanking?"

"I sure did."

She searched his face so long that he half expected her to come up with the right diagnosis of his soul sickness. "You can tell me the other stuff too," she said at last. "Not from when you were little."

He felt like an escaped convict with a persistent hound on his trail. "Nope. God and I belong to a mighty exclusive club, and you're not going to horn your way into it, young lady."

"Huh?"

"God and I are the only ones who know why I'm sad, and that's how it has to stay."

"If you talk to Jesus and say you're sorry, He'll forgive you."

"That's what I hear."

He checked his watch. He might as well risk running into Yvonne's father again, because Martha was nearly as bad.

"Tell your mother I'll be back in a while with the surprise," he said, swinging Martha down from the counter. "She'll know what I mean."

Martha needed something new to think about, and so did he.

Lost in drowsy memories as she leaned against her headboard, Miranda closed her eyes and pictured Auntie Lou's cheerful smile. She'd been so careful to be an aunt—a great-aunt, actually—instead of a replacement mother. A child should still love her mother, she'd said. No matter what Mom did, she was still Mom.

But when Karen Ellison didn't want to be a mom anymore, Auntie Lou stepped in. She was a rescuer from afar, like Jack, except she had volunteered for the job. She'd known what she was getting into.

"Mama?"

Startled, Miranda looked up to see Martha tiptoeing near. "Yes, sweetheart?"

"Mama," Martha whispered. "Uncle Jack told me he's bringing a surprise. What is it?"

"If I told you, it wouldn't be a surprise."

"You know what it is? Tell me."

"No, love. You'll have to wait."

Martha made a face. "Okay." Still in a whisper.

"Why are you whispering?"

"I know a secret." Martha climbed onto the bed and snuggled close. "Uncle Jack did something really, really bad. That's why he's sad in his eyeballs."

"In his...oh. You mean his eyes look sad sometimes?"

Martha nodded against Miranda's shoulder.

"You're exaggerating."

"No." Martha's head moved sideways this time. "He said nobody knows what he did. Nobody but him and God."

"Martha, do you know what you are?"

There was a long silence. "A tattletale?"

"Yes. And a gossip. You shouldn't have repeated what Uncle Jack told you. Now, scoot."

"Yes ma'am." Martha climbed off the bed again and ran off, leaving the door open.

"Ah, Jack," Miranda said softly. "We've all got secrets."

She knew what it was like to have a guilty conscience. Sure, she'd been obeying the authority God had placed over her, but she could have refused to go along with it.

Too late now.

She closed her eyes. With effort, she transported herself into a pleasant daydream of springtime, with flowers blooming and the girls helping her in the garden. They all wore jeans. Bought and paid for too. Not stolen. And pretty shirts. Martha would be adorable in pink....

Jolted back to the present, Miranda realized she'd dozed off. Outside, Jack yelped, his voice an octave higher than usual.

By the time she made it to the porch, the girls were there, gawking at Jack as he came up the walk with a kitten clamped to his shoulder. A squirming, gangly creature, it was all long legs and big ears, and obviously older than eight weeks.

Jack surrendered the kitten to Rebekah, who snuggled it to her heart.

"Who's it for?" she asked.

"Anybody who's brave enough to take her." Jack massaged his shoulder with a scratched hand. "The little monster clawed her way out of the carrier on the way over."

"Thank you, Jack," Miranda said. "I'm sorry you were injured in the line of duty."

"It was worth it."

Rebekah carried the writhing kitten to the middle of the rug and sat, cross-legged. The kitten looked around with big green eyes and stilled.

"Look at all her colors," Rebekah said. "Orange and black and brown and white, all swirled together like—like clouds."

"One of God's dappled things," Jack said, smiling.

Nose to nose with the kitten, Rebekah laughed. "Oh, she's sweet."

The other children got wind of the excitement through some mysterious communication system that brought them from all corners of the house. Timothy stood at a distance, but the others crowded as closely as Rebekah would allow.

Two years ago, Miranda couldn't have adopted a kitten. Carl wouldn't have allowed it. Now she didn't have to worry about his preferences. The realization was like the closing of a door in a series of doors. Life never stayed the same. Everything kept moving, kept changing.

Rebekah nudged Jonah away when he tried to lay his head on the kitten. "She's not a pillow."

He sat up and stroked the kitten with one finger, then gave Rebekah an inquiring look.

"Yes, that's good," she said. "Because kittens are fragile."

"Not this one," Jack said in a tone of grim amusement. He sat on the corner of the hearth and stretched out his legs.

"What's the kitty's name?" Martha asked.

"Miss Yvonne calls her Hellion," Jack said, "but your mother might insist we change it to something more genteel, like…Helen."

"That doesn't sound like a kitten name," Rebekah argued.

"Picture her as a grown cat," Jack said. "An elegant, snooty cat with a rhinestone collar. Helen. Beautiful Helen."

The kitten twisted onto her back and swatted Rebekah's dangling braid, then latched on to it with both paws. Rebekah squealed, hunching over and cuddling the kitten to her cheek.

"I think Hellion is appropriate," Miranda said.

Jack smiled. "Do you object to that, Rebekah?"

"I think it's nice." Rebekah kissed the kitten's head. "Beautiful Hellion."

The kitten flipped over again. She sat with her tail curled primly around her feet and scrutinized her new home with wary eyes.

Timothy moved closer. "We can't let her go outside," he said.

"Because of the wolves?" Martha asked.

"Coyotes." He scratched the kitten's white chin with one finger and smiled when she tilted her head to beg for more.

Martha giggled, her face smudged with dirt and her eyes shining.

They were so sweet, each one of them. So vulnerable. And their mother was so tired of living in the fear that she would lose them.

Fasting and prayer. For now, those were her weapons.

Blinking back tears, Miranda tried to focus on the moment and savor the pretty tableau. Six beautiful children and one homely kitten. Everybody was watching the kitten.

Everybody but Jack. From the corner of her eye, Miranda saw him, watching her.

twenty-two

After almost a week of fasting, Miranda didn't have the energy to join Jack at the window to watch the children as they blew bubbles in the yard. They'd used up the first refill jar already, and he'd produced another from the trunk of his car. It must have seemed like Santa's sack to the children.

The bubbles were cheap, of course, but his generosity drove her crazy. The photo developing. Construction paper and crayons. Replacement glass for the lily photo. Smoke alarms, carbon monoxide detectors, safety latches. A soccer ball. She was grateful, yet she hated to be in debt to him, and he refused her offers to reimburse him.

"School went well today," he said. He had Hellion tucked under his arm like a football, and she purred like a rattle-trap jalopy, in fits and starts.

"Yes, it did. Thanks to you." Another debt.

She would have laid her head on the table and wept except she couldn't let Jack see her weakness. Once he'd realized she was fasting, he'd made it abundantly clear that he disapproved of the practice.

At the moment, she wasn't too fond of it herself. Emptiness gnawed at her stomach. She felt faint, airy, disconnected. Every hunger pang was a sharp reminder of her goal: to overcome the flesh so she could hear what God had to say to her, if anything.

Hellion plunged to the floor and galloped out of the room.

"Ungrateful beast," Jack said, picking a black cat hair from his white shirt.

Except for the cat hair, he could have stepped out of an ad in a men's magazine. A fashionable bit of stubble on his jaw, a white button-down shirt, khakis. He jingled coins in his pockets. That habit, more than the faint family resemblance, reminded her of Carl. But Jack was kind.

There. She'd admitted it, at least to herself. Carl hadn't often been kind. Jack drove her to distraction with his teasing and his bossy arguments, but beneath it all, there beat a compassionate heart. He'd become a friend as well as a brother, and he treated her as an equal. That was something Carl had rarely done.

But Jack thought he had all the answers when he didn't know half the questions.

Miranda's stomach growled. She tried to pretend it hadn't.

"When are you going to eat something?" Jack asked, facing her.

"When I've finished fasting."

"Why do you fast? Are you trying to manipulate God into doing something for you?"

"I'm trying to hear God. There's a big difference."

"Personal messages from God don't fit into my theological framework."

"Neither does God, then. He's too big for any man-made box."

"Touché. But if God speaks to you, please tell me. I want to know if I agree with Him."

"Oh, listen to your arrogance. Just hush."

Again, he played with the coins. "I know your history, Miranda. Learned it from Dean, the sheriff's deputy, who heard it from Tim."

"Excuse me?"

"When you fast, you faint. When you faint, you fall. Falling isn't a recommended activity for someone who's recovering from a brain injury. I'll be spending less time here, shortly, and I want your word that you won't starve yourself when I'm gone."

"Your leave of absence is over?"

"I won't teach again until the May session, but my other responsibilities keep piling up. Some of them require being on campus."

"Of course. You've already spent days and days looking after us. I don't know what I would have done if you hadn't. Thank you, Jack."

He smiled and waved away her words. "That's what family is for." He looked out the window again. "Visitors. A big white van. Does everyone you know have a noisy vehicle?"

A big, noisy, white van. Wendy Perini's?

Miranda hurried to the front door with Jack close behind. It was indeed Wendy's van. Leah sat in the passenger seat, and several of the younger girls sat in the back, waving. Martha and Jonah hopped up and down on the grass, waving back, while Rebekah pumped her bike furiously up the drive after the van, her skirt hiked up to her knees.

Jack's arm brushed Miranda's back as he leaned against the door jamb. "Friends of yours?"

"That's Wendy—one of the elders' wives—and some of her children." Miranda edged forward, away from the disconcerting warmth of his arm.

Wendy parked her van beside Miranda's, making the Audi look tiny and outnumbered.

Miranda couldn't remember the last time she'd seen those two vans side by side. She and Wendy often joked that their vans were twins, so similar that sometimes the younger children climbed into the wrong van after church gatherings.

Leah climbed out, carrying a large covered dish, and shoved the door shut with her hip. Her cape flapped in the wind. Very pretty, that one. Mason had often complimented Robert and Wendy on raising such a beautiful and godly young lady. According to Mason, Leah would make a perfect wife for some lucky man who needed a supportive helpmeet.

Another innocent lamb who didn't know her pastor was a wolf.

The wind picked up. Leah's skirt billowed around her long legs, then clung to them as if it were made of flimsy gauze instead of sturdy denim. Sometimes, those baggy dresses were no more modest than jeans.

"They're bringing a meal," Miranda said, stating the obvious to help her focus.

"Too bad you're fasting," Jack said, oozing mock sympathy.

"Hush."

Wendy came around the van, and three more of her daughters spilled out of the back. She handed dishes and bags to each one, even little Mary, and the girls followed their mother toward the house. Five capes streamed in the wind like gray sails on a curiously disjointed ship. Wendy was the pregnant masthead, her delicate features drawn with fatigue emphasized by the gray streaks in her ash brown hair.

"Even the vans are clones," Jack said in Miranda's ear. *"Send in the clones,"* he sang softly, then went on humming.

She knew the original. Her mother had stolen the soundtrack.

Miranda stepped onto the porch with Jack right behind her. "Thank you, Wendy, but you should be home with your feet up."

"It's no trouble." Wendy gave Jack a wary peek as she climbed the steps. "We brought a couple of meals, and Leah baked her famous sourdough muffins and a loaf of bread." Wendy scrutinized Miranda's bruises and scrapes. "Abigail was right. You had quite a fall."

"Yes, I did. Wendy, this is my brother-in-law, Jack Hanford. Jack, this is Wendy Perini. These are her daughters. Leah, Esther, Rachel, and Mary."

"Glad to meet y'all." A dangerous undercurrent sharpened Jack's genial tone.

Mary, five years old, smiled at him. Rachel, a chubby nine-year-old, barely glanced at him before she started scanning the yard for Rebekah. Esther, a beauty at fourteen, greeted him politely, while Leah whispered a hello but kept her eyes downcast.

Rebekah ditched her bike and raced across the yard and up the steps to hug Rachel. Wendy gave her younger girls permission to stay outside and play. Jack relieved Rachel and Mary of the bread and muffins just as Gabriel and Michael ran around the corner and shouted their greetings. Timothy followed, more reserved, and agreed to stay outside to watch over the little ones.

Martha slung an arm around Mary's shoulders. "C'mon, let's blow bubbles. Uncle Jack bought 'em for us. He gave us a kitten, except she's really from Miss Yvonne, but I *love* having an uncle. Do you have an uncle?"

"Come on in, ladies." Jack held the door open. Wendy, Leah, and Esther swept in, their capes settling in the still air of the house. Then Jack motioned Miranda inside with a nod of his head and brought up the rear.

"Sit down, darlin'," he said as the others filed into the kitchen. "You're pale."

"I'm fine." She lowered her voice. "And don't call me darl—"

"You're about to pass out." He took her elbow and propelled her toward the couch. "Sit. If you faint, I'll force-feed you whatever they brought."

He would too. She obeyed, her knees nearly buckling as she sank into the cushion.

"I'll be fine, as long as you behave yourself." She tried to make him meet her eye, but he kept looking somewhere past her right ear. "Jack. Look at me."

Still, he didn't quite manage it. "What?" He sounded too vague, too casual.

"Don't stir up trouble. Behave yourself."

"Yes, Mama. I'll try." He took the bread and muffins into the kitchen.

He wouldn't make any off-color remarks, would he? Wendy had already looked at him askance, as if his presence created a scandal.

"Oh, no. Don't think *that*." Miranda got her legs under her and stood, but they went weak in an instant. She collapsed on the couch again and put her head between her knees. After a few moments, she straightened cautiously and listened, but she couldn't make out much from the muddle of voices.

They were only putting food away, after all. It wouldn't take long. Surely Jack could behave himself for a few minutes.

If he felt like it.

Miranda had questions—did the Perinis have any prospects for selling their house, had Robert given notice to his employer, was anyone speaking out against the move?—but hurrying Wendy out the door was more important. The Perini children must have heard about the move, and Miranda wasn't ready for that information to hit her own children's ears. Or Jack's.

When Wendy and the girls returned to the living room, Jack trailed behind, humming softly. *Send in the clones.* Miranda knew the soundtrack in her head would never return to the correct version of the lyrics.

Wendy took in the clutter of textbooks and library books everywhere. On the couch, the coffee table, the floor. She lingered longest on one that Timothy had brought home from the library. Its cover was a montage of famous faces, including Marilyn Monroe's.

"Thank you for the meals," Miranda said.

Wendy met her eyes. "You're welcome. Is there anything we can do for you before we go?"

Miranda shook her head, wishing she didn't have to hurry them away. "No, thanks. We're doing fine."

"We'd better run, then. I left Matthew in charge of Susanna and the boys, so we can't stay. No, don't get up, Miranda. Call if you need anything."

"Thank you."

Wendy and her daughters swept toward the door, their capes touching. Jack waved them out with slightly overdone gallantry and followed them onto the porch. There was no telling what he might say or do.

Miranda stood, swaying. By the time she made it onto the porch to stand beside Jack, Wendy and her girls were halfway to the van. Jack kept humming as he watched them climb into the van. Wendy backed it up and turned around, and the van rattled away.

Jack turned toward Miranda. "I have some questions."

"Go ahead."

"In the kitchen, I asked that pale young thing—Leah—if she's in school. She said no, she's waiting on the Lord for a husband, and while she waits, she's living with her parents. Serving them. How old is she?"

Trying to remember the number and ages of the Perini children who came between Leah and Esther, Miranda resorted to counting on her fingers. "Leah must be about twenty-six. Twenty-seven, maybe."

"Still living with Mom and Dad?"

"Yes."

"Not working? Not going to college? Just waiting for a husband?"

Miranda made a face. "She has some kind of home business or... something."

"That's all she's allowed, isn't it? Because higher education and careers are for men only. Women have to stay home and bake muffins and birth a baby every year or two. Leah's mother must be in her midforties, and she's expecting another baby. If I kept track of all the kids she mentioned, she has at least eight already. It's insane."

Ten, actually. "Which one of her children would you ask her to give up?"

"Not a one. Don't twist my meaning, Mrs. H. I'm just..." He shook his head. "Flabbergasted is the word, I guess. No wonder their van is falling apart. How can they stay afloat, financially, when the man's the sole breadwinner and the wife pops out babies as fast as she can?" He gave Miranda a cynical smile. "Some churches are known for their evangelistic efforts, but yours must be known for its reproductive excellence."

"Watch it, Jack. I don't want to hear your crude remarks."

"Mother?" Rebekah, her arms folded across her chest, slowly climbed the porch steps. Tear tracks marked her cheeks.

"What's wrong, sweetheart?"

"Rachel says we're moving—to North Carolina. All—all of us." Rebekah's choppy words came between sharp, miniature sobs. "The whole—church. What—was she—talking about?"

Miranda found it hard to breathe. Hard to think. A faraway siren split the silence, followed by a deeper sob from Rebekah.

"The whole church is doing *what*?" Steel edged Jack's soft question.

Rebekah came closer. "M-moving," she choked out. "Rachel said God told Pastor Mason to move the whole church."

Miranda pulled her into a hug and whispered in her ear. "We're not moving. Stay outside, sweetheart. I need to speak with your uncle in private, and then I'll tell you what's going on."

Her eyes huge pools of worry, Rebekah nodded. She pulled away and sank into the nearest rocking chair.

Miranda limped inside with Jack following so closely that his breath warmed her neck. When she faced him in the living room, his eyes glittered like cold black stones.

"So," he said. "An entire church has to pack up and move because one man claims he heard from God?" He started pacing the room. "The other day, Yvonne and I were talking about such things. Jonestown. Or maybe it would be Waco instead of Jonestown. Fire, not poison."

"Do you really think I'm that stupid?"

"If Mason hears from God, then I hear from Elvis every Tuesday." Jack scrubbed a hand through his hair, making it wild. "I've learned my lesson. This time, I don't care if I look like a fool. I can't stand by and do nothing. I won't let you do this crazy thing."

"Would you please listen to me?"

"You listen to me, Miranda. You can follow Mason to the ends of the earth, but the children aren't going. I'll take them away from you first. So help me God, I'll find a way."

She snatched a copy of his signed pledge from the shelf where she'd stashed it. "You promised you wouldn't take my children, and boy, am I glad I've got it in writing."

Jack sputtered something incomprehensible, ran both hands through his hair, and walked out. He slammed the door, making the windows rattle.

"I'm not moving anywhere!" she screamed after him, but he didn't come back.

⌣

Jack pressed his temples with his fingertips, feeling the darkness descend upon him like a bad headache. He had no right to tell Miranda how or where to raise her children. He was only the uncle. A half uncle, at that.

He was halfway across the yard when a transparent sphere drifted past his nose. Martha laughed and blew a new stream of bubbles in his direction.

She was a sight—her braids with their end-of-day messiness, her dress smudged with red marker, her mouth topped with the vestiges of a milk mustache. She looked beautifully normal except for the old-fashioned cape.

He tried to smile. "You must like bubbles." His voice cracked oddly.

"I *love* bubbles!"

Hearing a thud inside the house, he braced himself for his briefcase and duffel bags to come flying out the door. They didn't.

He kept walking, not sure where he was going. Away. Just away, before he said worse things and found himself banned from Miranda's property forever. Banned from the kids' lives.

She intended to take them to the boonies with Mason? It was the perfect setup for a small-scale Jonestown. Ninety instead of nine hundred.

And he'd thought he could breeze in, change their lives, and breeze out again. The visiting uncle, the man of the world, he was supposed to have all the answers.

He didn't have any answers at all, but he had to do something.

When a mother said, "You'd be better off without me," a wise son made sure she was all right. And when a woman said she was moving her family to some isolated spot with a cultlike church, a wise brother-in-law stopped her. By foul means or fair.

He didn't see Rebekah anywhere. The poor kid was probably holed up somewhere, crying. She couldn't become a clone of that pale girl who was pushing thirty and didn't know how to talk to a man.

Jack crossed the lawn. The archangels looked like whirling dervishes producing eddies of iridescent globes. Jonah squatted on the grass, blowing bubbles but not chasing them as the wind snatched them away. He hummed a few notes, lifted the wand to his lips again, and blew. Contented. Happy. Too young to have been warped.

Martha chased after Jack. "What are you doing? Where are you going?"

"To the cliffs." A gloomy place to suit his dark mood.

She hopped up and down in her boxy shoes. "Can I go with you?"

"May I," he corrected, like Miranda. "Yes. Come on."

As he and Martha walked behind the barn, he slowed so she could keep up with him, but his mind raced. They moved from the clearing and into the woods. The trees blocked most of the wind, producing a sudden calm that only emphasized the turmoil inside him.

Pushing through the dogwoods and laurels that overhung the path, he remembered finding his card, crumpled in the mud. So much had changed since that morning.

The path to the cliffs had grown greener; the bushes and trees had begun to leaf out. Thousands of violets rose above the black litter of last year's fallen leaves. Year after year, layer upon layer, green things lived and died and decayed. Each new spring was built upon the deaths of previous seasons. And each new season ended in death.

He tried to shake off his morbid thoughts. It wasn't even Friday, but the blues were about to hit. The infection was creeping up on him like a virus. There was no antidote. He would have to ride it out.

Martha started singing, her sweet voice jouncing as she skipped. *"Rock-abye, rockabye, sweet—Maya baby."*

That little jolt in the rhythm again. That imaginary baby who'd died but came back to life. She was sometimes an infant, sometimes a playmate, her age changing to accommodate Martha's playacting.

Martha raised her volume, belting out the lullaby so loudly that it jarred Jack's nerves.

"Didn't you tell me Maya died?" he asked, to make her stop singing. "So you're singing a lullaby to a ghost."

"What's a ghost?"

"We'd better not use that word. Your mama doesn't approve of ghosts."

"But what's a ghost?"

"The spirit of a departed—never mind. I don't dare try to work ghosts into your mother's theology."

What did it matter? Crazy talk about an imaginary friend who was dead and then not dead—none of it mattered when Miranda was trying to take living, breathing children into some weird counterculture in the hills.

"Uncle Jack? What's theology?"

"The study of God."

"That sounds hard. Like for big people."

"Yeah, most four-year-olds save it for when they're older."

"I'll be five pretty soon, and Jonah's going to be two. Maybe Maya's birthday is coming. Maya's going to be…I don't know. I'll ask Timothy."

"Hold on, now. Why would you ask him? I thought Maya was your friend, not his."

"Huh-uh. He gets mad when I ask him stuff about Maya. But sometimes he keeps saying 'Maya, Maya, Maya,' and it drives me crazy, but then he gets all grumpy and says I'm the one who drives *him* crazy."

"You mean Maya is *his* imaginary friend? Isn't Timothy too old for that?"

"I don't know." She skipped ahead, pointing. "We're almost to the cliffs."

They rounded the curve and faced the vista he'd first seen on the morning Miranda fell. The morning he met Timothy on the path.

A fierce wind bit Jack's face. He imagined Martha being blown into the air, her cape acting like Mary Poppins's umbrella, except it wouldn't carry her to a safe landing.

"Stay close to me, Martha." He took her hand as they went closer.

She slowed to baby steps, a funny shuffle that revealed her reluctance to go too close to the edge. "Is this where Mama fell?"

"It is."

They peered into the ravine. Water gurgled on the jagged rocks. It was a dismal sight, all those rocks and branches that must have punished Miranda's tiny frame as she fell.

A small brown bird flew from a bush and darted down the cliff to disappear into shrubs beside the water. That was one advantage birds had over humans; if they lost their footing, they could fly.

"That must have hurt so bad," Martha said.

"Badly," he corrected, feeling numb.

She squeezed his hand. "Are you sad, Uncle Jack?"

"Yes."

"Me too. It's shivery here."

"Let's go."

They began walking back. Her little feet trudged slowly in their clunky shoes, giving him more time to worry.

Wendy Perini and her crew wore shoes like that too, and those awful dresses. No makeup. They smiled a lot, though, like happy robots. He suspected that Wendy wasn't merely submissive; she was subservient. As Miranda must have been to Carl. And, no doubt, as Mason's wife was to him.

What's a half person? In Miranda's case, it was a woman who'd spent half her life under a man's control.

She must have been a cute teenager. Then Randi met Carl and became Miranda of the gunnysack dresses. She adopted his beliefs and devoted herself to raising a family on the outskirts of Slades Creek. A safe place to raise a family. A mountain paradise. Now, some burg in North Carolina was being advertised as a better paradise, but it could be hell on earth.

When they emerged from the woods and started across the grassy clearing, Martha glanced over her shoulder. Jack followed suit. The sun hadn't set, but beyond the first few feet of brush and dogwoods, the woods were dark and spooky. He could understand her fear of wolves.

She dropped his hand and ran ahead. Over the crest of the hill, the roof of the house came into view, the chimney puffing smoke.

Martha waited for him to catch up and took his hand again. "Our house is a strong house," she said fiercely. "We're safe there."

"Yes. So help me God, I'll keep you safe." Safe from her own mother. There was something terribly wrong with that concept.

He needed a plan. He needed to talk to somebody local. Somebody who knew Mason.

Jack pulled his phone out of his pocket, thinking of Yvonne or even Dean, the deputy, then decided to wait. Martha couldn't hear a conversation like that.

A high-pitched, faraway scream chilled his blood. He stopped in the path to listen.

Miranda.

twenty-three

Panicked young voices joined Miranda's, crying Martha's name like Jack had called for the archangels that day in Chattanooga.

He uttered a pungent phrase, not quite loud enough for her to catch. "Let's run, sweetie. Your mama thinks you've gone missing. She'll want my head on a platter."

"The turkey platter? The big one?"

He couldn't even laugh. If Miranda dragged Martha off to the hills, he couldn't teach her about figures of speech. Or read stories to her. Or protect her from wolves in shepherds' clothing.

Her cape billowed as she raced through the tall grass of the clearing. Jack stayed right behind her. He imagined stuffing the kids into the van and driving off somewhere, anywhere. But he wasn't the official guardian as long as Miranda lived and breathed, and kidnapping was a felony.

If it saved them, it would be worth it.

Timothy and Rebekah barreled across the clearing and shouted in unison as they spotted Martha. Timothy picked up speed, beating Rebekah by yards.

He slid on to his knees, nearly knocking Martha over when he grabbed her. "Mother thought you went to the cliffs," he said, panting. "You're in deep trouble."

She let out a howl and started rubbing her eyes with her fists. Timothy hugged her, hard, but she was beyond consolation.

"It's my fault." Jack tried to make himself heard over Martha's caterwauling. "I'm sorry."

Timothy shot him a look of unadulterated hatred. "No, you're not. You're just an interfering bully. You're always bullying my mother. All the time."

Jack opened his mouth to protest, then remembered talking over Miranda, being blind to her tears, deaf to her protests. Trying to control her. He'd been acting like—

He wheeled around, feeling as if he'd received a physical blow to the gut. He was no better than Mason, that manipulative, self-righteous misogynist. A tyrant.

When Jack faced Timothy again, the boy had scooped Martha into his arms. He jogged away, her head bouncing against his shoulder. Sick inside, Jack followed at a slower pace.

He pulled out his phone, endured Yvonne's interminable recording, and left a terse "Call me" at the beep. By then, he was a few yards from the barn, where Miranda had just hit her knees in the straw-colored weeds to embrace Martha.

Timothy watched, his arms locked across his skinny chest. Rebekah stood beside him, her cheeks wet and her shoulders heaving.

Still wrapping herself around Martha, Miranda glared up at Jack. She'd had the cuddle-quilt around her shoulders like a shawl, but it had fallen. The stiff stalks of the weeds held it up in peaks and valleys.

"I'm sorry," he said. "I should have told somebody she was with me."

"Didn't it occur to you that a mother needs to know where her four-year-old is? Especially when there are cliffs?"

"I'm sorry. I shouldn't have assumed anyone noticed she went with me."

"There are a number of things you shouldn't have assumed." Miranda cupped a hand around Martha's chin and gave her a tremulous smile. "Sweetheart, go back to the house with Rebekah and Timothy. Uncle Jack and I have some talking to do. Rebekah, if everyone's hungry, go ahead and eat. We'll be a while."

Rebekah sniffled. "Yes ma'am." She took Martha's hand. The girls started back with Timothy close behind them.

Miranda stayed in her awkward crouch. "You cannot imagine how terrifying that was."

"No, I can't. May I help you up?"

"I don't need your help." She straightened, biting her lip. "And don't assume that you know my plans." She shivered and swayed, the wind almost blowing her over.

He picked up the quilt and draped it around her shoulders. She sagged beneath its weight as if it were chain mail instead of soft cotton.

"Tell me your plans, then," he said. "Please, talk to me."

She grasped the corners of the quilt, holding it tight under her chin. Her face was tense, her shoulders stiff. A gust of wind hit hard, and she lurched sideways.

"I'll talk," she said, "but not in front of the children. The barn."

She led him through the sturdy old structure's yawning entrance. The thick timbers above them exploded with flapping wings as roosting birds fled the intrusion. Then the birds were gone, and he and Miranda stood in a sudden calm, the wind reduced to a faint whistling in the cracks between the wide planks. Shafts of sunlight slanted onto a broken wheelbarrow, a pile of rotten lumber, and a rusty harrow. The residue of long-ago animal residents filled the place with the age-old smell of farming.

Miranda wheeled to face him. "I'm not moving. Do you hear me? I'm not moving."

"You're not? Thank God!" Relief boomed through his blood. He started toward her, but the look in her eye brought him to a halt. "What's going on?"

"When Mason said he was moving the whole church, I told him I didn't want to go. He put so much pressure on me that I pretended to back down. He thinks I'm going along with the idea—or at least he thought so until I started dragging my heels."

"Why don't you tell him to take a hike?"

She returned to the doorway and looked toward the mountains. The sun, low in the sky, blazed into the barn, touching her hair, her cheek, her right shoulder swathed in the quilt.

"For now, I need to lie low."

"Why? Are you afraid of Mason? He's nothing but a two-bit preacher from a two-bit town. He's not some all-knowing prophet of God."

"You're right, he isn't," she said. "But I have to think about the children."

Jack moved to the doorway. Leaning against the massive timbers, he studied her profile. Her lower lip trembled.

"What about the children?" he asked, assailed by vague fears. "Why do you mention them and Mason in the same breath?"

She faced into the gloom of the barn again, silhouetted against the sunset. "It's nothing sordid."

"What is it?" He moved closer, wishing physical proximity could help him drag the truth out of her. "Tell me."

Breathing fast and shallow, she said nothing.

He realized he was framing her, as if he were the photographer now. Memorizing her. In case she sent him away for being a bully. In case he never saw her again.

The sun caught the quilt on her shoulder in a golden spotlight. The fabrics in the wide border of the quilt didn't quite match the worn and faded fabrics in the center section. In one corner of the center piece, the sun highlighted small holes where someone had pulled out stitches that must have been made with thick thread. The stitches had left ghosts of themselves, perhaps the remnants of lettering. Like the names she'd embroidered on crib quilts.

Drawn closer still, Jack traced the ghost stitches with one finger. Seven or eight letters, maybe.

He stopped breathing.

Everywhere, sets of seven. Seven dried roses in the wreath on the door. Sets of seven drawn on the cover of the attendance book. Six angels in the Christmas cupboard and one more hidden in the kitchen. Six baby quilts, and this one—but only six children.

"Dear God," he said.

Miranda said nothing.

"I have a strange little habit," he said. "I count things, all the time. Can't stop myself. I've counted sets of seven all around your house. In quilt patterns. Needlework. Flower arrangements. Even in the doodles on your attendance book."

He stopped. Was he crazy? Or was she?

"There are five baby quilts hanging on the kids' walls," he said. "Jonah still sleeps with his. That makes six." He touched her shoulder. "And this one—the center portion of your cuddle-quilt—makes seven."

She inhaled a quick breath, then another one. And then it seemed as if she was the one who'd stopped breathing.

"Miranda, how many children have you had?"

Her shoulders rose and fell. She turned to face him, and his hand skimmed lightly over her as she moved.

Tears like rivers. Eyes like deep wells of sorrow. And more than sorrow.

She'd lost a child, that was plain, but he couldn't understand why her grief was mixed with so much fear.

The children were all in bed—Rebekah's worries relieved, Martha's tears dried—and Miranda had finally stopped shaking, at least on the outside. The wind snarled at the windows. Timothy, then Jack, had stoked the fire, but she was still cold in spite of the blaze.

Curled up in Carl's chair with the cuddle-quilt, she met Jack's worried look. The poor man had waited all evening for her explanation. He sat in the center of the couch, his hands gripping the edge of the cushion.

"I've been praying about how much I could tell you," she said. "Or whether or not I should tell you at all, but Timothy isn't our firstborn."

Jack nodded, eyes narrowed as if in cold-hearted calculation.

"Jeremiah," she said, the name familiar to her heart but foreign to her tongue. "Jeremiah was our first child. When he was five years old, just after we moved here, he fell from the cliffs."

Horror dawned on Jack's face. "Oh, Miranda."

She closed her eyes and recalled the familiar scripture. "'If any man has a hundred sheep, and one of them has gone astray, does he not leave the ninety-nine on the mountains and go and search for the one that is straying?' But I couldn't, even though I only had three lambs then. Two by my side. One at the bottom of the cliffs."

"What happened?"

"It was late afternoon. I was upstairs, getting Rebekah up from her nap. I heard the front door slam and I knew Jeremiah had run outside. Twice before, he'd gone all the way to the cliffs by himself.

"I hurried to get jackets and shoes on Rebekah and Timothy. We went after Jeremiah, calling his name. We'd had some rain, and everything was muddy. We tracked his footprints past the barn. Through the clearing. Through the woods. I carried Rebekah and I tried to make Timothy hurry. We followed Jeremiah's footprints to the edge of the cliffs. I didn't let the little ones see, but—"

She opened her eyes. It was easier to look at Jack than to see the scene that still burned on the inside of her eyelids. "He lay at the bottom. So still. I couldn't leave Timothy and Rebekah alone at the top of those tall, slippery cliffs. They might have fallen too. And I couldn't take them down with me. You've seen how steep it is. And how far it is from the house. Tell me, what would you have done?"

He studied the floor. "I don't know."

"I had to make a choice. I abandoned one lamb on the mountain to be sure the others would be safe. I ran back to the house, carrying Rebekah and dragging Timothy. Carl was just getting home from work. He ran all the way to the cliffs, but it was too late."

"Oh, Miranda," he said again.

With her forefinger, she traced the holes left by the stitches she'd made when Jeremiah was a tiny baby. "We buried Jeremiah two weeks before you came to meet Carl."

Jack's head came up. "You'd just lost your son?"

"That's why Carl wouldn't let you stay. He was afraid Timothy would say something. He'd been asking for Miah—that's what Timothy called him—and Carl wanted Timothy to forget."

"Do you mean the other children have never known?"

"Never. It's best that way."

A log shifted in the fire. It thudded in the quiet, in the space she left in her story.

Jack's face had that calculating look again. "I think I understand. Timothy and Rebekah might have blamed themselves one day. For being there, for keeping you from reaching Jeremiah in time. And Carl wanted to spare them that. That softens my heart toward him, a little."

"Good." Never mind that his theory was wrong.

"And that's why you have no mementos, no photos of Jeremiah. Nothing but his quilt."

"I have one photo of Jeremiah, but everyone thinks it's of Timothy."

"The little guy in overalls? The one where you look like a teenager?"

"I was nineteen, almost twenty."

"So you were about twenty-four, twenty-five, when Jeremiah died."

"Yes. I loved him so much. If I could have taken his place, I would have."

"I believe you."

She nodded, remembering that terrible, sleepless night, ringing with the sounds of Carl's saw and hammer, and then the cruelest of mornings when the sun came up on a world that no longer held her living, breathing son.

"Jeremiah. The name means 'God will raise up,'" she said. "But God didn't raise him."

Jack knelt beside the chair and drew her hand to his chest. His heart beat steadily under her fingers.

That kind heart. His kindness might have persuaded her to tell him the rest, but it wouldn't have been fair.

Jack stood in the kitchen, slicing into a loaf of Rebekah's whole-wheat bread and trying to put the puzzle together. He was still missing a few pieces.

Why had Carl insisted on keeping Jeremiah's death from the younger kids? They didn't need to know the details, but surely they needed to know about their brother.

Anyway, it seemed that Carl's plan had failed. Timothy remembered. Miah, not Maya. A boy, not a girl. Real, not imaginary. Miranda wasn't ready to hear it, though.

First, she needed to eat.

When Jack brought her the bread and a glass of apple juice, she'd moved to the couch. She still had the quilt wrapped around her.

"I have no idea what's good for breaking a fast, but I'm gambling on bread and juice." He sat beside her and placed the glass in her hand. She fumbled, nearly spilling, so he took it back and held it to her lips. "Once you have some food in your stomach, you won't be as shaky."

He broke off a piece of the bread for her. She chewed and swallowed mechanically, but she seemed very far away.

"Miranda, where'd you go?"

She focused on him with unnerving force. "Back to about AD 33, and I met you there. And I met Jesus—" She touched his chest with her forefinger. "Here. In you. And in Yvonne."

Bewildered, he shook his head. "Far be it from me to comprehend the workings of a woman's mind. Eat, please."

"I'm seeing so much. Hearing so much. Hearing from God, inside. I was 'naked, and you clothed me.' That was Yvonne, bringing those hand-me-downs. 'I was hungry, and you gave me something to eat; I was thirsty, and you gave me something to drink.' Even if you spiked my food with pain pills, sometimes."

"Guilty as charged."

She smiled, blue eyes drowning in tears. "And 'I was sick, and you visited me.' You dropped everything and showed up to take care of me. 'I was in prison, and you came to me.' I wasn't in a literal prison, but—"

"Hush, now. I'm no saint. Not even close. More of a bully, it seems. Eat—and there I go again, telling you what to do."

She took a tiny bite of bread. "It's all right, now and then."

"I'm very thankful that you and the children won't be moving." Jack ducked his head. "I've become quite fond of the whole kit and caboodle, including you."

He handed her a tissue. She blew her nose and pushed her hair out of her eyes. She was a mess, dripping tears like a leaky faucet.

"But I have some more questions," he said.

"I knew you would."

"Are you sure Timothy doesn't remember Jeremiah? Because I've heard him mumble 'Miah.' I thought it was a girl's name. Martha's imaginary friend. I thought Timothy was imitating her, but it might have been the other way around. Martha might have heard him talking about Miah and made an imaginary friend out of the name. And she must have heard him say that Miah fell and died, because that's what she told me."

Miranda passed her wadded-up tissue from one hand to the other, squeezing and shredding it. "No. Timothy was so young. How could he remember?"

"It's quite possible, and it could be unsettling if he remembers his brother but you've led him to believe there was no brother."

She shook her head, hard, and a lock of hair fell across her face. Her hand trembled when she tucked the hair behind her ear. "Timothy doesn't remember."

"I'm not so sure about that, and if I were him, I'd feel cheated. That's how I felt about never knowing Carl, but the brother Timothy lost was actually part of his life, if only for a few years. That must be even harder than losing a brother you'd never met until the day you lost him."

"I don't believe Timothy remembers."

"The lady doth protest too much, methinks." Jack searched her eyes and saw growing uncertainty. "But why not tell him anyway? Why not tell all the kids? You don't have to share anything that would make Timothy and Rebekah believe they were somehow to blame. Give them the short version. Jeremiah was your first child. When he was five, he fell from the cliffs and died. That's all they need to know."

She looked away, pressing her lips tightly together, and he could have kicked himself. A grieving woman needed comfort, and he'd offered another lecture instead.

Thinking back to eighth grade, he remembered hating the hollow expressions of sympathy people had given him when his mother died. Some claimed to know how he felt. Some had the gall to say all things worked together for good, and God wouldn't have allowed it to happen if it hadn't been for the best.

Wiser souls, though, had the wisdom to make one short, truthful statement, wrapped in heartfelt sympathy, and then shut up. His favorite teacher, Mrs. Hurst, was one of them. She'd known what to say. It was so simple, and he'd loved her for it.

That lock of hair had fallen across Miranda's face again. He brushed it back and tucked it behind her ear. Putting his whole heart into the words, he repeated in its entirety what Mrs. Hurst had said to him.

"I'm so sorry."

Those simple words opened the curtains that hid Miranda's heart. She gave him the tearful version of her Princess Diana smile and dropped her head to his shoulder. He cupped her cheek with his hand as if she were a weeping child, and like a child, she wet his shirt with her tears.

It must have been two or three in the morning. Miranda didn't want to know.

Jack paced the porch, smoking one of his smelly cigars, and she was alone. Although her feet were planted on the rug in front of the wood stove, she felt lost. Disoriented. Like a tourist in a foreign land who didn't know the language or the laws. Or maybe there were no laws.

She only knew she was done with Mason's church. Done with obeying his rules.

She wasn't sure she knew who she was though, apart from the church. Already, she'd been nobody's daughter, nobody's wife; now, she was nobody's disciple.

No, that was wrong. She wished Jesus were there in the flesh though, to stand between her and Mason. And to reassure her He was real. Sometimes, she just didn't know anymore. All those things she'd told Jack about seeing Jesus in him and in Yvonne? They'd sounded good at the time, but now nothing felt good or solid or real.

The children had been asleep for hours. Still, Miranda tiptoed to the bookshelves as if someone might be listening.

She pulled Carl's books and pamphlets off the top shelf. They were thin. They didn't look dangerous.

She stood still, chasing elusive memories, tracing out the maze of the past. They'd meant well, both of them, but they'd gone so far wrong that some things couldn't be mended.

"Oh, Carl," she said. "You did the best you could. I did too."

The home-printed booklet on top was bound in a translucent plastic folder. The title showed through: *Raising Your Family God's Way—Heaven in Your Home.* Carl had always referred to this one when she expressed an opinion about discipline. After a few years, she'd stopped trying to change his mind. She'd simply handled things her own way whenever possible.

She carried the pamphlets to the wood stove and opened the door. The blaze toasted her face as she threw Carl's treasured teachings into the fire. She closed the door and backed away as the stench of burning plastic filled her nostrils. The scent of freedom.

She shut off the living room light, leaving the room in darkness except for the fire. Out on the porch, a small orange glow bobbed in the night as Jack moved his cigar to his lips and lowered it again. He was a sentry, standing guard.

Soon, though, he would return to Chattanooga to stay. She would have to stand alone against Mason.

twenty-four

The house reeked of burned plastic in the morning, as it had when Jack had come inside at three. Miranda must have smelled it, but she had neither complained nor explained.

He poured coffee into two mugs and glanced over his shoulder at her red nose and puffy eyes. She'd cried, off and on, for hours.

When a woman's husband died, a specific word defined her; she was a widow. But a woman who lost a child had no special title. She was still a mother, whether or not she had other children, and she had to carry on.

Jack took the coffee to the table, where he ran one of the mugs under her nose. "Where in the Bible does it say herbal hay water is godly and coffee isn't?"

She let out a long, appreciative sigh. "It doesn't."

"Exactly. Take anything in it?"

"Just a little sugar, please."

"From the forbidden sugar bowl in the cupboard? Yes, I've already learned most of your secrets."

He stirred in a generous spoonful of sugar. She took her first sip and smiled as if he'd given her a brand-new Mercedes.

"Pretty decent coffee?" he asked.

"Perfect. I haven't tasted any in years. Carl wouldn't allow it in the house. He even threw away my favorite coffee mug."

Overnight, she was talking more and talking faster. Like a spring that had been paved over and broken open again, she bubbled. These were bitter waters, some of them, and they needed to run and run until they ran clear and clean.

He sat across from her, and Hellion jumped into his lap. "Why did he trash the mug? You could have used it for your hay water."

"It had my unfeminine nickname on it."

Beneath Jack's hand, Hellion's bony back vibrated with a purr. Lucky animal, so far removed from human craziness.

"How long have you doubted Mason's teachings?" he asked.

"For a long time, but especially after Carl died. I…I sort of fell apart after Jonah was born. I clashed with Mason. He told the men to keep their wives away from me so I wouldn't contaminate them with my rebellion."

"And did they stay away? They made you a pariah?"

"Yes. Abigail stayed in touch though. She stuck with me even when I was really down. When I probably wasn't quite rational."

"Postpartum depression, maybe," Jack ventured, "after the shock of losing your husband. But I suppose Mason told you to pray your way through it?"

"How did you guess?"

"I've run into his type before. You should have told him to get lost."

"I needed Abigail." Miranda's eyes sparkled with tears. "I was on my own, with six children including a colicky newborn. If Abigail hadn't stood by me, I don't know what I would have done."

"I would've taken Mason behind the barn and shot him right into a pre-dug grave. Like they do with old horses."

She gave him a crooked smile. "I'll pretend you didn't say that."

"Yes ma'am. Back to your clash with Mason. It was about…?"

"My camera. I wanted to earn money with my photography, but Mason said I had to be a keeper at home and trust God to provide." She stared into her coffee. "Robert Perini said that if the church wouldn't let me earn money, the church should make up for it. Mason has mailed me a small check from the benevolence fund every month since then, but he never lets me forget that I'm a Jezebel."

"You don't believe it, do you?"

"I try not to. I've tried to find scriptures that show he's wrong, but I've found just as many that seem to show he's right. Sometimes, I don't want to read my Bible because I always seem to hear Mason in my head, putting his spin on every verse."

"Enough about Mason. I'd like to hear more about Carl, if you don't mind. I don't even know what he did for a living."

She leaned the coffee mug against her cheek. "He drove a truck for one of the textile mills."

"What was he like? What were his hobbies, who were his friends, what did he do in his free time?"

"He liked woodworking and fishing. His friends were the men in the church. He spent most of his free time serving the church, being Mason's disciple. I know you don't like Mason—and neither do I, now—but he straightened Carl out about a few issues."

"Like what?"

Miranda lowered her coffee to the table and studied it as if it held answers. "Carl wanted to be separate from the world's systems as much as possible. He didn't want to buy insurance, for instance. If Mason hadn't told him to buy good life insurance, I'd be in a tough spot."

"When you met Carl, did you realize his beliefs weren't exactly mainstream?"

She lifted her shoulders in an offhand shrug. "He seemed very spiritual. When he asked me to wear more conservative clothes and throw out my jewelry and my music, he said it was about consecrating our lives to God. He made it sound good and holy. When I married into his church, everybody believed the same way he did."

"You've been in Mason's church since you were nineteen, then?"

"No, we didn't move to Slades Creek until Carl's mother died and left the property to him. Before that, we lived near Ellijay and went to a church that wasn't too different from Mason's. Small. Strict. Very similar teachings."

"Did it all seem normal after a while?"

"Not really, but I was trying to be a good wife. I was trying to be"—she fell silent but her lips moved, trying different positions, different shapes, as she sought exactly the right word—"obedient," she said finally. "I was an obedient wife."

An obedient wife, forbidden to tell her surviving children about their late brother. Forbidden to grieve aloud for her son.

Jack stood, spilling the kitten onto the floor, and pulled the porcelain angel from the high cupboard. "Does this have something to do with Jeremiah?" He set it before her, half expecting a rebuke for having mended the wing against her orders.

She placed her fingertip on the hairline crack. "Last Christmas, I bought seven of these and put six of them on the mantel. I didn't know what to do with this one, so I hid it in the cupboard."

"I'm very sorry I broke it."

"It's all right, Jack. It's only a…a thing."

"When are you going to tell the other children about Jeremiah?"

The color drained from her face. "First, the children. What's next? The newspapers? The world?"

"Why would the world care? No, just tell the children. Before somebody else does. How hard could that be?"

"Hard. You have no idea."

"Still, shouldn't you come clean?"

She studied the angel in a stony silence that sent a prickle down his spine. Perhaps she wasn't telling him the whole story.

A minute or two late for supper, Miranda stood in the hallway and peeked around the corner. The one dark head among the blond ones gathered around the table, Jack was about to say grace. With his shirt sleeves rolled up to the elbow, he joined hands with Rebekah and Gabriel.

Jack's quick smile landed on Martha and became a warning glance. She was squirming.

She ceased wiggling. Holding perfectly still, she gave him an angelic smile.

He closed his eyes. "For these and all Your gifts to us, we thank You, Lord Jesus. Amen."

"Amen," the children echoed, simultaneously opening their eyes and dropping each other's hands.

Martha picked up her spoon and examined her reflection in it. "Uncle Jack?"

"Yes, Miss Martha?"

"If my daddy went to heaven, and if babies come from heaven, and if Jonah came from heaven after my daddy went there—" She sucked in a melodramatic breath. "Then they knew each other for a while." She grinned, pleased with herself for figuring it out.

"I'm sorry, sweetie, but babies don't come from heaven."

Martha lowered the spoon and studied him. Miranda could almost hear the dangerous question forming in that little blond head.

"Where do they come from?"

All the children trained their attention on Jack. Timothy laughed softly.

Jack cleared his throat. Picked up his fork. Put it down. Stumped by a simple question from a four-year-old, the brainy professor stared at the ceiling. He swallowed.

Any other time, Miranda would have laughed, but she couldn't enjoy it. She couldn't enjoy anything until she'd told Jeremiah's story.

Jack was right. If she didn't tell the children, Mason might. Even if she told them, he could still supply the ugly details, but at least the children wouldn't have been completely blindsided.

"Babies…ah…well." Jack scratched his chin. "Most often, babies come from a conflagration of desires. Gabriel, would you please start the bread basket? Thank you, sir. Rebekah, how's that new quilt patch coming?"

Rebekah launched into a detailed description of her troubles with her slant-star patch, and Miranda slid into her chair without anyone taking much notice.

Martha gave Jack a puzzled frown. "What's a con…con…that big word you said?"

"A conflagration? It's a fire. A big one, like a bonfire. We'll have another bonfire sometime, and maybe your mom will be up to joining us." He gave Miranda a friendly smile.

She nodded, feeling strangely detached from him. From the children. Even from herself. As if she didn't know anymore how to act. Who to be.

Just be Miranda Ellison Hanford, she told herself. Widowed mother of six.

No. Seven. And if she could be honest about it, even with the children, it might help her remember where she'd come from, how she'd arrived at this time and place. How an ordinary Ohio girl came to be in a mess like this. Maybe that would help her find a way out.

There had to be a way out. A way that didn't put the children at risk.

She took a careful breath, mindful of her ribs. "Children, there's something I need to tell you. You're not to share it with anyone outside the family though. This is our business and no one else's. Our family history."

Jack set down his fork. He picked up the saltshaker, then the pepper shaker, and scooted them around like chess pieces, his food forgotten.

Timothy had also abandoned his supper. He put his elbows on the table, his chin in his hands. His wary expression told her he remembered more than she'd given him credit for.

twenty-five

Jack's sleep shattered into shards of garish orange noise. His nerves shot in an instant, he sat up, throwing off his covers in the dim light of early morning.

The cacophony came from the coffee table. From his phone.

"Gabriel! You little devil!" He fumbled for the phone and sent it into blessed silence. "Hello."

"Hi, it's Yvonne. Sounds like I woke you. I'm sorry. I thought you were an early riser."

"The little barbarian. The little—no, not you. Gabriel."

Jack smelled coffee. That meant Miranda was up. Sure enough, she and Timothy sat at the table, talking in low voices.

"Hold on a second, Yvonne." Jack wrapped the quilt around his bare shoulders, unfastened the deadbolt, and stepped onto the porch. The mountains were still streaked with fog and nearly blended in with the pale sky.

"Sorry about that," he told her. "Last night, Gabriel discovered the joys of messing with my phone. He set it to the most obnoxious ring tone imaginable—at the highest volume—stop laughing. I want to go back to bed. Except I don't have a bed. I only have a couch and a kitten that wants to sleep on my face all night."

"Well, that sounds like fun. Seriously, Jack, is everything all right? Somehow I missed your message until now."

"Long story. Everything's pretty much okay now."

"You sure, hon?"

Jack paced the porch with his feet freezing on the damp, rough planks as he answered Yvonne's questions. Yes, Miranda was doing fine; she was cutting her ties to Mason. Yes, she might try Yvonne's church someday.

If it were up to him, though, he would steer Miranda away from any church that encouraged its members to spout impromptu prophecies.

Once Jack had extricated himself from the conversation, he set his phone to a civilized vibrate setting and sat in his usual rocker, his feet like blocks of ice.

His brain was frozen, unable to make sense of anything. Why had Miranda kept quiet about Jeremiah for so long? After Carl's death, she could have told the children about their brother. In fact, they might have noticed Jeremiah's grave marker when they'd buried Carl.

Jack rubbed his chin, considering. Jeremiah's remains might have been cremated. Carl's too. Maybe there were no markers.

The church's mass move was also odd. Jack couldn't understand it unless Mason believed his own hype about hearing from God. Or wanted control or money or kids to molest. In an isolated church that revered authority figures, the potential for abuse was staggering. Even if it was "only" psychological abuse, all those families were at risk.

Jack went inside. He grabbed a T-shirt and pulled it on, then wandered past the table and into the kitchen to pour himself a cup of coffee.

"Mornin'," he said.

Timothy said nothing.

Miranda's smile trembled, but it held. "Good morning. I've been telling Timothy more about Jeremiah."

Jack directed his question to Timothy. "May I join you?"

After a moment's hesitation, the boy nodded.

Jack sat at the head of the table, between them. He played with half a dozen of Martha's paper hearts while Miranda gave Timothy a rundown of his big brother's life and times. Jeremiah's personality. His habits. His likes and dislikes. The way he'd loved ketchup and hated mayonnaise.

"Like you do," she told Timothy. "Maybe you learned that from him. In looks, he resembled Jonah, with the gray eyes that don't look blue until he's wearing a blue shirt."

It was like watching a morning begin, going from darkness to full day. A light dawned inside Timothy, softening his countenance.

"Jeremiah loved everything about the outdoors," Miranda continued. "He loved to cut daylilies from the yard and put them in a jar for me."

"All this time, I thought I was losing my mind." Timothy wiped his nose on his shirt sleeve. "But I knew I remembered him. I *knew* it. He fell. And we cried and cried. It was all foggy in my mind, though, and I was afraid to ask you."

"I'm so sorry," she said. "I should have told you, years ago."

"Yeah, you should have." Timothy pushed back his chair and headed toward the stairs.

"Timothy, wait." Miranda's shoulders sagged as she watched him go.

"He needs time to adjust." Jack reached for her hand. "Listen though. Hear that?"

"Maya, Maya, Maya," Martha sang upstairs.

Except it was *Miah,* and Timothy didn't tell her to shut up.

Jack squeezed Miranda's hand. "I still have questions. Lots of questions."

She frowned. "Can't they wait?"

"Please, just one. Not about Jeremiah. About Mason. If you've been a troublesome member of the church, why does he want to drag you off to the boonies? Why does he want the whole church to move?"

She freed her hand from his, ran her forefinger back and forth across her chin. The sound of toe tapping came from under the table. "Does it matter?"

"Maybe. Here's a theory. Sex, money, and power are the forces that drive nearly every conflict on earth. Out of those three, I'd bet on sex. Could he be running from some scandal? And maybe he wants one-hundred-percent compliance, even from troublemakers like you, so this won't happen."

"So what won't happen?"

"What we're doing. If a few of his sheep stay behind, they might put their heads together, compare notes, and realize their shepherd is a scoundrel. There goes his gravy train, right off the track. Forgive the mixed metaphors. And what if—"

"You said you had one question. You've asked about ten. You're done."

"No, Mrs. H., I've only asked three, and you've given me zero answers." He waited, giving her a chance to speak.

She shrugged.

"Fine," he said, "but if I catch Mason at anything that has even a whiff of criminality to it, I'll call the cops so fast it'll make his head spin like Ezekiel's wheels."

It might have been his imagination, but he could have sworn that her face paled.

After another long school day and a weary evening, Miranda longed for her bed. Jack wouldn't follow her there with his endless questions.

All the children were down for the night except the youngest, who'd tumbled from a kitchen chair and bumped his head. After a long, drawn-out howl, he'd snuggled up on the couch with Jack and a handful of picture books. Jonah had finally fallen asleep, and Jack carried him cautiously across the living room.

Almost too tired to smile, Miranda managed it anyway. "Don't worry. He's out until morning."

"Are you sure?"

"Positive." She looked from Jonah's slumbering face to the arms that held him. Jack's shirt sleeves were rolled up, revealing his wrist bones and a portion of the dark hair on his arms, a particularly masculine beauty that sent a shiver to her stomach.

But he would soon return to his own life. Back in Chattanooga, he wasn't Uncle Jack who blew bubbles with the children and sang goofy songs in the shower. He was R. Jackson Hanford, PhD, who felt right at home in a lecture hall, addressing scores of students instead of wrangling, one on one, with six. His nephews and nieces.

They needed his sanity and his craziness. His laughter and his love.

Discreetly, with one finger, she dried the corners of her eyes.

Jack leaned toward her and sniffed. "You smell good. I can't quite identify…" He inhaled again. "What's that scent?"

She ducked her head, hiding a smile. "A custom blend."

Tonight, she'd tried three different fragrance strips from the hand-me-down magazines. One scent on each wrist, one on her throat. The combination must have bewildered his nose.

A clatter on the stairs proved to be Gabriel, followed by Michael, Martha, and Rebekah, all in their pajamas. Timothy brought up the rear, still fully clothed and holding a dog-eared paperback.

Miranda squinted at the book's title. *To Kill a Mockingbird.* She'd loved it in seventh grade. She'd have to read it again sometime.

"We want to make sure Jonah's okay," Gabriel said. He came close and stroked Jonah's messy hair. "He still doesn't know about Jeremiah."

"We'll tell him when he's old enough to understand," Miranda said. "And I'll tell all of you more about Jeremiah, as time goes on. You would have loved him. And he would have loved you."

Rebekah wanted to know Jeremiah's birthday. The archangels wanted to know exactly where he fell, and what time of year. Timothy only listened, but Martha asked more questions than everybody else put together.

"Was he a good reader, Mama?"

"No, Martha. He didn't live long enough to become a good reader."

"But I'm only four, and I'm a good reader."

"Yes, but some children don't learn to read as early as you did, even if they're very smart. Boys often don't read as early as girls do. Did you know that? But Jeremiah was a nature lover, like Jonah. Jeremiah always walked around with stones and sticks and even dead beetles in his pockets."

Martha grimaced. "Ew! Dead things are bad."

"No, they're not," Timothy said. "They're like everything else. Molecules. Elements."

"Like bread and grape juice?" Martha's uplifted face held astonishment.

Timothy smiled tolerantly. "That's a different kind of element."

"And that's enough questions for one night." Miranda's voice cracked from a combination of emotion and exhaustion.

"It is indeed," Jack said, leaning against the wall with Jonah a dead weight in his arms. "It's late, and y'all are turning this into another bedtime-avoidance ploy. Get to bed, the whole lot o' ye rampageous rapscallions."

The funny words took the sting out of the order, and the children trooped off to bed without argument. Timothy went too, although he was still five minutes from his new, later bedtime.

Jack remained against the wall, holding her baby. She didn't know what she would have done over the last few weeks without Jack to carry some of her burdens.

"Thanks," she said, keeping her voice steady. "It was getting hard to handle."

"I could tell."

She inspected Jonah's forehead. "That's quite a bruise."

"And he milked it for all it was worth. Three stories, three times each, but it was fun. I've always loved Mike Mulligan."

She lifted Jonah's chubby hand and kissed it. He didn't stir. "You teach literature on the college level, but you're always talking about children's books. Why is that?"

"That's where everybody starts. Besides, the whole time I was married to Ava, I was surrounded by kids' books. She bought them for her kindergarten classes. We both bought them for her niece and nephews. And for the kids we thought we'd have someday."

"Someday, you'll be a good father to some lucky children."

"That's what Ava thought when she married me. Or at least that's the excuse she used when she decided to leave me."

"You couldn't have children?"

"She could. I couldn't. And don't try to tell me it's because I don't tithe, darlin'. The fertility doctors said it might have been because my mumps vaccination didn't take. Maybe that's why I'm so stuck on wanting family connections. Because I don't have any, and I don't have real prospects of creating any."

Jack couldn't have children? How terrible. How lonely.

She plucked a cat hair from his shirt sleeve. "You have us. If you want us."

Their eyes met in a silence that sizzled with questions. She held her breath, her fingers poised an inch from his shirt. What a fool. So forward.

"If I want you," he said softly. "Miranda, I'm very fond of your whole family, but when it comes to you in particular, it's a good thing there's a two-year-old between us, acting as chaperone, or I'd be tempted to demonstrate how I want you."

Her throat dry, her heart pounding, she managed a smile. "Oh, really?"

"Really. There's just one problem."

"What's that?"

"Sometimes, I get the feeling there are a few things you're not telling me." He raised his eyebrows. "True?"

She captured another cat hair and let it drift to the floor. "Don't you like a woman to have a bit of mystery to her?"

"A bit, yes. Not a whole truck load. Good night, mystery woman." He turned and carried Jonah up the stairs.

"Good night," she called belatedly, then walked to her room and shut herself in.

She longed to be the kind of woman Jack would want. Her heart ached with the impossibility of it all.

She caught her reflection in the mirror above her dresser and grimaced at the baggy dress and unflattering braids. She could at least stop dressing like the kind of woman he *wouldn't* want. When he'd called her clothing utilitarian, it must have been the kindest adjective he could find.

She opened her closet and saw Abigail's sweater neatly folded on the shelf. The perfect color to bring life to Abigail's face. Her sister in Nebraska knew her well.

Leaving the sweater where it lay, Miranda started yanking ugly dresses and skirts off their hangers, dumping them on the floor. She saved a few of the better skirts and shirts, but she was done with Mason's rules about dress.

"Done." She salvaged a good hanger from a hideous floral jumper. The skirt ballooned as it sailed through the air to land on the growing heap of discards. "Done, done, done."

She worked her way toward the back of the closet, toward clothes she hadn't worn in years. The further she went, the closer the memories came until finally she leaned against the back wall, hiding her face in a faded blue dress she hadn't worn in nine years.

Carl never knew she'd laundered it and hidden it. The stains hadn't come out, and she was glad. They proved Jeremiah had existed.

Holding the dress to her heart, she stumbled out of the closet and faced the bed where she'd given birth to her first baby, in a different house. On the same bed, here, five years later, she'd held him for the last time. The bed had seen blood and anguish at the beginning of Jeremiah's life and again at the end of it.

He's gone, Carl had said, over and over. *He's gone. Crying won't bring him back. Shut up, shut up, shut up!*

But Carl had wept when he'd thought she was sleeping. He'd blamed himself for everything. He'd loved Jeremiah too.

Miranda curled up on the bed and pressed the dress against her face. She tried to muffle her crying at first, but Carl wasn't there to silence her. He wasn't there to forbid her to speak Jeremiah's name.

"Jeremiah," she said softly at first, then louder and louder. "Miah, Miah, Miah!"

She heard footsteps. Then Jack was kneeling by the bed, stroking her hair and letting her cry. Her grief finally broke out of her in a wail that she wished could wake the dead.

twenty-six

Voices filtered through the open windows to the porch where Miranda sat rocking. Martha sounded out a story about a bear while Jack explained the Jacobite rebellions to Timothy. Jack seemed to know something about everything.

The door creaked open and shut. Jonah came out onto the porch, clutching a picture book to his belly. Rebekah had already read it to him, over and over. It was a silly tale about a friendly family of dragons.

Mason would have said the dragons were demonic. Miranda didn't care.

"Read, Mama?"

"Yes, sweetheart. Sit on my lap. Gently."

He climbed into her lap and opened the book. The print was large, and her vision had cleared enough to make the reading easy.

Jonah pointed to the smiling dragon on the first page. "Good dragon."

"He's a good dragon and you're a good boy." She kissed the top of his head. "Did you know your birthday is coming up soon?"

"Cake?"

"Yes. Cake. With two candles."

She smoothed his curly blond hair against the curves of his skull. Leaning her head against his, she inhaled the smell of baby shampoo. Her last baby, so much like her first.

Jonah pointed at a splash of water on the page. "Rain?" He giggled. "Mama's raining!"

She wiped the tear from the paper and began reading. Jonah let out a happy sigh and slumped against her, then straightened again, no doubt remembering Jack's earlier warning: *Hold still as a stone or lose lap privileges.*

"The baby dragon laughed and laughed," she read. "Even the daddy-dragon laughed and laughed." On she went, scarcely comprehending the story but quickly reaching the end.

Satisfied, Jonah slipped off her lap. Giving her a sweet smile as good as spoken thanks, he ran for the house with the book.

Jack held the door open for him and stepped outside, pulling his phone from his pocket. He sat beside her and pushed the phone's buttons with his thumb. "Marvelous invention, text messaging. Ever tried it?"

Stealthily, she wiped her eyes. With her emotions firmly in check, she faked a smile. "Don't try to bait me. You know I've never even owned a cell phone."

"You should get one. The signals aren't always reliable in the mountains, but it's better than nothing. Especially in an emergency."

True. With a cell phone in her pocket, she would have been able to summon help within moments. Jack's tiny phone looked like a toy, but maybe it could have saved Jeremiah's life. She would never know.

Trying to escape those unanswerable questions, she watched Jack's thumb flying over the buttons again. Texting. Another skill she'd have to learn.

The first time she used a cell phone, she would feel as if she'd rejoined modern life. That day would come soon, Lord willing. If she could outsmart Mason.

"Did Jonah ask for the dragon story again?" Jack asked.

"Yes, it's his favorite."

"The new stories aren't as good as the old fairy tales, like St. George and the dragon."

Miranda shivered. "I don't like the gory ones."

"No? I do. Speaking of dragons…" He went back to texting. "Farnsworth. Good Lord, deliver me."

And me, Miranda mouthed silently.

While Jack dealt with his messages, she imagined herself as a modern St. George—except she was a woman. St. Georgia.

It was no laughing matter. She couldn't let Mason slither out of town with his lies intact. She had to finish him off or live the rest of her life in fear.

Jack sat on the porch's top step, watching the kids wash his car. Again. He'd never thought of car washing as a privilege, but their enthusiasm was inspiring. If life itself was a privilege, so was every mundane part of it.

Michael had appointed himself boss of the operation. He rinsed the car with enthusiasm, making a stream flow down the driveway and into the grass. Jack was drawn into the bad memories of his thirteenth year, but he shook them off.

Rebekah ran outside with old towels, and the kids swarmed over the car, drying it. Even Jonah tried to help.

Timothy, however, was nowhere in sight. He'd been doing that. Disappearing for hours or retreating into long silences that bothered Jack more than the occasional flare of temper.

"Somebody's coming," Gabriel yelled, slinging his towel over his shoulder.

Jack prepared himself for a van full of clones or the head guru himself, but a sheriff's cruiser came around the bend. He stood and walked down the steps, his heart lifting as if the cavalry had come thundering in.

Dean flashed the car's blue lights and whooped the siren to make the kids laugh, then pulled up next to Jack and lowered the window. "I just thought I'd check on the family. How's everybody doing?"

"Very well, thanks." Jack checked to make sure nobody had wandered within earshot, but all his helpers were still drying the Audi. "Miranda's leaving Chandler's church, so everything's changing for the better."

"Good."

"But I'm going to be spending more time in Chattanooga soon. Could you swing by now and then? Create a little more police presence out here?"

"Is this just about a widow who's spooked about living on a back road, or do you have particular concerns?"

"I don't know. I'm a worrywart."

Dean smiled. "Nothing wrong with that. We'll keep an eye on her. To protect and to serve, that's what I'm here for."

"I'm very grateful, sir. And I'll be here, off and on. Next weekend, I'm going to borrow a big tent so we can camp out in the yard."

"Just check the weather first. Those spring rains can be frog chokers."

"Will do."

"Good man. Take care now," Dean said.

It sounded like a farewell. Like he thought everything was fixed, as fast as glue could mend a porcelain trinket.

Jack wanted to say, *Not so fast there, we might still need you,* but he settled for shaking hands. The car pulled away, the kids and Dean waved at each other, and Jack sat down again.

Miranda opened the door a crack and peered out. "I heard a siren."

He rose and motioned toward the rockers, but she didn't budge. "That was Deputy Dean, showing off for your young hoodlums. He'll swing by now and then to make sure you're okay."

"Jack, no! I don't need the sheriff's department on my doorstep."

"There you go again, acting like you're allergic to law enforcement."

"I just don't like...interference from the government."

"You've absorbed a little too much of Carl's attitude. Repeat after me, darlin': the policeman is my friend."

While she was still rolling her eyes at that, tires ran through the gravel again. Yvonne's car pulled around the curve.

"It's like Grand Central Station around here," he said. "Were you expecting Yvonne?"

Miranda stepped onto the porch, smoothing her skirt with one hand. "Yes."

"What's up?"

"You'll see."

Hauling a sequined tote bag, the family's gum-chewing guardian angel climbed out of her car, and the kids mobbed her. "Hey, everybody," Yvonne said. "I just saw Tom Dean leaving. Isn't he the nicest fella? He's been through a lot, that man." She smiled at Miranda. "Ready, hon?"

"I think so."

"Okay, clear the decks. Men and boys, y'all need to skedaddle."

"Excuse me?" Jack said. "Why?"

Yvonne parked her hands on her hips. "Because I said so."

He tried to sneak a peek into her tote. She whipped it behind her back.

"But what are you up to?" he asked.

"None of your beeswax." Yvonne popped her chewing gum. "Men and boys, shoo. Stay out of the house until you get the all clear. If you need a drink of water, there's a hose. If you need to eat, go to town. If you need to pee, pee in the woods. We don't want any men underfoot, but the girls can stay if they want."

"Stay, stay!" the girls shouted.

"I'm sorry, Jack," Miranda said. "It was a last-minute, now-or-never idea, and I thought it was important."

"Fine. Carry on."

"We will," Yvonne said, smiling. "As soon as the menfolk get out of our way."

Out of the corner of his eye, Jack saw that Timothy had come close enough to listen. "Is there a decent pizza place in town? Or Chinese?"

"Both," Miranda said.

"Do the boys like Chinese?"

"I don't know. Carl didn't like Chinese, so the children have never tried it."

Jack turned to Timothy. "What do you say? Chinese or pizza?"

Timothy surveyed his siblings with those cool blue eyes. "Pizza."

Of course. He was his father's son.

"Because if the girls aren't coming with us," Timothy added, "we should wait to get Chinese sometime when they can try it too."

Something melted in Jack's heart. He gave the boy a gentle cuff in the shoulder. "Good thinking, man."

Timothy was Miranda's son too.

Yvonne had brought another load of hand-me-downs. She asked the girls to fetch them from the car. When they raced outside, their braids swinging, Miranda knew she might never see them that way again, dressed alike in denim jumpers and braids. Another door was closing on the bittersweet past.

The girls struggled inside, lugging one huge, black trash bag between them. They dumped the bag's contents on the rug and began pawing through the clothing.

"There are some jeans that might fit you, Miranda," Yvonne said. "And some light sweaters, just right for spring. There's a beret. Some women can't wear hats, but I think you can."

Miranda's eyes misted. Auntie Lou had loved her hats. The other church ladies never wore hats except on Easter, but Auntie Lou wore them whenever she pleased. Plenty of jewelry too, inexpensive and glitzy. And flirty shoes.

"See how pretty?" Martha held up tiny jeans, embroidered with pink roses on the pockets and hem. Her face fell. "Oh. I forgot. Jeans are for boys."

Yvonne laughed. "Would your brothers wear jeans with pink flowers?"

"No!"

"Well, then. Those must be girls' jeans. Try 'em on, baby."

"Can I, Mama?"

"*May* I. Yes, you may. You too, Rebekah. Try some jeans. You may wear anything that's modest and appropriate for your age."

After a brief, shocked silence, the girls squealed. Rebekah pounced on a pair of flared jeans, slung them over her shoulder, and dug through the pile for more.

With no embarrassment about changing clothes in front of Yvonne, Martha wriggled out of her jumper and sat down to pull on the jeans. She stood up, conquered the zipper and snap, and ran a hand down her thigh. "It feels funny. Hey! We can climb trees better now."

"And ride bikes without getting our skirts caught," Rebekah said, running toward the bathroom with an armload of clothes.

Martha picked up a bright red T-shirt. "Is this one okay to wear? Pastor Mason says red isn't for ladies."

"You may wear any color that you find in creation," Miranda said.

"Huh?" Martha frowned, tilting her head first to one side, then to the other. "That's all colors."

"Exactly. God didn't make any bad colors."

Martha smirked. "See, Rebekah?" she hollered. "All my Valentine colors are good." With lightning speed, she stripped off her white turtleneck and replaced it with the red shirt. "Now I feel like a regular kid. I mean, child."

"It's all right to say 'kid,' too," Miranda said. "I know you're not a baby goat, even if you smell like one sometimes."

Martha went into gales of giggles, then found a pink beret, set it at an accidentally jaunty angle on her head, and ran off to look in a mirror.

"You'll have to steal that beret back," Yvonne said. "It'd be cute on you. Now, what's this business about red not being for ladies? Is that more of Mason Chandler's foolishness?"

"Do you know him?"

"Not personally, but word gets around. The man has a few screws loose."

"I think you're right."

"Why have you put up with his rules, then? Did your husband go along with them?"

"Yes. In some ways, Carl was stricter than Mason."

"Stricter than *that*? And I suppose you obeyed him, no questions asked."

Miranda checked to make sure the girls were out of earshot. They were, but she lowered her voice anyway. "Sometimes I disobeyed. Not often enough."

"Well, like my daddy used to say, if you obey God with your whole heart, you'll usually scare off the folks who want you to obey them." She chuckled. "I haven't heard him say that in years. He's like a broken record now, says the same thing every time and thinks it's a new word from the Lord. At least it's a good word."

"What do you think?" Rebekah romped around the corner, wearing a black T-shirt and sequin-spangled bell-bottoms that were years out of style.

"You're beautiful." Miranda's vision blurred. "No matter what you wear, you're beautiful, inside and out."

"I sure feel prettier in pretty clothes." Rebekah scooped up more clothes and ran for the bathroom again.

"You're beautiful too," Yvonne said, taking Miranda's chin and tilting it upward. "Inside and out. Hold your head high. There. That's it. I'd love to get a look at that preacher's face when he sees the new Miranda."

Miranda swallowed. Her new streak of independence might make Mason think twice about tangling with her, or it might only infuriate him. "Don't take too much off. Be careful."

Yvonne let go of Miranda's chin and began undoing her braid. "You've spent half your life being too careful. It's time to go for broke. Now, I've done hair for years. You let me have free rein, and I'll do you up right. I'm thinking something flippy and wild and a little on the messy side. You know what I mean? Good messy, not bad messy."

"Just leave it…long enough to play with."

Yvonne moved behind Miranda, freeing the last of her hair from the braid. "Jack will play with it, all right. He can't take his eyes off of you."

Miranda's face warmed. "You're crazy." Her scalp tingled, a strange combination of relief and pain.

"No, *he's* crazy." Yvonne lowered her voice when Martha came back. "He's crazy to be interested in the mother of six kids. But wait till we're done with you."

Miranda cleared her throat. "Martha, the bags of hand-me-downs Miss Yvonne brought us earlier are in my room. You and Rebekah may go ahead and see what you can find."

"Can I have the pink party dress?" Martha asked with longing written all over her face.

"Yes, sweetheart. You may have it."

Martha's mouth dropped open. She let out a squeak and ran for the bedroom. A normal, all-American girl in jeans.

Again, Miranda wanted to cry but couldn't understand why. "They'll never want to wear denim jumpers again."

"No great loss. Let's get started. My, my, this'll be fun. Jack won't know what hit him." Yvonne fluffed Miranda's hair and clucked like a cheerful hen. "I brought makeup. I brought nail polish. I brought perfume. Poor Jack. He's a goner."

Afraid a reply would lead to more teasing, Miranda didn't answer. She pulled a chair into the middle of the kitchen and sat, her pulse speeding. She hadn't had a real haircut since she was eighteen.

Yvonne reached into her tote and pulled out scissors, a comb, a squirt bottle, and a thin cape of shiny black fabric that rustled as she draped it over Miranda's shoulders.

"This is the only kind of cape I intend to wear for the rest of my life," Miranda said.

Yvonne laughed. "Amen. Face forward, baby. Chin up."

Miranda obeyed. She focused on a crooked line of hearts of all colors, taped to the refrigerator door, then on Martha's crayon drawing of a spiky yellow sun over a strip of green grass and gigantic pink flowers.

Directly below, under a daisy-shaped magnet, was the business card of R. Jackson Hanford, PhD, also known as Unkul Jack. A man who loved to dig for the truth.

Below Jack's card was Thomas Dean's, with a phone number scrawled in the white space between the simple silver-foil star of the sheriff's department and the intricate design of the county seal. She remembered him as a kind man, but he was part of the justice system. He had sworn an oath to uphold the law of the land. Like Jack, Dean was committed to digging up the truth. It was a lawman's job to bring lawbreakers to justice.

No doubt about it. She should have disobeyed Carl more often.

As Jack sat on a log a few feet from his latest fire, a sense of foreboding hung over him. Over the next few weeks, he had to make a gradual return to his normal life, and that meant leaving Miranda and the kids to their own devices, for the most part. He couldn't be in both places at once.

Besides, it was a Friday. The night that meant loss and grief and regrets.

Ava left him on a Friday. He'd found his mom on a Friday. His dad died on a rainy Friday afternoon. Even Jesus died on a Friday. Sometimes, it took until Sunday to remember that Sunday always came.

Jack checked his phone for the time, the silvery light nearly blinding in the darkness. He and the boys had come back from the pizza place an hour before, but they were still banned from the house. He didn't mind; it forced Timothy to participate in the outdoor festivities. The girls had joined them too. Everyone but Miranda and Yvonne had gathered around the fire.

Once in a while, Martha and Rebekah shared mysterious smiles with each other, then giggled and clammed up. They thought their secret was safe.

As if Jack hadn't noticed they wore jeans.

A great encouragement, those jeans. Now that Miranda's posse knew what freedom tasted like, they would wage war if she ever tried to drag them back to Mason's legalism.

As the fire's orange tongues licked the night sky, Jack entertained the bitter notion of burning Mason in effigy. Not a Christian thought, but it would have been a satisfying way to celebrate. Lord willing, the man's tyranny over Miranda and her family was over.

Jack had grand plans. He would come back on weekends. He'd take them to church—a mainstream church. He'd take them to Chattanooga sometime, to the aquarium. To the school, where Martha's eyes would light up at the sight of all those books in the library. There was the zoo. The Cooledge Park carousel. The river, the caverns, Lookout Mountain. They could spend the night at his house. His bachelor digs would come alive with noise and laughter.

He closed his eyes, imagining Miranda in his bed.

He pictured himself sleeping on the couch. The perfect gentleman. That couldn't last forever.

A minor commotion startled his eyes open. Over Jonah's grumpy protests, Timothy hauled him away from the fire.

"Not so close." Timothy situated his baby brother on one of the logs and returned to the outskirts of the circle to stand guard.

Jack tried to relax and absorb the peace of the mountains. Crickets chirped, the wind rustled the pines, and the children chattered around the fire.

Back at the house, an engine turned over. Headlights and red taillights wavered against tree trunks and vanished into the darkness. Yvonne had left.

Jack waited, not knowing if Miranda would stay inside or join them.

Time crawled. He couldn't stand it.

"Timothy, would you mind being in charge for a few minutes?"

"I don't mind."

"Thanks." Jack started toward the house. Nearly there, he looked behind him. Timothy, silhouetted against the fire, hadn't budged from his post.

Then Jack turned the corner, going around the house, shutting out the dim orange glow. Alone in the soft darkness, he found his way to the front. The porch light was off.

Then it was blazing in his eyes and he was blinking at a gorgeous blonde in jeans and a pale green sweater. Her hair swung freely, falling just to her shoulders in a sassy cut that simply couldn't have sprung from the scissors of a great-grandma.

Miranda shut the door behind her and stopped there, exactly where they'd first met. He'd been coming up the steps to knock when she'd ventured onto the porch. Upbeat, excited about meeting his brother, he'd talked about wanting family connections. Miranda had smiled, served lemonade, juggled two toddlers, and said how nice it was to meet a surprise brother-in-law. She hadn't said a word about having just lost her son.

Now her eyes asked...something. Jack stood motionless, trying to hear her unspoken question. What did she want from him? Or what did she want to give?

An invitation into the invisible box she'd built around herself. That was it. His doubts gathered wings and darted away like bats, back to the darkness where they belonged.

"Wow," he heard himself say from an echoing distance. "Jeans."

"I had to try on half a dozen to find some that fit."

As he urged his clumsy feet up the steps, he inhaled a light, flowery scent that challenged the smell of smoke on his clothes. Placing his hands on her shoulders, he thought he could feel the merging of their invisible boxes into a heady little universe of their own.

He leaned toward her but hesitated, giving her a chance to escape. Instead, she stretched up for a quick, awkward kiss that was all the sweeter because she'd initiated it.

"I'm out of practice." She let out a low, breathy laugh. "But practice makes perfect." Her hand found his shoulder and slid up toward his neck, and she tugged him into their second kiss.

It was much better than the first. Solidly on target. Warm and willing, on both sides.

He pulled away to study her. To savor her. Her face framed with a wild abundance of silky hair. Her lashes longer than ever, her big eyes shimmering with tears.

"A buckwheat cake was in her mouth," Jack sang, so softly that his voice cracked and wavered. *"A tear was in her eye. Says I, I'm comin' from the south. Miranda, don't you cry."*

"You didn't come from the south. You came from the north. But you came. You came when I needed you." She clamped her lips together, parted them long enough to say, "Thank you, Jack," and clamped them shut again like a dam against a flood.

He couldn't answer. He wanted to give back everything that had been stolen from her. But that wasn't something a man could say out loud. It was just something he would try to do.

For now, there was nothing to do but tease those pretty lips into a smile and kiss them again.

And again. And again. Forever and ever, amen.

twenty-seven

Saturday sped by, a blur of long conversations and stolen kisses. Miranda and Jack sat up late, talking, and when she'd finally gone to bed, she hadn't slept well. Plagued by nightmares of being trapped in a closet under a pile of stolen sweaters, she woke on Sunday with a stabbing headache.

Two reddish brown ibuprofen tablets lay on her palm. Jack had fished them out of his shaving kit for her. If she took them, they would be the first bit of *pharmakeia* she'd taken voluntarily since she was eighteen.

Of course she would take them. They might help her survive the Sunday service at a mainstream church Jack had picked from the phone book. He kept using that word, "mainstream," as if it were a guarantee against heresy.

He stood before the hall mirror, fussing with the tie he'd borrowed from Timothy. They were funny, those two. They were learning to get along, almost as if they'd always wanted to like each other and had now decided they could, except Timothy still retreated into sullen moods sometimes.

Miranda popped the tablets into her mouth with a swallow of water, then looked down at her dress of periwinkle blue. A matronly style from the hand-me-down bags, it was years out of date but better than the sacks she'd thrown out.

"I love, I love my twirly dress," Martha sang. Spinning in circles, preening and pirouetting like a little pink bird, she was oblivious to the fashion faux pas of wearing clunky brown shoes with a lacy dress.

Rebekah wore a simple jacket and skirt in a soft blue. Her shoes were wrong for her new outfit, and it was even worse in her case. Partly because she had big feet, partly because most girls her age would have known the shoes were wrong, but she didn't have a clue.

Miranda was afraid she'd ruined her children. They would be misfits forever. Other children would laugh at them.

She turned quickly to hide her tears from the girls and nearly crashed into Jack. She spun away before he could inspect her, but paid for it with a flash of vertigo.

"Lookin' good, y'all," he said. "Except for some cat hair here and there, everybody looks reasonably respectable."

She looked down at her own frumpy shoes, evidence she was living half in her new world, half in her old world. Her heart and her head were still making the transition into unknown and terrifying territory.

Jack picked a cat hair from her shoulder. "It's chilly out. Do you and the girls have coats?"

"Just capes. The girls would rather go without. They don't want to hide their pretty new clothes."

"And what about you, Mrs. H.?"

She made a face. "I guess I'll wear my cape. One last time."

He lifted the cape off its peg and draped it over her shoulders. Its weight was familiar. Comforting.

Stifling.

About to fasten it at her throat, she balked. "I'd rather freeze."

"I won't let you freeze." Jack whipped the cape off of her and dropped it on the floor. He took his rumpled raincoat off its peg and held it up by the shoulders. "May I interest you in the latest style? The menswear look." He waggled his eyebrows. "Capes are so last year, *dahling*."

She smiled and let him help her into the coat. He cuffed up the sleeves, fastened a few of the buttons, and motioned with one finger for her to spin around. She complied, laughing. Feeling like a little girl in a spinny dress.

Jack kissed her forehead and nudged her toward the door. "Let's go, troops," he called.

As Jack pulled the van onto the road, Miranda looked both ways for familiar vehicles. She let out a sigh of relief when the road was empty.

"Afraid someone's going to see you sneaking off to a different church?"

"Sometimes you're a little too perceptive, Jack."

"Trying a new church doesn't make you a rebel or a backslider or a traitor." He looked in the rearview mirror. "You need a little more of the rug rats' perspective. They're as excited as if we were headed for a carnival."

"I know, but it feels wrong. Like I'm abandoning my friends on a sinking ship."

"So? They can jump ship too."

Miranda lowered her voice. "What if this church's pastor is no better than Mason?"

"I'd guess that nine out of ten pastors are better than Mason. Most clergymen aren't in it for money or power. They're in it because they love God and people."

"I wish I could believe you."

"And I wish I could drag you up to 'Nooga this morning to meet my pastor. He's one of the good ones. I'd trust him with my life."

She stared ahead at the winding road, remembering the day she'd met Mason. She'd thought she could trust him. "How did you decide on the church we're trying this morning?"

Jack coughed. "I, uh, opened the phone book to the church listings and took a stab."

"You what?"

He ran a finger under his collar as if it had grown too tight. "You heard me."

"You steered me away from Yvonne's church because they believe in prophecies but you'll trust your fingers to pick the right church?"

"Yes ma'am. I'll let you have your hang-ups if you'll let me have mine. Deal?"

Miranda smiled and offered her hand. "Deal." They shook on it.

Neither of them spoke again until he pulled off the county road to a side road, and from there to the parking lot of a small, brick church surrounded by shade trees. At the front entrance, a man and a woman handed palm fronds to adults and children alike as they arrived.

"It's Palm Sunday," Jack said, swinging the van into a parking space. "I'd almost forgotten."

While he explained the tradition of palm fronds to the children, Miranda watched a middle-aged man help an elderly woman exit the passenger seat of a beat-up car in a handicapped spot. He maneuvered her walker so she could lean on it. Once she'd started moving, he pulled a black Bible and a large, pink purse from the front seat.

Then Miranda noticed his clerical collar. Matching the woman's slow shuffle, the pastor escorted her toward the building. He let her take her time, as if ministering to a frail and needy lamb took precedence over everything else.

In nine years of knowing Mason Chandler, Miranda had never seen him perform such a simple, humble task. Carrying a woman's purse was beneath Mason's dignity, even if that purse wasn't large and pink.

A purse-toting pastor certainly wasn't looking after his own interests.

A smile started deep within Miranda and made its way to her lips. Jack's fingers might have picked just the right church after all.

Jack knew he was leaving something undone. He just couldn't think what.

It wasn't as if he'd be gone for weeks and weeks, but an unfortunate con-fluence of deadlines and committee meetings required his presence in 'Nooga for at least four days. Maybe five.

He walked into the kitchen and cleared paper hearts from the refrigerator door so he had room to affix his phone number at a four-year-old's eye level. "Martha asked me to teach her how to leave a message," he told Miranda. "So I did. I'll leave my number here, just in case."

"Okay." Miranda paused in tidying the counter. "I hope she won't abuse the privilege."

"I don't think she will." He smuggled the hearts into the trash. Martha would never notice.

Sunday had slipped through his fingers in a hurry, half of it taken up with going to church. It had gone well, for the most part. Miranda liked the pastor, Jack's built-in heresy detector hadn't gone off, and they'd caught Jonah just before he pilfered a twenty from the offering basket.

Jack had spent the afternoon collecting his belongings, rounding up every last paper and sock and book that had migrated there with him. Now his bags were packed and loaded into the car. Only minutes remained before he had to leave. Only minutes to nail down whatever it was that he'd forgotten.

Circling the kitchen, mindlessly counting rafts of paper hearts, he remem-bered. "Microwave. That's it. I was going to run to Clayton and buy you a microwave."

"I haven't had one since college. I'll get along fine without it."

"It's the principle of the thing. You need to get over your fear of—"

"Fear? Jack, I've never been afraid of microwaves. That was Carl's notion. I just never got around to shopping for one."

"Sorry. I'll—I'll bring you one."

"You don't have to do that."

"But I want to. Will you remember to lock up at night?"

She gave him a wan smile. "We'll be fine. And don't start lecturing me again, professor."

"No, I won't. I've been thinking though. I'm glad you like this new church, but maybe you should ask Yvonne to put you in touch with some good, sane homeschoolers. They're everywhere. Big families, little families. Conservative and not so conservative. Most of 'em are some variety of nonconformist. You'll find some new friends."

"I'd say that nearly qualifies as a lecture."

"I'm sorry. Old habits die hard. Miranda, if you can only—"

"No wonder I have a hard time hearing God speak." Her voice rose. "There's always some man telling me what to do, and I can't hear God for all the noise!" She seized the broom that stood in the corner and started sweeping the floor.

"I'm sorry," Jack said. "Here, let me sweep."

"No."

"Please. It can't be good for your shoulder."

He moved behind her, encircling her with his arms and taking charge of the broom, his hands over hers. Bits of construction paper, crumbs of dried Play-Doh, even stray grains of rice from Martha's bridal spree several days ago. The floor was a mess, and he was inordinately grateful because it gave him more time to waltz across it in a broom dance with Miranda.

"*Waltzing Miranda, waltzing Miranda,*" he sang softly. At the last moment, he remembered to turn the line into a question: "*Will you come a-waltzing, Miranda, with me?*"

Her shoulders shook in a tiny, carefully controlled sob.

He stopped moving and leaned his head against hers. "Everything's going to be all right, darlin'." He brushed his lips against the nape of her neck and felt her shiver. Encouraged, he nuzzled her again. "You smell delicious."

Timothy walked in, quiet as a cat. Something flickered in his eyes. Surprise or anger or something worse.

Miranda froze. Jack held her more tightly, his lips poised to nibble her ear.

Jack took a breath. "Timothy, you can be loyal to your father but still let your mother move on with her life."

"Oh, yeah. You two are a great combination." Timothy curled his lip. "The guy who harps about digging for the truth, and my mother, who lied to me for years about Jeremiah."

"Show your mother some respect, young man, or you'll answer to me."

Miranda twisted out of his arms, and the broom clattered to the floor. "You're not in charge of disciplining my children."

Jack raised his hands. "Sorry. I was treating him the way I'd treat him if he were my own son."

"He's not your son, Jack."

"Yeah, *Jack,* I'm not your son." Timothy swaggered out of the kitchen.

Miranda's face was white. "I can't believe he said that."

"It's true. He's not my son."

"Not that. He called me a liar."

Jack rubbed his face with his hands, trying to squelch the doubts that kept plaguing him. Maybe it was better to be blunt.

"That's true too," he said. "You lied for years by keeping quiet. You deceived Timothy. You made him think he was going insane. He has every right to feel betrayed."

A small sound behind Jack proved to be Timothy at the table, his hands white-knuckling the back of one of the chairs and his eyes pleading. He wasn't a guard dog or the alpha male. He was a gangly, half-grown puppy.

"That's what I tried to say before, but it didn't come out right." Timothy's voice was rough but held no hint of mockery. "Thanks, Uncle Jack."

Uncle Jack. He was finally in, but he sensed that in some terrible way, Miranda was out.

"People die all the time," Timothy said. "Mrs. Perini's mother died, and the Tenneys' baby died, but their families still talk about them." Still gripping the seatback, he hunched his shoulders, shrinking into a younger, smaller version of himself. Frightened—yet brave enough to keep talking. "Why didn't you ever talk about Jeremiah before?"

Jack waited. If Miranda explained the fear that Timothy and Rebekah would have blamed themselves, Timothy surely *would* blame himself.

"That was your father's decision," Miranda said. "I didn't agree with it, but I obeyed."

"You mean he told you not to talk about Jeremiah?"

"Yes, he did."

"Why? What happened? Did you…hurt him or something?"

Raw pain flashed across her face. "We never would have hurt him. We loved him. We *loved* him, Timothy. We'll talk about it again, soon, and I'll tell you more. But not now."

Timothy nodded, leaving the room with his questions unanswered. Jack had never felt more kinship with the boy or more distance from Miranda.

His doubts winged back to roost in his mind. There were too many questions she had never answered to his satisfaction.

Even her good-bye kiss was tentative. When he let go of her, his heart felt as empty as his arms.

He walked down the steps and made the rounds of the children, giving each one a hug and steeling himself against Martha's tears. When he reached Timothy, they shook hands, man to man.

"You have my number," Jack said. "Call anytime. I mean that. And would you like some of my dad's history books? I'd like to pass them on to you."

Timothy shrugged.

"You're his grandson," Jack said. "I think he would have liked for you to have them. I can bring them next time I come."

"You're coming back?"

"Of course. I couldn't not come back."

Slowly, Timothy nodded. His eyes warmed. "Okay. I'd like the books."

"Then I'll bring them." Jack surveyed the semicircle of grave faces. "Cheer up, y'all. I'll be back in a few days. Be good."

He climbed into the car amid a chorus of good-byes. Miranda stood alone on the porch, leaning her shoulder against one of the pillars.

He turned the key in the ignition, then looked back at the porch and counted the blond heads he'd first counted in a family photo, before he met the younger kids. He'd wished then that Timothy had a smaller number of siblings.

Jack shook his head. Now, he wished Timothy had just one more. Jeremiah.

The younger kids were still clumped together, waving, but Timothy stood apart. As wary and watchful as a Border collie guarding a flock of sheep. Quiet, canny, determined. He might have been capable of helping his mother stand up to the wolf, except he was only twelve.

twenty-eight

I n the checkout line at the Slades Creek Kroger, Miranda tucked her checkbook into her purse and imagined drawing a big red *X* across another day on her calendar. In a little over twenty-four hours, Jack would be back in town.

She dreaded his visit.

She hated the way he'd looked at her just before he left for Chattanooga. Timothy was acting chilly too. Neither of them trusted her, but she couldn't offer apologies or explanations until it was safe or at least until it was over.

The red-haired bag boy made short work of pushing her cart out to the van in the warm sunshine, then loaded the bags into the back and closed the door. "Have a nice day, ma'am."

"Thanks." She dug in her purse for keys. "You too."

The boy looked so nice and normal. And—she smiled despite her worries—so did she. Even the checker had noticed her new haircut and the jeans that felt like her personal Declaration of Independence every time she put them on.

"Miranda, wait!" Abigail scuttled between parked vehicles, her long skirt flapping and her face as pink as if she'd run a block.

Miranda scoped out the parking lot, her heart pounding, but didn't see Mason anywhere. Not that her jeans should matter, but a Declaration of Independence could start a war.

"I can't talk long," Abigail said, breathing hard. "Mason's at the bank. He'll pick me up in a couple of minutes." She stopped a few feet away. "I didn't recognize you at first."

"Is it too much?"

"No. You look wonderful." Abigail waved her hand at her hot cheeks. "Mason's still fixing up the house to sell. He's scheduled another workday on Saturday. I'll try to slip away while he's distracted. Even if he figures it out, he can't stop me with people watching."

"*This* Saturday? The day after tomorrow?"

"Yes, and if you'd like to tell everybody why, be my guest. Just wait until I've had a decent head start."

Miranda felt faint. She'd wanted it to happen soon, but now it was happening too fast. And she was losing Abigail.

"Does Mason keep the notes he takes in counseling sessions?" she asked.

Abigail frowned. "I suppose so."

"But does he hang on to files from years ago? If he does, could you find mine? And Carl's?"

"I don't know. He has so many file cabinets, and I don't know how they're organized."

"Could you look though? Please? Just open some drawers, take a quick peek?"

"If he caught me at it… Miranda, they're confidential. I've never even wanted to look."

"I'm not asking you to read anything. Just bring me anything with my name or Carl's. Why would Mason need them anymore? Abigail, please."

Abigail regarded her doubtfully. "All right. I'll call if I find them, but there's not much time left. Not many chances to call either. He's always there, always listening." She moved closer, lowering her voice. "Don't share my plans with anybody until I'm on my way. Promise me."

"I promise."

"Thank you." Abigail was still breathing hard.

The bag boy had rounded up half a dozen stray shopping carts. He pushed them past, their wheels rattling and shaking on the rough asphalt.

A louder rumble drowned out the racket of the carts. The pale blue flank of Mason's truck crept forward, taking the empty parking spot beside Miranda.

Her fingers like ice, she dropped her keys. She stooped to pick them up, then straightened, turning her back on the truck.

She was torn. Part of her wanted to tell Mason she knew what he was doing. It was all about sex, money, and power, like Jack had guessed.

Part of her only wanted to run.

"Go," Abigail said. "Or he'll take it out on me."

Miranda moved faster than she'd moved in weeks. By the time Mason climbed out of his truck, she was behind the wheel of her van. She started the engine, looking through the dirty windshield.

Abigail stood stolidly in her baggy dress and old-lady shoes. Mason hurried around his truck's hood and stopped beside her, trim in his black trousers and white shirt. The wind ruffled his hair, softening his immaculate appearance and giving a glimpse of the handsome young man who'd married homely Abigail. She must have loved him so.

Miranda had once thought his eyes were a striking, silvery blue, but they were only the same faded shade as the peeling paint on his truck. His hold over her had weakened. He had no authority over her.

Yet he had all the power he needed. He knew about Jeremiah.

Moving closer, Mason held up his forefinger as if to ask her for a moment of her time.

She hit the gas. She would not give him one more moment of her life until Abigail was safely away.

The campus, nearly deserted on Good Friday, had been the perfect place for catching up on writing, research, and administrative paperwork. Jack could breathe easier again.

His mental energies had already shifted toward the weekend and a ramshackle log home rich with children. A domain ruled by a peasant-princess with dazzling blue eyes and heavy burdens.

He missed her. And the kids. Even Timothy. Miranda's oldest boy had called with a question about a school assignment, and they'd progressed from awkward silences to a friendly argument about the necessity for book reports. Neither of them had mentioned the tension between Timothy and his mother.

"It's quittin' time," Jack said, shuffling piles of papers on his desk.

An early escape meant hitting Slades Creek while he still had some daylight for pitching the tent. And he'd be so busy that the Friday night demons wouldn't have a chance to catch his ear.

He gathered a batch of papers and stuffed them into his briefcase. Once he'd locked up, he strode toward the side exit.

"Jack!"

Farnsworth. Farther down the corridor, between Jack and the exit, she conversed with a custodian but held up one finger to tell Jack he'd better not run off.

He suppressed a groan but told himself to be patient. In five minutes, tops, he'd be out of Farnsworth's clutches. On his way to Miranda.

He walked down the hall, remembering her curves in her jeans. How her waist felt in his hands. The downy blond hairs at the nape of her neck. The way her shoulders relaxed when he kneaded them with his fingers. Her shoulders were always so stiff.

Your shoulders are hard as bricks, he'd told her once.

Life is hard as bricks, she'd answered with a—

"Jack."

"Uh—huh?" He'd almost walked right past Farnsworth.

Her eyes bored through the thick lenses of her black-rimmed glasses. She'd dismissed the custodian. "Are you catching up on your work?" she asked.

"I'm getting there."

A short woman, she could still make a man feel she was looking down on him. "Last time I saw your desk, it was a disaster."

"There's always a backlog."

"You're more trouble than you're worth."

"I know. Thank you." He consulted his watch with exaggerated interest. "If you'll excuse me, I need to hit the road."

"I presume you're going down to Georgia for the weekend."

"Yes, I am." His phone vibrated, and he checked it. Miranda's number. One of the kids, probably; they called more often than she did. He let it go to voice mail. He'd call back once he'd ditched Farnsworth.

She dogged him down the hall, slowing his flight. "It seems you're quite smitten with your hillbilly homeschoolers."

"They're not hillbillies. The six-year-old reads on the high school level. The eight-year-old has a flair for writing like you wouldn't believe, if you can make him sit still. And the four-year-old…"

He patted his shirt pocket to hear the rustling of the blue paper heart. Miss Martha loved her Unkul Jack. It was one of the highest honors he could ever hope for. He might even consider finding work closer to Slades Creek. Closer to Miranda and the kids. Jobs were scarce, but so were good women, and it wasn't as if he'd be giving up a position at Yale.

He'd be giving up Dr. Vera Farnsworth.

She snapped her fingers. "Jack! You're drifting off. Acting like a teenager in love."

"I'm in love with the whole family. Good night." He broke into a run before she could think of some complication to throw in his path.

Outside, unlocking his car, he checked the sky. A storm had been threatening all day, but it kept backing off, changing its mind. With some luck, it wouldn't hit Slades Creek, miles away.

The trunk and the backseat of his car were crammed with borrowed camping paraphernalia, sleeping bags, and an eight-man tent that smelled of old suns and old rains. In the trunk, he'd stashed some of his dad's history books and the impulse buy for Miranda.

No, he couldn't call it an impulse. He'd hovered over eBay for days, nervous as a cat until the prize was his.

He was only two miles from the turn for Slades Creek when he remembered the incoming call from Miranda's number. Keeping one hand on the wheel, he put his phone to his ear and listened to the recorded message.

"Uncle Jack?" It was Martha, still timid about this new voice mail business. "Hi? Uncle Jack? Hurry up and come home."

"I'm almost there, sweetie." He wished she could hear him.

The recording continued. "Mama's been crying a lot. She's sad and she's mad, but she won't tell me why." Martha sniffled. "Okay, bye."

He stomped on the gas, trying to outrun his doubts about Martha's mama. Those doubts mingled with memories of his own mama, who'd done most of her crying in private.

Eleanor Hanford hadn't had a tender-hearted four-year-old to help her through. She'd only had a thirteen-year-old who'd let her down.

"God, help," Jack said. It was a Friday. Good Friday.

Catching a glimpse of Miranda just around the first bend of the driveway, Jack made the engine growl through a downshift to grab her attention. She turned, holding a handful of mail. Her hair whipped by the wind, she put up her thumb to hitch a ride and gave him a smile that seemed artificially bright.

He braked beside her and reached over to open the door. "It's a blustery day for hitchhiking, Mrs. H."

"It's a blustery day for anything, Dr. H." She climbed in, the puffiness around her eyes confirming Martha's message.

Still hanging on to his smile, he pounced, trying to lose himself in the warmth of Miranda's embrace. She cradled his head in her hands and kissed him as fiercely as he was kissing her.

She drew back and studied him. "What's wrong? The worry in your eyes…it worries me."

"No, you've got this all backward, darlin'. I'm fine, but Martha tells me you've been crying. May I ask why?"

"When did you talk to Martha?"

"I didn't, but she left a voice mail. Answer my question."

"As you like to remind me, I'm recovering from a brain injury, and moodiness may be part of the package. Let me be moody, please."

"There's moody and then there's moody. Martha said you were sad and mad but you wouldn't tell her why."

"I'm more mad than sad, and you're making me madder."

"Good," he said. A woman with a lot of fight left in her wasn't as much of a worry. "But who are you mad at, besides me?"

"None of your business. You're not all sweetness and light either. What's wrong?"

"Nothing."

"Baloney. If you're going to use Martha's gossip against me, I'll use it against you. She told me you did something really, really bad, and that's why you're sad."

"I am not—"

"In your eyeballs," Miranda said, leaning closer. "She told me you're sad in your eyeballs, and she's right."

He drew back, afraid she would try to poke his eye like her daughter had. "Everybody has something to be sad about sometimes. Everybody makes mistakes. Or call them sins."

"Oh, no. You don't mean…"

"Whatever you're imagining, it's wrong."

Turning away from her penetrating stare, he flashed back…how many years? Forty minus thirteen. Twenty-seven years had passed since a nerdy kid walked through the door of his mother's house with his books and clothes for the weekend.

Hey, Mom, I'm here. Where are you? Mom…Mom?

The blue parakeet, dead in its cage. The cat, frantic with hunger. The light left on in the bedroom.

The neighbor was the first to realize something terrible had happened. Mr. Olson dropped his garden hose and raced to the porch where Jack stood, screaming. The water ran endlessly to the street, into the gutter. Even after the cops came, the water kept running. That image was seared on Jack's brain as clearly as the other. He still couldn't see water swirling into a storm drain without remembering the rest.

Miranda touched his cheek. "Jack, tell me. Or did you do something so horrible that you can't?"

"It wasn't anything I did."

A squirrel flounced across the driveway, tail waving like a flag, then scrambled up the trunk of a pine. A crow cawed, far away.

Miranda took Jack's chin in her hand and tried to make him face her. "Why do you feel guilty then?"

"It was something I didn't do."

"What didn't you do? Come on. I told you about Jeremiah. It's your turn."

True. She'd leaned against him and cried, that night beside the fire. She'd told him a tale that had ripped her heart in two. She'd earned the right to ask for his honesty.

"It's nothing recent," he said. "It was years ago."

She moved her hand to his arm and squeezed it. "That doesn't make it go away though. Who was involved in this situation, whatever it was?"

"My parents." There was no retreating now. "They split up when I was thirteen. I lived with my dad—he was the fun parent—and spent weekends with my mom. I've heard you say Timothy and I have a lot in common. Well, we each had a mother who needed help. But Tim did the right thing, the responsible thing. He got out of bed, early in the morning, and followed you to the cliffs because he worried about you. Me? I couldn't be bothered to make one phone call for my mom's sake."

"Why? What happened?"

"She was all alone from Monday to Friday. Alone except for a cat and a parakeet. She took a wicked assortment of pills sometimes. Sleeping pills, antidepressants. And she was careless about dosages."

"No," Miranda breathed.

"I showed up on a Friday night and found her lying across the bed. There were pill bottles on the nightstand."

"Oh, Jack."

He adjusted the rearview mirror, tried to lose himself in the peaceful reflection of pines lining the driveway. "Maybe it was an accidental overdose. Maybe not. She didn't leave a note. But whether it was deliberate or accidental or accidentally on purpose, I could have stopped it."

"Maybe, maybe not."

"I could have tried at least. Some people say they listen when God speaks. I didn't even listen to my own common sense. Common sense told me my mother needed help. Common sense told me to tell an adult—my dad or a teacher—anybody—but I didn't want to look like a fool if it was all my wild imagination. I didn't speak up; I didn't act; I didn't do anything. I kept quiet until there was nothing to do but pray for her. I still do."

"Pray for her? Isn't she…"

"Dead? Yes."

"You pray for the dead?"

"Don't sound so shocked. Luther prayed for the dead too. 'Dear God, if this soul is in a condition accessible to mercy, be Thou gracious to it.' That's in Luther's writings. It's no secret."

"You said it so mechanically. Like you've prayed those words a million times."

"Maybe I have."

Her hand tightened on his arm. "Oh, Jack. I see what you've been doing. You have such a tender conscience."

He frowned, flicking a speck of lint from his knee. "What are you talking about?"

"You haven't been praying for your mother. You've been praying for yourself. Asking God to have mercy on *your* soul. Because you feel responsible."

"Because I am." He escaped her grip, started the engine, and rocked the gearshift into first.

"Says who?"

"Says God, apparently. Yvonne's senile father keeps prophesying over me, and it's spot-on."

Miranda's expression held more amusement than was appropriate for such a grim conversation. "I thought you didn't believe in that. But if it was spot-on… Do you remember what he said?"

"'Silence is brother to lies,'" he said. "'The truth is sister to mercy. This time, say the words you've been given to say. Do the deeds you've been given to do. This time, hear Me and obey.'"

Miranda's smile faded. "That's almost generic. It could apply to you, me, anybody."

"Sure it could." He tried to speak lightly.

Her eyes were haunted again with that thing he couldn't name. "If anything happens to me, will you still be the guardian of the children?" she asked.

"Now you're both moody and morbid. The combination worries me."

"I'm not being morbid."

"That phrase, 'If anything happens to me,' popped into your head for no good reason?"

"Answer my question about being the guardian, please."

"Yes, of course, I would still be the guardian of the children, but why—"

"Thank you, and never mind why." She settled back in her seat. "I wish we weren't doing a campout tonight. I'm just not in the mood for it."

"Neither am I. Not while you're playing this game, Miranda. What's going on?"

"I don't know yet," she said, barely audible above the idling of the engine. "I don't know."

"That's hardly a reassuring answer. Look at me, please."

She wouldn't meet his eyes.

twenty-nine

Barefoot, Miranda slipped out of her bedroom at dawn. She wished she could fly to the end of the day with her children and keep them safe forever.

Abigail hadn't called about the files. Maybe she never would.

Holding her breath, Miranda tiptoed past the couch where Jack still slept beneath that ratty old quilt. The first one she'd ever made, before she'd started making baby quilts.

At the front door, she flicked off the security lights and unlatched the dead bolt. The door creaked as it swung open, but Jack didn't stir.

She stepped onto the porch and shut the door. Everything was a murky shade of gray except her van looming like a great white dinosaur. Jack's car sat beside it. Having decided to postpone the campout for a day, he'd smuggled the camping gear into the shed after dark. The children still didn't know a thing about it.

Miranda slipped her feet into her gardening shoes and crept down the steps. She longed to walk all the way to the cliffs, but the garden would be private enough if she kept her voice down.

She stole around the side of the house and made her way across the grass to the garden. Then, pacing up and down the rows where last year's crops had grown, she tried to pray.

Her worries refused to make room for prayers.

She stopped at the end of the row, where a few sunflower stalks still stood. Breathing deeply, she tried to clear the cobwebs from her mind.

She didn't want to uncover anybody's sins, but she wanted to live free. She wanted the church to live free too.

Birds were waking in the woods, in the brush, in the sky. As dawn began to color the clouds behind the black bulk of the mountains, Miranda lifted her face to heaven.

"God, that crazy prophecy...it's for me. I'll say the words You've given me to say. I'll do the deeds You've asked me to do. I'll do what I can—if You'll help me. Please help me."

She didn't wait for an answer. Committed to her plan, she walked back through the garden. When she was nearly at the house, she heard the phone.

Nobody ever called this early. It had to be Abigail.

Miranda clomped up the steps, no longer worried about noise. The phone would have woken Jack already. She kicked off her shoes, leaving them on the porch, and ran into the living room.

The couch was empty. The quilt lay crumpled on the floor with the kitten tottering across it.

Jack stood in the kitchen in his flannel sleep pants, the phone to his ear, his hair wild. He squinted sleepily at the kitchen clock.

"This is Jack," he said into the phone. "Who's this?"

She hurried to his side. "It's for me." She would have yanked the phone out of his hand except she recalled too clearly what it felt like to receive that kind of treatment.

"Mmm-hmm," Jack said. "She's right here." He handed her the phone.

"Hello," Miranda said.

"Sorry it's so early," Abigail said in a low voice. "I had to call before Mason woke up."

"Did you find—" Miranda stopped.

Jack moved across the room to turn on the coffee maker. And he stayed there, making no effort to give her any privacy.

"Yes," Abigail breathed. "Come over about ten."

"Thanks," Miranda said, trying to sound cheerful and calm. "See you then."

She hung up the phone. Avoiding Jack's eyes, she walked over to the refrigerator and rearranged a couple of paper hearts. And the two business cards.

"I need to run an errand this morning," she said. "About ten. I'll leave the children with you. It won't take long."

"What's going on?"

"I need to drop something off for Abigail."

"What kind of something?"

"Don't you remember what curiosity did to the cat?" She held her breath. The coffee maker gurgled. Bare feet padded up behind her.

Jack gripped her shoulders. "Hard as bricks. You're up to something."

"I'm dropping off a sweater."

"Yeah, let me get this straight. Abigail called about a sweater? At this hour? Must be some sweater."

"I'm dropping off a sweater," she repeated. "You can stay here with the kids."

Jack tugged her away from the refrigerator, turned her around, and searched her eyes at close range. "You want me to stay with the kids and be prepared to be their guardian in case anything happens to you?"

"Don't put words in my mouth."

"Those are your own words, and they're worrisome. And now you're going to Mason and Abigail's house by yourself?"

"I won't be by myself. Half the church will be there for a workday."

"Then you'll be outnumbered."

"Stop, Jack. You're making it sound like a battle."

"If 'it' is only an errand, you wouldn't even think in those terms."

Afraid of digging herself in deeper, she didn't answer.

"Has your doctor cleared you to drive?" Jack asked.

"No, but it's only a few minutes away. On back roads. It'll be fine."

"Tell you what." Jack put his arms around her and pulled her close. "I'll play chauffeur. I'll ask Yvonne if we can drop the young 'uns off at her house for a while."

Miranda opened her mouth to argue, then nearly cried with relief instead.

If the children were at Yvonne's, a social worker wouldn't know where to find them.

It was almost ten. Standing by the bedroom window with Abigail's red pullover tucked inside a Walmart bag, Miranda tilted her head and listened for the van. Jack would be back soon from delivering the children to Yvonne.

Springtime had arrived overnight. The sun shone, the air was warm, and the ornamental cherry tree had burst into bloom. Every year, when the pale pink blossoms were at their thickest, she loved to lie on the grass and stare up at them. Sometimes a gust of wind blew a flurry of petals into the air, and they would fall like pastel snowflakes.

They weren't quite at their peak yet. Maybe tomorrow.

She didn't know where she would be tomorrow, but within an hour, her conscience would be free. As free as the fresh air that streamed into her bedroom.

When Jack had muscled the window open for her, he'd said something about the smell of sunshine. Of course sunshine had no smell, but that was so typical of Jack.

He'd been laughing too much, talking too much. Stealing too many kisses. A kiss for *good morning* and *here's your coffee* and *one more time just to be sure.* Whatever he'd meant by that. She could see right through his flirtations to his worries.

It wouldn't be fair to tell him everything. He would know soon enough, but to keep him out of trouble, she had to go it alone.

She caught part of her reflection in the window and sized herself up. Jeans, a lightweight blue pullover, and a touch of the makeup she'd bought at Kroger. It was beginning to feel all right. Like it wasn't sinful.

She heard the van rolling up in front of the house.

"God, make me brave." Taking the Walmart bag and her huge, straw-colored purse, the biggest one she owned, she went outside. She locked up and tucked the house key into her pocket.

Having abandoned the van, Jack was lowering the convertible's top. He gave her a wolf whistle.

"Stop that," she said.

"Make me."

This, perhaps, was what Mason had always warned against. The lust of the eyes, the lust of the flesh, the pride of life. She and Jack had been acting like giddy teenagers, even in front of the children. But under it all, for her, lay the sharp taste of panic.

Then they were off. Her hair blew free in the wind, too short to be restrained in a braid.

She found herself clinging to the Audi's seat like she'd clung to it on the ride home from the hospital. She hadn't trusted Jack's driving. She hadn't trusted his heart, but she'd had no one else to lean on.

Today, she wished the ride could go on all day, with no worries. But they pulled onto Hollister Road in no time and wound around the curve that led to Mason and Abigail's house.

Jack parked at the end of a line of vehicles on the shoulder. Abigail had left her car at the foot of the gravel drive where she couldn't be blocked in.

Bringing her purse and the Walmart bag, Miranda walked up the steep slope, hand in hand with Jack. A chain saw buzzed and a hammer spanked wood. An extension ladder leaned against the side of the house; a couple of the men were on the roof, replacing shingles. Robert and Wendy's muscular teenage son, Matthew, knelt at the front door, painting it a dignified shade of dark green. Led by Wendy, a handful of women and girls planted lavender and yellow pansies along the walk and around the birch tree on the lawn. Judging by the number of vehicles at the road, there must have been dozens of people working inside.

Good people, all of them. Godly, loyal, hard-working, kind, they obeyed God the best way they knew how. Miranda wondered, though, how many of them had confessed painful, private secrets to Mason, as she had done. Half the church might be afraid to cross him.

Wendy and a few others smiled and said hello, but Miranda caught some curious glances as people sized up her new look and the man by her side. Thankful for the warm reassurance of his touch, she looked up at him—just as he looked down at her.

"You can't fool me, Mrs. H. You're not just dropping off a sweater."

"I'm picking something up as well. Do you see Abigail anywhere?"

"She's in the garage."

"Wait here. I'll be right back."

Abandoning him on the gravel, Miranda walked into the open garage, careful not to appear hurried. Abigail stood at the rear amid moving cartons. She held a large cardboard box full of odds and ends. A wicker basket, a tarnished copper tea kettle, a dented cookie sheet. Donations for the thrift store—or cover for the last few items she needed to smuggle to her car.

"I'm glad you made it," Abigail said, as serene as ever. "The things you wanted are tucked behind the cookie sheet. Go ahead, reach in. You'll find them."

"Oh, thank you," Miranda breathed.

She found two file folders labeled with her name and Carl's. She opened the one marked with her name and recognized her own words written in

Mason's crisp, square printing. He'd always been a stickler for neatness and accuracy.

Her hands shook as she hid the files in her gigantic purse. Without revealing the Walmart bag's contents, she tucked it into Abigail's box.

"Make sure you take the bag all the way to your destination," Miranda said, keeping her voice low. "I'm returning something that belongs to you."

"Thank you, dear." Abigail smiled, but the strain showed.

"Are you all right?"

"Yes. I've already said all I can say, but his heart hasn't changed." Her eyes snapped with anger. "I could have picked a different time, but this is perfect. He'll have to explain my disappearing act." She set the box down long enough for a hug so quick that nobody would have noticed if they hadn't been looking at exactly the right moment.

"Good-bye," Abigail whispered. Taking the box, she walked into the sunlight, right past Jack, who waited on the driveway. He nodded. She nodded back and kept going.

Miranda rejoined him, her heart pounding.

"What's going on?" he asked.

"Just watch. And don't get involved, whatever you do."

As casual as could be, Abigail proceeded to the middle of the lawn. She looked up at the men on the roof, then at the women working in the flower beds.

"I hope you all know how wonderful you are," she said.

Some of the women smiled at her; some kept their eyes on their work.

"I love you all," she added in a brisk tone, "and don't you ever forget it." She shifted the box in her hands. "Has anybody run across any more boxes marked for the thrift store?"

"Not me," somebody called back.

"All right then," Abigail said. "I'll put this one in my car."

It was hardly an award-winning performance, but it served its purpose.

Her shoulders squared, she walked down the steep slope, her skirt swaying with her gait and her old-lady shoes sending bits of gravel flying. She disappeared behind the curving line of dark pines. Moments later, the Buick's engine came quietly to life, its sound muffled by the belt of trees. No one paid attention.

Abigail was on her way. Miranda had no more excuses. Even if DFCS swooped down on her house, they wouldn't find the children, who would be either with Yvonne or with their legal guardian. Safe.

She heard Robert Perini's gentle voice and looked over her shoulder to confirm it. His gray hair sprinkled with sawdust, he'd joined Wendy on the lawn. They shared a smile of approval as they surveyed the flower planting.

Miranda looked up at Jack. "I wish I'd been able to tell you everything days ago," she said quietly. "Weeks ago. Years ago. But it wouldn't have been fair to you."

His forehead wrinkled. "Would you please speak in plain English?"

Define terms, she thought, lightheaded. *Dig for the truth. Earn it, and you'll own it.*

"The truth is coming out. About a number of things." She stopped, wishing she could halt time long enough to be sure she knew what she was doing. No. She could only proceed. "Jack, do me a favor, please. Take out your phone and dial a number."

He pulled his phone from his pocket. She recited the number she'd memorized as she'd sat facing the fridge with that shiny black cape over her shoulders.

Frowning, Jack placed the call and lifted the phone to his ear. "Who am I talking to?"

"Not you. Me. I'm doing the talking." She held out her hand. "Please."

"Darlin', I've just about had it with your little mysteries," he said, but he relinquished the phone.

Thomas Dean answered, and she spoke into a cell phone for the first time in her life.

thirty

Jack was convinced of it this time. His ears had gone bad. Miranda could not have called the cops—on herself—for some vague, generic crime.

"That's right, 3742 Hollister Road. I'll be here." She handed the phone back.

Numbly, he hit the "end call" button. "What do you think you're doing?"

"Taking away the weapon he's been using against me."

"Who?"

"Mason. They'll believe him, they'll follow him, unless I deal with him. Once and for all." She made a slashing gesture with her hand. Her purse gaped open, revealing manila folders.

"What the—"

She placed one finger on his lips. "Hush. It's my turn to talk. Let me handle this. I mean it, Jack. Don't get involved."

With her head held high, she walked across the grass and onto the porch steps. She drew some looks, but she also caught friendly smiles from the friend with the baby bump and her pale, shy daughter who'd baked those dreadful sourdough muffins. The Perini women.

Miranda stood tall on the top step, her jeans and bright sweater in sharp contrast to the drab dresses and skirts of the pansy planters. "Don't move to McCabe," she said in a clear, strong voice.

In front of her, a ripple of surprise ran through the pansy brigade. Behind her, the teenager lowered his paintbrush and frowned at her back.

"Ladies, don't let your husbands sell your homes," she said. "Don't let them quit their jobs. Mason never had a word from the Lord. Mason had a word from Mason, and it was: *Run*."

A tall woman, a formidable tower of denim, stepped out of the ranks with a pot of bright yellow pansies in her hand. "Miranda Hanford, you should be ashamed of yourself. Touch not the Lord's anointed."

All stony determination, Miranda kept going. "Mason is a wolf in sheep's clothing. He—" She stopped.

The wind had picked up, slapping the halyard against the flagpole in a repetitive, annoying jangle. Clamoring for attention, it competed with Miranda, but she'd stalled.

She looked at Jack, her eyes filled with tears and misery. "I can't do this."

"Yes, you can," he said, "if you should."

She studied her toes, then raised her head and addressed the crowd again. "Mason has been unfaithful to Abigail. I've spoken with her, and it's true."

Miranda's pregnant friend gasped, the color draining from her face. "It's Nicole, isn't it? I had a bad feeling about those two."

"Nicole," the woman's husband echoed quietly.

People standing nearby caught the name and repeated it on a dozen startled tongues.

"Nicole? What about Nicole?"

"I thought so…I saw things…"

"This explains…"

The pregnant woman, Wendy Perini, put her arms around her husband. They clung to each other. They were listening. They were giving Miranda her chance to speak, and Jack blessed them for it.

"It's over," Miranda told the crowd. "Mason's leaving town to keep it quiet. That's why he wants all of us to move. That, and he wants the tithes from the profits when we sell."

"Tithes," Jack said. "I knew it. Money, power, sex."

"Somebody needs to drag that man outside," Wendy said. "I want a word with him."

The teenager set his paintbrush on the lid of the paint can. "I'll get him, Mom."

He disappeared inside the house. One of the older women followed him at a run.

Miranda's shoulders sagged as if she'd spent all her energy. Jack tugged her toward the edge of the lawn. She gripped his arm with both hands, like Martha had clung to the newel post in fear of coyotes.

News of the drama in the front yard spread fast. People began to drift outside, through the half-painted front door and through the garage. One of the men on the roof climbed down the ladder and sat cross-legged on the grass, combing it with his fingers. Everyone watched the house and waited. The halyard smacked the flagpole again and again, clanging and banging like an alarm bell.

The tall woman in denim began gathering like-minded people to her side. She twisted her hands together, over and over, speaking quietly. Rallying her troops. But an equal number of people drifted away from her, toward Miranda and the Perinis.

The church divided itself into two camps, about equally matched. A few people, including the man who sat combing the grass with his fingers, remained uncommitted.

The Perini boy exited the house, leaving the door open. "He's coming."

Mason stepped into the doorway. His pleasant smile faded as he took in his waiting audience. "What's going on?" He zeroed in on Miranda. "What are you doing here?"

Miranda disentangled herself from Jack. "Mason, would you tell us about your relationship with Nicole, please?"

Mason shook his head. "What relationship? You have an evil imagination."

"How do you know I wasn't asking about a pastoral relationship?"

He spread his hands wide, appealing to the crowd. "You know Miranda," he said. "She has a history of this kind of thing. Lies and insinuations."

"Oh, really," she said. "I do remember disagreeing with you about a number of things, but I don't recall lying about any of it." She turned toward the Perini couple. "Robert, you're in the inner circle. Do you recall that I told lies?"

"No," Perini said bluntly. "Never."

His wife kicked an empty plastic flowerpot, sending it onto the sidewalk with a shallow clatter. "Never," she echoed. "Miranda's not a liar."

Mason smiled sadly. "Come now, Wendy. You aren't privy to everything that goes on in this church. Neither are you, Robert. Trust me, though, when I say that Miranda's rebellion has been brewing for a long time. She wants to malign my good name, after everything I've done for her, and that hurts." His voice remained steady. Calm. He knew how to work a crowd.

"Listen up, folks," he continued in that friendly tone. "Miranda's been through a lot, and maybe she's a little unhinged right now. She needs our prayers, not our condemnation."

Perini let go of his wife and closed in on Mason. "I don't think you're telling the whole story. I'm starting to understand why Nicole left the church."

"Nicole left because she's a rebel with an attitude problem," Mason said.

Wendy Perini put her hands on her hips, accentuating her pregnant belly. "I should call and get her side of it."

Mason's Adam's apple bobbed, and he clenched his hands into fists. "Don't—don't you bother that young lady," he said, his face turning red. "She has nothing to do with Miranda's crazy stories."

"We'll see," Wendy said. "We'll see." She turned to Miranda. "Where's Abigail?"

Miranda shook her head. No one else tried to answer the question.

Mason's eyes darted every which way as murmuring spread through the remnants of his flock. Several of the younger women sat on the grass in a semi-circle. Some of them began to cry. A handful of men drifted out of the garage and stood in the sun, talking in low voices.

Apparently satisfied with the damage she'd wrought, Miranda returned to Jack. Taking his hand, she whispered in his ear. "I almost feel sorry for him."

"Don't," Jack said. "He doesn't deserve mercy."

"Neither do we. That's why it's called mercy."

Jack didn't know how to answer that.

The man who'd remained on the roof came down the ladder. He retracted it with a great metallic rattling, tipped it sideways, and gave a mocking salute to Mason. "I've heard enough. I've seen enough. You can finish your own roof."

"You don't understand," Mason said.

"I do," said the Perini kid. "I understand." He ran lightly up the steps, right under Mason's nose, and replaced the lid on the paint can. He had the same pale coloring as his old-maid sister, but the set of his jaw hinted that he'd be making his own decisions. "I'm done," he said.

The door was half green, half brown, with a few stray brush strokes of green encroaching on the brown. He left the door open and joined his parents and his sister on the grass.

The tall, denim-clad woman stalked up the steps to stand beside Mason, and a few of his other supporters joined her. Five men and three women, they huddled there with Mason, speaking quietly. Jack strained his ears but couldn't make out what they were saying.

Down on the road, a vehicle slowed. Silence fell, like the dark hush before the first drops of a rainstorm. No one spoke. No one moved.

Mason squinted toward the road, and his face changed. Smiling like a crafty fox, he waited.

About the time Jack had reached the end of his patience and was on the verge of saying something—anything—Mason cleared his throat and struck a pose like a politician on the campaign trail. Head high, chest puffed out, hands relaxed.

"Let's get back to Miranda's problems, shall we?" he said. "Why doesn't somebody ask her about her son who died? Her first son. The one she never talks about."

Jack wanted to storm the steps and pop the guy in the jaw. "That's off limits."

"It shouldn't be. She concealed the death of a child. Her own child. Check it out, Jack. There's a secret grave on her property."

"What?" Jack sought Miranda's eyes. "Concealed? Secret?"

She nodded her head, barely.

Stunned, he tried to process it. He'd assumed Jeremiah was buried in a cemetery somewhere, beside his father's grave. Legally. Or cremated, legally.

"A secret grave," Mason repeated. "That's a felony. Isn't it, officer?"

Tom Dean walked slowly onto the grass. His gun hung from his hip. Handcuffs too. They glinted in the sun. He stopped a few feet from Miranda.

The cavalry had shown up again. This time, it was on the wrong side.

Dean had never looked more mournful. "Mrs. Hanford, is there any truth to this allegation?"

"It's true," she said in a steady voice.

"Let's walk down to my car, ma'am."

Jack's mouth filled with a metallic taste, and he wondered wildly if Dean would read Miranda her Miranda rights. A sick joke.

Jack seized her arm. "She's not going anywhere."

"I'm sorry, Dr. Hanford," Dean said. "I can't pretend I didn't hear what I just heard in front of a crowd of witnesses."

"Don't interfere, Jack," Miranda said. "Please. Don't do anything to get yourself arrested. The children need you."

Dean gave him a warning look. "Let me do my job. Don't even follow us down to the road."

"Jack, I asked him to come," she said. "Remember?"

Numb, Jack nodded. He let go of her.

She faced Mason, who still stood on the porch. "This is my choice, not your revenge. So don't enjoy it." She dug into her pocket, pressed something into Jack's hand, and brushed his cheek with her lips. "I know I can trust you to take care of the children."

He found her house key in his hand. Finally, she'd given him his own key.

"Don't lose it," she added.

"Miranda, you can't do this."

"It's done."

"My car's down at the road, Mrs. Hanford," Dean said. "If you'd come with me, please."

She gave Jack a hug so swift that he hardly had time to hug her back, and then she walked away, her head high. In jeans, with that cute haircut and her big purse slung over her shoulder, she could have been a suburban soccer mom, except a deputy followed her, slightly to her left and back a few paces. At least he hadn't cuffed her.

"Lord, no." Jack came out of his daze and started after them, but a firm hand clamped his shoulder.

"Wait," Perini said. "Don't run off. Let's think it through. What can we do?"

Jack looked between Perini and his wife. "Can y'all vouch for the fact that Jeremiah's death was accidental, at least?"

They shook their heads in unison. "I never even knew she'd had a Jeremiah," Perini said.

Jack's throat went dry, and he ran, his feet pounding down the slippery gravel to the road. The patrol car was double-parked beside a black pickup. Dean had already shut Miranda in the backseat cage like a common criminal.

He'd set her purse on the trunk of the car and was leafing through one of those file folders.

"Dean!" Jack skidded to a halt beside the car.

Miranda stared through the window, her eyes huge. He placed one hand flat on the cold glass. She matched her hand to his, just for a moment, then lowered hers and looked away.

He remembered his written statement. *I, R. Jackson Hanford, will not report Miranda Hanford to DFCS or to any other government agency, for anything, so help me God.* Fat lot of good that did now that she'd reported herself.

He turned to Dean. "Help me out. What can I do? Who can I talk to?"

"An attorney might be helpful." Dean continued examining her papers. Slow as Moses.

"What's in the files? Did she tell you?"

"Yep, she told me." Dean closed the file and picked up her purse. It looked small in his big hand. "We'll be at the station. On the back side of city hall, right downtown."

No mention of checkers and coffee now. Dean was all business. He climbed into the car, slammed the door, and drove away. In the rear window, Miranda's head bobbed like a bird's as the car rounded the curve and caught a pothole. Then she was gone.

Hamlet's words wept in Jack's head. *There is special providence in the fall of a sparrow.*

"Not my sparrow. No."

He ran for his car.

thirty-one

Alexander Whitlow was out of town, and Miranda declined to use another attorney. No legal advice could have swayed her into telling her story any differently.

She remembered the sheriff's name from the last election. Dixon Sprague. Carl had voted for him. A good man, Carl had said. A believer, even if he didn't have the whole truth of God.

As if anybody did.

The air was chilly in the conference room. Or did they call it an interrogation room? The walls were bare, and the floor was dingy. A bleak place. So many people must have sat in the same chair, clinging to hope. Or losing it.

About the same age as Thomas Dean, Sheriff Sprague had that same cautious, slow-moving way about him, as if he had all day to search for answers.

A female deputy named Lucy Silva had done most of the questioning. She was thorough but not harsh, and she had a way of biting her lip before she asked the difficult questions. She'd already heard the whole story, but she kept circling back for more details.

Lucy bit her lip now. "Why, exactly, did Jeremiah run for the cliffs?"

Miranda had been dreading that particular question. "He disobeyed me about some little thing. He was afraid he'd get a whipping when Carl came home."

"Was Jeremiah expecting a particularly severe whipping?"

"When Carl gave a whipping, he meant business. He wasn't abusive though. He loved our children."

Lucy Silva exchanged glances with the sheriff. "What did you do when you arrived at the cliffs and saw that Jeremiah had fallen?"

"I tried to reach him, but I couldn't. I took Timothy and Rebekah and ran back to the house, screaming. Carl had just come home from work. I started to call 911, but he—he yanked the phone out of my hand and then pulled the line out of the wall."

Sprague frowned and wrote something on his notepad. He hadn't been talking much. Just frowning. Making notes. And referring to the files from Mason's office over and over, although each one held only three or four sheets of paper.

"Carl ran for the cliffs." A spasm shook Miranda. "He came back carrying Jeremiah."

Sprague made another note. "Don't go on until you're ready."

"Carl helped me prepare Jeremiah's body. He built a little pine coffin that night and dug the grave in the morning. We had a funeral service while the little ones were sleeping. Carl said there was nothing morally wrong with what we'd done, burying our own child on our own property. Legally though…" She stopped, searching for the right words. "He was so afraid that DFCS would take the younger children. He was strict, but he loved them. And we knew of good families who'd lost custody of their children because of anonymous and false accusations. Carl said it would be even worse for us. Jeremiah's home birth with an uncertified midwife was illegal. Not reporting his birth was illegal. So Carl didn't report Jeremiah's death either."

Sprague looked up. "I don't understand how you kept a five-year-old child's life and death a secret. Didn't anybody notice he was missing? Friends, family, neighbors?"

"We had just moved here. We hadn't met the neighbors. We hadn't found a church yet. We didn't have family. We still hadn't met Jack."

"Was Jeremiah the only one whose birth wasn't reported?"

"Yes. Starting with Timothy, we reported them all."

"What made your husband change his mind about that?"

"I convinced him that we'd have problems if our children grew up without Social Security numbers, but he never reported Jeremiah's birth. Carl was so afraid of the law."

"Whew." Sprague scanned his notes again. "Let me sum it up. Based on his religious beliefs and what I might call paranoia about the government, your husband neglected to notify the authorities when your first baby was born at home. Five years later, when that child ran from a whipping and died in a fall, your husband was afraid you would lose custody of the two younger children. He buried your son on your property and forced you to live as if your firstborn child had never existed. Is that accurate, Mrs. Hanford?"

"Yes, it is."

"Was your pastor involved in that decision?"

"No, it was my husband's decision. We didn't meet Mason until later. Carl made me go to him for counseling."

"Made you?"

"Carl thought I was suicidal. I wasn't. I was grieving for Jeremiah, but Carl wouldn't let me cry, even in our own home. Carl wouldn't even let me say his name. He wanted Timothy to forget Jeremiah, so nobody at all would remember him."

"Now you have six children, and none of them know about your first child?"

"I told them, not long ago, but they don't know the details. Nobody knows all the details except Mason and me. Please don't drag Jack into it. He had no idea that Carl and I did anything illegal."

"And today, with most of the church assembled for a workday at your pastor's home, he shared in public what you'd confessed to him in private. That you'd helped your husband conceal Jeremiah's death."

"Yes. I had just accused Mason of...moral failures. So I knew what was coming."

"You knew he would retaliate by revealing the problems that you'd shared with him in confidence? And that's why you'd already called my deputy?"

"Yes sir. I needed to get it off my chest anyway." She inhaled so deeply that her ribs hurt like they hadn't hurt in weeks. "Maybe I'll go to prison, but at least my children will go to their legal guardian—a man I trust—and not to DFCS. And I won't spend the rest of my life worrying that Mason will turn me in."

"Because you beat him to the punch. My, my." Sprague picked up the files and stood. "Excuse us for a few minutes, Mrs. Hanford." He stopped at the door. "Can I bring you a cup of coffee? It's always cold in here."

"No, thank you."

He and Lucy Silva left the room, closing the door softly behind them.

Miranda bent over the table, cradling her head on her arms. It was a mercy Auntie Lou had passed away. She wouldn't have wanted to see her great-niece behind bars.

Miranda prayed for her children and for Jack. She prayed for Abigail and for Nicole. And for the church. It would fall apart, the sheep scattered for lack of a shepherd. Robert and Wendy might try to hold things together, but why bother? There were larger, healthier churches that could take in what was left of the flock.

She even tried to pray for Mason—*pray for those who spitefully use you*—but she couldn't. Not yet.

It was a long time before Sprague and Lucy Silva entered the room again. He'd abandoned his notepad, but he carried Miranda's files and her purse. His sandy gray hair stood on end as if he'd scrubbed through it with a horse brush.

"Mrs. Hanford, I'm sorry we had to put you through all that," he said.

"It's all right." She hardly recognized her own voice, flat and faint.

"Small-town cops don't always play by the rules. Thomas Dean, especially, tends to make up his own rules as he goes along." Sprague sighed. "I've known him all my life, and he's a good man. I remember the day his daughter died."

"His daughter died?"

"Yes ma'am. Tom lost his little girl to an accidental drowning, and I remember what he and his wife went through when DFCS investigated." He met Miranda's eyes. "I've been chatting with Tom. The way he sees it, you've already been dealt a harsher punishment than any parent deserves. And any penalty given to you by the criminal justice system would fall on your children too. The last thing they need is to be deprived of your love and care."

She nodded uncertainly.

"As Tom put it to me, you violated the law, but under duress and when you were in shock. One look at the contents of these files, and any defense attorney worth his feed would call this a clear case of psychological abuse. I may need to speak with the DA, but he's an intelligent man, not likely to waste the county's money on a shaky case like this when we've got real criminals to go after."

"What are you saying?"

"I may need to contact DFCS. Or maybe not. We've already broken every rule in the book, so what's one more?" He gave Lucy Silva a narrow-eyed scowl. "We don't intend to let them ride roughshod over this family, do we, Lucy? We can't let them do what they did to those folks over in the next county."

"No sir, we can't," Lucy said.

"And I am inclined to protect this family from God only knows what might come down the pike. We've still got a secret grave on private property though. And I'm not sure what to do about that." He slapped the files against his leg.

"Mrs. Hanford, I'd intended to write out a statement and ask you to sign it, but I'd prefer that we didn't put any of this mess in writing, if that's all right with you." Sprague placed the files on the table. "These are yours. You might want to hang onto them for a while, as evidence of what your husband put you through."

"What do you mean?"

"I can't make any promises, but I think you'll come out all right, even if the DA decides there's something worth prosecuting. I don't suppose you're a flight risk either. Not with all those kids. I've never seen such a lively bunch."

"They're here?"

"Yes ma'am, your gentleman friend brought them in to make a point, and he made it well. They're happy and healthy and swarming all over my itty-bitty lobby like bees in a hive. You'd better mosey on out there and tell them they've got their mama back."

"Do you mean…?"

"Yes, you're free to go. The DA may want to speak with you next week, but he's a reasonable man. He knows right from wrong, but he knows there are some shades of gray too."

She stood, lightheaded, hardly noticing when Sprague placed her purse in her hands. He tucked the files into the purse.

"Don't leave town, now, Mrs. Hanford."

"I have never wanted to leave town," she said. "Thank you. Thank you."

Smiling, he waved her past Lucy and out the door.

A short hallway brought Miranda out to the cramped, drab lobby crowded with hard plastic chairs and wilting philodendrons. Jack and Dean stood watching her children as they milled around by the windows that looked out on the rear parking lot of city hall. It was all so small, so casual, so human.

But humans were all God had to work with, and how beautiful those humans could be.

No one noticed her; Jack and Dean's backs were half-turned to her. Those stubborn, merciful men.

Dean looked neat in his uniform, but Jack was as unkempt as the teenagers she saw sometimes at Walmart. His shirttail was out, and his hair was wild.

"She's a good mother, Dean," he said quietly. "The kids are living proof, aren't they? I wouldn't haul a passel of young 'uns to the sheriff's office if we had anything to hide, would I?"

"I don't suppose you would." Dean shook his head. "If it were up to me…" His melancholy voice faded into silence.

Miranda was swimming in air or walking on water, her feet not quite touching the ground as she moved closer to her precious children. They could all go home. Together.

Timothy glanced her way. His eyes grew huge. He hurried across the room. "What happened? Do you have to go to jail?"

"Everything's all right. I'll tell you the whole story tonight. You and Jack both."

Timothy hugged her. Nearly as tall as she was. A young man, growing straight and true.

Gabriel saw her and whooped. "Mother's here!"

She fell to her knees and opened her arms. The children surrounded her, but Dean and Jack hung back, regarding her with worried expressions.

"Careful," Jack said. "Be gentle, ruffians. Half hugs."

"No, I want whole hugs. Lots and lots." Laughing and crying, she savored each rib-scorching squeeze.

Finally, Jack herded the children away and helped her to her feet. He held her hands so tightly that it hurt. "What happened?"

"The sheriff turned me loose."

Jack's frown began to ease away. "Lord, have mercy. Well, I guess He already did."

"He did. He does. Over and over."

Dean moved closer. "Mrs. Hanford, I wouldn't have been able to live with myself if it had come out any differently."

"You were only doing your job." She searched the lawman's face. "I understand you've lost a child too."

His eyes shimmered with moisture. "Yes ma'am. Twenty-six years ago this summer, my little girl drowned in our own backyard."

"I'm sorry."

"Thank you, ma'am. And I'm sorry about your son. You never—" He cleared his throat. "You never quite get over losing a child."

"No. Never."

Dean studied the floor. "Accidents happen. They happen to good people, and life isn't about divvying up the blame. It's about—" He stopped short.

"What's life about, Dr. Hanford?"

Jack looked into the distance, perhaps seeing pill bottles on a bedside table. "If I had a quick answer, it wouldn't be the right one."

Dean's lined face eased into a smile. "You're a wise man. Now, if I recall correctly, you said you planned to pitch a tent tonight. I wish you luck, considering the weather forecast. On the other hand, I think you're the kind of man who gets things done, regardless of difficulties."

Jack let go of Miranda's hand and shook Dean's. "So are you. Thank you, sir."

"Call if you need anything, and take good care of those youngsters. Keep countin' noses. Good-bye, Mrs. Hanford. Bye, kids. I'll come see y'all sometime." He walked down the hall and disappeared into one of the cubbyholes that masqueraded as offices.

Taking Miranda's hands again, Jack searched her face. "Why didn't you tell me the whole story? Did you think I would report you?"

"No. I knew you wouldn't. I didn't want to put that on your tender conscience."

He shook his head, then drew her close and planted a long, firm kiss on her lips. She kissed him back, her knees weak and her whole body weightless with freedom.

Somebody groaned. Somebody giggled. Somebody—Michael?—said, "There they go again."

"No wisecracks, please," Jack said. "Kissing is perfectly acceptable behavior under certain circumstances, so get used to it. Now, we have a lot of work to do this afternoon if we expect to camp out tonight."

Exploding with questions, the children led the way out of the building. Miranda's van waited only two spaces from the squad car that had brought her there. Into the lion's den and out again.

She lifted her eyes to the mountains. Dark clouds grew in the west, sweeping across the sky in a brisk wind. They were every shade of gray, but they were rimmed with sunlight. And Jack's arm lay across her shoulders as if it belonged there.

thirty-two

The sun had barely risen in a cloudy sky when Miranda crossed the kitchen in the half dark. Through the window, the tent was a black bulk in the gray. She imagined Jack out there in the cold and the damp, spending a virtually sleepless night just to make her children happy.

He'd sat up late with her and Timothy, talking about everything. Carl. Jeremiah. Her mother, the jailbird, who wanted nothing to do with her.

Don't give up on her, Jack had said with a smile. *Persistence pays off, sometimes.*

Miranda walked back across the room and turned on the light. On the counter, a big pink gift bag sat beside the coffee maker. Jack had written directly on the bag: *A very happy Easter to Mrs. H. Open immediately and see the world with new eyes.* He'd scrawled a sloppy happy face beside the words.

Easter. How could she have forgotten it was Easter?

Reaching into the bag, she grasped a familiar shape. Her hands trembled as she drew out a camera case. She opened it and began to cry.

A vintage Nikon in mint condition. A twin to Jezebel.

Except for the tears, her vision was clear as she aimed the empty camera toward the sunrise, framing it in the window pane. Off center, to make the eye pay attention. Like stories that didn't have neat endings, Jack had said. They left doors open. They made him think about possibilities.

Oh, the possibilities.

She reached into the bag again and discovered gadgets, filters, and film. Lots and lots of film. Bless the man, he'd known that a camera without film was like a car without gas.

The kitten growled and scampered crablike across the room, her tail puffed up in defiance of some imaginary enemy. Hellion was another of Jack's gifts, just to make the children happy.

Now, just to make her happy, he'd bought her a camera. Her dream camera. He'd tried to replace the irreplaceable.

Sometimes that was possible. Sometimes it wasn't.

Sometimes you just had to wait for eternity.

She turned on the living room light and took Jeremiah's quilt from the couch. With one finger, she touched the square of red calico where she'd once stitched eight letters in blue embroidery floss. She'd pulled them out again, five years later, weeping over her husband's harsh decree to forget Jeremiah, to hide him in the earth and never speak of him again.

God hadn't forgotten Jeremiah. God never would. God would raise him up. Jeremiah was home free.

Carrying his quilt, Miranda went into her bedroom to find her embroidery floss.

The rains had come, but the tent held.

Barefoot, because the only shoes he'd brought were soaked, Jack lifted the flap and ventured onto the soggy grass. A few lights shone inside the house, so Miranda was up.

With his feet freezing, he took a few steps and looked back at the tent. It listed to starboard and held a reservoir of water on top. If anybody jostled anything, they'd have a flood.

In the gray light of a stormy morning, rain-driven petals from the cherry tree lay on the grass like pink snowdrifts. The driveway was a river of mud. The sun hid behind a dark cloud like a coquette flirting behind a black fan. It was wild, glorious weather. The kind of weather that bred rainbows.

The kids were still zonked out in a chaos of sleeping bags and pillows, like a litter of kittens. Jack had hardly slept, and his back ached. It had been worth it, though, to lie awake and hear the archangels whispering their plans for a bear hunt someday.

Miranda had spent the night in her own bed, for the sake of her still-tender ribs or perhaps for the sake of her burdens. Jack didn't know how to lift them. He was reasonably certain she would escape scot-free, but her fears ran deep. At least she wouldn't face them alone.

Several times in the night, he'd felt in his pocket for the house key. Evidence that she trusted him, not only with her house, but with her family. Maybe she was in it for the long haul.

Was he?

Yes. He could sell his tiny house and buy a big one—except she would never move. Her firstborn child was buried somewhere on her land.

What was he thinking anyway? Matrimony? He gave his head a quick shake but it didn't dislodge the idea from his brain.

He ran from the tent to the porch with mud squishing between his toes. After stealing some dry wood and kindling from the stash there, he hustled back to the fire pit the boys had made. He would cheat and use matches and the paper scraps he'd stuffed in the pocket of his jacket last night. None of that hard-core Boy Scout stuff for him.

The kindling lit quickly. He coaxed it into a higher flame and fed it with small branches. Within a few minutes, the fire began to cooperate.

Miranda stepped onto the porch, wearing jeans and a pink shirt.

He greeted her with a loud wolf whistle. "I knew I would like you in pink."

She blushed to match her shirt. "Hush. You'll wake the children."

"Oh! Miranda," he sang, *"don't you cry for me!"*

In the tent, the children laughed. The flap swayed, and Gabriel popped his head out.

"Uncle Jack, can we wash your car?"

"Now? Again? Before breakfast?"

"Yeah."

"In the rain?"

"Yeah. It'll be fun."

"Sure. Go ahead. Get that thing as clean as an angel's undershorts."

Gabriel spread the news, and the rest of the kids poured out of the tent like fire ants out of a hill of sand. Timothy took charge this time, and soon they were scurrying around the Audi. Everybody but Martha.

The valiant little fire kept burning through the drizzle as Jack headed for the porch with Martha at his heels.

"Gotta check on Hellion," she said, passing him. She raced up the steps and kicked off her shoes beside Miranda's mud-caked gardening shoes, then frowned at Jack's feet. "Uh-oh. You better not go inside like that." She slipped inside, the door slamming behind her.

"I need an ol' fashioned footwashin'," he said, reaching for Miranda. "And a good-morning kiss."

She obliged with gratifying enthusiasm, then drew back to scrutinize him as if she'd never seen him before. "You're almost too good to be true. Thank you."

"You're welcome. Is it—she—the right kind?"

"She's perfect. Where did you find her?"

"On eBay."

"I hope you didn't pay too much."

"That's none of your business. What's her name? Jezebel II? Esther? Pocahontas?"

"You can help me decide." She patted his cheek. "I'm cold. Back in a minute."

As she disappeared inside, he settled into his rocker. He smiled at the idea of his-and-hers rockers. It felt exactly right.

Martha poked her head out. "You want me to wash your feet, Uncle Jack?"

"No, I can just turn the hose on 'em."

"But I want to. Really, really bad."

On the verge of correcting her with "badly," he laughed instead, weighing the gift.

Priceless. "Have at it."

Two minutes later, Martha was back. He held the door open while she came out with a big pan of hot water. She had a dishcloth and a kitchen towel draped over one shoulder.

Ordered back to his chair, he sat, rolled up his pant legs, and lowered his muddy feet into the pan. The hot water was bliss to his frozen feet as she gave them a quick once-over with the dishcloth. Her mother wouldn't want it back.

The other kids were having a grand time washing the car in a light sprinkle of rain. Timothy was soaked and smiling. He tormented his siblings with a soapy sponge but defended Rebekah when the archangels teased her.

Timothy was one fine kid. All of them were. Messy and noisy and full of life.

The rain began to fall in earnest again, tapping on the porch roof and filling the air.

Water, water, everywhere. The stuff of miracles. Water, walked on. Turned to wine. An ark tossed about on it.

Water and earth made mud. Mud to heal a blind man's eyes.

Earth to entomb a man, and the voice of God to call him out.

Jack had begun to make some adjustments to his thinking; he was ready to admit that God might send personal messages, if a man had eyes to see and ears to hear. But if a man—or a boy—ignored the messages…

"There," Martha said. "Finished."

Out of the mouths of babes. Finished, indeed. Clean all over.

"Thank you, Martha." Awash in unearned love, Jack could hardly speak.

"You're welcome." She peered intently at him. "Your eyeballs don't look sad anymore."

"That's because my heart's not sad anymore, sweetie."

Martha smiled. She slipped her feet back into her shoes and ran into the rain, abandoning the foot-washing gear.

The rain had doused the fire. He didn't care.

"I'm a sinner, Lord," he whispered, "but I'm Your sinner. May I always be in a condition accessible to mercy. So may we all."

The water kept running down the driveway, like life kept running, and he couldn't change any of it. No more than he could retrieve the water that had run from a garden hose so many years before. It was over.

He'd loved his mother. He still did. He could only hope that God still did too. Jack closed his eyes and made a conscious effort to place her in the Almighty's hands and leave her there.

The door creaked, startling his eyes open. Miranda came out, wearing Jeremiah's quilt like a shawl. She stood at the railing to watch the children, and Jack moved to stand behind her, absorbing her warmth as his feet turned to ice again on the damp planks.

He placed his hands lightly on her shoulders. Not hard, but strong. So strong.

"Miranda—"

"Randi, please. My mother only called me Miranda when I was in deep trouble."

"Randi," he said, loving the tomboy sound of it. "Turn around, Randi. Please."

She did, and he sized up his peasant-princess with that shy and winsome smile. Something felt different. It was a bit of a shock to realize that for quite some time, he'd been looking not *at* her eyes, but into them. Connecting.

"I owe you so many apologies," he said. "I bullied you. I mocked you. I even drugged you. Please forgive me."

"Don't be silly, Jack. Of course I forgive you."

"Thank you. I—I like you. A lot. I want to go on learning who you really are."

He cleared his throat. "Obviously, I don't see you as my sister-in-law anymore—I mean, you're still my sister-in-law, but I also see you as a...I want to..." He stopped, flustered. His glib tongue had abandoned him. "May I court you?"

She examined his shirt and gave her head a tiny but definite shake. "No."

His heart seemed to stop. "No?"

"I associate the word, the concept, with certain teachings I don't like. Call it anything but courtship, please."

His heart resumed beating. "Randi, you're a brat and a tease, but I'm a fool for you anyway. I would like to pursue your affections. May I?"

Her dimples blossomed. "Aren't you doing that already? With some success?" She stretched up for a quick kiss, then turned to watch the children.

Jack leaned his head against hers and tried to take it all in. The children in the rain. The pink petals like snow. The water running like a river, the washing of feet, the holy communion of saints. And every day was Easter.

He tightened his hold on the fragile strength of the shoulders that had carried such heavy burdens. Miranda—no, Randi—reached up and placed her hands on his. Her head moved against his cheek as she followed the flight of a handful of sparrows against the dappled sky, their wings edged with light.

So many sparrows. Only God could count them all.

Readers Guide

1. Who are the sparrows of the title? How many physical or spiritual falls did you notice, including those that happened before the story opens?

2. Jack wants freedom for Miranda's children, starting with good literature to open their hearts and minds to a wider world. Which works of fiction have changed your perspective on life?

3. Do you think Miranda homeschools for the right reasons? If you could give her only one message or ask her only one question about her choices, what would it be?

4. Even the most fiercely protective parents can't, and maybe shouldn't, shield their children from every danger. When does a parent cross the line from protection to over protection?

5. Timothy, at twelve, is the man of the house, and he resents Jack for stepping in. What developments help Timothy let go of his too-large responsibilities and allow him to be a kid again?

6. When Carl told Miranda to do things that violated her conscience, how could she have persuaded him that being the head of the house didn't necessarily make him a good decision maker?

7. Victims of spiritual abuse often experience anger, depression, and a loss of faith when they attempt to break away from their abusers. When Miranda couldn't pray or enjoy reading her Bible anymore, did she have other options for rekindling her faith?

8. Spiritual abuse can be subtle, leaving no physical evidence. Should an outsider ever dismiss or diminish a victim's experience because there's little evidence?

9. Jack and Miranda fall in love within a fairly short time. What experiences or personality traits may have primed them to warm up to each other so quickly?

10. The fact that Jack is uncomfortable with a "word from God" shows that he takes such things more seriously than he claims to. Even if the elderly preacher isn't a prophet, how might Jack still benefit from the old man's exhortation?

11. What leads Miranda to think she can't hear from God? Are there any events she might interpret as being divine guidance?

12. Which of Miranda's new freedoms do you think mean the most to her?

13. As a photographer, Miranda is aware of perspective and focus. What changes her focus and perspective on life? Could she have made the journey to freedom without help from friends like Jack and Yvonne?

14. Can you be a friend to someone like Miranda? Or are you a Miranda in need of a friend?

Acknowledgments

I owe my start in publishing to my agent, Chip MacGregor, who not only understands the book business but also understands people. Thank you, Chip, for championing my writing and for giving me time to grow.

Jessica Barnes and Shannon Marchese have my undying gratitude. I have loved the privilege of learning from them and from the copy and production editors who also worked their magic on my writing. The whole team at Multnomah has inspired me with their enthusiasm and hard work. My heartfelt thanks go to each one of you.

In researching the story, I became acquainted with *Quivering Daughters* author, Hillary McFarland; Karen Campbell; Cynthia Kunsman, RN; and therapist Sandra Harrison, MA, LPC/MHSP. Thank you for your courage in confronting modern-day patriarchy and for your compassion toward the families who are trapped in it.

I have so many friends to thank, starting with my original posse of local writing buddies: Lindi Peterson, Maureen Hardegree, and Missy Tippens. My dear friends and mentors Deeanne Gist and Sherrie Lord live in distant states but stay close in spirit via phone and e-mail. I don't know what I would have done without you two. Other treasured writing compatriots include Cindy Woodsmall, Sally Apokedak, Mark Bertrand, Suzan Robertson, Carla Fredd, Mae Nunn, Mirta Ana Schultz, Amy Wallace, and Ruth Trippy.

I owe a debt of love to my church family too, and to my pastor and his wife. John and Ellen, thank you for your encouragement and your faithful prayers for my writing career.

Michelle Truax, you're another one who prays for me, understands my hermitlike ways, and loves me anyway. Thank you for being there. And Hampton and Susan…a certain thread of this story took me by surprise but seemed to have your names on it. I hope you'll receive it as a token of my family's love for yours.

I'm very grateful for my kith and kin by blood or marriage, all across the country. David, thanks for introducing me to Sayers and Chesterton and for always being willing to talk books. Lesley, the steadfast one who does whatever needs to be done, thank you for believing in me and cheering me on. Mom, an artist who taught me to see beauty, thank you for loving your family with your whole heart. I love all of you.

My biggest thanks go to my husband and our children, who've made many sacrifices on my behalf. From the days when our world revolved around 4-H and homeschool, you've always given me the freedom to hang out with my fictional friends. You've helped me in a million practical ways too. Husband, sons, daughter, son-in-law, and granddaughter: I love you, always and for so many reasons.

Above all, I'm thankful to Jesus my Savior, God's grace incarnate.

About the Author

Although I've lived more than half my life in other states, I grew up in California and am still a California girl at heart. I love vintage bungalows, twisted oaks on rolling hills, and the rocky beaches of the central coast.

We lived inland, in a sun-baked town that was tiny but fortunate enough to have received an Andrew Carnegie library grant—and our house was within walking distance. I've read that all the Carnegie libraries had grand entrances with steps leading upward to symbolize the self-improvement that comes with reading. My hometown library, which was built in 1908, had a second set of steps that led down to the children's room, and it was a wonderland of stories. Once I'd read everything that interested me there, my dad made a deal with the upstairs librarians to let me use his card to check out books from upstairs. I took full advantage of the privilege.

A few blocks away stood the Lutheran church where I came to faith, first through Sunday school teachers whose kindness drew me to the kindness of God, and then through confirmation classes. The Bible verses that had been drilled into my head came to life in my heart.

After moving away from home as a teenager, I worked at a variety of jobs, from candle maker in a tourist town to administrative assistant at a Christian college. I married a wonderful man from Michigan, and we lived north of Detroit for seventeen years. That's where we started homeschooling our three children, a journey that we finished here in Georgia when our youngest graduated from high school in 2009.

My husband and I live near Atlanta, close to the foothills of the southern Appalachians. His motorcycle often carries us to the mountains of Georgia,

Tennessee, or the Carolinas. Sitting on the back of the bike, I can pray, enjoy the beautiful views, and plot new stories. Fiction still makes my world go 'round, whether I'm writing it or reading it.

You can find me on the Web at http://megmoseley.com.